SUZIE JOHNSON

WhiteFire Publishing

This is a work of fiction. All characters and events portrayed in this novel are either fictitious or used fictitiously.

SWEET MOUNTAIN MUSIC

WhiteFire Publishing
13607 Bedford Rd NE
Cumberland, MD 21502

ISBN: 978-1-939023-41-4 (print)
          978-1-939023-42-1 (digital)

To my father, Bill Smith:
Dad, you inspired this book when you gave me the 1909 book,
Wanderings in South America by Charles Waterton.
Thank you for a lifetime of adventure,
and most especially for loving me and believing in me.

To my husband, Keith Johnson:
Thank you for all of the weekend drives up to Index, Skykomish,
and the Cascade Tunnel while I was researching and writing this book.

To my son, Kirk Johnson:
You are my inspiration now and for always.

Chapter One

Cedar Ridge, Washington
Cascade Mountains, 1896

"I think we should have him take off his shirt."

Several delighted *oohs* and *aahs* followed the sugary, yet authoritative voice drifting through the slightly opened window.

Standing below the window, Chloe Jane Williston recognized the voice of Trina Clark. From the sounds of it, every young woman in Cedar Ridge sat inside the town hall.

What could they possibly be up to in there? And why didn't she know about it? There was a story in the making, she could tell; one that would hopefully sell more copies of *The Cedar Ridge Reporter* than usual. Chloe stretched up on the tips of her toes and tried to see through the open crack. It was much too narrow. Disappointed, she scrubbed at the window's filthy panes with the sleeve of her gray and white pinstriped shirtwaist.

Her only success came in dirtying her sleeve.

Chloe frowned and stood back to once again survey the window. She found a clearer spot higher up but wasn't tall enough to reach it.

Glory be. If only she had something to stand on, she'd be able to see better.

Quickly, pulse jumping, Chloe looked around the wooded area surrounding the meeting hall. Nothing.

Scanning the early summer sky, dusty blue with traces of wispy clouds, she smiled. Thankfully, it wouldn't be dark for a few more hours. It stayed light so much later here in Washington than it did back in Boston.

Kicking at a bed of last year's pine needles, Chloe stubbed her toe on a partially buried rock. She stood back and sized it up. Boulder was more like it. It appeared wide enough for her to stand on and yet not so huge she wouldn't be able to move it. It was worth a try.

At least the town of Cedar Ridge was good for something. There were plenty of rocks, if nothing else. A deep breath filled her lungs with the rich sappy fragrance seeping from the surrounding trees. After prying, tugging, and then kicking at the rock, it finally broke free.

Blood-red worms squirmed forth when she rolled it over. An army of potato bugs scurried every which way. Chloe allowed herself to shudder just once before kicking and rolling the rock toward the meeting hall.

Each direction she looked, snow-tipped mountains and lush fir trees rose to greet her. The Skykomish River, racing down from higher elevations, thundered in the background. Grudgingly, Chloe admitted to herself that Cedar Ridge was more than a pile of rubble and too many trees. The mountains were higher, the sky bluer, and the air headier than any place she'd ever lived.

More than once she'd tried to describe this place on paper but failed. It wasn't possible to put words to the majesty of her surroundings. Her father had chosen well when he'd moved the family this time.

Life would be almost perfect, if only she had a friend or two. As for the *almost* part, she didn't want to think about it right now.

"Just think about it." Trina's voice drifted through the window as Chloe chugged the rock into position. She gave a few swipes at the glass, a little harder than earlier, and was rewarded with a somewhat distorted view of Trina flouncing her right hand back and forth at her peers. Chloe couldn't quite make out the look on Trina's face, but she was certain it was no less than prissy.

Trina, the self-appointed leader of the Cedar Ridge Young Women's Guild, was a feisty little blond tornado hurling along a path of destruction, and every young and otherwise sensible lady in town seemed to follow right along behind her.

Except Chloe.

Her presence wasn't welcomed by this tight-knit group, and hadn't been from the day she moved to the small mountain town. Whether from her initial shyness upon her family's arrival, or that her father was a well-to-do newspaper publisher from Boston, Chloe had been ascribed as pretentious—a fact that couldn't be further from the truth. Chloe's interests may not reflect those of most young women her age, but she still had the need for friends and acceptance.

"When will you ever be able to have such a delectable time?" Trina's tone was smooth and manipulative. "I can guarantee you'll never have the chance again."

Chloe's heart raced as she leaned closer. Her earlier suspicions were correct. She had known something was amiss when she first saw Trina headed this way, looking over her shoulder too many times not to be guilty of something. There was a story here.

The rock she stood on tilted to the right, catching Chloe by surprise. She regained her balance, but not before banging her hip against the building.

"Glory be!" Too late, she remembered the women inside. She held her breath, praying they hadn't heard her. She'd die if they caught her eavesdropping. Not only that, she'd ruin the opportunity for a story the town wasn't likely to forget anytime soon.

Shaking dirt and pine needles from her skirt, Chloe brushed her hands together then gingerly rubbed her sore backside. Disgusted for almost ruining things, she tiptoed back to the window.

A good reporter maintained control no matter the situation. She'd heard that directly from Nellie Bly's own mouth, and Nellie Bly was nothing if not a good reporter.

"I'm sick and tired of my Russell spending every Saturday evening in the saloon, watching those *girls* sing, dance, and shake themselves at him," Trina said. "If he thinks I'm going to marry him without having a little harmless pleasure like he does, well...I want some merriment, too." There was one collective, scandalized, in-drawn breath, followed by silence.

Certain even the youngest of the women present must be wearing that sour-faced look, suggesting they'd been sucking lemons all afternoon, Chloe wished she had a clear view of their faces. This story had the potential to be big. Imagine, the mayor's daughter hiring a man to take off his clothes.

It might not be the type of story worthy of Nellie Bly, but it was juicy enough to sell papers and grab readers' interests. And really, wasn't that the goal of every writer?

"Ladies, it'll be positively luscious. It's just a lark, nothing harmful. All he's going to do is sing for us. It's not like we're going to touch him or anything...unseemly...or..." Trina lowered her voice. "Naughty."

"Truly, Trina, it's undignified and immoral." A timid-sounding woman spoke, her voice unnaturally high.

Chloe's hand flew to her mouth and she stifled a groan. What was her sister-in-law doing here?

Leave it to poor Sarah to have the dubious misfortune of disagreeing with Trina Clark. Chloe was shocked Sarah even spoke up. People disagreed with Trina so rarely, she certainly wouldn't let it pass without a squabble of some sort. Not when there was an entire group of women looking on.

Chloe stepped down from her rock just long enough to flex the tingles out of her feet before she was up again. When next she looked, Trina was marching toward Sarah, hands on hips, bottom lip pushed out dangerously. Trina stopped when her nose was only half an inch from Sarah's. Sarah would be lucky to get out of this one with her dignity intact.

"Think about your husband and his little habits, Sarah Williston. Could this be any worse?"

Trina took one hand from her stick-straight hips and shook a finger in Sarah's face. "I happen to know for a fact, your Charles Jr. is first in line when Pete unlocks the saloon each afternoon."

Every woman in the room gasped, shocked Trina would dare say such a thing.

Shame washed its ugly truth over Chloe. Her oldest brother, Charles Williston Jr., was a drunk and treated his wife abominably. Poor Sarah. What she must be feeling right now? Humiliated publicly, made a fool in front of all her friends. Chloe's heart went out to her.

Sarah was infinitely more timid than Chloe could ever dream of being. That Sarah dared speak out against Trina meant she believed resolutely against what the silly girl had planned. Chloe understood. She'd been forced to speak out a time or two, herself. Her stomach churned at the thought of doing it again. Still, Sarah needed rescuing and, much as she didn't want to be the one to do it, Chloe had to help her.

She reached back, absently rubbed her backside, and winced. She must have banged the wall harder than she thought.

"From the looks of things, it must be mighty interesting in there." Behind her, a deep male voice came out of nowhere.

Chloe jumped, missed hitting her head on the window sash, and came down crooked, once again struggling to retain her balance.

The man was beside her in an instant, but instead of looking at him, Chloe ducked her head. Heat rushed to her cheeks.

"Are you all right?" His voice was rich, mellow, and vibrated through her senses.

Too flustered to make eye contact, Chloe wished a little band of wood nymphs would appear to whisk her away. Why must she be caught like this? Eavesdropping, rubbing a most delicate area, and then stumbling like an ungainly oaf?

Aunt Jane, whom she admired so much, would've opened her mouth and snapped out a retort. Not Chloe. Feeling sheepish, she glanced up into the greenest eyes she'd ever seen. Her voice caught. She doubted if she could get one word out.

In a feeble attempt to look away, Chloe found her gaze riveted on the rich red wool shirt that stretched across his solid chest. Glancing further downward, his long legs were nicely encased in wheat colored trousers.

There was no safe place to look. She squeezed her eyes shut.

"Miss? I asked if you're all right."

For one lengthy, embarrassing moment, Chloe couldn't open her eyes. Finally she did and was struck with a sense of weak-kneed wonder that mortified her. She couldn't take her eyes off him. His hair, neatly trimmed, was the color of rich, dark honey. Though it was combed back from his sun-bronzed forehead, a handful of springy curls fell forward.

"Miss?"

Glory, why couldn't she answer him? Tongue-tied, wondering if he thought her an idiot, she could only nod.

"Good. Now maybe you could help me." His mouth curved in a spirited, playful manner. "When you're finished looking me up and down, that is." His smile grew wider, cockier, and her heart began to pound.

Cheeks burning, Chloe tore her gaze from his.

"No." Humiliated, Chloe could do little more than whisper and started to turn away.

"Please wait." He reached out to stop her. Firm, big, and warm, his hand encased hers, and a dozen sensations, all pleasant, raced up her arm.

This was foolhardy. She should be frightened but didn't sense any danger about him. Her heart flittered. Chloe jerked her hand away.

"Let me apologize for my bad manners. I shouldn't have teased you." His voice fairly rumbled with sincerity, although his sea-green eyes didn't reflect the grin on his face.

"I-it's all right." Chloe hated that she stammered. Did she sound all breathy and flirty like Trina? Or was it her imagination?

"I'm Benjamin Kearny." He extended his hand in introduction.

Could he be the new doctor everyone was expecting? Now his sudden appearance made sense. Chloe stared at his outstretched hand, not sure it was wise to touch him again. This man was a far cry from the craggy old physician who had just retired. Cedar Ridge would do itself proud with him as their physician.

For one crazy upside-down moment, Chloe entertained the notion that if she had an injury Dr. Kearny could examine her. What would happen if she suddenly turned her ankle? The blush burned back to her cheeks and she closed her eyes for a brief second. When she opened them again, Dr. Kearny studied her closely as if expecting a response; his hand still extended. Had he read her thoughts?

Her throat suddenly dry, with butterflies flitting in her stomach, Chloe took a steadying breath and ignored his hand.

And wasn't this just superb? She thought she'd gotten better about this stupid inability to talk with people. Obviously not. She opened her mouth to speak, horrified to find she had to try twice before the words came out in a rush.

"Are you here to set up your practice, doctor?" There. That wasn't so bad. Except he now stared at her in a funny way and withdrew his hand. She'd spoken too fast. He probably hadn't a clue as to what she'd said.

"Practice?" He sounded puzzled.

"Yes, your medical practice." Was he daft?

"Oh. I see. You think I'm..." His voice trailed off and he gave her another trace of his devastating smile. "I'm not a doctor."

"You're not?"

"You sound disappointed."

"Not disappointed, I just assumed..." She felt like a fool. "We don't get many strang—um, visitors, and we are expecting a new doctor soon."

"I'm a scientist, actually. An ethologist. I do field work, studying animals in their natural environment." The smile grew broader and made him seem warm and somehow very inviting. Obviously he loved his work.

This would be a great interview. Once the stray thought burst into her mind, she knew she had to muster up the nerve to ask him for one. It would make a most interesting story for *The Reporter,* much more interesting than anything to do with Trina Clark.

"Do you know everyone around here?" He raised his honey colored eyebrows with the question, and Chloe found her gaze drawn to the dark blond curls that kissed their feathery tips.

"Yes." She swallowed hard. She didn't want to tell him it was because the town was so small. "Are you looking for someone?" Even before he spoke, Chloe had a sickening hunch what his answer would be.

"A young woman"—*don't say it, don't say her name!*—"by the name of Trina"—*she knew it*—"Clark." Trina had all the luck. How, where, *when* did Trina meet this man?

"Well?" Ben stared at her, obviously curious as to why she took so long to answer. Only then did Chloe realize her mouth hung open like a blowfish.

Humiliated at the impression she must be making, she could only whisper. "I know Trina. She's in there." Chloe nodded at the building behind them.

"Ah, good. I'm supposed to meet her at the town hall and wondered if this was the right place."

There was only one building in their small town large enough to hold an assembly of any sort. Surely a scientist like Benjamin Kearny was bright enough to see that. Then the import of what he'd said dawned on her, and she gasped.

"*You're* the one they're all in a dither over?"

No wonder Trina was so determined to have her way over this man taking off his shirt. She couldn't believe it. The pea-brained women of this town had actually hired a man to entertain them for the evening, and he turned out to be the only man ever to set her heart a-flutter.

"What do you mean, 'all in a dither' over me?" His lips quirked in the most appealing way.

Hmmph. "As if you didn't know. I can't believe you're going to take your shirt off for them."

"Take my shirt off?" He sounded offended as well as horrified. "That infuriating Clark girl and her silly notions. No, I'm not—" He muttered a few words that would have had her mother racing for a cake of lye soap. He broke off suddenly and stared at the ground for a second before glancing up. "Sorry."

At least he had the good graces to realize his language left little to be desired. Not that she was offended by his choice of words—she had two brothers. But it was nice to see Benjamin Kearny had some manners.

Chloe nodded, accepting his apology. "I'm glad you're not planning to be their afternoon entertainment." Though she wasn't sure she actually meant it. The heat threatened her cheeks once again.

"Yes, well, unfortunately I am. I'm going to sing for them." His voice hardened along with the muscles in his face.

It was on the tip of her tongue to ask why he would sing for them since he so obviously didn't want to. Instead she said, "I have to go."

"Wait. You haven't told me your name yet. Are you sure you won't stay?"

"I wasn't invited."

"Oh." He blinked, obviously surprised. "I was certain Mayor Clark said every young woman in town was invited to his daughter's birthday celebration."

"Not me." Chloe stared at the ground, hating to admit she was the only one not welcome. Bitten by curiosity, she battled with herself, dying to know but still frightened to speak. Curiosity won out. "Are you a relative?"

"No. Her father is a friend of a friend, and I'm sort of stuck in the middle. Between you, me, and that rock you were standing on, I'd just as soon not be here. I was more or less coerced. Business type favors, and all that. You understand?"

"Um...right." He didn't look the type to allow himself to be coerced into anything. "I'd really better go now." She looked up into his eyes, wanting one last look before she left.

"I thought I heard voices out here."

Chloe turned, dismayed to find Trina on the steps with a dozen other women crowded behind her. They all stared. She wasn't surprised in the least when Trina tossed back her blond head, gathered her skirts, and tiptoed daintily down the steps.

"Why, Ben." Trina batted her eyelashes a few times. "Ladies, this is the man I told you about. Benjamin Christopher Kearny."

"Ben will do fine."

Trina blinked, clearly pleased. "Oh, yes. *Ben.* At any rate, I'm so glad you've arrived. I was ever so fearful you may have changed your mind."

I'll just bet you were. Chloe thought briefly about uttering her sarcastic comment out loud, but refrained. Her mere presence was usually enough to incense Trina Clark.

Ben Kearny. Benjamin Kearny. Benjamin Christopher Kearny. Chloe rolled the names over in her mind. She peeked up at him. He seemed larger than life. Yes, the name Ben fit him perfectly.

Ben stepped toward Trina, who watched him with the look of a woman ready to devour a dish of berries covered with the richest cream. Feeling suddenly possessive and not quite knowing why, Chloe shoved back her intimidation and stepped right along with him. Besides, there was still the matter of helping Sarah out of a tough situation. Shamefully, she almost forgot about her sister-in-law. Perhaps with Ben beside her, she'd have the courage to speak up for Sarah's sake.

Before she realized what happened, Chloe found her hand caught up in his.

The impropriety of his action caught her off-guard, and she froze. He watched her, his spirited smile still there. The fact that it didn't reach his eyes tugged at her heartstrings. Chloe lowered her gaze. Staring hard at the pinecones on the ground, she tried to extract her hand from his. He wouldn't let go, and she started to look at him again but knew if she did she'd be lost. One more look into those eyes and Chloe suspected she would end up making an even greater fool of herself. She had to concentrate on other matters, like helping Sarah.

Determined, Chloe took a deep breath and stepped forward. When they stopped at the stairs of the building, she mustered her courage. "Trina Clark." There. That wasn't so bad. Her voice didn't squeak. It only sounded a little higher than usual. She swallowed hard. Ben squeezed her hand.

She opened her mouth again. "I can't believe you're contemplating such a thing. What are you thinking, hiring a man to entertain a gaggle of women in the town meeting hall?" She lowered her voice to a whisper. "The very same hall where we worship the Lord every Sunday morning, in case you've forgotten."

After a lengthy glance at the rest of the women staring at her from the wide double doors, aware of Ben so close to her—watching her, holding her hand—Chloe's voice stuck in her throat and she could say no more. She caught her sister-in-law's horrified eye. Sarah, bless her heart, looked like an under-ripe raspberry.

Trina slapped one hand to her hip. "Save your moralizing for someone who cares, Chloe." Twisted in self-righteousness, Trina's face was no longer sweet. "You know very well you're not concerned with what we're planning this evening. You're just upset because we didn't invite you."

That part was true, though not for the reasons Trina might think. She'd long ago given up any hope of having friends in Cedar Ridge. She was upset over the lost chance for an interesting story.

She sighed. Caleb would be out of luck on this edition unless she came up with something new. Somehow she'd lost control of the entire situation. Even more, she'd lost the nerve to say anything further to Trina.

She cast one last glance at the growing crowd of young women and furrowed her brow. A young, waif-like woman stood back near the door.

Felicity Jepson. Married to the meanest man in town, Felicity often wore her husband's wrath on her jaw or upper check.

Despite being stared at, despite wishing the earth would swallow her up,

Chloe extracted her hand from Ben's and hurried to the girl's side. "Felicity." Chloe spoke softly. "Why don't you leave with me? When Josiah finds out you were a part of this, he'll be most upset."

Felicity's plain face transformed into a cloud burst. Clearly, she hadn't thought her presence here could well put her in jeopardy.

"Don't worry." Chloe gave Felicity's hand a gentle squeeze. "If you leave now, you won't have done anything wrong, and he'll have no reason to be angry."

Trina quickly rushed over and seized Felicity by the arm. "Josiah won't know a thing about this. No one will if *you* don't tell them, Chloe." She spoke so rudely, Chloe wondered if somehow Trina knew what she'd been about.

No one knew Chloe wrote the newspaper articles and her younger brother submitted them. Especially not their father, the publisher and editor. The word *anger* couldn't even begin to describe what would happen if he found out.

It wasn't as if they lied, really. Chloe didn't actually put Caleb's name on the articles. She signed them C. J. Williston. Her father just assumed this was Caleb's pen name, and she and her brother were happy to leave it that way.

"Besides," Trina continued in that sugary tone of hers. "We're sick and tired of our men thinking they can run off to Pete's whenever they want; drinking and eyeballing every entertainer who happens along. It's high time we get even with them. If we have a little fun while we're at it, so what?" Trina shrugged then walked over to Ben and held out her hand. "Coming Mr. Kearny?"

From where she still stood next to Felicity, Chloe looked at Ben. He searched her face, his expression shaking her to the core. He seemed almost...interested. It had to be her imagination. Then he stepped toward her, reached out, and squeezed her hand. His mouth curved slightly.

"Good night, Chloe." Her name was a whisper on his lips. He released her then, and for a second, the imprint remained against her palm—warm, firm, and comfortable. Then it was gone, an emptiness left in its place. Chloe felt abandoned as she watched him walk up the steps with Trina, though pleased he hadn't taken Trina's hand. He glanced back long enough to flash a grin before he stepped through the door.

Sarah. She'd quite forgotten about Sarah. Chloe raced up the steps only to have Trina slam the door right in her face. She tried to work up the courage to bang it down. Instead she opened it wide enough to poke her head inside. Maybe she could get Sarah's attention quietly.

Before she could even glance around, Trina appeared. "You'd better not breathe a word of this, Chloe Williston. If you do I'll be having a talk with that father of yours. And you can be sure he won't like what I'll have to say."

That only confirmed what Chloe feared. Somehow Trina found out about C. J. Williston. Before she could reply the door slammed again.

In a huff, Chloe stomped down the steps and searched for something sturdier than the rock to stand on. She found an empty bucket—admittedly a little rusty, but the bottom was wide enough to stand on comfortably. She placed it beneath the window and climbed up.

The first words to drift through the window set Chloe's senses reeling.

"We want you to take your shirt off, Mr. Kearny."

Chloe couldn't wait.

Chapter Two

Ben coughed, startled by the shocking request, still trying to understand why these women didn't like Chloe. She seemed nice enough, intelligent. She hadn't blinked an eye when he'd said he was an ethologist. "Wh-what did you say?"

"We want—"

"I heard what you said. That isn't what I meant. The answer is no!" He didn't like the fact that he had to sing for them in the first place. By no means would he take off his shirt.

He wouldn't even be in this predicament if Trina's father hadn't been such a good friend of the colonel's. Colonel Wilkes had hired Ben to lead the hunt of a lifetime. There was such an exorbitant amount of money at stake that when Wilkes asked Ben and his team to stop and look up his old cavalry pal, Jase Clark, Ben could hardly refuse. He certainly never intended to end up singing for the man's flirtatious daughter's birthday gathering.

Ben set his jaw angrily. This was no birthday party. He'd been duped, and this new request was certainly not one he'd expected. Neither was Chloe, he thought suddenly. Her determined attitude and wide, curious eyes caught him totally off-guard.

"But Mr. Kearny..." Trina's whine grated on his nerves.

"No!"

Trina flinched, but he didn't care. Every woman in the place watched him expectantly. If they thought he was going to strut around with a swelled chest like some peacock, they could just think again.

"But you agreed!" Trina's bottom lip stuck out in a way that suggested she was used to getting what she asked for. Not this time. Not with him. He never gave in to anyone, and he wouldn't start now.

Well, he corrected himself wryly. He *had* given in to Trina's father. But he laid the blame squarely at the feet of one person—Gus. Father figure, mentor, fellow scientist, and blabber-mouth extraordinaire.

Once Gus mentioned Ben's musical talent, the man insisted Ben sing for his daughter's birthday party. When he refused, Clark threatened to send a telegram to his good pal the colonel. Ben had visions of all funds for this project disappearing, and this project meant more to him than anything ever could, so he finally gave in. When Ben finished here and returned to the hotel, he planned to cheerfully wring Gus's neck.

"The agreement was for me to sing, nothing more. The shirt stays on. Now if you want to hear some music, I suggest you all take your places and be quiet."

He looked at the sea of faces and wished Chloe hadn't left. If he had to sing for anyone, he'd rather it be her. If he had to look into a stranger's eyes, he'd prefer they were hers. Chloe's eyes were a deep, rich blue, a shade which he'd only seen once before—on a fleeting bird he'd been lucky enough to catch a glimpse of in South America.

Could that be why she kept creeping to the forefront of his mind? Or was it her hair? Thick and wavy, it was a vibrant golden-brown, not unlike the grizzly bears that inhabited these very mountains.

"Do you have some songs prepared, Mr. Kearny?"

"I write my own music. I have the sheets right here. If your pianist feels she can play them, I'll go ahead and sing." He leveled Trina Clark with a stare so fierce, wild animals had backed down from it. "But I'm not taking off my shirt!"

Trina pursed her lips, plucked the papers out of his hand, and strutted to the front of the room. "Follow me. We have an organ Mr. Kearny, not a piano. I hope you don't mind." She turned and fluttered her eyelashes in a way that could rival any young woman from Florida. "*I* am the organist."

"I'm not surprised." Ben grumbled under his breath as he followed Trina, wishing for a moment that he'd never heard of Cedar Ridge, Washington, or the Cascade Mountains. He was used to singing for people, an audience. He often sang for other scientists when they were out in the field for months at a time on various projects. But he'd never sung for a group of women who looked hungry enough to devour him.

Trina struck the first chords on the organ, sour and very off-key. Ben winced then opened his mouth to sing.

Haunted. That's what she was. Haunted.

The moment Ben began to sing, any hope Chloe had of fabricating a new article for the paper disappeared. Her brain turned to mush.

She stood on the rusted bucket, her face plastered to the window. Chloe, along with every woman inside the building, was mesmerized. She didn't know it was possible for a man to sing like that. She didn't even know if the law permitted it.

Ben's voice, low and devastatingly alluring, seemed to roll over each woman, touching them, sending tingles up their spines, darn near causing them to swoon. It must have affected them that way. That's what happened to her when he started singing about his lonely heart and begging her to look into his eyes. Of course she knew, logically, he wasn't telling *her* to look into his eyes. He wasn't really singing to *her* at all. He didn't even know she had herself stuck to the window, panting for breath, in an attempt to see every move he made and hear every word he sang.

Not that she could see him all that clearly through the window. It didn't matter. The minute Ben opened his mouth and began to sing, Chloe became the only woman on earth and the walls between them faded.

It was just her, Ben, and the lonely heart he sang about. She wanted to reach out to him and make his world right, make his loneliness disappear.

He sang to her, begging her to soothe his troubled soul. She ached to do just that.

He needed her. No one could help him but her.

She floated on a cloud.

An instant later, Chloe saw stars.

Somehow her foot broke through the bucket and she crashed to the ground. She gasped and struggled to regain her breath. Then, slowly, breathing raggedly, she sat up.

The haunting sound of Ben's voice tantalized her ears.

Chloe cradled her head and tried to shut out the sound. She must be sensible about this situation. She couldn't become distracted by such a man. She had work to do; an article to write for Caleb so their father wouldn't be angry with him.

Devastating voice or no, Chloe had to put Ben Kearny out of her mind.

"I'm telling you, Gus, it was the most bizarre thing." Ben tipped his head back, drained the mug, set it on the sticky table, and wiped his mouth with the back of his hand. The hotel's dining area was closed, and this dimly lit saloon was the only place in town where he and Gus could sit down and talk strategy. "If not for Clark's threat to our project, I would have walked away without a backward glance."

To his dismay, Gus had been asleep when he'd arrived back at the hotel last night. By morning, Ben's anger had faded and he could see the humor in the situation. Well...maybe just a little humor. At any rate, the desire to wring Gus's neck had faded.

"Thanks to you, I felt I had no choice but to entertain that screeching woman and her friends."

Gus, an elderly gentleman with a shock of white hair and eyes the color of weak tea, guffawed loud enough to draw stares from the other patrons in Pete's Saloon.

"So?" Gus raised one silver eyebrow. "Did you take off your shirt?"

"You raised me better than that, old man." Ben looked at his friend affectionately. Gus Pieper had stepped in and raised him when his parents stepped out. "I think I learned what a saloon singer must feel like, what with all the leers and comments."

Gus laughed again and slapped the table.

Ben drew his eyebrows together, slightly annoyed. "It's really not that funny."

"What did you think Clark would do if you refused to sing for that so-called birthday party? Send a wire to Wilkes and tell him to stop the funds before we ever get started?"

"That's exactly what he said he'd do."

Gus considered the thought for a moment. "Do you think he really meant it?"

Ben shrugged. "Probably not, but Clark talks a good game. I just don't want a confrontation."

"If I didn't know better, I'd bet you did it for the attention." Gus grinned then gulped down the rest of his ale.

Ben swore under his breath. "Gus if you weren't so old, I swear I'd—"

"You'd just better hope Clark's little girl doesn't decide she wants more of you than your singing."

"It won't matter because tomorrow we're heading up the mountain, and we'll never set eyes on Clark or his princess again." Nor would he likely set eyes on the comely Chloe.

"Hey! Why do you look so cow-eyed all of sudden? Are you going to miss that Clark girl?"

"Not likely." But Ben wouldn't have minded spending a little more time with Chloe. He didn't even know her last name.

"Then wipe that frown off your face. The next time Wilkes asks you to look up an old friend, I'll bet you'll think twice about it."

"There won't be a next time, Gus. Wilkes doesn't have long to live. That's why we're here. He's too frail to go after it himself. I'm not happy he's dying, but I am glad he chose me to lead the hunt."

Ben studied Gus's weathered face a moment, knowing he was the same age as Wilkes. He couldn't imagine Gus frail and dying like the colonel. He shrugged the image away. "I can only hope we get it back to him before that happens."

Gus hooted. "That old codger has had one foot in the grave for as long as I can remember. He's just too lazy to go a-hunting himself."

"I don't know. He seemed pretty sickly to me. Whatever the reason, we're here. If we succeed, it can only mean bigger and better things for us. Maybe even a sponsorship for my snow gorilla project."

The bartender, a balding man with a salt-and-pepper mustache, stopped wiping mugs and tucked the bar rag in his apron pocket. He approached the table with a quizzical expression. "You fellows with the railroad?"

"The railroad? Not a chance." The instant Gus spoke, Ben kicked him in the shin. He didn't want to arouse curiosity amongst the townsfolk. The less people knew, the less chance this expedition had of turning into a poodle act in a three-ring circus.

"We're here on a special mission." Gus clearly ignored Ben's warning. "We're going on a hunt."

Ben scowled in frustration, knowing it wouldn't take much encouragement from the bartender for Gus to talk about their plans.

"A hunt?" The bartender's blue eyes grew wide.

"Gus." Ben's tone was low, serious.

Gus merely winked at Ben. "Sit down and I'll tell you all about it."

The barman took a quick glance around the room to make sure no one was waiting for a refill. Satisfied, he grinned from ear to ear, showing off the town's lack of dentistry.

Gus waited while the man took a seat. "Are you Pete?"

"That's me." Pete stuck his hand out, and Gus pumped it up and down a few times.

"I'm Dr. Cygnus Pieper, Gus to you."

"Doc? Hey, listen." Pete placed a hand on his lower back. "I've been meaning to talk to someone about this crick I've got here—"

"No, no," Gus interrupted before Pete could list off a bunch of ailments. "Not that kind of doctor. I study animals. Not like a veterinarian, either. I'm a scientist." Gus beamed and chuckled. "So, like I said, call me Gus. And this here's Ben Kearny. You can ignore his frowning face. He looks like that all the time."

Ben scowled harder. Why couldn't Gus ever keep his mouth shut? And why did he have to be so impossibly good-natured? While Gus aggravated the dickens out of him more times than not, Ben still loved the old coot.

The two older men bent toward each other over the tabletop—Gus's preferred position for filling someone's head with malarkey. Ben drummed his fingers on the table, restraining himself from his sudden urge to knock their heads together.

Gus made a poor attempt to whisper. "Now you can't breathe a word of this."

"Neither can you." Ben itched to clap his hand over Gus's mouth and drag him from the saloon.

Delight twinkled in Gus's eyes and Ben turned away with a grumble. It wouldn't matter what he said, Gus wouldn't put a lid on his enthusiasm.

Though he was exasperated with him and could pull rank since he was the one in charge this time, Ben wouldn't. To do so would hurt and humiliate the man he loved like a father. Besides, he thought with a painful reminder that never seemed to leave him, he was single-handedly responsible for the ruination of Gus's career.

"So what's this hunt you fellows are talking about? You hunting for silver?" Pete cradled his chin in his hand, his blue eyes bright, expectant. "There are a lot of silver mines around these parts. Lots of fellows have made a fortune and moved on."

"Yeah, and I'm sure lots of them have gone home without the shirt on their back, too. Mining's for sissies. We've got more important things to find." Gus's face positively glowed with anticipation, a look that warmed Ben inside but did nothing to ease the guilt. Was there really any harm in the guy talking about his adventures?

"Naw. Get outta here. What's going to make you richer than hitting a vein of silver or gold?"

"Pete, my friend." Gus slapped him across the shoulders. "There are things of this world that are of far greater worth than money. Far greater."

"Get outta here." Pete laughed as he repeated himself. "If you believe that, you're the first folks crazy enough to declare it around here."

"Just sit back, my friend. I'll tell you all about it." Gus looked at Ben and grinned. The corners of Ben's mouth twitched and his mood perked up just a bit. "It's not what's under the mountain that we're interested in, it's what's on top. We're going hunting."

"Hunting? For what? Grizzlies? You'd best be careful." Pete's expression changed from interest to fright.

"Grizzlies?" Gus fairly cackled. "Ha! What we're after will make your grizzlies look like a bunch of pussy cats."

The excitement rose. Ben couldn't help it. Talking about their upcoming adventure started his blood racing and, like Gus, he was eager for the hunt to begin. He could no longer keep quiet. Ben also loved sharing tales.

"I don't suppose you've ever heard of a gorilla?"

Pete looked at Ben, clearly surprised he'd spoken up. "Can't say's I have."

Ben didn't doubt it. It amazed him, the number of people he'd come across who, after thirty years, still hadn't heard of or seen pictures of the fearsome gorilla. "Let's just say my gorilla can out do your grizzly any day." Ben looked at Gus and grinned.

Pete looked doubtful. "Where do you find this grilly creature?"

"Gorilla." Ben couldn't help correcting him. "Africa."

The barman's blue eyes widened. "Africa? You've been all the way to Africa?"

"Yes." Ben took a last swig from his mug. "Gus and I went on an expedition there several years ago. We were lucky enough to be with a party whose leader was there when they discovered the gorilla back in fifty-six."

"What does this here grilly look like?"

Ben loved this; the telling of a tale, sharing his adventures, describing a find. "First off they walk on two legs like we do. But they're huge. Bigger than you can imagine. Some are taller than most men and, like the monkey, covered with hair—lots of hair. And they're completely fearless. Their eyes flash like fire when they're scared, and they like to beat their chests with huge fists." Here, Ben couldn't help himself. His fingers curled into his palms, and he pounded his chest a couple of times. "They have a roar that'll curl your toes."

Pete drew his eyebrows together, listening, watching intently. "Sounds mighty fearsome. Were you scared?"

"No. I walked right up to him." Truth be told, they were one of the most beautiful creatures Ben had ever seen.

"And he didn't hurt you?" Pete sounded skeptical.

"Not at all. He grabbed some branches from my hand. He was really rather playful. I think he thought I was just another animal from the lowlands."

Pete let out a low whistle. "You don't say?"

"Ben here has also tangled with a Bengal tiger and wrestled with an anaconda." Gus pulled his shoulders back with pride.

Ben didn't bother to tell Pete he was scared spit-less both times.

"Your bear isn't likely to scare me." Not exactly true. Ben considered himself to be a sane man. But as an experienced tracker, he knew how to conduct himself in the wilderness areas. If he happened across anything dangerous, he'd know how to handle it.

Pete pulled thoughtfully on his chin. "It appears to me you're a couple of pretty well-traveled fellows. You've seen a lot more interesting places than our Cascades here. These mountains are going to seem mighty boring in comparison."

"Oh, but you're wrong." They wouldn't be boring at all. Ben knew what they'd find up the mountain, and it was far from boring. "I'm sure they'll prove very interesting indeed."

"Well, I'd think twice about going up there if I was you." Pete's eyes lost their twinkle of anticipation, and Ben heard the fear enter his voice. "There's a wild creature up there. Sounds kind of like your grilly. I hear tell he's half-man, half-animal. He's a gigantic creature covered with hair. Has the face of a man and walks upright on two legs." Pete pressed his lips together and shook his head. "One other thing. He's got the biggest footprints you ever did see."

Gus grinned. "You've seen the prints yourself?"

"Sure have. Why, the prints were so big, I could almost lay down in one of 'em."

Ben knew that to be an exaggeration, but of course that was to be expected with a legend. The stories just grew and grew. He almost laughed out loud with joy. It wasn't enough just to be here. Hearing Pete's words, hearing it confirmed by yet another human being, stirred the excitement.

"Sasquatch." Ben let the name roll off his tongue, savoring it, unable to keep the smile from breaking across his face. "That's his name. Sasquatch. And that's why we're here, Pete, to find your Sasquatch creature."

Never take your eyes off the goal. If you take your eyes off
the goal for even a second, you won't reach it.
I love you, sweet pea. You can do it.
Always, Aunt Jane

Chloe carefully folded the well-worn letter and tucked it into the hem of her sleeve. Though her aunt was gone from her life, Chloe still drew courage from her words.

She stood on the wooden sidewalk just outside the open door of Pete's Saloon where she'd been seeking her brother Charles Jr. She wanted to speak with him about the abominable way he treated Sarah. Even though he would probably yell at her, Chloe felt the need to stand up for her sister-in-law.

Realizing Charles Jr. wasn't there, she'd been about to leave when she recognized the deep rumble of Ben's voice. Yesterday evening, his voice found a permanent place in her memory. Now, hearing him mention the name Sasquatch, her reporter's ear became instantly alert.

Sasquatch! Ben was looking for the giant creature rumored to roam the deepest forest area.

Tales of the horrid half-man, half-animal creature had terrified residents of the North Cascades for years. Only a handful of people claimed to have seen him. He was legend among natives all across the country, with more names than she could count. It impressed Chloe to hear Ben call him Sasquatch. Not many even knew the creature by that name. She'd learned the native name from a Salish man—whom her father met shortly after they'd moved to Cedar Ridge—and immediately wrote an article about it. As C. J. Williston, of course. Her father liked the article so well he even sent it to the newspaper in Boston, where it was reprinted.

Chloe's fingers tingled, and a familiar sensation sizzled through her veins. She knew a story when she heard one. This was most definitely a story. Bigger than any story that had to do with Trina Clark. An interview with Ben now seemed much more urgent.

Running a finger under her sleeve, she traced her aunt's letter. Could she double the courage she'd drawn to confront Charles Jr. and ask Ben for one?

"Well, hello again."

Ben's resonating voice pulled Chloe out of her thoughts. She straightened and smoothed her sleeves. She looked at his feet first, handsomely encased in tan hiking boots. Faded denim trousers covered his long legs, and she recognized the red wool shirt he had on yesterday. Finally lifting her eyes to his face, Chloe swallowed hard. Ben towered over her by at least a foot. Amusement touched his lips, and fine lines crinkled the corners of his eyes.

A fascinating man—a fascinating mission—the story would make a great read.

Usually, once Chloe got started with an interview, she relaxed enough to talk comfortably. She thought perhaps it was because she tried so hard to put the other person at ease, she ended up forgetting about her own self-consciousness.

Gazing up at Ben, Chloe didn't think she'd ever have enough nerve to ask him for an interview, let alone ask any questions. Still, she must try.

For the story.

To be a reporter of the same calibre as Aunt Jane and Nellie Bly, to make her father realize women reporters could be every bit as good as men, she had to remember the goal. She had to concentrate on the story, not on what Ben might be thinking while she spoke.

"Why, Mr. Kearny. Imagine meeting you here."

"Yes, imagine." His tone told Chloe he suspected her of eavesdropping again. Twice caught, twice embarrassed. She closed her eyes and tried to unjumble the words she wanted to speak aloud. When she opened them again, she found him staring most intently. She hushed the annoying voice in her head, the one telling her to shut up because nothing she had to say was of importance.

"Uh...Mr. Kearny, I'd like to talk to you if you'd so kindly give me a moment of your time."

The words came out so rushed, she was sure he didn't catch any of what she said. He continued to study her face, which brought the nerves raging back to life. Her heart pounded in her ears. She averted her eyes then smoothed the front of her sky-blue skirt, taking one slow, steady breath after another.

Never one to be fashion-conscious—though her father could afford it—Chloe wished she'd worn her cranberry skirt and jacket. Its tailored look was much more professional than this everyday skirt and shirtwaist. She smoothed her skirt one more time and paced her breathing back to normal, which finally helped lessen the thrumming in her ears.

"I'm sorry you couldn't stay for my performance last night." His honey-rich voice set off tingles of awareness, unnerving her, and her gaze was drawn back to his face.

"Oh, but I..." *Oops.* Chloe looked at the ground, heat warming her cheeks. She spoke quietly, but loudly enough, she hoped, for Ben to hear. "I mean, I am too. I'm not very welcome there, as you obviously saw. But that's not why I want to talk to you. There's another matter we need to discuss."

"Why aren't you welcome there, Chloe?" Ben spoke softly, and Chloe looked up into his questioning gaze.

She tried to see into the depths of his green eyes, to see if there was a hint of the loneliness she'd heard in his voice when he sang. Her breath caught in her throat. It might not be loneliness, but she imagined there was some hidden emotion there, and it tugged at her heart. Unable to help herself, she stepped closer.

"I—they don't like me very well."

"Any particular reason why?"

Why? Because words choke in my throat, and they think I perceive them as beneath me. "It's not important." The goal. She had to focus on the goal and ask for an interview before her nerve disappeared altogether. "I couldn't help but overhear your conversation with Pete and the other fellow. I'm interested in the Sasquatch creature also. I..." Chloe stopped and took a breath. *Please, please, please let it come out right.*

"I wonder if you would do me the kindness of granting me an interview."

She hoped the tremble in her voice wasn't as noticeable as the trembling in her hands. Her heart pounded in her ears while she waited for his answer. And though she wanted to find a safe haven by looking at the ground again, she held his gaze, scarcely breathing while she willed him to say yes.

Ben raised his brow. "You want to interview me? Surely you're not serious."

Was that amusement she saw at the corners of his mouth?

Chloe blinked and clenched her fists, fighting to keep her expression passive. She couldn't let him know his attitude bothered her. Why couldn't men ever take women seriously? Why did they think women belonged in a kitchen baking bread, or sweating over a wash pan of smelly socks?

"Yes, I'm serious." She wasn't looking for a laugh. With a story like this, she would finally gain some respect in this town. Or at the very least, prove something to her antiquated father.

"No." Ben shook his head, his friendly tone gone. A brooding look clouded his face.

No? Did he, like her father, think women incapable of writing a decent article?

"But Mr. Kearny, my father owns a newspaper office. The readers—"

"Will all be stomping around the woods ruining our chances of finding the creature once your article goes to press. The answer is no. No interview, no article, no mention of Sasquatch. I warned Gus not to say anything."

He turned to go, and Chloe saw her big chance slipping away.

Her heart thudded. She had to speak up, but the words lodged in her throat. Her dream was about to die.

"Mr. Kearny, wait."

He stopped and looked back at her. She hated to beg. Worse, she hated to sound like a whining ninny. "Please reconsider. I promise, I won't even submit the article until after you and your party have left Cedar Ridge. And I won't say where you're headed."

"Why are you so interested in this?"

"I've been interested in the Sasquatch since I first heard about it." She explained about her father's Salish friend and the article she wrote. He listened with interest, and the more she talked about the article, the more comfortable she felt. "It's an important story, one people know relatively nothing about. Educating the public, being able to capture their attention with my words...it means everything to me."

He considered her for a moment with his startling green gaze. Then he shook his head. "I really do have to go."

She couldn't let him leave without agreeing to the article. "How much do you need?"

"Excuse me?"

"Money." Surely he needed some. Scientists always needed money. "How much do you need?"

"None."

"Mr. Kearny, if you give me the opportunity to be the first reporter with proof of the Sasquatch, I'll pay you however much you ask. I'll even supply you with a train ticket home. Wherever home is."

"Florida." He drew his eyebrows together in a scowl. "You're certainly persistent, aren't you?"

"Is it a deal then?" Her excitement brimmed, and her mind worked furiously to figure out how to get the money from her father.

Ben exhaled in a huff and looked away. The spirit seeped right out of her. Chloe knew what that meant. Defeat. Plain simple defeat.

"I don't want your money, Chloe." Ben's tone was quiet, final, and very clear. "I'm not doing an interview."

Chloe swallowed back her disappointment, wishing she could disappear from sight. Nellie Bly would never give up. Aunt Jane would never have given up. Neither would she.

"I'm sorry you feel that way. My article could have gained you all sorts of publicity. I'll bet there's not a single person in this town who knows what an ethologist is or does. I would think you'd want all the publicity you could get."

"That's exactly what I don't need." He stomped away without looking back.

Feeling incompetent, Chloe stared after him, angry for making a muddle of the chance of a lifetime. Why did she always say the wrong things? Why couldn't she be well spoken like her father?

Or better yet, like Aunt Jane? She would have had Ben Kearny begging to be interviewed, or whatever else she wanted him to do. Chloe failed to understand why she could express herself through her writing so much better than she could with her speech.

As if it mattered to Ben whether or not Chloe was a babbling idiot. Once he left Cedar Ridge, he'd never think of her again. Not that he had reason to now. He probably forgot her the moment he walked away.

Chapter Three

"I would think you'd want all the publicity you could get."

Why had he ever told her he was an ethologist? Of course, Ben hadn't known Chloe was a reporter when he'd said it. He hadn't even expected her to know what the word meant.

A reporter! He slapped himself upside the head. When word spread around and reporters were dogging their every footstep, this sure wasn't one he could blame on Gus.

He slouched on the wooden bench outside the Ridgeview Hotel, elbows on his knees, face plopped in his hands. The sheer granite side of Cedar Ridge loomed behind the hotel. The Skykomish River roared in front of it. Beyond him, across the river, rose an extensive range of mountains; some heavily wooded, some walls of granite like Cedar Ridge, others with snow-covered peaks. There were too many to count. He'd tried repeatedly but lost track. He just couldn't concentrate.

Thoughts of Chloe swirled in his head. Their encounter left him dazed and confused. Why? He couldn't figure it out. In trying to determine what so drew him to her, Ben's mind kept coming back to one thing: her spunkiness. Yes, she seemed a bit shy. But her initial timidity quickly gave way and wasn't enough to hide the heart of a spunky, effervescent woman who wanted to seize life in every way possible. He knew it as well as he knew the Sasquatch roamed these mountains. One look in her sassy blue eyes and he'd seen a zest for life and learning.

Never before had he felt a pull toward a woman like he did now. He was intrigued by it. Deep in his gut, he sensed Chloe was someone who shared his love for nature and its gifts.

That was why he had to put as much distance between himself and this little town as possible. Thoughts like this could only spell one thing—danger. Trouble. There was no room for thoughts of Chloe to be filling his mind. He could never see her again—especially since she was a reporter. What would happen if she found out the truth?

Chloe walked behind Pete's Saloon and headed up a well-worn path that led to the outskirts of Cedar Ridge. The heels of her shoes dug sharply into the dry ground, and her skirt swished around her legs, threatening to trip her as she quickly covered the distance to her destination.

Ben Kearny didn't want publicity? He didn't want a write-up in the paper, and wouldn't talk to her. Fine. There were other ways to get a story, and Chloe intended to do just that.

The path followed the Skykomish River. Usually the river calmed her, even when it was turbulent like today. But this time the waters offered no peace to counter the troubling emotions churning inside her. The way Ben had abruptly stalked away left her feeling ill at ease and defeated.

"When you want something bad enough," Aunt Jane used to say, *"you rush right out and do whatever you can to get it. If you have to go out on a limb, you go out as far as humanly possible, and then you go a little farther. That is the only way you ever get anything in this life."*

Chloe had learned long ago that Aunt Jane's words of wisdom were too valuable not to be heeded. No matter that her father thought her aunt a fluff-brain—his only sister had been a very wise woman.

A touch of sadness slivered through Chloe as she climbed the hill and gazed at the heavily forested mountains all around her. It was breathtaking.

Aunt Jane would have loved it here. Though Chloe hadn't seen her aunt in many years, they communicated through letters. Jane always promised to come and visit them, but a story never failed to keep her away. Still, Washington was a place she always wanted to see, and she'd promised in a letter that she would come visit them as soon as she could. Before she could join them, Jane had word of some story and took off for Florida, where she disappeared without a trace. Her father said she was likely dead, though Chloe didn't want to believe it.

Closing her eyes for a moment, she tried to picture her aunt as she'd last seen her more than ten years ago. Outfitted in men's trousers and a short haircut that framed her face in the most delightful way, she'd been ready to head off on yet another adventure. Chloe didn't know for sure if the memory was real or based on a lonely girl's dreams. But that image of Aunt Jane was always comforting.

"So what would you do in my situation, Aunt Jane?"

I'd follow that man with the green eyes and never let him get away.

Chloe could almost hear her aunt's voice whisper along with the breeze. And it surprised her. Follow a man? She'd never heard Aunt Jane say anything of the sort. Men usually followed Jane, but she didn't have much use for them. Her aunt said there wasn't a man around who appreciated a woman with spirit or a passion for adventure.

Could Aunt Jane have been wrong? Ben seemed different than other men, and certainly seemed the adventurous sort. But did Chloe have the spirit and pluck necessary to capture his appreciation? An inner smile lifted her heart. Maybe she should try to find out.

Lengthening her stride, Chloe realized her discouragement had given way to hope...and to a plan. She reached her destination, a towering oak—her brother's usual spot beside the river's rocky bank. Caleb could often be found here, just as he was now, leaning against the gnarled tree trunk, pencil in hand and sketch pad on his lap.

Caleb's gray corduroy vest was unbuttoned, as were the top buttons of his shirt, and his cap was tossed haphazardly on the grass. Intent on sketching something within the branches of the tree, he didn't acknowledge Chloe's presence. She kneeled at her brother's side and tipped her head back, trying to see what he did. Not sure what to look for, she peered at Caleb's pencil drawing before she looked back up in the tree.

After a moment spent searching, she spotted the jumble of twigs woven together to form a bird's nest. "I see it now."

"You should have been here half an hour ago." Caleb smiled before shoving his mop of blond hair out of his eyes. Though much lighter than her own, her brother's hair was as thick and wavy, and always seemed to be in need of cutting.

"An hour ago? Why's that?"

"It was feeding time." Caleb shuffled through his stack of sketches to reveal several stunning drawings of four hungry little birds with their mouths open wide.

"Did you have to stand up to get this view?"

"No. I climbed the tree." Chloe knew Caleb was teasing, and his grin did wonderful things to her heart. She loved to see her brother happy, and in this environment, he was. Sitting in *The Reporter* office only seemed to turn him rather melancholy.

"You didn't see Elizabeth anywhere, did you?" There was more than a hint of that very gloominess in Caleb's tone.

"No. Trina Clark is having one of her silly quilting parties, and I'm sure Elizabeth is there right along with Mother, Sarah, and every other female in town."

"Except you."

"Except me." Chloe nodded. "I see no reason to waste my time doing something I care nothing about. Important things might be happening somewhere else." Chloe could see the traces of gloom almost lift from her brother's appearance. She pressed her lips together, shaking her head. After a moment she sighed.

"What?" Sounding defensive, Caleb stared at her wide-eyed. The sheepish look was so typically Caleb when he knew exactly *what*, that Chloe almost laughed out loud. But though his eyes were unblinking and the look on his face attempted innocence, a hint of unhappiness remained. No. Her younger brother's unhappiness was not a laughing matter.

"You know exactly what I'm thinking about, Caleb Williston." Chloe paused for effect. "Elizabeth."

That one word was enough to prove her point. Caleb set his stack of drawings face down on the ground and stared at something down along the river, silent for several minutes before he spoke again. "I don't want to talk about her."

"She's not the girl for you."

Caleb tucked his knees to his chest and rested his chin on them.

"She's not." Chloe was earnest in her belief. "She makes you unhappy."

"No she doesn't." His voice was low, filled with pain.

"Then why were you so relieved to know she's not coming down the path anytime soon?"

Caleb didn't have to look at her for Chloe to know there was a hurt in his eyes that reflected his soul. He was her baby brother only by a year. She knew him as well as she knew herself. He hurt, and she felt it. Elizabeth was too judgmental of him. If Caleb wrote newspaper articles, he was like gold in her eyes. But if he dared waste precious time on the drawings she regarded with disdain, she called him a frivolous wastrel.

Chloe reached out and rubbed her palm against her brother's shoulder. She could feel the tension there. Elizabeth wasn't good for him. Chloe bit her lip. Voicing the thought to her brother only made him more miserable.

"I really do love her." Caleb's plaintive whisper tugged her heart. "I just can't do anything to please her."

Chloe understood that well enough. That was the position she found herself in with her father. She loved him, yet she couldn't please him. She either talked too much or not enough. And she never wanted to do the things a woman should aspire to do. Baking, cooking, sewing, needlework, gardening, quilting.

Nice girls weren't newspaper reporters, he always said. Then he'd remind her of Aunt Jane. *Just look at her now,* he'd say. *Where is she? What has a lifetime of speaking her mind gotten her? Nothing. She's gone, disappeared off the face of the earth. Do you want to end up like her?*

Chloe sighed. "What you need, Caleb, is something to take you away from Father's demands and get you out from under Elizabeth's scrutinizing eye. How would you like the opportunity to draw whenever you want without worrying about Elizabeth coming around the corner and catching you?"

Caleb gave her a lazy smile, but she did catch the gleam of interest in his eyes. "I'd say it sounds like your imagination is getting the better of you."

"Well, it's not." Quickly Chloe filled her brother in on Ben Kearny's big hunt.

"Yes." His smile lifted, no longer lazy, and spread across his face in delight. "I'd say your imagination has definitely taken over."

"Caleb, don't you see? This is a wonderful opportunity for us. If we can talk Mr. Kearny into letting us go along."

"Mr. Kearny? What about Father? How do you propose to get him to agree to me being away from the paper?"

"Just leave Father to me. It's Ben we have to convince. He's already told me no reporters. We have to figure out a way to convince him that he needs us—or rather, you."

"So it's Ben now, is it? Chloe, are you sweet on him?"

Chloe flushed and looked at the ground. She didn't want her brother even guessing at how attractive she found Ben.

"I don't know." Caleb shook his head.

"Please, Caleb. Think about it before you say no. You'd be free from the paper. You could relax, draw, whatever you want."

"What do you want me to do? Ask this *Ben* if he'd like a reporter along for the big moment?"

"No, no." Chloe was quick to interrupt. "I told you, I've already asked him for an interview. He's made it quite clear he doesn't want anything to do with the press."

"Maybe he just said that because you're a girl."

"Woman." Chloe corrected her brother automatically. "And no, he was quite specific. No reporters."

"Let's think about this for minute." Caleb stared out at the river, lost in thought.

Chloe watched him, worried he'd say no. If he didn't agree, there wouldn't be much chance of her going along on this hunt. Perhaps she could hire on as a cook. She wrinkled her nose in distaste. That wouldn't be as much fun as reporting, but at least she'd be there.

"I've got it." Chloe had a sudden inspiration. "You'll be their guide."

Caleb's burst of laughter startled the birds in their nest overhead, and they set to chirping noisily.

"Chloe you're talking about miles and miles of mountain trails. Switchbacks. Up one side and down the other. Dangerous. Treacherous."

Chloe seized the opportunity to argue her case. "That's why they'll need a guide. All you have to do is convince them."

"I'm no expert on this area. It's not like we've lived here all our lives."

"I know, but we can't let that stop us. You've hiked with some of the men enough that I think you can pass it off. Caleb, we have to go. It will be so good for us." She didn't want to sound selfish. "I mean, for you."

Caleb lifted an eyebrow in disbelief.

"Okay, for us."

Finally Caleb smiled at her. "It's pretty important to you, isn't it?"

"Yes, it is, but you'll see. It will be for you too." She'd get her story, but her brother would be away from Elizabeth and could draw to his heart's content. Maybe then he'd see that he didn't really love the arrogant young woman.

"So how do I become a mountain expert, and won't he recognize my last name and get suspicious about you putting me up to this?"

"Don't worry about the name thing. He doesn't know my last name. Now, first you need to talk to Pete." Pete was her favorite source for all kinds of good information, and one of the few people in town she was comfortable talking with. Though her father didn't approve of her acquaintance with the barman, Chloe thoroughly enjoyed many interesting conversations with Pete.

"I'm sure he knows someone you can get a map from. Surely a map will help with credibility when you approach Ben. That and the warning they shouldn't go into the mountains alone without someone experienced should do the trick."

"But what about you?" Caleb didn't seem entirely convinced. "How will I talk Kearny into letting you join me?"

"I'll figure something out when the time comes. Maybe I'll be your assistant or something." She tilted her head and gave her brother a mischievous smile.

"All right. We'll do it." Caleb returned the smile. "But this better be worth it."

"It will." Chloe threw her arms around her brother. "Just think. You'll be able to draw for who knows how many days. And at the end of it, you'll have enough illustrations to fill books on everything from mountain wildflowers to the Sasquatch. And me?" Chloe smiled with triumph, leaned over, and planted a kiss on her brother's cheek. "I'll have an article that will be in every paper in the United States. Father will recognize my ability, and Elizabeth will look at you in an entirely different way."

"Yes." Caleb's tone turned dry. "She'll look further down her nose at me than she does already."

"Now see, Caleb? If Elizabeth feels so negative toward you, what are you two doing engaged?"

"We don't see eye to eye on things, but we love each other."

If love makes people this miserable, I don't want any part of it. Chloe knew her brother so well, but on this she was stumped. How could he be in love with a woman who so clearly disapproved of that which gave him his every reason for breathing?

Not me. I'll be accepted for who I am or I'll never fall in love.

Which is why you'll spend your life alone, whispered the hurt little girl her soul harbored.

She didn't care. Well...maybe she did. But she would never put herself in a situation like Caleb had with Elizabeth. In order for her to look at a prospective beau more than once, he'd have to not only approve of a woman who was a reporter, he'd have to be totally fascinated by her.

What about Ben and his green eyes? Would he be fascinated by her? He already said he didn't like reporters.

And she'd have to be able to wow him with words, before she could fascinate him.

A hard lump clogged her throat. Chloe vowed she'd get over her inability to express herself verbally and find her voice no matter what.

Chloe walked up a narrow cobblestone path, neatly bordered by a colorful array of pansies and petunias in shades of purples and pinks. The path led to a little white building that housed *The Cedar Ridge Reporter.* It was the newest structure in Cedar Ridge, a small two-roomed office. Her father hadn't wanted something too fancy lest he scare off the town residents. He was never one to flaunt his wealth, but most people were still usually aware of it immediately. Her father just had that kind of demeanor about him.

He also had the presence to intimidate people. Especially those who were easily intimidated—like her. She could talk quite comfortably to those she was close to like Caleb and her mother. But she had a difficult time mustering the words around those who didn't approve of her desires—her father, especially.

Just think of the Sasquatch. The story. What it will mean. Be like Aunt Jane.

Chloe sucked in a breath and stepped through the hand-carved door with its etched glass window and inhaled the familiar scent of pipe tobacco.

"Hello, Father."

Charles Williston Sr. sat behind his large mahogany desk in an oversized leather chair of rich burgundy. His wire-rimmed spectacles were perched on his nose, and he squinted at a mock-up of the next issue of *The Reporter*.

Chloe bit back her disappointment when her father didn't look up. Slowly she made her way across the oak floor and stopped in front of his desk. Standing quietly, she waited for him to acknowledge her.

Finally, he removed the pipe from between his teeth, and peered up at her over the top of his spectacles. Chloe almost laughed. The action made him look like a walrus trying not to frown. "Chloe. Sweetheart. Why aren't you at the quilting party with your mother and Sarah?"

Chloe wrinkled her nose, and her father sighed.

"I know. Why should you waste your time on frivolities when you can do something important like edit my articles?"

Amazed that he wasn't going to give her a lecture, Chloe smiled so huge her jaws ached. "You do have a point, Father."

This time her father's sigh was most heavy. "My dear, when will you understand? I was being sarcastic. Your place isn't in a dusty old print shop with us men."

What men? Her father and Caleb? He made it sound so pretentious. As if she'd ruin herself for all of society if she deigned to be seen in a print office.

Her father stood up behind the desk. "Your place is in the meeting hall, with your peers."

The meeting hall.

Chloe's mind didn't have to wander too far to recall last night's episode. Ben Kearny singing. She sighed. It was an image she wouldn't soon forget. "Father, I have some news you won't want to miss."

"Really?" Her father tapped his pipe on the edge of his desk then bit the stem before putting it back in his mouth. He watched her quizzically.

Chloe took his interest as a good sign. Maybe she'd be successful and get what she wanted for a change. "There's a team of scientists—they call themselves ethologists—in town. They're passing through on their way up the Cascades. You won't believe what they're after."

"Hmmm?" Removing the pipe from his mouth, her father pressed his lips together and glanced down at his mock-up.

Chloe hated that. She knew when her father pressed his lips together and diverted his attention, he was only humoring her. When would he take her seriously as a reporter?

"They're hunting for the Sasquatch."

"Hmmm." He didn't even look up. Instead, he sat back down.

"Father, listen. You remember. The *Sasquatch?* I—Caleb wrote a small article about the rumored sightings not too long ago. Surely you've not forgotten?"

"Oh, yes." Finally he glanced at Chloe. "Now I recall. I believe we even sent it to the paper in Boston. I wonder if Preston ever ran that article in his paper?"

"Father." Chloe tapped her foot impatiently.

"Hmm, yes. You say they're here looking for the creature?"

"Yes. They've been offered a large amount of money by some old game hunter."

"How did you say you learned of this?"

"I overheard them celebrating at Pete's."

"At Pete's?"

Chloe flinched at the loudness of her father's voice. Again, he stood up. This time he walked out from behind his desk to stand in front of her. He towered over her, but not by as much as Ben did.

"Chloe, a young woman with your upbringing does not belong anywhere near Pete's."

Chloe couldn't help but protest. "I was just walking by and heard the celebrating."

"And you were curious."

"Well...yes. You always say curiosity is the mark of a good reporter."

"That's true, my dear." Her father draped his arm affectionately across her shoulders. He edged her toward the door as if to dismiss her from his presence. "But you are not a reporter. You are my daughter. Leave the reporting *and* the curiosity to the *real* reporters—your brother and me."

Chloe was tempted to roll her eyes at the reference of her brother being the "real" reporter. She wouldn't betray Caleb's secret. Her father's hand was on the brass door handle but Chloe planted her feet, not about to be swept out the door before pleading her case.

"Seriously Father, can you imagine the kind of story we could get if this team actually finds the Sasquatch?"

"If it exists."

"What do you mean, if it exists? Father, are you telling me you ran the article then sent it to Preston but don't believe a word of it?"

"It's not as simple as it sounds, Chloe. But I suppose you have a point. My job is to sell papers. As I recall, the interview you mentioned sold quite a few extra issues."

He dropped his arm from his daughter's shoulder and flung the door open wide. The smile he bestowed on her made Chloe's heart leap. "You're on to something here." Then her father patted the top of her head like she was a little girl. "Sweetheart, go find your brother. He's going to do a little mountain climbing."

The excitement bubbled up from Chloe's toes and filled her near to bursting. "Oh Father, this is wonderful." She stood on her tiptoes and gave him an impulsive kiss on the cheek. "We won't disappoint you."

She started to step through the door.

"Just a minute, young lady."

Chloe halted in her tracks, and her heart quickly sank. She knew that tone.

"I said Caleb was going. I don't recall mentioning your name."

Bitterness formed a painful lump in her throat. "Father." She'd expected as much. She had to fight for every tantalizing bit of the newspaper business. If she didn't, she'd spend the rest of her life peeling potatoes and baking pies. "Caleb needs someone along with him." Chloe wasn't about to give up now. "You know, he always bounces his ideas off me. We're more of a team than you want to admit—or know."

Chloe's father sighed unhappily. "Perhaps you and your brother are too much alike."

Not as much alike as you think, Father. Caleb hates to write. Chloe just smiled. "Well, maybe we're not so much alike as we are good for each other. Don't you know, Father, that Caleb always looks to me for ideas and help while he's working on an article? Besides, I know it's foolish to go up there all alone. I doubt those scientists are going to let Caleb tag along. He might have to follow at a good distance. He *needs* me there."

Her father sighed and raked his fingers through his thinning hair. "Charles Jr. can accompany him."

"Don't be ridiculous. Father, haven't you been paying attention? Charles Jr. is always drunk. He'd be no help for Caleb. He'd probably walk right off a cliff and never realize it."

Her father made a hemming sound. "I just don't know. You have no business going up in those woods. And someone has to run the paper, so I can't really go. Perhaps it wasn't such a good idea after all."

"Oh, no, Father. No. It's a wonderful idea. We'll sell more papers than ever. The story will be so great it might get picked up and run in papers across the country."

She stopped at the look of pain that crossed her father's face. "I know the paper hasn't done everything you wanted it to."

Sympathy for her father pierced through her. The townsfolk of Cedar Ridge didn't seem all too interested in a newspaper. But if the story was one that grabbed them, they'd certainly be more eager to buy the next issue and the next.

Finally, her father smiled half-heartedly. He reached out and squeezed her hand.

"Please, Father. Let Caleb and me do this. I promise we won't let you down."

"Ah, Chloe, my dear daughter. You are going to be the death of me yet. Go." He made a shooing motion. Then an uncustomary smile spread across his face. "Go. Find Caleb. You have plans to make."

For the second time that day, Ben sat on the bench in front of his hotel. Sighing in disgust, he stood up from the bench and jammed his hands in his pockets. Rocking back on his heels he looked around at the river, the mountains, the hotel, then plopped back down. He had to rid his mind of the sprightly Chloe and think of other things...like the big trip.

Anxious to get started, he planned to leave tomorrow afternoon. He was so eager to feel the mountainside under his feet, he wouldn't mind leaving this instant if he didn't have to consider the rest of his companions. They still had a few supplies to gather together.

"Excuse me, sir? Mr. Kearny?"

Ben pulled his gaze from the rushing river and looked at the man who plunked down beside him. He looked to be in his early twenties, with shaggy light hair and blue eyes. Ben felt a startling sense of familiarity.

"Do I know you?"

"No sir."

In spite of the answer, Ben couldn't shake the odd feeling of recognition. "Then what can I do for you?"

"I understand you're planning a trip into the mountains."

Ben straightened in surprise. "Did you hear that from Pete?"

"I, uh, yes, sir." The man broke eye contact with Ben and stared at the river. "I was thinking maybe you needed a guide."

"Really?" Ben nodded in interest. The thought had crossed his mind a time or two, but his team was more than experienced, and secrecy for the mission was of the utmost importance. Advertising for a guide would have been like advertising for newshounds to follow their trail. Of course, that was beside the point now since apparently Pete had blabbed.

"What did you say your name is?"

"I didn't, sir. It's Caleb, sir."

"Why don't you dispense with the 'sir' and all the formal talk and tell me your full name." Did he imagine it, or did Caleb squirm and look uncomfortable?

"Caleb Williston."

"So you think I need a guide, do you?"

"Yes." Caleb looked Ben square in the eye. "It can be dangerous up there. Lots of strangers have disappeared never to be heard from again."

"Any unfamiliar territory can be dangerous. But my team and I are more than capable of handling ourselves."

"I'm sure you are. I merely wanted to offer my services because I'd hate for anything to happen to you or the people you're responsible for."

"Yes, well..." Ben kicked at a clump of dirt and weeds, no longer as eager or as sure of himself as he'd once been. "Are you from around here?"

"Yes."

"You know your way around the woods?"

"Yes."

"Been up there before?"

"More than once. I, uh, have a map too." Caleb produced a battered map from his pocket. The map looked well used. If Caleb had indeed put every wear mark on that map then he must be an experienced guide; although he did seem a trifle young to have so much experience.

"I appreciate your interest, Caleb. And I'll certainly give it some consideration." He was indeed interested, but Ben didn't want to seem too eager. "How can I get in touch with you?"

"You can leave word with Pete." Caleb grinned.

"I'll make a decision by morning."

"Thank you, sir. I mean, Ben."

After shaking Caleb's hand and sending the young man on his way, Ben trudged toward the hotel. He'd talk to the others about Caleb and make a decision.

"I'd hate for anything to happen to you or the people you're responsible for." Caleb's words echoed in Ben's mind, twisting in his gut.

He would only talk to the others out of respect. The decision was made. He wasn't about to make the same mistake twice.

They needed a guide.

Chapter Four

"I think that's everything your father ordered, Miss Williston. Would you like Robert to deliver these?" Mr. Fenton, owner of Cedar Ridge's only store, was a short, rotund man with a jolly face and a chipper attitude.

"Uh, not quite yet, thank you." Chloe stared at the neatly wrapped parcels stacked on the counter, feeling rather glum. The sight in itself was enough to overwhelm a lumberjack. But that wasn't the cause of her low spirits.

Hidden beneath the layers of brown paper lay the ugliest clothing man ever created. The shirts, jacket, and trousers were the smallest adult sizes the store had in stock. It was obvious they were all too big. But worse, they were the ugly shade of dead grass. Dead grass! She'd look like a walking weed out there in the woods with Ben.

Hardly a way to make an impression.

Not that this trip was about capturing the scientist's attention. Nor did she hold any notions that he might take a liking to her. Still, when a man like Ben Kearny was around, a woman wanted to look her best. It couldn't be done in clothes that were a sick shade of yellowish brown.

"Um, Mr. Fenton?" He'd gone to so much trouble to get this order ready for Caleb and her on such short notice, she really hated to be any more of a bother. However, she had her pride. No brown shirts. "I know you picked out exactly what my father ordered, but would you mind terribly if we unwrapped the shirts and exchanged them for something with a bit more color?"

"Color?" Confusion clouded Mr. Fenton's jolly features. "But Miss Williston, your father distinctly mentioned clothing for hunting. For that, you mustn't have too much color. Not that I approve of women hunting, mind you." Both his confusion and jolliness were replaced with a frown of disapproval.

"Many women hunt, Mr. Fenton, but this isn't that kind of hunting trip." She left it at that, not wanting to explain about the Sasquatch. If he believed women shouldn't hunt, what would he say about her hunting for the feared creature?

He responded with what sounded remarkably like her father tsk-tsking her whenever she expressed interest in writing about one story or another.

"My father won't mind my changing the shirts. Honestly he won't." The shopkeeper's expression didn't change, so Chloe cupped both hands under her chin.

"Look at my skin color, sir. Do you honestly think that ghastly brown will do one thing to enhance it? I'd look positively hideous with that color next to my face."

"Yes, well—"

"I'll accept the brown trousers, and the jacket. Hopefully I won't have to ever wear the jacket, but I'll take it just the same. But I'm afraid I've decided against the shirts. Now please, can't we exchange them for something else?"

Mr. Fenton blinked twice, maybe in surprise at her outburst—Chloe didn't know for sure. But after the second blink, he brightened and once again appeared his jolly self.

After unwrapping the parcel that contained the two unsightly shirts, Mr. Fenton carefully placed them back to the shelf where they belonged, then led her to the backside of the shelf where there were more cotton shirts in an assortment of colors.

Mr. Fenton picked up a bright blue shirt and held it against Chloe's face. He smiled with approval, and his blue eyes twinkled.

"This one will do quite nicely, Miss Williston. It brings out the blue of your eyes and adds a pink touch to your cheeks."

Heat burned the tips of Chloe's ears. She wasn't used to this kind of attention from the townsfolk. It was decidedly nice. "I'll take this one then."

The next shirt Mr. Fenton picked up, bright yellow, would have her looking like a sunflower. He held it up to Chloe and shook his head. "I think not. It's positively as bad as the brown. Not for you at all." He shook his head once again before pausing over a red and black checked shirt.

"Hardly the thing for hunting." He winked at her. "But it does even nicer things to your face than the blue."

Really! Was the man flirting with her? This wasn't like him at all. She opened her mouth to speak but was at a loss for words. Instead, Chloe took both shirts and walked back to the counter. Mr. Fenton quietly followed suit.

"There's one other thing." Chloe watched him wrap the shirts. "A parasol is totally out of place on a hunting trip. I know my father wants me to shield my face from the sun. It seems to be his one concession to frivolity in all these purchases. But really, sir, can you see me on a hunting trip carrying a parasol?"

Head tipped to one side, Mr. Fenton pursed his lips and studied her with one eye squinted, much as her mother's seamstress did. "Truthfully, no. Do you wish to exchange it for a hat?"

"Yes, please. Where do you keep your hunting caps?"

"Right over here. We'll find one that fits you." Chloe followed Mr. Fenton past the shirts and trousers, to the back of the store. She stopped short. All the hats were that same awful dead-grass-brown.

"You don't happen to have a Nellie Bly cap, do you?" She could tell by his drawn brow, he had no idea what she was talking about. "It's a jaunty little cap with a smart looking bill that will block the sun quite nicely without washing me out with that dreadful color."

"I could check into getting one for you, but it might take a while."

A Nellie Bly hat would have been nice but would be impossible to obtain by this afternoon. "I guess one of these will have to do then." Chloe tried to keep her voice light in hopes Mr. Fenton wouldn't see her dejection. Perhaps the blue and red shirts would give her enough color that the hat wouldn't matter much. She did need something to shade her eyes and keep her face from burning.

"I'll take this one." She handed the shopkeeper one of the ugly hats that sported a heavy bill down both the front and back. "I think I'm ready now."

"Very good. Now what about having these things delivered?"

"I don't think so. Thank you though." Much as she'd like to take Mr. Fenton up on his offer of a delivery, Chloe had to do this on her own. After all, no one was going to help carry her gear up the mountain. But that didn't mean she had to lug Caleb's stuff home too.

"On second thought, I'll only take part of it. I'll send Caleb around for the rest."

"Are you sure, Miss Williston?" Mr. Fenton frowned.

"I'm sure. There's no time like the present to get used to packing all this stuff." Besides, once she showed up with Caleb, Ben was sure to be none too happy. They'd stand a better chance of convincing him to let her go along if she appeared to know what she was doing.

Early this morning, Caleb had firmed up the plans with Ben. He'd told Chloe to be ready shortly after lunch. The group would get on a freight train just outside of Cedar Ridge and ride to Skykomish. From there, they'd start their ascent into the higher mountains.

It was now or never, and she was eager to get started. Brushing her hands together, she sized up her purchases. An arctic sleeping bag was neatly rolled and fastened with string. There were packages containing two deliciously scented bars of Pears soap, shirts, the funny looking hat, trousers, socks and boots, and finally a carry-all bag with straps that could be slung over her shoulders.

Opening the carry-all bag, she inserted as many packages as possible. Hopefully once everything was unwrapped it would all fit. It would be torture carrying all this up the mountain.

A tiny brass bell tinkled as the door opened. Chloe glanced over her shoulder and quickly turned back to her purchases, hoping she'd go unnoticed. Her heart thudded. Ben Kearny's presence filled the room, and she could scarcely breathe.

Yesterday's encounter and his abrupt dismissal of her still stung.

"Good morning, sir." Ben greeted Mr. Fenton. "I need to get a few more supplies before I head out." Mr. Fenton looked at Chloe expectantly. She kept her face averted from Ben's line of vision and nodded to let the shopkeeper know she was finished. She hoped he wouldn't dismiss her by name the way he usually did. Much to her relief, he didn't.

If Ben noticed either Chloe or her supplies, he said nothing. A small breath, an odd mix of relief and remorse, escaped her when Ben walked past. Sadly, she was as unnoticeable as the little brown cowbirds that lined the banks of the river. Mr. Fenton led him to the far wall, and Chloe listened to the low, pleasant rumble of Ben's voice as he conversed with the shopkeeper.

The prospect of finding the Sasquatch was exciting in and of itself, but trailing

Ben Kearny for days on end was like sweet cream on berries. It would be a lie to say she wasn't looking forward to it.

With a shaky hand, Chloe reached out to sling the bag over her shoulder. She scooped up the remaining packages and tried to hold them in one arm while grabbing hold of the sleeping bag. Her father ordered enough things for a year-long trip.

Chloe was almost ready to step away from the counter when the door opened and the bell tinkled once more.

"There you are, Ben. Did you get everything we need?"

It was a woman's voice, and much too sweet. Chloe's arm wobbled, and her packages dipped dangerously toward the floor. She fought to balance them and managed to land the packages back on the countertop, but not before she dropped the sleeping bag on the floor. She reached to retrieve it then dared a glance over her shoulder.

A long legged, voluptuous woman rushed over to Ben and grabbed him by the arm. Her hair was the same jet color of a raven's wing. Though it was cut surprisingly short for a woman, the chin-length hair framed her face in a most becoming fashion. Chloe's own hair looked like dirt by comparison. The woman was almost as tall as Ben. She wore the same horrid clothes Chloe had just turned her nose up at. On this woman though, they were stunning if not a little too snug. Inadequacy filled Chloe.

Ben appeared surprised to see the woman but didn't extract his arm from her grip. "What are you doing here, Monique?"

Who was she? His wife? Obviously she was dressed for the trip. For the first time, Chloe considered that Ben might be married. Surely he wasn't. No wife in her right mind would let Ben entertain a group of man-hungry women like he had the other night. Unless, of course, she didn't know about it.

Chloe frowned.

"We have to hurry, Ben." Monique tapped her tiny foot impatiently. "Daddy's waiting at the hotel. He wants to eat an early lunch so we can get things organized and in perfect order before leaving."

Her purchases balanced precariously in her arms once again, Chloe brushed aside her sudden dread of the adventure ahead of her. *No.* She had to dig deep to find her resolve. Nothing was going to ruin this trip. Not even a voluptuous woman named Monique, who defied fashion with her short, black hair.

"Ben, why are you walking so slow?"

He stopped on the path and looked up. Gus and Monique stood waiting for him to catch up. Rudy and Skip walked ahead, lost in conversation. They'd left town through the woods, on a path that would lead them to the railroad tracks.

Cedar Ridge didn't have a train station yet, so they had to walk to the site where the freight train would pick up equipment to be delivered further up the line where men were forging a tunnel through the mountain. The engineer had agreed to let Ben and his crew ride to the end of the line at a much higher elevation so they could begin their hunt.

"Hurry up." Monique's whine grated on his nerves. It was a sure reminder of the last time she'd been in the field with him. A reminder he was struggling to ignore. "You're the one who said we didn't have time to waste."

Ben kicked a pebble that lay ahead of him on the path and watched it skip down the hill and land in a patch of wildflowers. Berating himself over letting Gus talk him into bringing Monique along was of no use. It was over, done. Like the past. He needed to put it aside and move on.

"Why don't you go on ahead? I'll catch up with you in a few minutes." Yes he needed to put the past to rest, but he hadn't done it yet. It would be easier, perhaps, if he had a few minutes of solitude before their hunt actually began.

"Ben, what's wrong?" Monique's tone was full of concern, but it was one Ben could see right through. It was the one she reserved for times when she wanted people to think she cared—but she only really cared that they weren't blaming her for something.

"Nothing's wrong, really. I just need a little time to think."

"Think about what? I thought you were anxious to get started." The hunting cap Monique wore was tilted up off her forehead, high enough that he could see the concern in her brown eyes. Perhaps he wasn't being fair. Maybe she really did care about someone besides herself, and it could be he was misjudging her now.

Feeling guilty, he looked away. "I was. I mean, I am. It's just that after today there won't be much of an opportunity for quiet time. We're all going to be together constantly. I'd just like a few minutes alone before that happens."

Gus stared at him like he'd gone weak between the ears. Perhaps Gus was right. Monique pursed her lips in a way that he'd come to hate over the years. It either meant she was annoyed, or someone hurt her feelings. Right now he was certain it meant annoyed.

"I'm fine. Would you all just let me be for a minute?"

Gus let out a disgusted grunt and continued to stare at him.

"I suppose." If possible, Monique's lips pursed even tighter. "If you insist."

"I do. Now go catch up with Rudy and Skip."

"Jeepers." Gus stared at Ben and adjusted the packs strapped to his back. "You got a burr under your saddle or what?"

He wanted to tell Gus exactly what the problem was; that Monique was a constant reminder of their—his and Gus's—tragic failure. That she would whine and complain the entire trip and undoubtedly put everyone's lives in danger at least once. But he didn't. Instead, he planted his feet in the dirt and glared until Monique finally shifted uncomfortably and grabbed her father by the arm.

"Come on, Daddy. Let's leave him be." Her tone was so conciliatory Ben was left to wonder if something in his eyes had betrayed him.

Did Monique know? Ben leaned against the trunk of a Douglas fir and looked down the path that led back toward town. Did she know he still struggled on a daily basis with what had happened on that island? Somehow, Ben doubted it would matter to her if she did.

Though she'd never admit it, and though Ben bore the ultimate responsibility, Monique was also an inadvertent part of the tragic loss of one of the members of their field team. Not just any member, Ben reminded himself bitterly, but someone who should never have been there in the first place.

He stuffed his hands in the pockets of his hunting trousers and looked at the majesty surrounding him. Inhaling the mingled scents of tree bark, dirt, and the spray from the river, he tried to put his turbulent thoughts aside. There was a peace to be found here. Elusive, yes, but he could almost feel it within his grasp. If only he could reach it, it would be like a retreat for his soul. It would be like...like coming home.

A real home was something Ben had never had. Gus had done his best, raising Ben the only way he knew how, instilling in him the love of nature, of adventure. And though Gus loved him like a father should, and always treated Ben as his own, there was always a dark empty place in his soul that nothing could fill. A darkness that had descended when his parents abandoned him. As a boy he believed himself unworthy of love. Why else would parents leave a child? Of course, now he realized the failing was on their part, not his.

Heaven help him if he ever did such a thing to a child of his own. He'd love that child, give that child a family. He'd provide a home for his family in a place much like this one. That, he supposed, was why it tugged at him so. Because this was where he'd want to envision his children being raised. A place like this, a town like this.

A vision of sparkling blue eyes and wavy gold-brown hair danced in his head. Sighing, he looked longingly toward town one last time before trudging off to meet the others. Any thoughts of remaining in Cedar Ridge indefinitely were just that. Thoughts. And it was best for him if he'd tuck them away right now and forget about them.

Because nothing was going to change.

Not who he was, and not what he was.

As long as that held true, there would be no such thing as a family for him.

Chloe sat on the edge of her bed, trying not to wrinkle the delicate pink and white quilt her mother had so lovingly stitched for her last year. She stared at the unwrapped packages. They should have focused her thoughts, but they didn't. Try as she might, she couldn't get Ben and Monique off her mind.

Caleb hadn't said a word about this woman. He'd only mentioned there were a few other fellows along. Monique hardly fit that description, Chloe thought dryly.

Still struggling with the question of how to survive a week with strangers, Chloe slipped out of her skirt and tugged on the trousers. Way too big. She turned the pant legs up a couple of folds. A little better. She'd just have to borrow a belt from her brother.

Turning one way and then the other before the large French beveled mirror that was attached to one door of her wardrobe, Chloe decided the trousers wouldn't look half bad with her white shirtwaist if they fit her properly. Her gaze strayed to her dressing table.

Remembering the length of black Chantilly lace she wanted to use to spruce up her navy blue Sunday suit, she opened the center drawer. The Sunday suit would have to wait. Chloe snatched it up and threaded it through the belt loops.

There. She smiled at the mirror with satisfaction. A bit of contrast, it held the pants snug, and it didn't look bad at all. She removed her shirtwaist and carefully hung it in the wardrobe before putting on the red and black checked cotton shirt. A little big too, but if she tucked it in it would be all right.

It was doubtful she looked half as good as Monique, but at least she wasn't as drab as she would have been in that awful brown. Chloe sighed. Not that Monique could ever appear drab.

This trip might not be anything near what Chloe expected. She would never be able to totally relax for fear she would draw unwelcome attention to herself. The last thing she wanted to happen was to be compared to a beautiful woman like Monique.

Thank goodness for Caleb. With him, at least, she could feel completely comfortable and, hopefully, blend in. He didn't tell her that her ideas were stupid. Nor did he judge her by how articulate she sounded. He knew she was as intelligent as the next person. She just had difficulty verbalizing her thoughts at times, mostly when she was being stared at or talking to people she didn't know. Give her a pad and pencil, and she could express herself perfectly fine.

After tugging on a pair of the men's wool socks, Chloe worked her foot into the lumberman's pac boots. They were a bit big, too, but not by much. The socks would help. They were meant to come to the center of a man's calf, but on her the tops stopped just short of her knee. She tied the laces snugly and pulled the pant legs down over them.

Walking across the room toward the door, she stopped. The pants fit funny over the tops of the boots. She tugged the pant legs back up, unlaced the boots, and tucked in the hem before re-lacing.

Much better. Chloe finished packing and then took her things down to the foyer. Then she went to set the table for lunch. Since she always ruined the food, she didn't help with the cooking. Setting the table and washing dishes were her duties. Though she hated scrubbing up the dishes, it was good thinking time and a fair trade for not having to endure her father's wrath over ruined meals.

Caleb walked in the front door just as she cleared the bottom step. He dumped his packages onto the stairs and sat amidst the heap. Plopping his elbows on his knees, he buried his face in his hands.

"So what did Elizabeth say when you told her we were off to the mountains for a few days?"

"Barely a word." Caleb spoke into his hands, never lifting his head. "She was kind of upset that I might not be here for the Independence Day Celebration."

"Don't worry." Chloe pressed her hand to her brother's shoulder. "We'll be back. She won't go to the dance with anyone but you."

Caleb raised his head. His blue eyes held none of their usual sparkle. He looked worried. "It's not that. If she knew the real reason I was going, I'm sure she'd call off the wedding in an instant."

Chloe bit her tongue, not wanting to agree with him. "Wait until she sees

43

your drawings of the Sasquatch. She'll have more than respect for you. She'll throw herself at your feet and apologize for having ridiculed you. She'll like being married to a famous illustrator, just you wait and see."

"I don't want to be famous, Chloe. I just want to be able to earn a living doing what I love."

"You will. And Elizabeth will come to appreciate you for it." Though she spoke the words to reassure her brother, Chloe highly doubted them. Elizabeth was spoiled silly by her parents. She wouldn't appreciate much short of being treated like a fairy princess.

"Try not to worry." Chloe struggled to sound cheerful. "Everything will work out. You'll see. Now, if you're recovered from carrying all that gear, I'd suggest you go and get ready so we can eat lunch. We wouldn't want to be late."

Caleb's eyes widened as he looked at her, then he grinned slowly. "You look like a lumberjack."

"I know. Do you think Father will approve?" She twirled around.

"Definitely not. But Aunt Jane would have."

"Yes." Chloe smiled sadly. "Too bad she isn't here. A journey to find the Sasquatch would be just the sort of thing she would have loved."

"Chloe, Caleb. I thought I heard your voices." Cecily Williston was an older version of her children. Petite like Chloe, she had the same blue eyes and light brown hair. She dusted her hands on the white apron that covered her pink skirt.

"Lunch is almost ready. I'm preparing something light since you'll be doing all that walking. I don't want you to feel so full you won't be able to keep up with those scientists."

"I'll set the table in a moment." Chloe smiled at her mother. "I just want to help Caleb take his things upstairs so he can hurry and get ready."

"Chloe, just look at you!" Cecily looked at her daughter askance, as if seeing her for the first time. "What on earth are you wearing? Your father will never let you out of the house like that."

"Not to worry, Mother. He ordered the purchases himself." All except the shirts, Chloe silently amended.

"I don't believe it." Cecily stared in disbelief. "Nor am I finding it easy to believe you talked him in to letting you go along."

Chloe also found it hard to believe. But she had. Her dreams were finally being realized.

"It's common everyday hunting wear." Caleb came over and draped his arm across his mother's shoulders. "Well, all but that lace around her waist and that red shirt."

"Wait until you see my hat. It's positively the latest thing. All your friends will be hounding Mr. Fenton for one just like it." Chloe couldn't help but tease her mother. "I'll bring it down in just a minute."

"I don't care about the hat right at this moment." With her brow furrowed and hands on hips, Chloe's mother sounded positively scandalized. "I want to know what you're doing with that fancy lace tied around those despicable trousers."

"I needed something to keep my pants from falling down, Mother. These are the smallest the store carries, unless I buy the children's sizes. And if you think this is a scandal, just imagine what that would be like."

Her mother's look of horror indicated she could indeed imagine it. "Do you really think such a creature exists? And are you sure you'll be safe?" Eyes wide, Cecily clasped her hands together. "I would die if anything happened to either of you."

"We'll be fine, Mother." Caleb planted a kiss on her cheek. "There are women along, a cook and a scientist, so Chloe will be well chaperoned. And there are several strong men experienced in tracking. We'll be perfectly safe."

"I hope so. I just don't know what your father is thinking. He doesn't want Chloe to do anything improper or that could be misconstrued as such. And now this? How is this proper for a young lady?"

"Mother, you've always stood up for me before. Why aren't you now?"

"Because, Chloe. You're my daughter and I want you safe. In every manner. This exceeds the bounds of propriety far more than you wanting to write for the paper."

Chloe pulled her mother into a quick hug. "Don't you worry one bit, Mother. I have Caleb to look out for me, and I promise I will be careful and I'll stay far away from the men." Though when she thought of Ben, she wasn't sure it was a promise she could keep.

"You two just hurry up and get to the table. I've already set it, Chloe, so you needn't bother. I'll expect you in a few minutes, just as soon as your father gets here."

Chloe grabbed a couple of her brother's packages and raced him up the stairs, the heavy boots keeping her from reaching the top first.

"You know..." Caleb paused outside his bedroom door. "I don't think this plan of yours will work. Ben Kearny is smarter than you're giving him credit for. He won't believe for one minute that I need an assistant and the assistant must be you."

A point Chloe had dwelled on all afternoon. "I never figured you for a measle-brained chicken. But..." Chloe stopped and smiled. "I guess I am too. I've been worrying about the same thing. I thought about trying to disguise myself as a boy, but I don't think I could keep that up for very long. It would get extremely tiresome, what with all the physical exertion we'll be going through."

Caleb followed her through the open door. "What are we going to do when he refuses to allow you to come along?"

She smiled and dropped Caleb's things on his bed. "Cry a lot?"

Caleb laughed. "It might just work. Not many men can resist your tears." He reached for his knapsack and started filling it.

"I hope it won't come to that." Chloe couldn't stand the thought of crying to get her way. "I'm just going to pray he won't want to cause a scene with all those other people around." She thought about Monique. Ben wouldn't create a scene in front of her, would he?

Caleb sighed and sat on the edge of his bed. "There's something else. I've been thinking about it all day. I'm so tired of this entire game of you writing the articles and me putting my name on them. I'm through pretending. From here on out, your name should go on every article you write. Not mine."

Speechless, Chloe just stared at her brother. He nodded to show he meant it.

"Father can just get used to it. So can Elizabeth. And if she can't, I won't marry her. I want to be accepted as who I am, not who they want me to be."

Chloe silently agreed with Caleb. She knew only too well exactly what her brother was feeling.

"I'll move out if I must. My and Elizabeth's house will be framed up soon. I can stay there. I'll work for Stanley's mining company if nothing else."

Unable to picture her brother working in the mines, Chloe shook her head. "You'll have your drawings from the trip. Surely once you send them off to a New York publisher, you'll be able to sell them?"

"I certainly plan to try. And you'll have the Sasquatch article. Surely that will be enough to convince Father of your ability. Let's agree to tell him everything when we get back."

"Why don't you tell him now?"

Both Chloe and Caleb looked at the doorway, stunned to see their father standing there wearing his sternest of expressions.

Chapter Five

"Father!" Chloe's shocked outcry echoed the fear in her heart. He couldn't possibly have overheard enough to piece together—

"Now!" Her father kicked the door shut at the same time that he bellowed. Then he folded his arms across his chest, demanding instant attention.

Wincing at the anger in his voice, Chloe took a step closer to her brother. Never in her life had she been so thankful for his presence. True, she was the elder, and when it was just the two of them alone, she was usually the one in charge. But facing down their irate father, who apparently had some inkling of their deception, Chloe needed Caleb beside her.

"You, young lady. I want to know exactly what it is you're up to." A muscle twitched in her father's cheekbone as he stared down at her. She stepped backward and bumped into the bed. Caleb reached out to steady her.

"N-nothing, Father. We're just packing for our trip." She gave a false sounding laugh that would certainly do nothing to aid her in convincing him. "But you knew that. W-what are you doing here?"

"I came to see if you were almost ready. Instead, I overheard part of your conversation." He narrowed his eyes and spoke in ominous tones. "What is it you've been hiding from me?"

"N-nothing, Father." Chloe's knees quaked and her stomach knotted. "I—we were just discussing our trip into the mountains."

"A trip, you'll remember, I didn't want you to take. You talked me into it, caught me at a foolish, weak moment. I don't think, as a woman, you're qualified to go, nor, as my daughter, do I want you to go. Just remember that when you come crying to me about how tough it was up in the wilderness."

"I won't come crying to you, Father. I'm going to bring back something that will make you proud."

The words were out before she realized it, the result of years of spent longing to do something that would garner his praise. Chloe swallowed hard, knowing she had no choice but to explain. She didn't want to, but there'd be no way around it. Her father, stern and always intrusive, would demand an answer.

Being a writer, Chloe had all the capabilities of making something up.

However, with her father staring her down this way, she was totally incapable of thinking straight. She opened her mouth then shut it again while her mind groped around for something—anything—to say. The knots in her stomach tightened as she realized she couldn't come up with a plausible explanation.

Beside her, Caleb squeezed her elbow. Chloe looked back at him, trying to communicate with a questioning look. He blinked once, slowly, then nodded and squeezed her elbow again. He wanted her to tell the truth, she realized. For Caleb, it would probably be a relief. For her, she wasn't so sure. Would it be a relief, or the beginning of a nightmare?

Dreading every word about to come out of her mouth, Chloe swallowed past a huge lump in her throat before she began to speak.

"Father, I'm hoping to bring you back an article on the Sasquatch."

"Yes, Chloe, I know." He waved a hand impatiently, as if to brush away a pesky fly. "Caleb is going to write it. That's the entire purpose of this little escapade. Tell me something I don't know. Like, what are you hiding?"

"I'm going to write the article, not Caleb."

"We've been over and over this particular subject dozens of times. You, daughter, are a woman. Women do not write articles."

"That's not true. Nellie Bly—"

"Is not a Williston! The Williston women do not engage in such actions. Women belong in the home. And before you think to mention my sister again, just look where her unrestrained lifestyle has led her."

How could he mention Aunt Jane so derisively, so apathetically? Didn't he care in the least for his sister? His lack of feeling brought a rush of stinging tears to Chloe's eyes. Not wanting to be accused of manipulating him by crying, she blinked furiously to keep them from spilling over.

"Then why, Father, did you say I could go on the hunt? You know it's far more scandalous than writing a newspaper article could ever begin to be."

"Did you really think I was about to let you go?"

Her father's mocking laugh rang victoriously in Chloe's ears. Caleb, still beside her, sucked in a breath and squeezed her hand for support as their father continued his tirade.

"I hoped once you saw the hideous clothing and tried to carry everything home from the mercantile and couldn't, you'd realize the folly of you going up in the mountains. Since you're already dressed like a bum, you must have had Mr. Felton deliver the goods."

Her father had manipulated her. She shouldn't have been surprised. Manipulating the banker, manipulating the mayor, manipulating his friends. It was the way he conducted business.

"Now that you know you can't hold your own in a man's world, go put on some decent clothes. Mr. Fenton will be around shortly to pick up his merchandise."

"I suppose you had that prearranged, Father?" Not that she really needed to ask.

"Yes, and I hope it teaches you a lesson. A woman's place is tending to her husband. Which, I might add, is where you should be expending your energies. Finding a husband. Not pursuing some flight of fancy. "

"Father, I don't want—"

"No man worth his salt will accept a woman journalist as a wife."

"I don't plan to—"

"If you know what's good for you, young lady, you'll put this entire idea of writing out of your head and get on with finding a husband. If you were half as smart as you claim, you would have accepted Jackson Dahl's proposal and married him before we left Boston."

"Jackson Dahl is an idiot. He's scared to death of a woman with brains. He's afraid she might have a few more than he does." Chloe wasn't sure where she found the words, but they seemed to spill forth, and she paid no heed to the death-grip Caleb now had on her elbow. "Unlike mother, I have no intention of tying myself to a man who thinks women are only capable of cooking meals and sweating over laundry."

Caleb's fingers dug even tighter, and he tried to pull Chloe away. She shrugged him off and narrowed her eyes at her father. "In fact, Father, Jackson Dahl is a lot like you. And I have no intention of marrying a man like you."

"Why you—"

As he advanced toward her, his face now a shade of mottled scarlet, Caleb stepped in front of her in a gesture of protection. "You're not being fair to Chloe, Father."

"I'll thank you to stay out of it, Caleb. Your sister is nigh on to spinsterhood. And you don't help matters much with all of your daydreaming. You're lucky Elizabeth will have you in spite of it."

"Charles! Chloe! What in the name of heaven is going on in here?" Chloe's mother pushed through the door, practically shoving her husband aside. "I could hear you hollering all the way downstairs in the kitchen."

"Nothing is wrong, Cecily. Why don't you just get back to tending the bread, or darning socks, or whatever it is you do to keep yourself occupied."

Chloe cringed at her father's dismissive comments, which certainly proved her point. Her heart went out to her mother, who worked so hard to let her son and daughter know they were valued equally—by her, at least.

"Well!" Chloe's mother drew herself up in indignation. "You'd best be on your way, dears. You don't want to be late."

"Never mind that now, Cecily. Chloe isn't going anywhere, and Caleb isn't leaving until I get some answers."

"Come on, let's tell him." Unfortunately, Caleb's whisper in Chloe's ear was loud enough for their father to hear.

"Yes." Their father crossed his arms against his chest. "Do tell me. I'm waiting."

Her ears rang, and her voice stuck in her throat. She'd already told her father part of what she thought about Jackson. Why was it so hard to tell him this? She swallowed hard then dug deep for courage to open her mouth. "I'm not interested in finding a husband. And for that matter, Father, I've totally disproved your notion that women can't write. Every article you've printed in *The Cedar Ridge Reporter* with the name C. J. Williston on it has been mine, not Caleb's. Mine!"

"Is that so?" His heavy inhale swelled his chest so it puffed out like a rooster. His forehead furrowed so sharp the tips of his bushy salt-and-pepper eyebrows touched.

"Y-yes, Father. It's so. I've been writing the articles, not Caleb. You see, he hates—"

"You've spent the last several months deceiving me after I specifically told you over and over that you wouldn't be writing any articles for *The Reporter*?"

"It wasn't like that, it—"

"And you, young man, what exactly have you been doing with your time?"

"Drawing."

"Drawing! Pishaw! That's for women to do. You aren't some dandified Italian painter. You're a Williston. My son." Their father puffed out his chest and gave it a swift thump. "You don't *draw*. You *write*! Am I clear?"

As hard as it was for Chloe to stand up to her father on her own regard, she had no such compunction standing up for her brother. "No, Father, you aren't clear. Drawing is what Caleb loves. Writing is what I love. Why can't we pursue our dreams?"

"Then you can pursue them out of my house, out of my life. You are twenty-five years old, and it's well past time you found yourself a husband. And by everything that's in me, I'm going to see you married to Jackson Dahl so you can conform yourself into the woman we've raised you to become."

"Father!" Chloe's tear-choked protest fell on empty ears as her father pursed his lips and shook his head before he turned to Caleb.

"You too, son. I am so very disappointed in you. Here I thought you were making me proud by becoming a fine writer. Instead, you sit around drawing flowers all day. What kind of husband will you make for Elizabeth? If you don't come back from this trip with a story fit for Joseph Pulitzer's newspaper, then don't bother coming back at all!"

"Charles!" Cecily put a restraining hand on her husband's arm, but he shook it off.

"You stay out of this, Cecily. This is between my children and me."

As if she and Caleb only had one parent. Chloe shook her head. Had her father always treated her mother this way? If so, why had she never really seen it? Ashamed, she turned to offer some semblance of comfort to her mother. "Don't worry, Mother. There will be no more fighting. Caleb and I are leaving now."

"I have to finish packing," Caleb said.

"Hurry, Caleb. We're already late. Meet me by the bridge." Chloe turned, and her father grabbed for her arm. She was faster, though it was really only due to fear. She marched down the stairs, followed by both her parents. Her mother made tiny sobbing sounds, and Chloe had to dig deep for restraint to keep from rushing into her arms. Only the rumbling bellow from her father kept her feet in motion.

"Chloe! You get back here this instant!" He was loud, but not as loud as the blood thrumming in her ears. Would he come after her? Physically drag her back? Hit her?

She wanted to slam the door but didn't dare.

Halfway down the path, she heard her mother call her name. Risking a look over her shoulder, she paused, relieved to see her father wasn't with her.

"You forgot the food I made for you. Here." She thrust a parcel into Chloe's hands then threw her arms around her, squeezing her tight.

"My baby girl. My headstrong baby girl. You've always wanted to be just like your aunt, and now you are."

Tears Chloe had been holding at bay burned and brimmed over, spilling unchecked until her mother sniffled and gave her one last squeeze before letting go. Only then did Chloe wipe her eyes with the sleeve of her red shirt.

Her mother didn't turn back until she was halfway down the path.

Caleb met her there, with all of his gear strapped on his back, and drew their mother into a deep hug. Chloe watched for a moment, a large painful lump in her throat.

When Caleb finally let go of their mother and joined Chloe, she could see the sadness in her brother's eyes. It matched that of her heart.

"Chloe, where's your stuff?"

"My stuff?" She studied her brother for a moment, took in the pack and bedroll strapped to his back and a sick realization dawned. Her gear! She didn't have it with her! After all of the upset with her father, she'd forgotten the very items she'd need for this trip.

But she couldn't go back now. Her father might lock her in her room, or worse.

"I'll go get it for you." Caleb turned back toward the house.

"No, Caleb. I don't want you to get into another confrontation with Father."

Caleb started to protest, but before he could the front door opened.

"Chloe!" Her father's booming voice was loud enough for the entire town to hear, and she watched in disbelief as he pitched her carry-all bag as far as he could throw it. "Don't bother coming back until you're ready to announce your engagement to Jackson Dahl."

Never, Chloe vowed to herself as she inched close to the house to gather her bag.

She'd never marry a man like him.

Williston was late.

Ben stomped up and down the length of the boxcar, fuming. And the more upset he grew, the further he walked. Before he knew it, he was walking past every single freight car attached to the train.

A crew of rough and tumble men were almost finished loading supplies and equipment onto each and every car of the train, except the one Ben and his group would be occupying. The engineer was in the small railroad work shack, talking things over with the supply foreman. It was only a matter of time before he was ready to head up the mountain. And he likely wouldn't wait on an errant guide.

Where was Williston? Ben huffed out a breath and turned to march the length of the train again.

Everyone in Cedar Ridge loved Caleb Williston. They practically fell over their tongues to sing his praises. Based on that, Ben couldn't have made a better choice for a guide. So if Williston was so dependable, where was he? Why was he late?

A loud sneeze drew Ben's attention to the open boxcar behind him. He shook his head. Rudy, again. Ever since they'd been in the Cascades, the giant bald man had sneezed his head off. Each sneeze ricocheted through Ben's nerves like the sound of a bullet. He wasn't sure how much more he could take.

The moment they had their sights on the Sasquatch, just about to bag him, Rudy would undoubtedly go into one of his attacks. They'd have to trudge back to Colonel Wilkes empty handed. That would mean no money, no big game prize. No white gorilla project in northwest Africa. Not much hope for the future.

This was his one chance to redeem himself and salvage Gus's good name. Rudy better get over his sneezing soon. Nothing was going to ruin this hunt.

Nothing.

"Ben?" Monique perched in the open doorway of their boxcar. "Where's this so-called trail expert of yours?"

Ben rubbed the back of his neck. "He'll be here, Monique. Probably any second."

"I hope so. If not, I say we get off now and try again tomorrow." She arched one delicate eyebrow. "After you find us a new guide. You're the one, after all, who convinced us we need him."

Ben huffed under his breath. Turning away from the train, he walked up the path hoping to encounter Caleb.

The engineer wouldn't wait much longer before he left for Skykomish to deliver supplies to the men who were digging a rail tunnel through the mountain to eastern Washington. This would have saved Ben and his group at least a day's hike, if not more. From there they would head higher into the heavily wooded and hopefully Sasquatch-populated mountain wilderness.

His two assistants, Rudy and Skip, were already on the train, along with Gus, his daughter Monique, and the mysterious woman named Cookie whom Gus had hired to do their cooking. Though they'd all traveled together from Florida all the way to Washington, Ben didn't think he'd recognize Cookie's voice in the dark. He may have heard her speak to Gus once or twice, but that was about it.

As Ben studied his team, all seated together on the open platform of the boxcar, their gear stowed inside, he pondered whether to do as Monique suggested or just go on with no guide.

Still, as Pete said when Ben had questioned him about Williston, these mountains were treacherous. One wrong step off the trail and you could fall to instant death. It had happened to more than one miner and hunter.

Ben dug into the lower front pocket of his hunting vest. He pulled out his watch and flipped open its silver case. The train left in ten minutes. Tarnation! He had a map. Not that it would help them all that much. None of them knew these mountains. It took someone familiar with the Cascades to recognize potential danger. So why had he relied on one man's word? He knew better than to trust anyone.

He'd been blinded by his own eagerness to get up to Skykomish and get started. For him, finding the Sasquatch wasn't just about monetary purposes. It was something he'd dreamed about since he was a boy. He'd been thirteen years old when he'd received the Canadian newspaper clipping and letter from his father. Thrilled to have some word from his father, he'd eagerly opened it.

WHAT IS IT? screamed the boldly printed headline in the July 4, 1884 edition of Victoria, British Columbia's *Daily Colonist*. The paper went on to tell about a strange creature captured near the town of Yale, B.C. After crewmembers of a Canadian passenger train traveling along the Fraser River spotted the creature, the train stopped and a mad, dangerous pursuit set about before the creature was finally trapped on a rocky cliff.

Knocked senseless with a rock, the creature was bound with the train's bell rope and deposited in the baggage car. He was taken to the town of Yale and promptly caged.

Jacko, as he was named, was described as something of a gorilla-type. His body covered with long, black hair, his forearms longer than any man's, Jacko proved to be a creature of extraordinary strength despite measuring in at four feet seven inches tall and weighing one hundred twenty-seven pounds.

In his letter to Ben, his father went on to speculate that Jacko was a baby Sasquatch. This was the first time Ben had heard the strange sounding name. His father explained that Sasquatch was a name given by the natives of the Fraser River Valley in British Columbia to an elusive, gigantic creature covered with hair like an animal but which walked on two legs like a man.

Several things happened when Ben read the letter. He realized the full scope of his parents' betrayal and finally understood they were never coming back for him. There'd been no mention of love or missing him, or of seeing him soon. He'd tried to drown out his heartache with his bittersweet enthusiasm understandable only to a thirteen year old boy; an emotion that remained within him today, along with a determination to one day find this elusive creature for himself.

"Hall-oo! You folks about ready to roll?"

Just great. The engineer. And Caleb still wasn't here. Ben snapped the watch case shut and shoved it into his pocket. He shot one last glance up the path before trudging back to the train where a short, stocky man stood rubbing his forehead with his thumb and fingertips. Ben waited while the man ran his fingers through his dirty black hair then picked at something on his head. Seemingly satisfied, the man put on a filthy blue and white striped cap. He glanced at Ben and stuck out his hand. Hoping his revulsion didn't show, Ben raised his own in a wave of greeting before saying hello. The engineer frowned. "The lady says you're missin' someone. I figure another five minutes before we pull out. You think your fella will show up 'fore then?"

"I sure hope so." Ben glanced back at the path.

"If he don't, you folks still 'tend on headin' up?"

"Yes."

"I don't know." The engineer shook his head.

"What?" Ben's irritation grew.

"Without a guide? This isn't the place to be without one. It ain't safe."

So he'd already heard, one time too many. "I'm well aware of the dangers, sir. But we're experienced. We've been over mountain terrain before."

Ben didn't intend to sound defensive. He knew to be too cocky in the mountains was foolhardy, and he had no intentions of letting that happen. But he was sick of being told he couldn't go up without a guide. Once again he cursed himself for hiring the first guide he came across.

"Even the lady?" The engineer tipped his head.

"What?" Ben wasn't sure what the man was talking about. The lady? Monique?

"The lady." The man looked at Ben like he was daft. "You said you was all experienced hikers. She experienced too?"

"I suppose she is." Ben would admit, only grudgingly, that yes, Monique was experienced, too. Though in his opinion, experience did not equate with ability. Especially after the last time. Again, he bristled over his obligation to Gus, wishing he'd never given in to the older man's pleas that his daughter be allowed to come.

The engineer pressed his thin lips together and nodded as if to accept the unspoken apology. "Look, sonny. If I was you, I'd hold off for another day. That way you can either find out what happened to slow up your guide then give him what for, or you can get yourself a new man."

Maybe he was right. Perhaps they should hold off another day. Although not fond of the idea, Ben didn't want to put anyone at unnecessary risk.

"I suppose you're right." Disappointment laced his words. Jacko's relatives would have to wait for another day.

A series of groans came from the boxcar, and Ben took a small measure of joy in knowing he wasn't alone in his disappointment. He resisted looking back at the five people watching him, not wanting to see the glumness in their expressions.

"No!" Rudy jumped down from the boxcar with a loud shout. "Look. Someone's coming. Is it him?" Ben turned and saw his errant guide coming down the path at a fast clip. Relief flooded him.

"Hurry up, man. What the devil took you—" Ben broke off when he saw the person trailing Caleb.

Chloe.

Through narrowed eyes, he watched her duck along behind Caleb. No wonder he'd looked so familiar. Seeing them together, though her hair was darker than his, it was obvious the two were related. Brother and sister, undoubtedly. He'd been duped. Ben cursed under his breath then stalked toward them, never taking his eyes off Chloe. She carried the same amount of gear as her brother. A hefty looking carry-all slung across one shoulder, and her bedroll across the other. And though she was small in stature, it didn't appear that she was having any trouble managing things. Except her hat which was way too big and, at the moment, threatening to slip off her head entirely.

The hat, shaped almost like a pith helmet, shaded her eyes from the sun. The back of it dipped low to protect her neck from the sun, though at the moment her hair was doing a fair job of covering her neck since so much had escaped the confines of the hat.

"No. No way." He shook his head and noticed Chloe tense as if expecting his reaction.

She reached up and caught the hat before it slid to the ground, and the rest of her thick brown waves slipped free to cascade around her shoulders. Her wide blue eyes were shot with red, the tender skin beneath them swollen. She looked woebegone and bereft, like she'd lost someone near and dear to her. Some tiny bit of emotion tugged at his heart. He didn't want to add to whatever had caused her pain.

"She can't go." Ben tore his gaze from her face, telling himself it wasn't hurt that he saw there. Even if it was, it didn't matter, he told himself. Hurt or no, she couldn't go with them.

"What?" Caleb planted his feet in a defiant stance that matched the challenge in his eyes.

"I said she isn't going with us."

"No. Please don't keep me from going." Chloe's words were breathy, barely loud enough to be heard, but Ben heard the desperation and couldn't help the stab of guilt that sliced him when he looked into her eyes. He tore his gaze from their blue depths and steeled himself against what he'd seen there, certain that look would haunt his dreams.

Ignoring Chloe, he spoke directly to Caleb. "She can't come with us."

"We're a team. We work together. Chloe is as much a part of this as I am."

Ben admired Caleb's loyalty, but he wasn't about to give in. "I doubt she could find her way out of a burlap sack."

Chloe gasped and Ben wanted to kick himself. But the fact remained, they'd tricked him. He'd told her no once before. He didn't want any reporters along. Particularly this one. Each time he saw her it became harder to banish her from his thoughts.

"She should be home knitting slippers, not traipsing through the woods trying to get the scoop on us."

"Listen here, you sorry—" Caleb's eyes blazed in anger. "You hired me as your guide. We had a deal. My sister is part of that deal."

"You never said one word about your sister."

"Mr. Kearny."

Ben raised a brow at the sternness in Caleb's voice. It surprised and gratified him that the younger man stuck up for his sister. He respected that, but he wasn't about to give in.

"I wonder about something." Caleb's voice grew louder, as if he knew Ben's mind was made up.

Pretending to study the iron wheel under the boxcar while the man talked, Ben tried to blot out the sight of Chloe's wide, hurt-filled blue eyes.

"When you were preparing for this big 'hunt' of yours, did you tell the man who hired you about all these extra people you brought along?"

"That's a little different, Williston." Ben turned toward Caleb again, but his gaze strayed beyond his shoulder to Chloe's unhappy face.

No. He looked away. She couldn't go. She did terrible things to his concentration.

"How is it different?"

One last look at Chloe then Ben spoke to Caleb. "Simply put, these people are all professionals. It's expected that there would be more than one of us. When we go on a hunt or expedition of any kind, it usually takes more than one person. An expert tracker, an expert in preserving specimens, one or two people to help document the finds, and a cook. All are equally indispensable."

"And which are you?" This, softly spoken and quite unexpectedly, from Chloe.

Ben looked at her, surprised to find her cheeks almost as red as her shirt. She made an appealing picture in men's trousers accented with a bit of black lace. Even before she'd blushed, the shirt had brought out a hint of color in her face and eyes.

Unable to help himself, Ben smiled. "Any and all, but more importantly the boss. A big outing like this requires more than one person, for safety measures if nothing else. Which brings me back to my point. You, Miss Williston, are not going. And if we didn't need a mountain guide, Caleb, you wouldn't be going either. Especially after this little stunt."

Chloe appeared uncomfortable. Her mouth opened then shut again. Finally she spoke, her voice still soft. "I'm quite certain I know this area much better than you."

"You might think so, but *I'm* quite certain your brother knows it even better than you."

Chloe's face had taken on a sassy expression. She bit her bottom lip and blinked once as if to challenge him.

"Let her come, Ben." Gus spoke in a quiet, fatherly voice.

Turning from Chloe, Ben glared at him. Nothing was going the way he'd planned. And most of it was Gus's fault. If possible, he glared harder. First Gus insisted Monique be allowed to come, then he had to go and get Ben involved in that entire fiasco with Jase Clark and his loony daughter. Now he planned to interfere in this matter with Chloe.

His plan of tracking Jacko's descendants was quickly unraveling. He wouldn't stand for it. Having Monique along was bad enough. But Chloe, too? No. He'd have to hover over them the entire time to make sure no tragedies occurred.

"No." This time he said it aloud. Rudy sneezed. Gus frowned. Monique and Skip both stared at him like he was a crazy man, and Cookie hovered quietly behind them.

Ben looked back at Caleb, whose face was set in a hard-edged, determined manner, then beyond him to Chloe. She chewed on her bottom lip, her shattered dreams reflected on her face. Maybe he really was crazy, because he found himself longing to draw her into his arms. And if he wasn't mistaken, fresh tears hovered at the brink of Chloe's eyes just waiting for a chance to spill. Not while he watched. He turned his back on the Willistons.

"They're not going. Either one of them." Ben stalked toward the boxcar before he could entertain any further thoughts of Chloe in his arms.

"But Mr. Kearny." Protesting, Caleb followed on Ben's heels. "You hired me as your guide."

"Not you, Williston. The women. No women on my trip."

Monique gaped at him and pointed at herself in question.

"Yes, that includes you, Monique."

"But, Ben—"

"I mean it. I've had it with everyone's interference. I'm in charge here. Colonel Wilkes hired me to bring back the Sasquatch. That's what I intend to do. The fewer people slowing me down the better."

Monique stuck her bottom lip out in a pout he'd seen one time too many. Gus, Rudy, Skip, and even the cook, all looked stunned by his tirade.

"How is my presence slowing you down?" Monique spoke through gritted teeth.

He didn't have to think hard to recall what happened the last time she was along. "If you think I've forgotten the past, Monique, you can think again." As soon as he spoke and saw the hurt pierce Monique's eyes, he regretted it. "I'm sorry—"

"No you're not, Ben Kearny. You're going to make me pay for the rest of my life. I'm sorry, do you hear? Sorry!" Monique's voice rose to a shrill shout. "I can't do enough to make up for what I did. Why do you torture me with it every time we're together?"

"Let's not talk about this in front of the others, Monique. I don't want to make a scene. Now, gather your things. You can walk back to town with Miss Williston then stay at the hotel until we get back."

"I most certainly will not." Monique's tone was indignant.

"She most certainly will not." Gus echoed his daughter's indignation. "And I don't like the direction of this conversation, son."

Ben loved Gus, but he wasn't in the mood to keep discussing this. "No women!" He looked at Cookie, whose blue eyes, shaded and barely visible beneath the brim of the double-billed hunting cap she constantly wore, looked distressed. "Except you, Cookie. We need to eat and none of us can make a decent cup of coffee." That was that. He was through arguing. He looked at his friends gathered in the doorway.

"Monique, get your things. The rest of you step aside. I'd like to get aboard please." He glanced back over his shoulder at Chloe and her brother. "Coming, Williston?" He hoisted himself into the wooden interior of the boxcar. He brushed past his friends and stalked to the back of the car where he sat on his bedroll and buried his face in his hands.

This was turning into quite the fiasco. If it weren't for the money and the chance at redeeming his reputation, he'd get on a train and head back to Florida.

"Who do you think you are?" Monique's question echoed in his ears. She just wouldn't go away. "I'm just as much a part of this as you've ever been. You're not leaving me out."

"I'm not leaving either."

Startled, Ben looked up to see Monique and Chloe standing in front of him... inside the boxcar.

He started to open his mouth, perhaps to curse. He wasn't sure because before he could get a word out, the train lurched forward and he fell backward. Slowly, loudly, the wheels began to turn and the train eased its way out of Cedar Ridge, two short, ear-piercing whistles splitting the air.

Ben struggled to right himself but ended up sprawled on his rear at Chloe's tiny feet. Ignoring the guffaws from Rudy and Skip, Ben let his gaze travel up a pair of hunting trousers that looked entirely too good on this woman, up past the flash of black lace at her waist, past the shirt that dwarfed her small figure, to her face—all angles, cheekbones, and wide, expressive blue eyes.

She appeared almost concerned. About him? The man who didn't want her along? *Well I'll be.*

It didn't matter. Ben looked away and struggled to sit up. He glanced across the spacious wooden car and frowned. With each occupant staring at him, he felt as if *he* were the Sasquatch. "You all can think whatever you want. I'm in charge here. I make the decisions. Me."

Gus seated himself on the floor next to Ben. "Just what in tarnation are you so touchy about?" Gus spoke in a concerned fatherly tone, a role he'd slipped into all those years ago.

The train jerked its way up the mountainside.

Across the rail car, Chloe had put her hat back on and seated herself near the open doorway. Ben tipped his head in her direction. She gave all the appearance of one concentrating on the passing scenery, but she was unnaturally still, and Ben was quite certain those dainty little ears of hers were attuned to his every word. So what? Let her hear. It didn't really matter to him.

"She's a reporter. I already told her she couldn't come with us." He waved his hand toward Chloe in a sweeping gesture. "And yet here she is." He pressed his lips together and shook his head. Out of the corner of his eye, he saw Monique.

"Don't gloat, Monique. Just because you two are on this train doesn't mean you're going with us. As soon as we get to Skykomish, you and Miss Williston are heading right back to Cedar Ridge."

Chloe whipped around so fast, her hat tilted to one side.

Seated so close to the open doorway, Ben feared she might lose her balance and fall off the train.

He opened his mouth to warn her just as the train jerked around a sharp corner.

Monique screamed.

Chloe tumbled off her seat, sprawling toward the open doorway. Ben sprang forward and grabbed for her. Somehow he managed to pull her toward him. Struggling to retain his balance, he staggered away from the door's opening. Another sharp lurch of the train threw him off balance and he fell against the wall. Chloe ended up plastered against his chest.

Time, it seemed, had stopped. He had Chloe right where he'd wanted her from the moment they first met; in his arms and face-to-face. Her mouth was open in a startled little gasp, and her hat was tipped far enough to the side that he could see how her blue eyes widened. Another stray hair had escaped the confines of the hat, teasing her rosy cheek. Ben couldn't help but brush it away. It was only mere coincidence that his fingers lingered against her soft, silky skin for a few extra heartbeats.

A sudden movement startled him out of his moment of senseless insanity, and he found Chloe rudely removed from his arms.

"Get your filthy hands off her, Kearny."

"It's all right, Caleb. Really." Chloe shrugged out of her brother's grasp. It was obvious by her soft-spoken tone and averted eyes that she didn't like the sudden attention.

Ignoring the challenge blazing in Williston's eyes, Ben shook his head in disgust. He'd just saved the man's sister from being thrown out of the train. What was wrong with him? "Are you hurt, Chloe?"

She lifted her eyes, and their gazes met. Ben caught his breath. She was so tiny, so fragile. Her bones would have been crushed had she actually fallen out. It was a good thing Caleb stood at her elbow. Otherwise, Ben feared he'd pull Chloe into his arms and never let her go.

She couldn't go with them. If for no other reason than to preserve his sanity.

Chapter Six

Chloe stared up into Ben's eyes, green as the trees that whirred past as the train ascended the Cascade foothills. She caught her breath and allowed him to lead her to a spot on the floor, well away from the open doorway. Her heart pounded louder than the wheels of the train. From almost falling off the train? Or from being in his arms? She couldn't be sure. The only thing she was sure of was that her emotions were in a downward spiral and threatened only to get worse.

Once she was seated, Ben stooped down in front of her. "Are you all right?" His brow furrowed as he searched her face.

"Yes, I am." Aware that everyone was looking at her, Chloe's voice came out in a cracked whisper. "Thank you."

Ben nodded once, stood, and walked away. He kept perfect balance in spite of the jerk and rattle of the train, as if he'd done this more than once. He stopped near the open door and leaned against the frame, then glanced back at her. To make sure she was really all right?

Not wanting to be caught staring, Chloe quickly looked away. She knew he really didn't want her here. No one did. She could feel everyone staring, so she kept her eyes fixed on the dusty floor in front of her.

This day wasn't turning out at all as expected.

Just as she could understand her father's anger, she could understand Ben's. She could tell there was something more than anger there. But it didn't make her feel any better. It just didn't seem fair. Why were men so bullheaded? Why couldn't they ever admit women might have a few brains and capabilities?

And her brother was no better all of a sudden. Couldn't he give her a little more credit than to think she'd fall into Ben's arms at the first possible chance?

Of course, she had. There was no denying it. For that one heartbeat in time, as Ben gently brushed his hand against her face, she seemed to forget that anything or anyone else existed.

Heavy-hearted and trying to go unnoticed, Chloe glanced around the confined space of the boxcar. Beyond her shoulder, Ben leaned against the wall. He held his hunting hat in one hand, and absently bent the flaps up and down. That lonely, haunted look that had appeared when he'd argued with Monique still filled his green eyes, but he also appeared disgruntled—like a boy who couldn't go on a buggy race with the rest of his friends.

Chloe bit back a sudden urge to smile. It appeared Ben had a touchy side.

On the floor in the corner nearest Ben was the elderly gentleman with a shock of snow-white hair. Ruddy cheeks and dimples on either side of his mouth softened his weathered face. Gus. Dr. Pieper, as she recalled. He had been with Ben at Pete's Saloon. Next to Gus sat an older woman. At least she appeared older. It was difficult to tell because the hat she wore—much like Chloe's—was tilted low and shadowed most of her face. She held herself still and quiet, staying close to Gus's side, almost as if she didn't want to be noticed. Ben had called her Cookie when he was all in a dither earlier.

In the center of the floor perched on her bedroll sat Monique. The curvaceous brunette cast her unblinking eyes on Chloe. Chloe stared back with a flash of unwelcome jealousy. She was dying to know what *past* Ben had been referring to and what lay between them now. The only other time she'd seen Monique was this morning in the store when she shoved her hand in the crook of Ben's arm and batted her eyelashes at him.

Apparently she was also unwelcome on this trip. Chloe should be feeling some sort of kinship with Monique, not envy. Ashamed, Chloe looked away and allowed her gaze to drift to her brother.

Caleb couldn't seem to take his eyes off Monique. Watching her in a way he'd never looked at his spoiled Elizabeth, his eyes were sort of glazed over and dreamy. Chloe was certain if she waved a hand in front of his eyes, he wouldn't notice. She couldn't reconcile this with her brother's recent bouts of pouting and moaning over Elizabeth.

She sighed. Would she ever understand what went on in a man's head? Did she really want to? And what would it be like to have Ben look at her with the same male interest and appreciation?

Against the back wall, seated cross-legged next to her brother, were two men Chloe didn't recognize. Nor did she have any desire to get to know them. The first, a huge man with a shiny bald head, sneezed like his life depended on it. He was positively frightening, and the red goatee he sported only added to that image. Though his eyes were bloodshot and his nose red, Chloe was certain that given the right circumstance, one look from him could freeze even a grizzly's blood.

By contrast, the other fellow wasn't much taller than Chloe. His dark goatee looked to be an imitation of the other man's. But instead of being bald, he had a head full of dark curls shot with an occasional streak of silver. His face was hard and unfriendly and reminded her once again of the ugly confrontation with her father.

Hot tears stung her eyes, and she fought to keep them from appearing. This whole thing with her father would work itself out. It had to.

Papa, oh Papa. Why can't I ever please you?

Aunt Jane never pleased him either. *"He'll get over it,"* she always said whenever her father would get angry over her aunt's latest escapade. In fact, more often than not, Aunt Jane would simply tell Chloe's father to stick it in his pipe if he didn't like it.

Chloe wished she had a little of her aunt's gumption and outlook on life right about now.

A sad sort of heaviness settled in her heart as she mulled over the early afternoon events. She thought about her father's reaction to her and Caleb's deception. Would he really get over it? She hoped so but doubted it. The little girl long buried deep inside her—the one who had always yearned for her daddy's approval—ached for him to draw her into his arms and say it was all right; to say he loved her anyway, loved her for who and what she was.

She couldn't bear it if her father remained unforgiving when she and Caleb returned to Cedar Ridge.

From the time she was a young girl, Chloe had been frightened of her father when he became angry. Her first awareness of his hard side was when she was ten and Aunt Jane had taken her for a carriage ride.

Any event, when partaken with her aunt, turned into a wild and woolly adventure. That particular day, they'd come across a traveling circus. Aunt Jane knew one of the members of the troupe, and he'd given them a firsthand glimpse of activity behind the scenes.

She'd come home, eager to share with her father about the day's adventures, certain he'd want to write an article about it. Chloe had unwittingly interrupted some sort of gathering of men, and her father turned on her. She'd glimpsed small bits of his temper before, but never this cold iciness. This was the first time she'd ever been a recipient of it, and it all happened while in the company of strangers.

Now, closing her eyes, she recalled every word in all its humiliating detail.

"Chloe, dear." He'd laughed then, an odd high-pitched laugh, not the belly laugh she was used to. Then he looked at his friends who all looked like they smelled something bad, took a few puffs on his pipe, and turned back to her. "When are you ever going to learn, my little one? Women, and you will grow up to be one, are not to interrupt the men. They only speak when spoken too. And children, especially girls as pretty as you, are to be seen and not heard."

"But Papa." Up to that horrible day, she'd always called him papa. Never again, though. From that day forward, he was *Father*. "You have to hear about this. The tightrope walker—"

"Chloe." Her name had been spoken low, ominous. It should have been her warning.

"But Papa, really, if you would just liste—"

"Shut up, Chloe!"

She'd stumbled backward at his explosion.

"Just shut up. You're always prattling on and on like my sister, Jane. Why can't you just look pretty and be seen for a while? That's what children are for."

It probably wouldn't have seemed so bad, had she been a little older, but it happened at a time when Chloe, for whatever inexplicable reason—her mother termed it female changes—was emotionally vulnerable.

That was the exact moment when Chloe stopped talking. No one would ever tell her to be quiet again. She couldn't be sure, looking back, exactly how long she remained silent. But it was long enough for her father to grow concerned. She remembered an endless parade of doctors, her father trying to cajole her, apologizing. She also remembered wanting to talk, but there was this horrible fear that if she spoke she'd be hollered at and humiliated again.

Ironically it was Aunt Jane who coaxed her into talking again, and Aunt Jane whom she grew to idolize and longed to be like. Even now, as an adult, the shyness threatened to overtake Chloe unless she was entirely comfortable. She had to fight to keep that from happening, and she'd grown leaps and bounds in her efforts and wasn't about to crawl into a corner now. She would make her father proud. No matter what it took, she would succeed.

Two short blasts, followed by the high-pitched squeal of the brakes, snapped Chloe out of her doldrums.

"We're here." Ben sounded a touch excited, and Chloe couldn't help but feel it, too. But his next words were a sore disappointment. "Everyone is to get off except you, Chloe, and you, Monique."

"I'm not going back." Monique jumped up and practically rubbed noses with Ben. Chloe's mouth dropped open, and she wished she could be so brave. Why didn't Ben want Monique along? Herself, she understood. After all, she and Caleb had tricked him after he'd made it clear she wasn't welcome.

"I've made up my mind. No women on my trip. Especially"—he glared at Chloe—"reporters."

The others watched, waiting for a response. She didn't want to give one. Not while they stared at her. Still, not trying meant failure.

Slowly closing her eyes, Chloe inhaled.

One.

Two.

Three.

Chloe breathed out as she opened her eyes.

With her next set of breaths she studied the dusty floor of the boxcar and searched her heart for the words to say, praying they wouldn't stick in her throat.

Finally, finally she was ready to speak. "What if I promise not to write the story?"

"You think I'd believe that for a minute?"

"Well, believe her, Ben. She's going and so am I." Monique looped her arm with Chloe's in a united display.

Shocked, Chloe could hardly believe Monique was closing ranks with her. Would it work? She felt the first glimmer of hope.

"You can't make me go back." Chloe drew courage from Monique, even though her stomach twisted. "I mean, you *can* force us to stay on the train. But who's to stop us from jumping off once you're gone? We could follow you, or for that matter, we could go on our own search for the Sasquatch."

"If you want to jump off the train and break your blamed fool neck, I won't be around to watch. So go right ahead. But you will *not* come back and follow me. You will not do *anything* to jeopardize this blamed hunt."

"Do you suppose you're intelligent enough to come up with a few words more interesting than *blamed*? You've used it twice in one breath." Shocked at her own audacity, Chloe snapped her mouth shut and her stomach twisted even more.

Aunt Jane, maybe I'm not a lost cause after all.

Caleb gaped at her, obviously stunned. The bald giant picked his nails with a mammoth hunting knife. Monique squeezed her arm for support. Gus and the dark-haired man looked everywhere but where they might meet someone's eye. And as for Cookie, Chloe could almost swear there was a hint of a smile on the cook's face before she busied herself with a strap on her pack.

Chloe might not have a delivery like Aunt Jane's, and she might be quaking in her boots at her own boldness, but at least she'd stood up for herself.

"Just stay on the train." Ben glared at her then turned away. But not before he tossed another threat over his shoulder. "Or I'll personally throw you both back up here."

Caleb turned toward Chloe, a question in his eyes. Just as he opened his mouth to say something to her, Ben practically bellowed in his ear.

"Let's get on with it, Williston. Or stay on this train with your sister."

Caleb turned toward Ben, fists clenched. Chloe knew she had to do something before their chance was lost. She gently tapped his arm.

"Please don't argue with him, Caleb. I'll be fine, but I need you to go so you can gather information on the Sasquatch."

He studied her for a moment as if questioning whether she really meant it. When she nodded, he chucked her under the chin then turned away.

Chloe watched sadly as her brother was the first to depart the train, followed by Gus and the two goateed men. Gus stopped and helped Cookie safely to the ground.

Ben turned to her and Monique again. There was something in his eyes. Regret? He opened his mouth to say something, but shook his head and jumped off.

The engineer had to scramble out of his way so he wouldn't be squashed. "Everybody off." His earsplitting roar rang in Chloe's ears.

"They're not getting off." Ben spoke in measured tones.

"*Everybody* has to get off."

"They're going back." Ben remained adamant. "No women on this trip."

From behind him, Gus cleared his throat.

"Except the cook," Ben amended. "But she's quiet and doesn't argue." He glared up at Chloe and Monique. "And she knows how to stay out of the way."

"Well now, sir." The engineer spoke slowly and removed his hat. Absently, he ran his fingers through his hair. "Perhaps you should have thought about that before you allowed them along in the first place."

"I didn't 'allow' them along." Ben jerked his thumb at Chloe, and she resisted the childish urge to stick out her tongue at him. "This one snuck on the train. She's not supposed to be here." He sighed heavily and indicated Monique. "The other one, well, let's just say I've decided it's better if she doesn't go either."

"It's going to be a mighty long walk. I hope you plan on escorting them back yourself." The engineer rubbed his chin and his fingers inched dangerously close to his nose. Chloe squeezed her eyes shut and hoped the man's nose didn't itch on the inside.

"Walk?" Ben sounded incredulous. "What do you mean? Can't they just ride back with you?"

"'Fraid not, son." The engineer's hand moved toward his ear, and Chloe grimaced. She resisted a look at her brother. Another time and another place, she and Caleb would have dissolved into gales of laughter over this man's habits.

But not today. The situation was too serious for poking fun at someone. Not that they should be doing that anyway. *Sorry, Lord.*

"This train isn't going anywhere for at least three days, maybe four. We're here to work on the tunnel, not haul any freight or passengers. When the supplies run out, we'll go back down for more."

Ben muttered and kicked the ground. Whatever he said was muffled. Chloe was quite certain it was another curse though, because as soon as his boot hit the dirt he glanced up and flashed a look of guilt.

She smiled down at him, satisfied. Ben was stuck with her—and Monique. Whatever reason he wanted to send her back, he wasn't going to win. And for that, Chloe was happy. But Ben wasn't. His guilty look turned to one of affront as he faced the engineer.

"They can stay with you then."

Outraged, Monique shrieked a string of words that were totally incomprehensible.

"I sure hope you didn't mean that, Kearny." Caleb took three long strides and faced off with Ben. "My sister isn't staying here with a bunch of railroad workers who probably haven't seen a woman in months."

Ben folded his arms across his chest and stared down at Caleb, who clenched his fists and raised them dangerously close to Ben's jaw.

"Caleb, stop."

Chloe jumped off the train, her heels stinging as they made contact with the hard dirt. She pushed her way between Ben and her brother. "This is getting us nowhere."

Caleb looked at her for a moment then back at Ben. Lips pressed together, fire blazing in his eyes, Chloe knew he wasn't about to give up easily. She tapped his arm.

"Let's talk privately for a moment." She turned and walked the length of two rail cars, expecting Caleb to follow. He did, albeit slowly.

"What?"

"Don't fight with him."

"Why? You heard him. He thinks you're just going to sit around here with a bunch of strange men."

"He's a man who feels he's been duped. He's not thinking very clear at the moment. Give him time, he'll come around."

"You don't know that. You barely know him."

"I know human nature, and I'm certain that given time to cool down and think things through in a clear manner, he'll see the reality and give in."

"And if he doesn't?"

"Then you can give him your best pop in the nose. Just don't hurt him."

Caleb grinned. "I'd like to do both. He has a lot of nerve. Insisting you stay with that nose-picking engineer."

He laughed then, the kind of laugh they shared as children when they were up to mischief. The sound was infectious, washing over Chloe's topsy-turvy emotions. Before she knew it she was laughing right along with him. But it wasn't enough to make her forget about the fight with her father, or how much she wanted—needed—to go on this expedition. What if Ben sent her away? She couldn't go back home and be forced to marry Jackson. She simply couldn't.

Every dream she'd held dear had been stomped on and shattered today—first by her father, then by Ben.

Tears bit the back of her eyes, and she turned from her brother.

"Hey." Caleb gently touched her shoulder. "Look at me."

She couldn't. If she did, the tears would surely fall.

Her brother, bless his heart, must have sensed what she was thinking. He pulled her close and wrapped his arms around her, letting her cry until her sobs turned to hiccups and a large damp patch of tears soaked his shoulder.

"Here." Caleb pulled her away from him and held out one of his brand new handkerchiefs. Chloe took it and dabbed at her nose.

"Caleb, look at it this way. Even if he doesn't come around, he can't stop me from hunting for the Sasquatch on my own." She shrugged. "I'll just follow you. Maybe I can talk Monique into joining me."

Caleb frowned. "I don't think so."

"Why not? I'll be at a safe distance, so if anything were to happen, I'd just scream loud enough for you to hear me."

"I'm not worried about that. It's him." He tilted his head to where Ben stood glaring at them.

"What do you think he's going to do? Chase me down and throw me off a cliff?"

"You never know about people, Chloe. We know nothing about him."

"Williston?" Ben interrupted them, snappish and impatient. "Are you two about done over there? We need to figure out what to do with these women and be on our way."

Caleb took Chloe's arm. "Let's go see if we can reason with him."

She didn't want to reason with Ben. His tone was entirely too condescending. May God forgive her, but she wanted to kick him in the shins. He'd stood there and watched while she'd cried and made a fool of herself.

Holding her brother's arm, thinking about how Ben wanted to keep her from realizing her dream because he had something against women, Chloe marched toward Ben intent on holding her ground.

With the exception of the cook, the rest of the small group had gone back to the boxcar and unloaded the belongings. Cookie was talking to the train engineer well away from where the rest of the group stood just behind Ben, loading their gear onto their backs. Approaching them, her resolve fizzled and disappeared. She'd had a tantrum in front of these people. What did they think of her now? She slowed her pace then stumbled once, slowing Caleb along with her.

"Think of Aunt Jane." Caleb's whisper brought a fresh round of tears to Chloe's eyes.

Blinking them back, she sent her brother a grateful smile. He knew her too well, knew what she'd been thinking, and knew just how to help her through this. She did as he suggested and called to mind an image of Aunt Jane standing up to her father.

Perfect. She could be like Aunt Jane. It didn't matter one whit what these people thought. It just didn't matter!

Chloe straightened her shoulders and marched toward Ben, who stared at her with his arms folded across his chest. She stood as close as she dared, much like Monique had done a few minutes ago. She didn't let herself stop to think lest the words twist her tongue into knots.

"Monique and I are going with you, and that's all there is to it. If you have some kind of problem with it, you can just pretend we don't exist. And that's all I have to say on the subject."

She tried to breathe shallow and easy when she finished her tirade, willing her heartbeat to slow down.

It didn't.

Ben stared at her in silence, his face impassive, his foot tapping up and down impatiently—or perhaps irritably.

She sucked in a breath, waiting for Ben to bellow in her face.

Her lungs burned and threatened to burst before he finally opened his mouth. And when he did, Chloe was so stunned by his words her breath came out in a woosh.

"Williston." Ben's voice came out in a low growl. "Do your job and lead us out of here."

Victory at last.

She was here. She won. Ben hadn't sent her away.

In spite of the heavy pac boots, Chloe's step was light as she traipsed along the path leading away from Skykomish and higher into the evergreen-dense Cascade Mountains. It didn't seem possible, but the air had a heavier, more fir-laden fragrance than it did in Cedar Ridge. She inhaled as deep a breath as she could. *This is real.* She'd dreamed for so long of actually being part of a story, rather than writing from a distant perspective.

She'd been so worried Ben would find some way to keep her out of the group. She'd meant what she'd said though. If he had sent her back, she'd have found a way to follow behind him.

And now, as if to make things perfect, the most beautiful sound she'd ever heard drifted back from the front of the group to tease her ears.

"The moon was bright, the night was clear, no breeze came o'er the sea."

Ben. Singing.

"When Mary left her highland home and wandered forth with me."

Chloe sighed so deep she almost swooned.

Earlier, before they'd gone very far up the trail, Ben had stopped to give everyone instructions. There was no need to walk in silence because no matter how quiet they were, the Sasquatch would still hear their steps. It was more important, therefore, to keep an eye out for signs of the creature. When tracks were spotted, they'd stake out the area and sit in silence to wait for the Sasquatch to come out of hiding. If no tracks or other signs were spotted, they'd stop several times throughout the day to stake out different areas.

It wasn't quite what she'd expected, and she wasn't sure what "other signs" meant, but she was more than happy to watch for tracks and listen to the smooth rich sound of Ben's singing. "Do you mind if I walk with you?"

Startled, Chloe looked up to find Monique on her left. Torn between walking up at the front of the pack with her brother or lagging behind, Chloe chose the latter. Walking up front meant all eyes would be on her. She'd rather hang back and be unobtrusive.

"Well?" Monique's brown eyes were inquisitive. "Do you?"

"I—um, sure." Confused as to why Monique would want to walk with her, Chloe gave the taller woman an uncertain smile.

Monique fell into step beside Chloe. The old mine trail was well-worn and fairly free of gravel and debris. Their footsteps were silent save the occasional snap of a stray twig or pinecone, which allowed Chloe to concentrate on the unfamiliar words to Ben's song. She was pleased to find that, in spite of the stretching sensation at the back of her thighs, she could match Monique's long strides without much effort.

The trail wound uphill, through the trees. Occasionally it led them into the open, where the sun beat down and a dangerous rocky slope loomed to their right. For the most part though, they were without the sun.

Chloe removed her hat, brushing the hair out of her eyes as she did so. It wasn't really necessary to wear it if the sun wasn't in her eyes. It slid all over her head anyway, and she preferred to just carry it. The crisp mountain air left her feeling invigorated. Like a small child on a journey, eager to get there. It almost made her troubles with her father fade into the distance. Almost. Until she could make him proud, there'd always be a smidgen of disappointment tucked deep in her heart.

Up ahead, Caleb appeared the seasoned guide. And if he was confused as to his whereabouts when he consulted the map, he didn't show it. Ben appeared satisfied with Caleb's ability, and for that Chloe was glad. They didn't need any more trouble today.

"You've really upset Ben, you know."

Chloe was surprised more by the sound of Monique's voice than her words. Much to her relief, they'd walked in silence for at least a mile. That had saved Chloe from having to make small talk with someone she barely knew.

"I'm sorry, Monique. I didn't intend to. It's just that this story is so important to me." And the way Ben had most of the others singing along with him, he didn't seem very upset.

"Hmm, yes. The story." Monique appeared to mull something over in her mind. "We're not talking made up stories here, are we?"

"No." Chloe was surprised at Monique's apparent interest. Talking about her work always helped put her somewhat at ease, even with strangers. "I write fact-based articles for a newspaper." She didn't think it necessary to tell Monique she'd never had her own byline.

"Have you ever tried writing tales? You know, adventures? Stories about love, romance?"

"No." Chloe shook her head. "I just stick to the facts. I do keep a journal though."

"Really? So do I."

This surprised Chloe. Monique didn't seem the type to keep a journal. Chloe supposed though, that there was no real *type*. A lot of people found satisfaction in recording their daily thoughts and activities.

"I've never met a woman reporter before."

Chloe tried to read Monique's smile, not exactly sure the other woman was sincere. Instinct told Chloe to take it slow. Much as she wanted a friend, someone she could converse with comfortably, she needed to be extremely cautious.

After a moment's silence, Monique spoke again. "Ben doesn't like reporters." She pursed her lips and studied Chloe through narrowed eyes; eyes with a cat-like gleam. She'd worn this same expression at least half a dozen times while on the train.

Chloe wasn't sure what to say. Though she was dying to know why Ben didn't like reporters, it was best not to appear too nosy. Besides, it seemed as if she were being taunted. She'd just bite her tongue and let Monique give her more details without any prodding.

Turning away from the other woman's scrutiny, Chloe focused instead on not falling too far behind the others.

Quiet for several minutes, Monique's voice was unusually low when she did speak. "I suppose I can tell you."

Chloe looked up then, surprised to see Monique's mouth down-turned, her lips no longer pursed. She appeared disturbed, frightened. Of what? Chloe's heartbeat quickened.

"Just don't tell Ben I mentioned it." Monique's voice quavered as she spoke. "He gets quite upset when we talk about it."

About what? Chloe checked herself before she spoke. She stole a glance at Monique, willing her to hurry up and speak. Excitement tingled through her senses. This might have to do with Monique and the reason Ben wanted to leave her behind.

Unwittingly, her gaze sought out Ben. No longer singing, he was deep in conversation with her brother. The two had apparently put aside their differences, appearing to chat amiably as they navigated the trail.

Quite unexpectedly, Ben glanced over his shoulder. Their gazes met. Chloe's footsteps faltered.

How would he feel if he knew Monique was about to spill his secrets? She learned enough in church to know gossip was a sin. Heat burned her cheeks, and she looked away, down the rocky slope that melded into a thick tree line. She put her hat back on her head. It was only because they were back out in the open sun. But her heart said differently, and she knew she really had to hide her face from Ben's breath-catching green-eyed stare. When she glanced back up, Ben was talking to Caleb again.

She did want to know why he didn't like reporters. But she also wanted to know more. Like why finding the Sasquatch was so important to him. And why he appeared so intense, eager and zealous—almost like a little boy—whenever the subject was mentioned.

But mostly, she wanted to know why that haunted lonely look raged in his eyes when he thought no one was looking.

"Oh, I hate this." Monique's overly loud declaration drew Chloe's attention. One hand rested against her chest in a dramatic fashion, the other was pressed to her forehead as if willing away some terrible memory.

"Monique?" Instantly she reached out and touched Monique's hand, her desire to know more about Ben quickly replaced with concern. "Are you all right? Do you need to stop and sit down?"

"No, no, no." Monique shrugged Chloe away, dropped her hands to her side, and kept walking. "It's fine. I mean, I'm fine."

If she was so fine then why were her hands balled into bloodless fists? Whatever Monique planned to tell her was obviously traumatic.

"If you'd rather not tell me, you don't—"

"No. I'll tell you. I want to tell you. Maybe I'll finally be able to get over it if I talk about it."

"Well." Chloe didn't want to do anything to cause the girl more grief. "If you're sure."

"I'm sure." Monique spoke with fierce certainty.

"All right. I'm here to listen." As Chloe nodded in encouragement, her hat fell to the ground and landed dangerously close to a steep incline. She squealed and scrambled after it, thankful when she was able to retrieve it before it went any further. It was a long way down that hill, and something told her Ben would have been quite upset if the group had to wait while she scrambled downhill then up again.

"That was close." Chloe plopped the hat back on her head and brushed her hair out of her eyes. "Now, what were you saying?"

"That will never do." Monique was staring at her with a bemused expression.

"What?"

"Your hat, your hair. It'll never do. You've spent more time putting that hat on and shoving your hair out of the way, and we've not even made it through one day."

She was right. "I can braid it, I suppose. I just hate to do that because I get headaches from it being pulled tight." She frowned at Monique. What did her hair have to do with Ben not liking reporters? "Forget my hair for a minute. Let's finish—"

"There is another answer, you know."

"Oh?" Chloe wasn't sure she liked the critical way Monique was studying her. Her expression wasn't unlike Caleb's when he was trying to figure out which angle to draw something from.

"It may not help the problem with the hat. It's much too big. However, it will give you one less thing to worry about."

"What are you talking about?"

"Your hair." Monique reached out and touched a strand that had already worked loose.

"My hair? You don't mean...no." Chloe shook her head and reached up to steady the hat at the same time. "Do you mean cut it short like yours?"

"Exactly." Monique beamed at her. She no longer seemed pensive, afraid. Whatever had been bothering her about Ben and reporters was clearly gone, replaced by a strange enthusiasm over possibly cutting Chloe's hair. Were her moods always so changing? Chloe began to suspect Monique might be equal parts supportive companion and irritating tagalong.

Chloe was about to comment on her change in mood when she heard shouts from the men, prodding them to hurry up. Only then did she realize how far they'd lagged behind.

She grabbed Monique by the hand, encouraging her to run so they could catch up. When her hat flew off again, she scooped it up but didn't bother to put it back on. It wouldn't do to give Ben the impression they couldn't keep up because of a hat. Or any other reason for that matter.

It wouldn't do at all.

His impression of her mattered far too much.

Chapter Seven

"What do you think, Williston? Are you about ready for food and a rest?" Ben wasn't asking, really, as he turned to face his guide.

Though they stopped earlier for a short rest and to watch for signs of Sasquatch, his stomach told him it was well past suppertime.

Off to their right was a winding stream, dotted here and there with giant boulders and downed trees. Ben came to a stop near a wide patch of soft grass. To his way of thinking, with the evening sun warming it, this clearing near the stream was likely the best place they'd come across this evening.

Whatever Williston said was drowned out by shouts of agreement from the rest of the group as they shuffled to a stop.

"If you think you're tired now, just you wait." Ben spoke to no one in particular, but his eyes rested on Chloe, who had come to stand at Caleb's side. "This is nothing compared to what tomorrow will bring."

Though Chloe didn't address Ben's remarks, she did pull her shoulders back and flash him a look of disdain before turning to Caleb. "Let's go sit on those rocks by the water."

Did that mean she wasn't tired? Or merely that she wasn't about to let on if she were?

"Do you want to join us, Ben?" Caleb actually sounded as if he meant it.

Ben glanced at Chloe, who quickly looked at the ground. He held his breath and waited for her to look up. When it became apparent that she didn't intend to, he was surprisingly disappointed. "No. Thanks. You go ahead."

He glanced around, looking for the others. Monique and Cookie were nowhere to be seen. Rudy, Skip, and Gus had plopped themselves in the center of the clearing. They looked happy, if weary, joking amongst themselves as they dug through their packs.

Oddly, Ben felt like an outsider. "I'll just sit over by those trees. I need to, uh, make some plans." No one responded, and he knew that meant they weren't listening because they didn't care if he ate alone. He shouldn't care either, but somehow he did.

Settling down under the base of a rough-looking cedar tree, his gaze as well as his thoughts turned to Chloe. Her trousers gently caressed her luscious curves as she wandered with her brother to the rocks where she'd wanted to sit and eat. Turning away when she laughed at something Caleb said, Ben opened his hunting bag and pulled out the neatly wrapped supper he'd ordered from the hotel dining room earlier that day; cold chicken, sliced potatoes, and a slab of corn bread that would have been perfect had it been heated and topped with melting butter.

This was to be their last bit of decent food for a good long while. From here on out Cookie would be in charge of meals, but each person should have a supply of dried fruit and beef in case things got rough. Though Gus swore by the woman's cooking, Ben had yet to taste anything she'd prepared. He wondered at their relationship—before he hired her Gus had never once mentioned her. If she was a romantic interest, it would be the first since Monique's mother died several years ago.

More curious than the relationship between Cookie and Gus was the woman's manner. She was quiet and kept to herself. She never initiated a conversation, and usually spoke only to Gus.

Then there was the hunting cap she constantly wore with her hair tucked so far under it he wasn't even sure of the color. Usually the cap was pulled low, keeping most of her face in shadows. But on occasion, when it wasn't, her eyes peeked through. Clear blue eyes that never seemed to miss a thing and hinted at intelligence. She was either hiding something or hiding from someone. But there was no one here she needed to be afraid of.

Why hadn't Gus assured her of that? He didn't want anyone on this field expedition to feel they needed to live in fear. He'd have to talk to Gus about it.

When Monique and Cookie materialized from the bushes, Cookie went over and sat down near Gus. Ben would be curious to see if she interacted with Skip and Rudy.

Monique was currently making an attempt to wiggle into the open space between Chloe and her brother. Ben pressed his lips together and shook his head. Was she trying to get close to Chloe, or Caleb? Perhaps he should go warn Caleb right now.

A pang of guilt struck him. He shouldn't be so judgmental. She probably just wanted to be friends with Chloe. And who could blame her? It wasn't like she'd grown up with a whole passel of girlfriends.

He supposed it was only natural that the two women would gravitate toward each other, especially after his earlier blowup. Still, their budding friendship stuck in his throat along with the dried-out corn bread. Not because he cared if the women felt a line was drawn between him and them. But because the entire situation reminded him of the South Pacific and what happened the last time Monique tried to be friends with someone.

This was ridiculous. He took a generous gulp of water from his canteen. Nothing like that would happen again. But he'd have to keep an extra cautious eye on things just to make sure.

Monique pulled off her hat and shook her head, running her fingers through ebony hair. Though he'd once thought her the most beautiful woman in the world, Ben now paid her no attention. Instead he watched, entranced, as Chloe followed suit. Sun-kissed strands the color of rich, dark honey streamed through her fingers. Next to Chloe, Monique appeared a faded wildflower at the end of its season.

Chloe tilted her head back, and the corn bread stuck in Ben's throat again. After another swallow of lukewarm water, he frowned. This certainly wasn't how he'd envisioned this trip; sitting alone, brooding, while the rest of the group had easy conversation and laughter.

It wasn't like him to sulk, but the more he watched the camaraderie between the others, the more left out he felt. Through narrowed eyes, his gaze settled on Chloe, her brother, and Monique.

Rustling through her pack, Chloe laughed and pulled out a tin can. Obviously her brother hadn't told her about the weight factor. Either that or she hadn't listened to him. Point proven, he thought wryly. She doesn't belong here. And perhaps that meant Caleb didn't belong here either. What kind of mountain guide doesn't ensure they're packed properly for an expedition?

He watched Chloe turn the can over and over in her hand, peering at it as if it were a puzzle. Ben scowled and again felt left out when she said something and her companions burst into laughter.

What were they laughing at? A joke? A cute story? Not that it mattered. No woman had ever captured his attention so fully just by laughing. Chloe's mouth curved upward, captivating him. Her cheeks were rounded like peaches while the corners of her eyes crinkled as she smiled. What would it be like if she looked into his eyes and smiled and laughed like that?

Slowly, not sure what had come over him, Ben stood up and sauntered over.

His gaze never left Chloe's smiling face as he approached, but the closer he got the slower his steps became. What was he doing? He stopped when Chloe looked up at him. Her smile disappeared and her mouth opened slightly as if in surprise.

"Hi, Ben." She spoke softly and looked down. "You're welcome to join us if you'd like."

Ben watched her for a moment, waiting for her to glance back up. She didn't, and he finally turned to Caleb.

"How much sunlight do you figure we have left?"

Chewing on a bite of sandwich, Caleb scanned the sky. "About four hours, I suppose."

"Good. When everyone is ready to go, we'll move on. Another three hours and we'll find a place to make camp for the night."

Monique's groan sounded from behind him.

Ben turned and looked at her. As usual, she exasperated him. "What's wrong?"

"Nothing." She stuck out her bottom lip. "I just thought we'd stop here for the night. I'm tired."

Forever the complainer—Monique would never change. Why had Gus insisted she come along? "You'd better get used to it. This is just the beginning. I told you before you aren't physically up to this."

"I'm as physically capable as you are, Ben Kearny."

There was fire in Monique's eyes, and Ben didn't plan to argue with her. Not that she was right, just that he'd rather avoid a scene with Chloe watching. And that's exactly what she was doing. Watching. With interest? Or puzzlement? Perhaps both. He couldn't be certain.

He turned to the rest of the group. "We started at noon. Tomorrow we're going to walk twice as far and twice as long. Anyone who wants to turn back, do it now. Otherwise, I don't want to hear any complaining."

Chloe stared at him with an unreadable expression. Did she want to turn back? Somehow he doubted it. She was tough, a hundred pounds of raw determination. Nothing but spunk. She'd proven she could keep pace with any of them.

A couple of times today, he'd purposely driven the group faster and faster, just to see what she was made of. The only time she fell behind was when Monique yacked her head off.

Breaking eye contact with Chloe, Ben stared at the tin can she held. The label identified its contents as plum pudding.

"Didn't your brother tell you to travel light?" He nodded at the can.

Chloe looked surprised. "Um, yes. He did."

"Then why did you load up on canned goods? By tomorrow your shoulders will be aching so much you'll want to throw every last can in the creek."

"But I..." She looked away, but not before a flush tinged her cheeks. He watched as she swallowed hard and bit her bottom lip.

When she glanced up again, his stomach flipped. "I didn't intentionally *load up* on them. I didn't even—"

"Just don't say I didn't warn you, and don't expect someone else to carry your load." Disconcerted with his reaction to the mixture of spunk and hurt in her eyes, he turned to walk away then paused to look back over his shoulder. "We leave in ten minutes."

Monique dogged his heels. He stopped and turned around. "What?"

"That wasn't very nice."

No, it wasn't. That's why he was so angry. Not at Chloe. At himself. But since when did Monique care about anyone but herself? Why was she sticking up for Chloe?

"Don't start with me, Monique. Just go finish eating so we can leave."

She spun on her heel in a huff and stalked off. Frustrated, and not exactly sure why, Ben grabbed at the cone-laden branch of a nearby tree. The branch bent, but didn't break free of the tree. Cursing none too softly, he kicked at the trunk instead then walked away. Not that he got anything for his trouble but a sore foot. He certainly didn't feel any better.

Why hadn't he minded his own business? Why was he so attracted to Chloe that he couldn't keep to himself? He squeezed his eyes shut, trying to will away the memory of Chloe's hurt look.

Blamed women.

Nothing but trouble.

Twigs and small pebbles crunched under Chloe's feet as she marched up the hill. She winced when one of the larger rocks jarred the arch of her foot. Breathing deep, she tried to rein in her emotions. Ben just assumed she was too stupid to pack her bag. She didn't want to tell him her mother had wrapped the tins in with the sandwiches she'd handed Caleb when she'd run after them.

That would only make her think about the fight with her father and the pain in her mother's eyes. She didn't want to think about it at all. To do so would distract her from paying attention to the trail and watching for Sasquatch tracks.

Because she still smarted over Ben's comments and was just plain irritable, she soon found herself ahead of the others. She just wanted to find the Sasquatch and write her article.

Cresting the hill, a flash of golden light caught her eye, and she turned to look over her shoulder. She stepped off the winding path to get a better look.

"Oh glory be!" She could only stare in amazement and breathe in the sight.

Far off in the distance, towering above the other mountains, was a snow-capped peak that seemed to reach heaven. From somewhere deep in the craggy rocks and juts, water raged toward a huge drop where it spilled into a stunning waterfall. Its crowning glory was a burst of sun glimmering through the spray to form a perfectly arched rainbow.

Sounds from the path told her the others were getting closer. She couldn't wait to show them. Especially Caleb. Not only could he do a drawing, but when they got home he could use charcoals or watercolor to capture the vivid hues.

There had to be a way to work this into the article somehow.

"Caleb, hurry. You need to see this."

Never taking his eyes off Monique, Caleb waved his hand close to his ear as if shooing away a pesky gnat. They were deep in conversation about something. At least, Monique was. Caleb simply stared at her with his jaw half open.

If he didn't pay attention, he'd likely trip over one of the gnarled tree roots that bumped up from under the dirt every so often.

Drinking in one last look at the falls, Chloe turned to go, regretting she couldn't share this with her brother.

"They don't know what they're missing."

Startled by Ben's sudden appearance, Chloe jumped back, immediately tense.

"Sorry. I didn't mean to scare you."

"It's..." She took a breath and willed her shoulders to relax. "You didn't. I'm all right."

Glancing up at him, their gazes locked. Ben smiled. "This really is amazing, isn't it?" He looked back at the waterfall, the look in his eyes reflecting the same wonder she felt.

"I could stay here all day."

Still smiling, Ben nodded. "Me, too. We stopped to eat too soon. This would have been the perfect spot."

His easy manner was similar to the night they met outside the town hall. This was certainly the most pleasant he'd been all day. Chloe rather liked it. But just as she began to feel comfortable, the moment passed.

"We'd better get going before the others get too far ahead."

After one last long look at the waterfall and misty rainbow, Chloe turned and followed Ben.

With him in this mood, she could easily follow him wherever he led.

Chloe slugged along behind Rudy and Skip, uncomfortably aware of Ben's presence behind her. It didn't help that he was alternately singing and humming. *"Oh Rose, oh Rose of Allendale, sweet Rose of Allendale."*

The sadness in his voice drew her and made it hard for her to concentrate. The uphill path grew steeper and rockier, leading them deeper into the trees.

Every once in a while she'd try to peer around the men in an effort to see her brother. She didn't want to shoulder her way past the men for two reasons. She didn't want to attract unwelcome attention to herself, and, more importantly, she needed to figure out why Monique walked so close to Caleb. He was engaged, for goodness sake.

What did Ben think of this little turn of events? Chloe pressed her lips together in disgust and turned to look at him. She didn't meet his gaze right away since he wasn't watching where he was walking. Instead, his eyes were practically pasted to a certain part of her body she'd rather he didn't observe.

Perturbed, she stopped. Not until he almost bumped into her did Ben look up. His expression sheepish, his already flushed cheeks deepened another shade.

"What?" He shrugged. He didn't even have the gumption to apologize. The audacity!

"Keep your eyes on the trail, mister, and look for your Sasquatch tracks!"

Shocked at her own gumption, she put an extra effort into each step she took. Still, Ben wasn't here to stare at her backside. He was supposed to be searching for signs of the Sasquatch. *And* keeping an eye on his girlfriend.

Stomping up the trail in a huff soon took its toll on Chloe. Before long, she found muscles she didn't know existed. Her legs ached until she feared they might fall off. As the sunlight began to fade, she also had the eye-opening realization that her lungs didn't work quite as well as they should. Finally, panting for breath, she stopped and leaned against a tree.

She needed a rest. Just a small one. Never mind the others. She'd catch up with them once she rested for a bit.

Her eyes drifted shut.

"What's wrong?" The husky whisper tickled her ear.

Ben!

Chloe's eyes flew open.

His voice was soothing and he stared down at her, concern in his eyes. Chloe squirmed under his gaze. She didn't want to give him any reason to think she wasn't up to the trek, but right now she was plain exhausted.

Struggling to catch her breath, she tried to keep her answer nonchalant.

"Nothing's wrong, really. I think I have a pebble in my boot." Chloe dropped her bundles to the ground and lowered herself to the soft earth. It felt so good to sit. After struggling to get the boot off, she wiggled her toes around and luxuriated in their temporary freedom. Finally, taking as much time as she dared, she dumped the boot upside down to shake out the imaginary rock before slowly putting it back on.

"Ah, that feels so much better." Did Ben know she was exaggerating? She rolled a kink out of her shoulders, somewhat disconcerted that he never took his eyes off her.

"Too much for you, huh?"

She hadn't fooled him a bit.

Chloe narrowed her eyes. "Of course it's not too much. I told you, I had a pebble in my boot."

"Oh, that's right. You did." Ben's tone belied his words.

Perhaps she should have shaken the boot a little harder. Perhaps she should have dropped it on his foot.

At the sound of heavy footsteps, she looked up.

Caleb stood there, glowering.

"What?" Chloe feigned innocence.

"How come you allowed yourself to get so far behind?" Her brother stared at his map for a moment. "I wanted to reach Money Creek before dark. We're never going to make it now."

"Don't be ridiculous." Chloe glared up at her brother, indignant. "We're not *that* far behind. And what do you mean, *allowed myself*? You were the one who walked right past me when I wanted to show you the waterfalls." Why were they talking this way to each other? She and her brother rarely fought.

"Waterfalls? Where?" Monique stopped at Caleb's side.

Chloe groaned and went back to lacing her boot.

Monique was the reason Chloe and her brother snapped at each other. Why was Caleb acting all friendly with her, and why wasn't Ben doing something about it? Didn't he care that his love-interest was spending so much time with another man?

"I'm mad at you, Ben Kearny." Monique stuck her bottom lip in a pout.

And he should be mad at you. If Ben and Monique were in love, why were they acting this way? Trying to make each other jealous, perhaps?

"Why are you lagging back here with *her*?" Monique indicated Chloe with a toss of her head. What had happened to their earlier camaraderie? "We're walking as fast as we can. It's not easy to keep up the pace *you* instructed Caleb to set, while carrying these heavy packs. Are you really so sure we couldn't have brought a couple of horses?"

"Look Monique." Ben huffed out a heavy breath. His tone was harsh. Much harsher than seemed warranted, by Chloe's estimation. Maybe he really did care that Monique walked with Caleb and this was his way of taking it out on her.

"We're on a journey to track a Sasquatch." Ben sounded exasperated. "Only a few people have ever spotted one. We don't stand a chance of finding it if we have a horse clopping along beside us."

"One horse wouldn't be—"

"If you want to get somewhere decent before nightfall," Gus interrupted with a growl, "I suggest you listen to your trail-guide and get a move-on. Knock off all this senseless bickering and get going."

Grumbling under his breath, Ben reached out his hand and pulled Chloe to her feet. He turned from her and started back up the hill, the subject obviously closed.

It wasn't closed for Chloe. At least, not the subject of Ben touching her hand, pulling her up, and then turning from her. She looked at her hand. It felt cold where the warmth of his had been. She stared at his retreating back and felt oddly abandoned. It was absurd, she knew. But she felt that way, nonetheless. It also surprised her that the more she talked with him the easier it was to get the words out.

"Hello? Chloe?" Caleb waved a hand in front of her face. "You heard Gus. Get a move on, or you'll get behind again. This time I won't come looking for you." Then he turned and ran to catch up with Ben.

Chloe stared after him, amazed at his transformation from loving, companionable brother to rude, arrogant, and bossy.

Only after he disappeared from view did she start in the same direction, Monique close behind. She tried to lengthen her stride to distance herself, but the pesky girl's legs were longer. Like it or not, she was stuck with the woman who seemed determined to drive a wedge between Chloe and her brother with her ever-shifting moods.

Chloe inhaled the crisp, damp air and smiled. The river flowed swift enough that its spray misted across her face as she stood on the low bank waiting for Monique to catch up. Her brother was happy that they finally reached Money Creek before dark, and Ben announced they were stopping for the night.

She would be happy too, if she could soak in the view of Money Creek, which was really a river, as it cut its way down from higher elevations with such force that it displaced rocks and broke off cedar branches that bent to close. Instead, whenever she tried to steal a tranquil moment, the air was filled with whining and complaints.

"I don't know why *we* have to help gather wood."

Monique. Chloe gritted her teeth, suppressing the urge to shove Monique in the river.

They were hiking among the cedar and cottonwood trees near the river, looking for stray branches for the evening's fire.

Chloe's arms were nearly full, while Monique's were empty. And her constant complaining confused Chloe. If Monique was so miserable, why was she here? If she wasn't whining about Ben and his grueling tactics, she was trying to extract information about Caleb by peppering Chloe with incessant questions.

"Does he like to attend social dances?"

"Does he prefer women with dark or light hair?"

"Is he courting anyone?"

Even though Chloe made it perfectly clear that Caleb was engaged to Elizabeth, Monique continued with her questioning about utter nonsense until Chloe thought she would scream.

Funny, while Chloe hadn't been sure of Monique's motives before, now they were quite clear. Monique was after her brother.

Why, when she had Ben? Chloe didn't understand it at all. Again she wondered what Ben thought of it. Perhaps it was why he'd been so irritable.

It certainly annoyed *her* twice as much as it should have.

"Gathering wood is a man's job."

Was she serious? Wasn't she a regular part of Gus and Ben's crew? Did Monique think she could just sit around and expect the men to do all of the work? It seemed to Chloe that all conventions went by the wayside when they were this far from civilization.

"I'm sure the work will go much faster if we all share in it."

"You don't have to be so snappy about it." Monique sounded hurt.

Chloe sighed and gave her a wan smile. "I'm sorry. I didn't mean to be rude. I'm just tired." As soon as she made the admission, she regretted it. She didn't want to give anyone the impressions she wasn't up to the task.

"It's just that I've been looking forward to trying out my new arctic sleeping bag. Why don't you gather some of those broken branches?" Chloe nodded toward a few small branches not far from where they'd come to a stop. "They look thick enough to make good fire wood."

Monique gave her a petulant stare before bending to pick up a branch. As afraid as she was of work, how had she managed to get along all these years? Certainly Rudy and Skip didn't seem the type to wait on her hand and foot. And given Ben's attitude today, Chloe was certain he didn't waste his time pampering her.

Chloe lugged her armload of branches back to camp, satisfied that she'd returned with equally as much wood as the men.

Monique, however, only carried the one tiny branch. With a self-satisfied smile, she reached out and dropped it atop the pieces Skip was laying out for the fire.

"There." Monique brushed minute specks of dirt off her hands. "That ought to keep the fire going all night."

A look passed between Gus and Ben. Obviously this was classic Monique behavior. Again, Chloe wondered why they put up with her.

Though the camp was in a small clearing, which was good for the sake of building a fire, giant cedars surrounded them. Cookie was already setting out her bedroll on the side of camp where the trees were thickest. On the opposite side of the fire, the men had dropped their bags, packs, and bedrolls in a disorderly pile.

Chloe put her branches next to the fire pit then turned to Monique. "Come on. Let's get our sleeping area fixed up." She knew her tone was sharp but didn't care at the moment. After picking up her arctic sleeping bag and carry-all bag, she headed toward Cookie.

Looking around as she approached, Chloe was pleased Cookie had staked out this area for the women. It was close enough to the trees for privacy, yet not far from the fire and the men's side of camp in case anything went wrong.

Like bears that might decide they needed a meal.

Or the Sasquatch and his family members.

Now wait a minute. She wasn't a 'fraidy-cat by nature. But she wasn't used to the idea of not sleeping in her own bed. The thought hadn't bothered her earlier, but now that the time was near she was a tad nervous.

It would be all right. The fire would keep any unwelcome critters away. If that failed, she trusted Ben's ability to keep them safe.

Chloe hoped to settle in next to Cookie so they could get to know each other. As it was, she'd barely heard the woman say two words out loud. Cookie always spoke in hushed tones, mostly to Gus. Although Chloe did notice the lengthy conversation the cook had with the train engineer. The hat shading most of the woman's face made her seem standoffish and unapproachable. In spite of that, there was something about her that drew Chloe. And after observing Cookie's interactions with Ben and Gus, she sensed the woman was gentle-hearted and kind. Most likely she was shy like Chloe, which gave her one more reason to want to get to know her.

Just as Chloe reached the spot next to Cookie, Monique squeezed in front of her and plopped her pack on the ground. "You don't mind sleeping on the outside, do you Chloe?" Monique flashed a syrupy smile that struck Chloe as less than sincere. "I feel much safer in the middle."

Unwilling to let her disappointment show, Chloe nodded and unfastened the two ropes that kept her arctic sleeping bag rolled up. Made of waterproof duck down, it was a sickening shade of tan—almost as ugly as the hunting clothes. She carefully unrolled it, pulled a thin flat pillow from the bottom, then sat down to remove her boots.

Glancing up, she found Ben watching her. He quickly looked away and stared into the fire. The night air, though chilly, seemed alight with intimacy. With Ben? She shrugged the wayward thought into the recesses of her mind. It wasn't something she should dwell on.

Feeling guilty, Chloe looked at Monique to see if she noticed. She didn't appear to. Fully dressed, Monique slipped beneath the covers of her bedroll and settled in for the night. Surprised, Chloe stole a glance at the men, quite certain they would be changing into nightshirts.

Everyone still wore their clothes. Even Caleb. In fact, they weren't even getting into their bedrolls yet.

She caught Ben's gaze again. This time it was she who looked away.

If they were all going to sleep in their clothes, she would do likewise. She wasn't about to be the only one to change. Chloe thought about the white muslin nightdress neatly folded and tucked inside her pillowcase. It would stay there. She wouldn't even take it out and put it in her pack. No one need know she was foolish enough to think they'd be changing out of their clothes.

The woolly sheepskin lining of her sleeping bag looked inviting against the chill air, and Chloe burrowed deep, ready for a much-needed rest. A moment later she turned on her side in disgust. This wasn't the way she'd imagined it at all. The sheep's wool was scratchy, itchy.

She'd never get any sleep this way.

As if to make sleeping more difficult, Rudy started sneezing. A few seconds later, Ben broke out into song.

"Ye gentlemen and ladies fair, on my affliction pity take. The more I strive the worse it grows, this little sting, this tickling in my nose!"

Though some of the words were missing, and Chloe knew Ben was teasing Rudy in good humor, she could still detect the underlying sadness in Ben's tone.

Someone had hurt him.

The thought pricked her heart.

Before this trip was over, she intended to discover who was responsible for the grief that appeared to overshadow Ben.

Chapter Eight

It shouldn't be morning yet. Chloe peeked one eye open. It was still dark, yet something had awakened her.

Alert now, she heard rustling sounds coming from the direction of the fire. Slowly, holding her breath, she rolled over, prepared to see a bear or a wolf basking in the firelight.

Instead, the fire's glow illuminated five men struggling to pull on their boots. They seemed to be in a hurry. Why? Chloe glanced over at Monique who was sound asleep, oblivious to the goings on around her. Cookie lay on her side, her back to them.

Chloe looked back at the men, and a sense of excitement began to slowly course through her, building until it thundered in her ears.

The Sasquatch?

Had they heard it? Or better yet, seen it? She took a deep breath and forced herself to remain perfectly still. If she had any hopes of following them, it wouldn't do to be caught before they'd even begun.

Ben bent over his sleeping area. It wasn't easy to tell because of the shadows, but he appeared to be digging in his bag. When he stood back up, he took his hat off and twisted it back and forth. Next he struck a matchstick against his boot and held it close to the hat before putting it back on.

What...? Chloe frowned and strained to see.

As she watched, a light flickered, followed by a beam glowing from Ben's head. Chloe squinted against the sudden brightness to see he'd attached some sort of reflecting lamp to the crown of his hat.

This definitely had to do with the Sasquatch.

A tickle of anticipation rose in her belly, and her heart began to pound. Forget the itchy wool, the sore feet, the stiffening muscles. This is why she was here—the story, the Sasquatch. It was worth every bit of discomfort to find the creature that, until now, was just a legend.

She tried to stem her excitement so she could hear the words that drifted her way.

"I'm telling you, Gus, the noise came from over there." Rudy sneezed, then adamantly pointed to Chloe's side of camp.

Quickly, she plopped back down and squeezed her eyes shut lest they discover her awake. Just as quickly, she opened them again. They wouldn't notice whether or not she had her eyes open.

Gus didn't agree with Rudy at all. He shook his head of white hair and set his jaw in a no-nonsense manner.

"Whatever it was, it came this way and this is the way we're going." The older man elbowed Rudy out of his way and charged through the bushes in the opposite direction.

"Hey." Ben's whisper was loud enough Chloe could hear. "Try to keep it down."

"Well, I got a look at it, and I think Rudy is right." Skip's voice sounded almost as whiny as Monique's had. "Gus, you're heading us in the wrong direction. We should be going thatta way."

Gus planted his feet and turned to face the men behind him. "I've been in charge of more expeditions than you've even dreamed about, young man. I'm telling you, we're going this way."

"Quiet, all of you." Ben sounded angry now. "You probably scared it all the way to Bolivia with all this racket. Gus, I say we go the other way. If Rudy says he saw it over there then that's good enough for me."

"Hey." By the glow of Ben's lantern, Chloe watched Skip's face harden. "His word is good, but mine isn't?"

"I didn't mean that, Skip. I just meant—"

Skip raised his fist in Ben's face and drew himself up to his full height, which was still a head and shoulder shorter than Ben. "I know what you meant, all right. I'm a danged liar. Is that it?"

Chloe held her breath, wondering if their dispute would escalate into actual fighting.

"No, Skip." Ben's even tone sounded forced. "That's not what I'm saying at all. However, you're still a bit green at this business. And this is the first time you've been part of one of my expeditions. I've been around Rudy enough to know his sense for tracking is spot on."

Their arguing might not be such a bad thing after all, Chloe decided. It was, in fact, a blessing in disguise. She'd be able to follow them without being heard.

None too quiet, the men tromped through the women's side of camp. Ben tried to shush them, to no avail. Apparently they didn't think anything could wake a sleeping woman. When they neared Monique, softly snoring away, Chloe squeezed her eyes shut and waited for them to pass. Then she slipped from her covers and followed at what she hoped was a safe distance.

They were so busy muttering over who was right and who was wrong, their feet practically dragged. Chloe found it quite easy to keep up with them and, in fact, had to force herself to stop when she was about twelve feet from them. It wouldn't do to be caught and sent back to camp like a wayward child. After counting to ten, she let out a breath then fell into step behind them.

Several paces beyond the camp, Skip stopped. "Hey, what's that smell?"

The men all stopped and sniffed the air.

"Phew!" Gus waved his hand in front of his face as if trying to dispel an unpleasant odor.

Ben and Rudy made similar sounds of disgust.

"Skip!" Gus shouted. "I told you not to eat all them beans. I'm going to tell Cookie to limit your portion from now on."

Chloe clapped a hand over her mouth. The look on her brother's face as he pinched his nose, illuminated by the light on Ben's hat, was priceless.

Rudy snorted. "You'll chase old Sassy away before we ever get near him." This brought a round of guffaws from everyone except Ben.

"Knock it off and get serious." Ben looked like he wanted to bang their heads together. "Whatever we thought we were following is probably gone by now thanks to all of this horsing around. But I'm telling you all, we aren't leaving these mountains without that Sasquatch. Even if we're here so long you get to know each and every slime-riddled slug up here on a personal basis. Now unless you want me to kick each and every one of you in the rear, you'll shut your yaps and get busy."

With that, he turned and marched off in search of his elusive Sasquatch.

The others shuffled along behind him as he muttered words Chloe couldn't hear. Not about to be left out, she followed close behind.

"This is ridiculous." Disgusted, Ben swiped the back of his hand across his forehead. "There's no sign of him. Even if there was, he'd have headed for the hills by now. Let's just go back."

They'd been scurrying around in the dark for over an hour. For what? So these jokers could entertain one another with their stupid shenanigans? Tracking the Sasquatch was serious business. Not something to be laughed at. He had half a mind to knock their heads together.

He turned around, only to bump into Gus. "Aw come on, Gus. Why are you hanging on my heels?"

"Shoo-ee, Ben. Why do you have to take things so serious all the time? We're just having a little fun."

"Fun? You call tracking a Sasquatch only to have you blundering fools scare it off when our very careers hang in the balance, fun?"

Stuffing his hands in his pockets, Gus shuffled his feet and looked at the ground. "Sorry." He pulled a face that usually made Ben feel guilty.

Not this time. "Yeah, well, let's just go. We aren't getting anywhere tonight."

Somewhere up ahead, a twig snapped. Ben froze, instantly alert.

"Did you hear that?" Skip's whisper was a bit too loud.

Ben pressed his lips together and made a shushing motion. They'd better not scare it off again. Slowly he turned his head, moving the beam of light from side to side, and strained to see what caused the sound. Nothing. He couldn't see a thing.

Signaling to his team, Ben tiptoed in the direction of the sound.

"Over there." Caleb pointed off to his right. "I saw some branches move."

Rudy shook his head. "It could have been the wind."

Skip poked Rudy in the back. "There is no wind, dummy."

"Breeze then. Breeze."

"Shut up, you two." Ben clenched his jaw.

First nights on an assignment were always the same. Though Ben didn't drink, Gus always started things off with a bottle. Only one, though. It was a celebration of sorts. Man and nature and freedom. Only he should have put a stop to it tonight. Finding the Sasquatch was too important.

"There it goes." Excited, Caleb pointed again.

The beam from his reflecting lamp was supposed to reach out forty feet, but Ben doubted it really did. However, just on the farthest edge of light, he thought he saw movement. He tipped his head so the light's periphery would extend and hopefully illuminate the creature, critter, or whatever was out there.

Again, the object moved just as the light hit it. It certainly wasn't a rabbit. A round of sucked-in breaths came from his men. There was something large out there. Almost man-sized. Maybe a bear, or could it be...?

Sasquatch. One of Jacko's cousins. Anticipation trembled in his gut. Ben was about to realize a life-long dream.

He took a cautious step forward...only to be nearly knocked to the ground by his men.

"Good grief! What are you trying to do? Terrorize it back into hiding?" Ben recovered his balance and ran to catch up, hoping they wouldn't injure his Sasquatch. "Come on, slow up!"

The men yelled and hollered as they dog-piled on top of the animal. Imbeciles. They had no sense at all. If it was a bear—he reached into his inner vest pocket for his revolver, hoping it had a strong enough charge to stop an angry bear.

"Will you idiots get off me?"

Chloe?

Ben rushed over to the others.

"Stop it. Get off! You're hurting me."

The men scrambled to get back on their feet, elbowing each other, stumbling over one another, tripping awkwardly all over the place. From beneath the pile, Chloe's yelps and cries of outrage filled Ben with concern.

"Get out of the way, will you?" He grabbed Caleb by the collar and pulled him up, shoving him aside. Next went Gus.

"A little grabby, there, aren't you?"

Ben ignored Gus's indignant attitude. Instead, he shoved Skip and Rudy out of the way. It figured Rudy, the big clumsy oaf, would have been the first one down.

"Chloe? Are you all right?"

Looking dazed and angry, Chloe raised herself up on her elbows. By the glow of his lantern, Ben could see the flush on her face.

"I was perfectly fine until these dolts tackled me."

Ben reached out to help her up, but she shrugged away from his touch.

"What's wrong with you, anyway? Are you fools, or simply crazy?"

Unable to help himself, Ben grinned. Chloe was fine, just fine. It seemed she forgot all about being shy when she was mad.

"What are you laughing at?"

Why *was* he grinning? Because she looked angrier than a mama bear?

Yes. And he wanted to kiss the anger off her face until she melted, weak and trembling in his arms. He reached for her, ignoring the presence of the others.

She shrugged away from him. "I can get up by myself. Thank you very much." The light glinted off a flash in her eyes. It matched her impertinent tone.

So much for taking her into his arms and kissing the outrage from her face. Not that he would have gotten very far with her brother looking on.

As if reading his thoughts, Caleb none-too-gently shouldered past him. "Chloe, what in blue blazes possessed you to come out here in the middle of the night?"

"What possessed me? What possessed you?"

"We were following the Sasquatch," Skip piped up. "I saw it with my own eyes. Walked right by the camp."

"I saw it too," Rudy said.

"I think you all stayed up a little too late, having a little too much fun." She tilted her chin, indignantly. "There was no Sasquatch."

"Was too," Skip argued.

"You're delusional."

Ben blinked, surprised by the sharpness in Chloe's tone.

"Hey." Rudy looked at Caleb. "Are you going to let her talk to us this way?"

Chloe turned to Rudy and poked him right in the chest. Ben watched, amazed, as sassiness transformed her into a spitfire who wasn't afraid of anyone.

"He's my brother, not my master. No one tells me what to say or how to say it."

Rudy held his hands up in surrender and took two steps back.

"Come on, Chloe. Let's get you back to the camp where you'll be safe and sound."

Caleb reached for her arm, but Chloe slapped him away.

"I'm safe and sound right here, Caleb Williston. I can help myself back. I don't need you to do it for me."

"Fine." Caleb sounded hurt. "You just help yourself back."

"I will," Chloe snapped. "I'll bet I make it back before you."

Biting the inside of his lip to keep from smiling, Ben watched the looks being exchanged between the other men. Caleb, Skip, Rudy, and Gus nodded amongst themselves, shrugged their shoulders, and turned in the direction of camp.

He rather liked this side of Chloe. Anger made her shyness fade, but would it come back with the morning sun? "Coming, Ben?"

"I'll be along, Gus. I'll be along."

"You don't have to stick around and escort me." Chloe's sarcastic tone was directed at him. "I found my way here, and I can find my way back."

"I'm not planning to escort you. I want to talk with you."

"Suit yourself. Just don't look straight into my face anymore. Your light hurts my eyes."

"I wish there was a way to dim it. You're supposed to be able to trim it like a lantern, but it doesn't seem to work."

Chloe giggled, and her tone softened. "Do you know how ridiculous you look with that thing attached to your head?"

He didn't care. All he cared about was the way her eyes lit up when she laughed.

"So," Ben said as they slowly walked back to camp. "You thought you'd follow us, and get in on the action?"

He turned and smiled at her, careful not to tip his hat toward her.

She smiled back, and his heart skipped a beat before her tone turned half-serious. "I was hoping, like you, that there really was a Sasquatch around. Instead, I suspect you all had way too much fun before settling in for the night."

Though he didn't want to admit as much, it was most likely the truth. He nodded slowly. "I suppose you're right."

"This isn't going to happen every night, is it? If it is, you'll be way too tired to give much of a chase during the day."

"Naw. Gus brings a bottle with him every time we set out somewhere. It disappears the first night, and everything's normal after that." Thank goodness. Tonight's behavior had severely tried his patience.

"So they really didn't see anything?" She sound disappointed.

"I didn't say that." He didn't want to feel like a fool for believing Skip and Rudy's story. "I didn't actually see anything myself, but I kind of hoped they were right."

Chloe stumbled just then, and Ben caught her in his arms. He held her for a moment too long, soaking in the feel of her in his arms. Soft, warm, and tiny. A perfect fit.

He glanced down at her as she wriggled from his arms. "Are you all right?"

She winced, squeezing her eyes tight against the brightness of his light.

"Sorry." He took off the hat. "I'll just hold it while we walk. Now are you all right?"

"Yes." She sounded dazed, confused. "There was a dip in the ground. I stepped in a small hole. But I'm fine."

What would happen if he kissed her?

"Chloe?" He brought his face closer to hers. Her eyes widened, her lips parted.

"I..." As if she knew his intent, she turned her head away. "We'd better head back."

Disappointment laced his insides. Nodding, he placed his arm around her small waist and led her back to camp, enjoying the feel of her close to him. At the same time, he knew he had to guard against this very thing. He couldn't afford distractions.

Distractions caused carelessness.

Carelessness caused people to get hurt.

Or worse.

Chapter Nine

Hunkerd down in her sleeping bag, Chloe pulled her itchy arms out of the covers and turned on her other side. It didn't take much to imagine the wool prickling her through her clothes. Still it wasn't enough to distance her thoughts from the nighttime excitement. She needed to relax, needed to concentrate on something else or she'd never get to sleep.

Perhaps a quick prayer would be in order. Outside of church on Sundays, Chloe didn't pray a lot. She knew she should, but most times it just seemed so ritualistic. Her family prayed before meals, and sometimes she prayed before bed as she'd been taught when she was young.

Other than that, God was just an entity she met with on Sunday morning. And sometimes she even had to wonder about that. Especially up here in the mountains surrounded by the beauty she'd witnessed today—it lit a spark inside her, infused a trickle of awareness in her soul. If God made all of this, He had to be more than just an invisible being one prayed to in the church building—much more.

As the heat from the fire started to warm her and her thoughts of God began to soothe her soul, Chloe's eyes drifted closed. But before she could be lulled into a comforting slumber, the sounds of muffled laughter caught her attention. Turning back over, she saw that Rudy and Caleb were slapping their knees with their hands. Skip had produced a harmonica and was now blowing into it. Gus clapped his hands, and Ben—Chloe's heart fluttered—Ben counted time and looked like he was waiting for the proper moment to jump in with a song.

Seriously? They weren't tired after all their shenanigans?

"In a canyon, in a cavern..."

A tingling worked its way up from Chloe's toes, and a warm melting sensation centered in her chest. Tuning out the gleeful sounds of the men, she snuggled down in her sleeping bag, temporarily forgetting its scratchiness, and focused only on Ben's voice. He'd wanted to kiss her earlier. She could tell.

The memory of the moment, the sweetness of it, combined with the smoothness of his voice to wrap around her. It warmed her, soothed her, and she marveled at the way she felt—safe, secure—almost like she belonged.

Awake just as a tiny magenta sliver of sunlight glimmered atop the eastern peaks, Chloe sat up with a groan. Every inch of her body screamed in agonized protest over yesterday's workout. Worse, when she actually struggled to get out of the bedroll, her legs and arms were lifeless, useless limbs. She stole a glance at Monique, relieved the girl was snoring away.

Guilt pricked her. Clearly Monique had some claim on Ben. But it was Chloe he'd been about to kiss last night. Chloe knew it as surely as she knew the sunrise would cast its pink glow on the snowy summits.

And she'd wanted that kiss, ached for it. Awake most of the night, she kept imagining Ben's lips descending toward hers.

A glance to the men's side of camp told her they, too, were stretched out in an unconscious state. Judging from last night's antics, they wouldn't be waking any time soon.

Unable to help herself, Chloe stared intently at Ben. She couldn't quite see his face from where she was, and she wondered if he appeared peaceful in his sleep. Or perhaps there would be that hint of loneliness she sometimes caught raging in his eyes.

She allowed herself the luxury of one sigh. One long sigh, then she turned from Ben and tried to forget all those silly schoolgirl thoughts. He was Monique's. Her face burned at the thought of almost kissing someone else's beau.

Carrying her toothbrush, a tin of toothpowder, a bar of lemon-scented soap, and a towel, Chloe forced her aching bones down to the creek to freshen up.

"Hello." The deep voice boomed from out of nowhere.

Startled, Chloe dropped her toiletries.

Rudy! He stood three feet from her, at the edge of the creek. Even when they were with the others, his presence left her feeling nervous. Giant, bald, frightening. She'd thought he was asleep with the others. How could she have not noticed one missing body? Especially his?

For a moment she froze, recalling her audacity at poking him in the chest last night. She never would have done it, had she not been caught up in the excitement. It was something Aunt Jane would have done, but totally out of character for herself.

However, everything was different up here. The rules of propriety didn't seem to even exist. And away from her father, her confidence bloomed just a tiny bit. So was she going to lose it now? Most definitely not. Not when she was right where she wanted to be, chasing the most exciting story to ever come her way. *"Dream big dreams, seek them with big confidence."* That's what Aunt Jane always said.

Bending to retrieve her things, Chloe wondered what she should do next. Talk to him? Ignore him?

"Need some help with that?"

Chloe whipped her head up and dropped her belongings once again. Rudy now stood in front of her.

"Uh—no. Th—thank you." No matter what kind of pep talk she tried to give herself, she was as unsure about talking to this man as she was jumping into the Skykomish River in the middle of winter. He was positively frightening. And so very big.

"I see you're an early riser." Rudy smiled at her, a big, gap-toothed smile that she felt obliged to return. Her lips trembled as she attempted to smile back.

"I-I'm sorry. I didn't mean to intrude on your early morning thoughts. I'll just gather my things and go somewhere else."

"Let me help." Rudy squatted and picked up her soap and towel. "Here you go."

"Thank you." Chloe started to turn when she realized there was something very strange about Rudy. He wasn't sneezing, and his nose wasn't red, but that wasn't it. She peered at him through narrowed eyes.

His head was lathered with soap, all except one perfectly shaven spot.

Rudy's baldness wasn't natural!

Quickly she looked away, at the creek, and tried to hide her shock, praying he wouldn't notice that she noticed. A sharp glint of sunlight on metal caught her eye. There, by the creek, was Rudy's wicked-looking hunting knife.

Unable to help herself, she gasped.

Rudy looked over at the knife then back at her.

She stared at him, unblinking, trying not to show her fright. What would he do?

He stared back.

"I'm sorry," Chloe said. "I didn't mean to be rude."

"Uh." A sea of scarlet that almost matched his goatee washed over his face and ears before creeping down his neck. He didn't seem so frightening all of a sudden. "Uh, nobody knows about this."

Nobody knew he shaved his head? "Don't worry." Chloe was quick to assure him. "Your secret is mine to keep. I won't tell anyone." Though she didn't know why he wanted to keep it a secret. Still, it was none of her business. He must have a good reason for wanting to appear bald. But why wouldn't he shave that awful beard as well?

"Uh...thank you, Miss Williston."

He seemed so relieved, and so vulnerable, Chloe couldn't help but begin to relax. Perhaps he wasn't as fearsome as she first thought.

"Chloe." Hesitantly, she held out her hand. "You can call me Chloe."

"Sure will." Rudy beamed and pointed at large rock that rose out of the creek. "I found a real comfortable spot out there on that rock. It gives a perfect view of the sunrise. Would you like to join me? It's a great place to greet the morning and talk to the One who created all of this."

Chloe looked at the hunting knife and recalled her earlier fear of him. Then she looked at his lathered, half-shaven head and his crimson face. This man was going to sit on a rock and talk to God? Interest piqued, she smiled.

"I'd like that." Anticipating the view of the sun making its full and glorious appearance, Chloe followed him to the creek, mindful of her screaming muscles as she carefully navigated three protruding rocks leading to the larger one.

"You're holding up pretty well for a tenderfoot."

A tenderfoot? "Thanks, I think."

Rudy laughed. "Most newcomers don't do this well their first time out, and they're usually men. I'd say by the end of this trip you'll be a natural."

Once they were comfortably seated on the cold rock, Rudy indicated the direction the sun would ascend over the mountainous horizon. The sliver of sunlight she'd noticed earlier was now a raspberry wedge. It wouldn't be long before dawn-filled sky was replaced with a glory of color.

"How long have you been doing this?" She'd never before sat on a rock in the mountains, awaiting the sunrise. Giddy with eagerness, she found she had no difficulty talking with Rudy. "Field expeditions, I mean. Studying animals?" She stared, fascinated, as Rudy ran the sharp blade over his scalp neatly swiping a freshly shaved path. Then he dipped the knife into the water to rinse it clean before repeating the process.

"'Bout ten years now, I suppose."

"You must love it then."

"That I do." His gap-toothed grin made him appear boyish. "No matter where it takes me, it's the best way I know to get close to my Maker. What about you? How long have you been a reporter?"

Not sure how to answer the question, Chloe hesitated. It was probably better not to say anything. She couldn't begin to explain about her father, how she'd always tried to make him proud.

How she failed.

How she would be forced to marry Jackson Dahl if she couldn't go back to Cedar Ridge with the big story.

Even if she did get the story, she might still be forced into the marriage.

Unless she never went home again.

Tears choked her throat and stung her eyes.

"Never mind. You don't have to tell me if it makes you uncomfortable."

Unable to speak, Chloe rubbed at the small of her back and winced. She'd almost forgotten about the sore muscles.

"You okay?"

Chloe nodded.

"You sore from all the exercise yesterday?"

If possible, she had more aches than her body had muscles. It wouldn't really be a lie to let Rudy think the unshed tears were about sore muscles. Would it?

Conscience clear, she said, "Just a few stiff muscles. It'll pass before long, I'm sure."

"It will. I've got some healing balm that works pretty well. If you'd like, you can have it when we get back to camp."

"No, thanks. I'm sure I'll be fine."

"Well, if you change your mind, you know where to find me. Look." He waved at the horizon with his knife, his eyes lit with awe. "Oh, praise the Lord. Here it comes."

A beam of orange crested the mountain peaks, casting its brilliance across the sky. Chloe took a breath of sweet, fresh air.

Again, as last night, she thought of God—the God who created this beauty versus the God she never seemed in harmony with at the little church in Cedar

Ridge. Why had she never thought of Him in context of God the creator of beauty? Of course she knew, had known since she was a small child that God made the world and everything in it in seven days. She thought about the waterfall and the rainbow. Until this very minute, she'd never, ever considered Him as having given the world such a beautiful and amazing gift.

Oh, glory.

This new day suddenly brimmed with possibilities. She could hardly wait to see what it might hold.

Ben stood a few paces from camp, where he'd just witnessed the sunrise. This was usually his favorite time of day. Usually. But all peace shattered the moment Chloe emerged from the bushes with Rudy. She practically glowed with an inner smile he'd never noticed before. He clamped his teeth together in an attempt to rein in the jealousy.

"Thank you." Chloe looked up at Rudy. Her voice sounded much too breathy. She didn't even seem her usual shy self.

"You're welcome. And remember, Miss Chloe." Rudy winked, and his smile started Ben aching to add another gap to his teeth. "Our secret."

Secrets? So Chloe and Rudy were keeping secrets now. He slammed his foot against a tree. So much for the sunrise. Something about this new scene wiped out all the majesty of nature.

He stormed toward them.

"Don't you two have better sense than to run off without letting someone know where you are?"

Chloe looked up at him in surprise, eyes wide, mouth open. The desire to kiss her was as strong now as it was last night. He ignored it.

"Anything could happen to you. Rudy, I'm surprised at you acting so irresponsible. You—"

He stopped his ranting midstream, realizing he sounded like a fishwife, or worse, a jealous suitor.

"I'm sorry." He looked at the ground. "I was worried." So worried, he hadn't even known they were gone until they returned.

Chloe said nothing. She gave him an icy glare and turned away. Not that he blamed her. His behavior was shameful.

"Let's eat." Rudy spoke quietly, not meeting Ben's eye. "I know you're anxious to get up the trail."

Rudy was right. Getting up the trail and finding the Sasquatch. That's what mattered. Not this infuriating female who confounded him at every turn.

After breakfast, and before they finished packing up their belongings, Chloe decided to take advantage of Rudy's offer. The way her muscles ached, she wouldn't be able to match the pace of a turtle. Hopefully with his healing balm, she'd be able to keep up with the group without much complaint.

Under Ben's watchful eye, she walked to the men's side of camp to borrow the liniment. Why did he keep looking at her like she was stealing a horse or something?

"Rudy." She kept her voice low so Ben wouldn't overhear. "Do you still have that liniment you told me about?"

Not only did Rudy give Chloe the liniment, he handed her a tiny leather-bound Bible. Though similar in size to the one she had tucked into her nightstand at home, this one was well used—well loved. Much more loved than her own.

A prick of sadness swept through her at the realization that she'd never once considered bringing her Bible with her. It was a reflection of just how empty her life was when she wasn't writing or actively seeking a story.

Before they'd headed back to camp after the sunrise, Rudy quoted a scripture he said was from Ecclesiastes.

"He hath made everything beautiful in his time; also he hath set the world in their heart, so that no man can find out the work that God maketh from the beginning to the end."

After explaining that this meant God allowed people to have a glimpse of His perfect creation so that His people could trust Him, Rudy prayed out loud.

Now, Chloe wanted more. She couldn't wait to look up the scripture and read it for herself. She wanted to understand it. The peace, the sense of wonder and awe she experienced this morning—she wanted to be constantly filled with it. She pressed the Bible to her chest and looked heavenward.

"Are you there, God? Do you really care about me?" As she whispered the prayer, everything in her wanted it to be true.

Jar in one hand and Bible in the other, she approached Monique, who was busy rolling up her blankets. Monique had complained long and loud during breakfast about all her aches and pains. Why did she hurt so much if she was used to this kind of field action?

Uncapping the jar, Chloe sniffed and promptly wrinkled her nose at the rancid odor.

It reminded her of the time her brother decided to go hunting to try and fit in with the other young men in Cedar Ridge. Her mother had been none too happy about preparing the unidentifiable creature he'd brought home. Especially once the scent of it stewing on the stove filled the house.

No one had been brave enough to taste it, and whether or not it was a rabbit, as Caleb claimed, he never went hunting again.

And Chloe had never forgotten the smell.

"If it smells half as bad as the look on your face, I'm not using it," Monique declared.

"Here." Chloe held it out to her. "See for yourself."

"Oo-eew, yuck!" She turned her nose up and pushed Chloe away.

"It smells pretty bad." Chloe nodded in agreement. "However, I'm opposed to trudging along slower than a turtle and having Ben declare victory. He wants nothing more than to prove we're nuisances. I'd rather smell bad and keep up than suffer that humiliation."

Monique gave it a moment's thought. "You're right. If we stay at the back of the group, they'll never smell us anyway."

"Or if they do, they'll just think a skunk passed through the area."

Chloe and Monique both laughed then dipped their fingers into the odious jar. The friendliness probably wouldn't last, but she might as well enjoy it while it did.

The rain started not long after they set out. The grey sky seemed to darken the green of the trees to a stunning shade. To Chloe, the color of every tree and wildflower seemed more brilliant. And in spite of the dampness soaking her clothes, it was lovely.

After about an hour of drinking in every sight she could, a different sight caught Chloe's eye. Different and interesting. To her right, just off the trail, water puddled in several tracks the size of her palm.

"Look!" She shouted without hesitation, her heart quickening with her first real taste of the same excitement she knew Ben must feel about his work. At the same moment, something else dawned on her. She'd spoken up with a newly emerging confidence. One she'd always wished she had. Something about their late-night shenanigans and her occasional camaraderie with Monique seemed to lessen the power they once had to intimidate her. A warm glow spread through her chest, and she couldn't help but smile.

Ben rushed to her side, followed closely by the others.

"What is it?" someone asked as they all crowded around.

"Be quiet." Ben waved them away. "Get back. I'm trying to see." He stared intently at the ground.

Though he'd been grouchy all morning, his mood did nothing to dispel Chloe's thrill at making a discovery.

"So?" She waited none too patient. "What are they from?"

He looked up at her, and his grumpy expression softened. Light danced in his eyes. "They're not from the Sasquatch, Chloe."

"Oh." Not the Sasquatch. She bit back her disappointment. Were the others looking at her and seeing a fool? "W-what are they then?"

"Lynx."

A lump of embarrassment formed in the pit of her stomach, and she looked away, staring at her feet, unwilling to look up and see condemnation in the eyes of those around her. Memories of her father's voice flooded over her, shaming her, telling her she didn't know ink from paper because she was a woman. Obviously he was right. A Sasquatch and a lynx could stand side-by-side, and she wouldn't be able to tell one from the other. *What an idiot.*

"It's all right, Chloe." Though surprised by Ben's gentle tone, she still couldn't look at him. "We never told you what the prints would look like. How were you to know?"

Murmurs of agreement went around the group. They weren't condemning her. Did that mean they didn't think she was stupid?

"We've all made mistakes at one time or another," Monique said.

"All of us." Rudy smiled at her.

They were trying to make her feel better, not worse. To Chloe, the thought was almost unbelievable. She glanced at Ben, still crouched before her. He nodded to confirm what they said then winked at her. Winked! His green eyes danced with delight, and he motioned for her to kneel down next to him on the damp ground.

When she did, he pointed at the tracks. "See how faint they are?" She nodded, and he continued. "If you look closer, you can see a halo surrounding them. The indentation is soft, but it's there."

Following his finger as he traced one of the prints, Chloe could just make what she hadn't noticed before. A delicate circle around the print, difficult to see because it was eroding away under the rainfall. "I see it."

"Lynx are light on their feet. Their paws act like snowshoes so they don't sink too deep. It was probably already muddy here when the animal came through. That's why there's an impression in the dirt. It also means it couldn't have been that long ago."

Chloe studied Ben's face as he talked, mesmerized by the change in him. Earlier, he snarled and growled at everyone. She'd suspected he was still sore at the other men for their behavior last night. Now though, he was confident and seemed to delight in his explanations. And she delighted in watching him, watching the way his eyes lit up, the strong line of his cheekbones and the soft lines above it accenting his eyes, the way his mouth moved when he spoke...the way it might move gently over hers....

Shaking her head to dispel such thoughts, Chloe cast a wary glance over her shoulder, thankful to see that Monique wasn't looking at her. No one was. Caleb and Monique huddled near a tree, laughing. The other men were nowhere to be seen.

"Cougar on the other hand, will have prints the same size and almost the same shape, but no halo surrounding them. Their stride will be larger, too, since they are a much larger cat."

Ben, still in his element as the expert naturalist, was unaware that Chloe had been paying more attention to his physical features than what he was saying.

"Great job noticing the tracks, Chloe." His words caught her so off-guard, her heart skittered.

"Th-thank you." She took a breath and tried to gather her thoughts. "Um, what about the Sasquatch though? Shouldn't I know what his tracks will look like?"

"You want to take off your shoe and step in the dirt?" His smile was teasing. He stood then held out his hand and pulled Chloe up as well. Continuing to hold her hand, he said, "They're all different, of course, but most prints will look almost like yours. Only much larger and there's no arch. The Sasquatch tracks will be flat-footed. Do you have any more questions?"

Caught up in the sensation of her hand in his, Chloe could only shake her head mutely.

"Then I'd like to ask you a question before we get on our way." Ben gazed at her, intently, his eyes searching hers. She held her breath, all of last night's feelings rushing back to overwhelm her. He lowered his face toward hers, and wrinkled his nose. "Has Rudy been sharing his little brown jar with you?"

Brown jar? She blinked as his meaning struck her, and prayed the ground would open and swallow her.

She stank.

"I—uh—yes." Her face burned. The humiliation was too much.

"I thought so." Ben flashed a teasing grin. "I hope it does the trick. In the meantime you and Monique might want to bring up the rear."

"Insult me again," she said with a saucy tone worthy of Aunt Jane, "and you'll be reading all about last night's shenanigans in the newspaper." She pressed her lips together to keep from laughing as he went off to round up the others.

As she watched him talking to Gus, she realized she'd teased and acted sassy without feeling awkward. Whether she smelled of Rudy's rotten liniment or not, this day started out with an unexpectedly beautiful surprise and continued to be full of them.

Ben stared out at the snow-capped panorama. The Cascades were glorious. He inhaled the fresh mountain air, thinking once again how nowhere he'd ever been could quite compare.

Other than spotting Chloe and Rudy together this morning, and then Chloe spotting the lynx tracks, the day had been uneventful. Not that he'd expected it this soon, but there'd been no sign of the Sasquatch.

Still, he loved it here. He wished he had someone to share it with. Really share it, deeply, from the heart. Wished there was someone who understood without words everything that sparked his soul when he looked out at the wilderness both above and below them.

For perhaps the twelfth time since this trek began, he found himself thinking of Rosalie. Ben had so distanced himself from the hurt that it seemed an eternity ago. Even now, he wasn't sure he was ready to face the pain. But there was something about these mountains that reminded him of her.

Rosalie Faulkner.

Fresh-faced, with blond hair like spun gold, Rosalie had a zest for life that seemed endless. She was a journalism student at the University in Florida, an acquaintance of Monique's, the daughter of one of his professors. She had enchanted Ben. He might even have been in love with her. It was something he never had the chance to find out, thanks to his own selfishness.

While she wasn't a student of animal behavior, the subject fascinated her. She'd even been considering changing her major. Aware of that, Ben didn't hesitate to ask her to join them on Gus's South Pacific study project. The way he'd figured it, since Rosalie's father was on the board that held the purse strings for University-funded field projects, all she had to do was write a series of papers showing Ben's competency, and the grant money would be endless.

The only problem came in talking her father into letting Rosalie go to the South Pacific. To say Professor Faulkner disliked Ben would have been an understatement. He'd always referred to Ben as an upstart, didn't like it when Ben talked about the places he'd been with Gus and all the animals he'd observed. Indeed, for reasons known only to Professor Faulkner, he'd flunked Ben out of an important block of classes—the classes he'd needed to ace in order to graduate with honors. Instead, his graduation was delayed by a year so he could make them up.

No, it hadn't been easy to get the professor's permission for Rosalie to go along. They'd ended up lying to him, a fact that Ben hadn't been proud of—and was even less proud of today. The only mention of Ben that Rosalie made to her father was to say, *"Of course he won't be there. He's off in the Brazilian jungle. In fact, Dr. Pieper is quite disappointed."* If not for the lie, she wouldn't have been able to go. And at the time Ben had been quite certain there'd not only be scholarship money so he could finish school, but there'd also be plenty of grant money flowing his way when she returned from the South Pacific with her papers documenting Ben's expertise.

Things had a way of not turning out as planned. No one had ever learned that lesson better than Ben. And now, two years later, staring at the awesome majesty of towering mountain peaks, he promised himself history would not be repeated. Tragedy would not strike another of his field expeditions.

The sound of footsteps alerted him to someone else's presence. He struggled out of his dark thoughts and glanced over his shoulder.

Monique stared up at him.

He tensed and looked away. He certainly didn't need her around while trying to come to terms with what had happened to Rosalie. Certainly Monique played a part in it, but he bore the ultimate responsibility, and he didn't want the reminder.

If nothing else, this was the first time a woman had accompanied them since then. And what was worse, he didn't have just one woman to look out for. He had two. Well, three if he counted Cookie, but she did whatever needed to be done without hesitation, so there was no need to worry about her.

"Are you going to ignore me forever?"

"If you've come to complain, Monique, you can just leave."

"Why, Ben." Monique whined in a pampered little tone that never failed to agitate him. "I'm surprised at your lack of manners. You've treated me and Chloe positively ghastly." She cast him a woebegone expression he knew wasn't heartfelt.

"Leave me alone." He tensed when she reached out and took his arm.

"What's wrong with you?" Her tone was saucy, almost flirtatious, and she smiled.

For a moment he saw her as she used to be, as his childhood friend. The way she was before they were adults. Before Rosalie....

"Go on." Ben shrugged out of her grasp. "I just want to be left alone."

Monique dropped her hand, letting it fall to her side, and bowed her head. "You've never forgiven me." Her heartbroken whisper caused a lump to form in his throat. "And I've never forgiven myself."

Ben couldn't see her face so he could only imagine her expression. And what he imagined pricked at his heart.

"Aw, blast it all anyway." He opened his arms to her. "Come here."

She didn't come toward him. Instead, hesitantly and seeming almost shy, Monique lifted her face. All the answers were etched there. The hurts of the past, the burden of responsibility she also bore, the pain of her broken engagement to Avery. It was all there, and it was real. Her chin quivered, and Ben knew she was fighting to compose herself. This truly was the Monique of the past.

Again he urged her over.

This time she stepped into his arms and buried her face against his chest. As he stroked her hair, she said, "I really loved him." Her voice cracked. "Why did he do this to me? Why?"

"I don't know, Monique. I don't know." Ben held her while she sobbed.

"I just wanted someone to love me, someone who would love me above all else."

Exactly the same thing he wanted. Would he have found that with Rosalie? Ben shut his eyes against the thought, not wanting to think about his own hurt. He'd never had the chance to find out. Certainly he wouldn't find it with this mixed-up woman he held in his arms now.

Monique may be physically attractive, which was fine if that's all a man needed. But he needed more, much more. He needed a woman who wasn't clingy and needy like Monique. He needed a woman who would listen to him, who wouldn't object to the job he did. She might even enjoy what he did—but if not, a sense of adventure and passion for life would be kind of nice. He needed a woman who wouldn't try to change him.

One name danced through his mind, and he squeezed his eyes shut, as if that would make thoughts of a certain persistent reporter disappear.

"I know it seems like the end of the world." He tried to soothe himself as much as Monique. "But it'll be all right soon. You'll see. Everything will work out the way it's supposed to."

His words seemed to have their desired effect on Monique. After a moment she pushed out of his arms, dried her tears, and smiled shakily at him.

"Do you think you can ever forgive me, Ben? For Rosalie? Or will it always be like this between us?"

Unable to answer, Ben could only sigh with the heaviness his heart still held.

Heaven knew he tried to forgive her. But try as he might, he just couldn't get the tragedy off his mind. He couldn't shake the image of what might have been had Rosalie not fallen to her death.

"That's what I thought." Monique's voice was quiet, her tone sad, as if she could read his thoughts. She touched his hand, gave him a small smile then left him standing alone while she headed back to the others.

The others. A group he no longer seemed to belong to.

He might have been able to help Monique, but nothing seemed to ease his own lonely ache—the one he didn't think would ever disappear.

Chloe leaned against the rough bark of a towering tree. Its needle-filled branches surrounded her like an umbrella. And though it had stopped raining, the ground beneath her feet was damp and spongy.

Concern, not nosiness, had motivated Chloe to follow Monique. She had appeared troubled, and Chloe sensed Monique could use someone to talk to. So could she, for that matter. Despite Monique's frustrating moodiness, maybe if they got to know each other better, they could actually become friends. Chloe hadn't planned to stumble upon Monique cradled in Ben's arms.

She remembered the feel of Ben's arms when he'd saved her from falling off the train. His strength, his warmth, the magic of his touch. Was Monique reveling in those same feelings now, as Chloe was then? A flash of bitterness tore through her as she observed the tender scene with Monique crying and Ben comforting her. It was hard, but Chloe managed to turn away. Just because she felt a powerful pull toward Ben didn't mean she had a right to be jealous. No right at all.

Besides, it was ridiculous to be jealous. There was certainly no room in her life for a man. She needed to set any feelings she had aside right here and now.

There was an article to write, a career to pursue. And just like Aunt Jane, she had to prove herself to her father so she didn't end up married to Jackson. She couldn't do that if she was all wrapped up in chasing after a man.

The image of Monique in his arms rose up to taunt her as she stumbled along the path back toward camp. They seemed meant for each other.

When she neared the river, shouts and splashes caught her eye. Caleb, Gus, Rudy, and Skip laughed as they tried to catch a fish without using a pole. Cookie silently looked on from the shore, and Chloe couldn't help but wonder why the woman kept her distance from everyone.

Was she as shy as Chloe? Did she feel as alone?

Because right now, Chloe felt more alone than ever. This longing to know Ben wasn't part of the plan. She had to focus her thoughts on the article and stop thinking about him.

She especially had to stop thinking about him with Monique cradled in his arms.

After a sleepless night, Chloe dragged herself from her sleeping bag eager to wash up so she could be ready when Rudy arrived at the creek. He came down the path just as she pulled the drawstring tight on the small linen bag that held her toothpowder, a few grooming items, and the jar of Rudy's liniment.

"Good morning, Miss Chloe."

"Hello, Rudy."

"I'm sorry they gave you such a bad time over the liniment." He avoided eye contact as he spoke.

"It was worth it," she reassured him. "It really did help."

Rudy sniffed the air and studied her with a measured glance.

"Yes, Rudy. I washed and then put more of it on. If I can put up with the smell, so can everyone else. I'm just thankful for the relief it offers."

Now Rudy beamed. "Fair enough. It'll get easier after a couple more days." He flashed her a smile of encouragement then gestured toward the grassy hillside near the creek. "Will that do for our scripture reading? Seems we're fresh out of rocks today."

Whether they sat on a rock in the middle of a creek or on a patch of grass, Chloe didn't care. She was eager to simply listen to Rudy pray and read the scriptures. She handed him the little Bible he'd lent her.

"I found the scripture we read yesterday and read it again. Ecclesiastes three, verse eleven." She couldn't believe she found it so easily given the only time she looked up scriptures was when Reverend Howard called for them to take their Bibles out of the church pews. And even then he gave them the page number. This may well have been the first time she'd ever looked a scripture up on her very own. Any Bible verses she'd had to memorize as a child were written out and handed to her on a slip of paper. So looking this up, finding it herself, was a sheer delight. She'd even read some of the scriptures surrounding it.

"It's beautiful, but I found myself wanting to know more."

Nodding, Rudy smiled and gestured for her to sit. Then he followed suit. "That's precisely what I think is hidden in that message; the desire to know more. God has given us this perfect creation, but we can never be satisfied. We'll always want more, and God desires us to seek Him for that knowledge. Only through Him can we truly be satisfied."

The image of God wanting her to learn more about Him, providing a way, wrapped her in a blanket of warmth. She closed her eyes and leaned back in the grass, propping herself on her elbows, listening while Rudy read from the Gospel of Luke.

"For the Son of Man is come to seek and to save that which was lost."

When they finished praying, and Rudy had once again tucked the Bible into her hands, they scrambled up the hill. It wouldn't do to be late when Ben was ready to get back on the trail. And judging from the scowl on his face when he saw her emerge from the trees with Rudy, she knew he was already in a mood.

Still, she wouldn't let his grouchiness rob her of the image of God loving her, seeking her, wanting to show her more.

Once on the trail, Chloe soaked in everything around her, unable to suppress the delight she felt after the morning scripture and prayer. From the dampness of the air to the heavy pine scent of the breeze, she knew it all was God's creation. She found herself looking at everything with fresh eyes in a renewed way that poured more meaning into her heart. Perhaps that's why the moss on the tree bark appeared brighter green, the color of the trees more vivid and varied, and the sound of Ben's singing even more tantalizing than yesterday.

Moss and lichen danced up the rough bark of most of the trees. Gnarled roots bumped up through parts of the trail, causing a trip hazard for those who weren't paying attention.

Ben, it seemed, was always paying attention even as he hummed a tune or sang a song. His eyes constantly searched out everything, sweeping back and forth in his search for the elusive Sasquatch. There wasn't much chatter between the men up front, and Chloe wished Monique would follow the same example.

It was difficult to tune out the other woman and focus on every sound of nature while at the same time scanning the woods and hillsides for birds, waterfalls, and of course Sasquatch tracks. With each step she took, in each sound she heard, and in each wildflower she spotted, Chloe could see evidence of God's handiwork. She was bursting to write it in her journal but, since they were nowhere near stopping for a meal or to rest, she prayed she'd be able to retain this feeling until they did so she could capture every feeling on paper.

A slight breeze carried Ben's tune straight into her heart, and the only thing that could be more perfect about this moment was if they were to find the Sasquatch and she could thrill her father with a prize-winning article.

Something on the trail, off to her left, caught her eye. Stopping, she slowly scanned the bushes for a sign. When the slight movement came again, she almost burst into laughter. Under a bush, two young kittens—fuzz-balls, really—tumbled and rolled as they nipped at each other. They were light in color, with sharp peaks of dark fur on their ears. These were no ordinary barn cats. In fact, if she weren't mistaken, they were lynx.

"Chloe, don't!" Startled by Monique's shrill pitch, she looked up. Ben was rushing toward her, his face tight with concern. Or was that fury? Caleb was right behind him, ever the protective baby brother. She wrinkled her brow. Why were they so concerned? And what was Monique yelling about?

Unaware of the humans observing them, the little kittens took turns jumping on each other's back then tumbling like circus performers. Chloe scanned the area. Wild babies meant an even wilder mama was sure to be nearby. Maybe even the lynx whose tracks she'd spotted before. Her pride still smarted over that little *faux pas*.

They definitely didn't want to be around when the mother cat showed up with her evening meal. She turned to tell Ben they should hurry up the trail, but before she could get a word out, Monique shrieked again.

"I warned her, Ben. I told her not to go near them."

Chloe turned to Monique. "What are you talking about?"

"They're wild, Chloe."

As if to affirm that Monique was a genius and Chloe was an idiot, Ben nodded in agreement. "Their mother is probably out hunting. And if that's the case—"

"We need to leave before she comes back. I know. I was just about to let you know that very thing when she"—Chloe shot a spearing glare at Monique—"started screaming."

She wanted to say more, wanted to defend herself. She just had to breathe deeply and steady the thumping of her heart.

One. Breathe in.

Two. Hold it.

Three. Breathe out. There. She could do it.

"Do you think I'm so stupid, Monique, that I don't know a wild animal when I see one? Or I don't know better than to mess with a baby?"

"B-but I heard you." Monique's voice quavered and Chloe looked at her sharply. "I was just trying to protect you." Her wide eyes were filled with tears, and her bottom lip actually trembled. Trembled! "You looked right at me and said we should take them with us. You said you'd love nothing more than to take them home to your mother."

Chloe blinked, stunned by the outright lie. Maybe Monique belonged on the stage. Either that or Blackwell's Island or some other asylum for the deranged.

"I don't know what you're trying to do, Monique. I never said any such thing. I know a wild animal when I see it, and I certainly know better than to pick one up." Chloe paused to catch her breath and realized it wasn't just Ben and her brother listening while she defended herself. Rudy, Gus, Skip, and Cookie had joined them. Each pair of eyes trained on her—their respective owners listening, staring, forming assumptions.

She didn't want to know what they thought of her. She wanted them to go away, to stop looking at her, to stop staring, to stop listening. She tried the breathing technique again.

"I..." It wasn't working. Awash in self-consciousness, she looked helplessly at Caleb, beseeching him with her eyes. *Please get me out of this.*

Luckily her brother could read her expressions, having rescued her from many situations in the past.

"Come on, Chloe." He took her hand and tugged gently. "Walk with me for a while, would you?"

She nodded, thankful, and walked up the path with her brother, painfully aware of the whispers behind her as they all tried to figure out what had just happened.

Monique lied. Flat-out lied. And Chloe was at a loss to understand why. If the other woman's intention had been to humiliate and embarrass her, it worked. Now everyone thought she was a lame-brained, helpless female, and she'd be lucky if Ben let her anywhere near the Sasquatch story once they found the creature.

Chapter Ten

Overcast skies were a disappointment the next morning, perfectly matching Ben's mood. He hoped today would be free of strife and hurt feelings.

After the incident with the kittens yesterday, Chloe had walked by her brother's side, stone-cold silent. Other than insisting that Monique had lied, she never spoke the rest of the day.

Unfortunately, his thoughts weren't nearly as quiet. They continually turned to Chloe and the way her silence needled at him. Out of everyone besides himself, she had shown the most enthusiasm for the trip, and he felt a prick of guilt that her enthusiasm had been snuffed out. The eager sparkle, the ambitious spirit— gone; dissipated into thin air with Monique's exaggerations.

Lies.

He should just call them what they were. For whatever reason, Monique felt the need to constantly make things up in a way that drew the attention she seemed to constantly crave. Could it be she was trying to fill up that lonely spot just like he was?

This morning he headed toward the riverbank below their camp, where he was certain Chloe and Rudy would be holding their prayer meeting. He wanted Chloe to know he believed her, and he felt it best if he told her away from the others so Monique wouldn't interfere.

Soft laughter drifted toward him on the air, and he rounded the corner to see Rudy and Chloe seated side-by-side on a giant rock that jutted out into the river. A series of smaller rocks led to the larger one, almost like a stairway.

Heads close together, Chloe laughed again and Ben felt a pang of jealousy that Rudy was the one to reach her. But when Rudy took Chloe's hand and they bowed their heads to pray, he felt like a lowlife. Rudy did what no one else could—coaxed Chloe out of her quiet, hurt mood. And he did it with the purest of intentions.

As he drew close to them, his eyes drank in the sight of her, and his heart lifted at her laughter. Digging deep, he tried to remind himself again of all the reasons she shouldn't be here. The most important one being the hazard Monique and her lies created for Chloe's—and everyone else's—safety.

He approached the shore quietly and stood waiting for their prayer to end then called across the rocks. "May I join you?"

A sense of peaceful purpose infused Chloe when Rudy finished praying. And now Ben was here to ruin it.

Instead of turning and telling him to get lost, she let Rudy handle it. She looked at him with a plea, silently begging him to send Ben away.

"Of course, Ben. We'd be happy to have you to join us."

Chloe started to open her mouth to protest, but Rudy was just as capable of communicating with his eyes. His were telling her to mind her manners.

"We were just about to read from Matthew." His tone dropped to a stern manner as he flicked his eyes away. "*Whatsoever ye would that men should do to you, do ye even so to them.*' I believe that's known as the Golden Rule. Isn't that right, Chloe?"

"Um, yes?" Her voice sounded weak to her own ears, thanks to Rudy. He'd just succeeded in filling her with shame. "Please join us, Ben."

"Great." Ben sounded less than enthusiastic. No doubt he noticed the dynamics between her and Rudy. He shot her an unreadable glance. "I'm not familiar with that one."

Chloe was. Only because she'd had to memorize it as a child for one of her many Sunday school teachers, not because she'd taken it to heart. Now she wanted to do just as it said, but still couldn't quite feel it in her heart.

She ducked her head while Ben climbed across the smaller rocks, willing her heart to stop pounding so she could get that peaceful feeling back.

Once Ben was seated next to her, Rudy opened his Bible.

She tried to concentrate on the words. She really did. But Ben, it seemed, had settled as close to her as propriety would allow. The clean scent of soap wafted from him, and she figured he must have just washed up. Intentional or not, it did strange things to her—like make her wish he'd scoot even closer.

Ben watched as Rudy closed the Bible and then looked from him to Chloe. The look he gave her was slightly different than the one he gave Ben, and Ben wasn't quite sure how to interpret that.

"I'm glad you decided to join us this morning," Rudy said. "I think I can speak for Chloe when I say we hope you'll join us tomorrow by whichever side of the river we happen to make camp. Maybe we can even have a campfire meeting with the others, if you think they might enjoy it."

"I don't know, Rudy." Ben kept his tone non-committal, not wanting to hurt the other man's feelings. He didn't want to tell Rudy it was highly improbable that Gus or Monique would want to take part.

Ben brought up the rear as they walked along the river on their way back to camp. Rudy's invitation intrigued him. And stranger still, he wasn't sure it was entirely due to sitting so near Chloe on the sun-warmed rock. The tug of the Bible's words as Rudy read them, the sincerity that emanated, plucked something in his soul, and he wanted to think more on God—the Creator of the world, the Creator of nature that Ben so loved.

He quickly put aside those thoughts so he could motivate the group to be on their way—his intended conversation with Chloe would have to come a bit later. As he planned the day in his mind, he was starting to worry that they wouldn't find the Sasquatch. So far there'd been no sign of the creature. And while Caleb was doing an okay job of documenting different specimens they'd come across, he didn't think it likely that they would pass muster with the colonel without evidence of the creature he'd been hired to find. Then he'd be back to scrounging for small jobs and his dream of the gorilla project would slip further into the future. His hair would be whiter than Gus's before he ever found his way back to Africa.

"I never did finish telling you about our trip in the South Pacific and Ben's history with reporters."

Well past lunch and on the way to supper, Chloe wanted to scream. She had listened to Monique's incessant chatter for the better part of the day. After what she'd pulled yesterday with the lynx kittens, the only thing that kept Chloe from turning her back on Monique was the memory of Rudy's chastising look just before he'd quoted the Golden Rule.

However, the very moment Monique mentioned Ben, Chloe was more than ready to listen. Talking about Ben was a nice change of pace from the endless questions she kept asking about Caleb.

Part of her wanted to dislike Monique for her apparent betrayal of Ben. Chloe couldn't forget seeing Monique in Ben's arms. Why, when she so obviously had him, was she so interested in Caleb? That Caleb returned her interest was a point of contention with Chloe. He seemed to forget all about his engagement to Elizabeth. Admittedly, Chloe didn't think Elizabeth was the right woman for her brother, but they were engaged nonetheless, and he shouldn't be entertaining notions of Monique without first breaking off with Elizabeth.

"Chloe?"

"What?" She looked up from her musings to find Monique staring at her, waiting to tell her about the South Pacific and why Ben was against reporters. "Oh. Sorry. I'm afraid my mind was wandering. Go ahead, I'm listening."

"We were in the jungle on an island in the South Pacific." Monique spoke in a hushed tone, her footsteps growing slower. She appeared thoughtful for a moment. "At least, I think it was the South Pacific."

Despite the intensity of the suddenly charged air, Chloe's interest was immediately piqued. Her feet ached to walk faster, not slower. Her pulse jumped with excitement.

Not because Monique seemed unsure of where the island was, but because she sensed a story that would have readers hanging on every word.

She waited, breath held, for Monique to continue.

"We were on this island studying the wildlife, documenting each species we found. There was this reporter, an eager sort. You know the type. Pad always at the ready, pencil stuck in the cap."

Chloe nodded and smiled faintly. "Yes, I know the type."

"Well, Ben wasn't the least bit hesitant about the fellow coming along. He thought the publicity would earn him favor in the eyes of several universities and he'd be awarded money to fund a couple of projects he'd always been interested in."

"Like this one?"

"Yes." Monique nodded then hurried on with her story. "Anyway, this reporter, his name was Avery, proved to be too eager. There *is* such a thing as too eager when it comes to trips like this, you know."

Sensing she was supposed to give some sort of acknowledgment here, Chloe nodded. But was Monique hinting that she was over eager?

"Avery was always bumbling about, getting in the way and scaring off the animals before we could have them properly documented. Or, in the case of animals we'd never seen before, scare them off before we could have them properly, uh, preserved."

Preserved? A sick feeling churned the pit of Chloe's stomach. What exactly did *preserved* mean? She refrained from asking, not certain she was ready for the answer.

"So, as you can imagine, Ben soon became quite testy with Avery. He threatened over and over to pack him up and send him back to the boat."

Yes, Chloe could just imagine.

"But Avery was able to talk him out of if each time."

Somehow Chloe didn't think it had been too easy.

Monique's tone turned dramatic. "Until the last and final time."

Monique's earlier interest in Chloe's writing had her now wondering if Monique harbored some deep desire to be a writer. Despite her doubts that the other girl was telling the unvarnished truth, Chloe felt herself pulled right into the story and waited with bated breath for Monique's next words. They didn't come.

Finally she could wait no longer. "What happened?"

"They argued, Ben and Avery. Loud enough to wake the dead." Monique shuddered. "That's exactly what happened. Or at least that's what appeared to happen."

Monique's hands shook. Was she frightened? Or did it happen purposely? Chloe couldn't help but wonder.

"They wore these hideous masks." Monique shuddered again, her feet barely moving now.

"Who?"

"The dead jungle men."

The hair prickled at the back of Chloe's neck, and the sensation traveled down her spine. Surely Monique was joking?

"Actually, they weren't dead. I think they were supposed to represent the dead or something. I never did understand. I almost fainted clear away when I saw them. Ben told us to run. Run for the ship as fast as we could. But Avery—"

Chloe was horrified. She could only imagine what Avery had done. He stopped most likely, to write down every detail.

"Did they...?" She squeezed her eyes shut for a brief moment, not wanting to finish the thought. "Did they capture Avery?"

Monique's eyes were wide now and she swallowed visibly hard before giving a tiny nod. "And that's not all," she whispered. "When Ben saw that he wasn't behind us, he went back after Avery. He said he would drag him back by the hair if he had to."

Chloe could just imagine it. She could sense, just by looking into his eyes, he would be fiercely protective of those he cared about. Or those he felt were his responsibility.

"Ben didn't speak when he came back alone. He tried, but couldn't. We were well out to sea when he was finally able to tell us what happened."

"Do I want to know?" Though in reality, Chloe did.

"I don't think so." Monique shook her dark head.

"Tell me anyway, Monique." Chloe's stomach clenched, and she waited for the shock she was certain to hear.

"They cut off his head."

Stunned by the blunt statement, Chloe stopped walking. Her stomach churned, and she prayed she wouldn't lose its contents.

Monique dragged her feet to a stop, too. She nodded; eyes still wide, lips pressed together in a bloodless line.

Chloe's heart welled with instant compassion for Monique. How could she have doubted her? The fear etched on Monique's face shamed Chloe. What a nightmare this poor girl had experienced.

She reached out and patted Monique's arm. "Don't worry. There's nothing like that around here."

"Yes there is. The Sasquatch." Monique shuddered and rubbed her arms.

"I don't understand." Chloe grew more and more confused by this strange girl. "If you're so frightened, what are you doing here?"

"Dr. Pieper, Gus, is my father."

Chloe nodded. She looked to the group ahead of them, way ahead of them, seeking out the ever-chipper Gus. Chatting with Rudy, he was doing his best to keep up with the other man's long-legged stride. Which is what they should be doing as well, she realized with a start.

"Come on, Monique. We'd better get to walking before we lose sight of them. This is one place I don't fancy being lost."

They picked up their pace, just enough to keep the others in sight. Once she was satisfied that they wouldn't be left behind, Chloe encouraged Monique to finish what she'd been saying.

"Daddy and Ben have been working together for years. Where Daddy goes, I go."

Why aren't you married and living a normal life? Chloe wanted to ask, but didn't. Perhaps her father wanted to marry her off to someone like Jackson. Or perhaps, like herself, Monique had dreams she longed to fulfill and didn't want to give them up by getting married.

"And you, Monique?" Chloe couldn't help but ask. "Are you a scientist too?"

"Oh, no. I've no real interest in animal biology. I've just always been with my daddy, from the day my mother walked out on him. And I've always helped with the documentation. But that doesn't mean I like it."

From the sounds of it, she'd been around Ben for a long time.

"And Ben? How long has he been with you and your father?"

"Ever since he was a little boy. Daddy raised him after his parents left. Family life is an endangered species when you're a scientist, especially where the wives are concerned. But no one ever figured Ben would be abandoned by his father as well as his mother."

Chloe's heart went out to the little boy Ben had once been, abandoned by his parents to be raised in a nomadic lifestyle by anyone who would care for him. "What if your father hadn't been there to take care of Ben? What would have happened to him then?"

Monique shrugged. "I don't know. Fend for himself, I guess. It's hard to say."

"How old was he?"

"If I recall correctly, I believe he was around six or seven."

"How sad." Chloe noticed a change in Monique's expression. She had a wounded look in her eyes. "Monique?" Chloe stopped walking and touched her shoulder. "Are you all right?"

Monique nodded. "I was just thinking about my mother."

Chloe couldn't imagine being abandoned by her mother. "Did she just grow tired of the traveling?"

"Yes. Mother threatened to leave many times, but I always thought she'd take me with her."

"I'm sorry. How old were you at the time?"

"Five."

Five. So young.

"Oh, Monique."

She shrugged and reached out to tug on the needles of a low-lying tree branch. Though she acted as if it no longer mattered, Chloe knew otherwise. She recognized the ploy as one she'd used many times when her father had brushed her aside. Being abandoned by your mother at such a young age—any age, really—was a huge hurt to carry around. And Ben, abandoned by both parents. It was good that Gus had been there. Apparently the older man had a heart full of love. Chloe warmed to him in an instant.

"Did you know Ben was engaged?"

Monique's words seemed to come from nowhere, and Chloe blinked, trying to make the adjustment in the conversation. How had they gone from parental abandonment to marriage in the space of a few seconds?

"E-engaged? To be married?" Somehow her voice managed to find its way past the shocked lump filling her throat.

The wounded Monique who was there a moment ago had transformed back into an enigma. She nodded at Chloe, her eyes once again gleaming.

The lump in Chloe's throat plunged to settle in the pit of her stomach. She dug her toe at a rock that was stuck fast in the hard ground, and struggled to keep her tone light. "When—"

"Hey! Are you girls coming, or are we leaving you behind?" Skip's irritated voice drifted back to them. Chloe realized with a start that she and Monique had fallen so far behind they'd have to run to catch up.

"Hurry up!" Skip bellowed. His voice boomed louder than she'd ever heard it.

Chloe took off at a run. She didn't need any further urging. She'd never prove she was capable of being here if the men had to spend all their time waiting on her.

Ben was getting married. It was good she didn't have time to question Monique. She didn't want to hear the details. Especially not from the woman he'd apparently chosen.

Ben was getting married.

Nothing else mattered.

They'd gone half the day without seeing any sign of the Sasquatch.

Not so much as a track or partial footprint. Disappointed, Chloe hoped the rest of the day would go by fast. She may have learned the truth about why Ben objected to having a reporter along, but this hadn't been one of her better days.

Monique was oddly silent after dropping her stunning piece of news. And though thankful for the silence, Chloe had to wonder at the reason. Monique was either plumb worn out or rejoicing with satisfaction over the shock she'd delivered.

There were a few times when Ben made them stop and sit in silence, watching, listening, certain they had to be getting close. But they were far from close, and Chloe found herself whispering a prayer of thanks. She was still trying to absorb Monique's comment about "preserving" the Sasquatch. She couldn't be party to a killing, if that was the plan. Somehow she'd have to make Ben aware that while she was writing the article, she wouldn't stand around and let the creature be killed.

"What did you think they were going to do with it?"

Ignoring that little voice in her subconscious, she bit her lip and tried to focus her thoughts elsewhere. Had she really known that was their intent? Did she ignore that fact for the sake of a story? If the stories her father's Salish friend had told her about the Sasquatch were true, then killing it would be akin to killing a man. The thought made her almost physically sick, and she stumbled as her foot hit a half-buried tree root.

"Are you all right?" Monique reached out to help steady her before she lost her balance.

"I'm fine. Just tired, that's all."

"Why don't you ask that darling brother of yours if we'll be stopping soon?"

"It's much too early to set up camp." Chloe tried to keep her tone light, though she was irritated and a bit perplexed over Monique's interest in Caleb.

Why, when she had Ben?

Monique might only be toying with her brother's affections, but Chloe saw a spark in Caleb that she hadn't seen in a long time. She didn't want to see him hurt, but he would be when Monique's attentiveness went by the wayside.

Chloe's gaze shot to Ben. How would he feel if he lost Monique to her brother? And why did her heart skip a beat when she thought of Ben as being unattached?

This was not good. She wasn't here to play games. She had a job to do, an article to write. She had something to prove to herself and to her father. And even to Ben, since he hadn't wanted her along in the first place. She was glad he seemed to lighten his attitude on that point.

"Ben." Monique used a simpering tone reminiscent of Trina Clark. "Do you think we could stop early today? Chloe's tired."

Chloe bit the inside of her lip. It wasn't even close to dark. In fact, it seemed like they'd just finished lunch. They had several hours left before the sun would slip behind the mountainside.

Ben turned to Caleb, and they whispered together before Ben finally answered. "We'll stop within the hour. We just need to find a good place. Do you think you can handle it that much longer?"

Though her hands cried out to find their rightful place around Monique's skinny throat, Chloe valiantly fought the urge. Instead she concentrated on placing one foot in front of the other. Whatever the reason, she was thankful they decided to stop early. Though Rudy's ointment gave her screaming muscles some relief this morning, by afternoon the pain was back, and it was quickly growing unbearable.

Ben chose a shady spot, set far enough back from the creek that she could go down and bathe in private.

Once she had her arctic sleeping bag laid out, she grabbed her towel and soap from her pack. Then she turned to Monique. "I'm heading to the creek to wash up. Would you like to join me?"

Not that Chloe relished Monique's company at the moment, but she knew she'd be far better served to be civil. And if Monique's sparkling smile was any indication, Chloe did the right thing by asking.

"Would you like to try my soap?" Monique dug a towel from the knapsack. "It's a French milled rose bouquet. I bought it at the general store in Cedar Ridge. I'm anxious to try it."

Truthfully, Chloe was partial to her own lemon-scented soap. However, Monique looked eager to share, and perhaps this was a good way to build on their budding, if sometimes precarious, friendship.

"All right, let's go." Chloe smiled and shoved her hair out of her eyes.

"Aren't you getting tired of fussing with your hair?" Monique asked as they started down the hill to the creek.

"Actually, yes, I am. It's a mess. It slips through anything I tie it with and won't stay under this hat no matter what I do to it."

"Remember earlier when I asked you about—"

"Hey, where are you two going?" Caleb's shout cut off whatever Monique had been about to say.

"We're off to wash up." Chloe didn't like the way her brother and Monique were looking at each other.

"Getting tired of smelling like a polecat?"

Monique giggled at Caleb's teasing, much to Chloe's contention. She turned to Chloe. "You go on to the creek. I'll be right there. I forgot something."

I'll just bet you did. Whatever Monique had forgotten, it was a sure bet it had to do with Caleb and not bathing.

Chloe wandered down to the creek, feeling only slightly guilty that Cookie and the men were doing all the work in preparing camp. They were tired too, but they didn't smell like she did. There was no chance she'd go through the rest of the day stinking up the place. Not that there was much chance of Ben getting close enough to know what she smelled like. But she did have her pride.

Once her boots and socks were off and her bare feet hit the cold damp ground, Chloe thought twice about undressing. None too eager to soak in the cold creek, she contemplated putting her boots back on. Would smelling like a polecat really be so bad? She heard the snap of a twig behind her and turned to tell Monique what she thought about actually bathing.

But Monique didn't appear interested in whether they jumped in the creek or not. A determined look on her face, she held Rudy's huge knife in her right hand, twisting it first one way and then the next so that the sun glinted into Chloe's eyes.

For a moment Chloe stood frozen in place, mesmerized by the shiny metal as it turned from side to side. Then, swallowing a scream, she backed away from Monique. She didn't know what had gotten in to her, but she wasn't about to stand around and find out.

An icy chill laced through her as her feet hit the water. Monique stepped forward at that same moment, her laugh reverberating in Chloe's head. Still facing her, Chloe backed away from the knife-wielding lunatic until she stood waist deep in the water. Between the tug of the current and the weight of her water-logged pants, she fought to maintain her balance. Desperate, she glanced around, wondering if she should call for help or try to out-swim Monique.

Was it her attraction to Ben or her disapproval of Monique and Caleb that provoked this? And how would Monique have known about either one? Thoughts ran rampant as Chloe continued to back away. She was almost chest deep now; the decision to swim or yell would have to be made. But, in that split instant when the thought entered her head, Chloe's heel hit a rock on the creek's bottom, and she stumbled, plunging backward under the water.

She came up, gasping for air, slapping at the water in an attempt to keep from going back under. As soon as she caught her breath and glanced around, she shrieked. Monique was nowhere in sight. That could only mean one thing. She was under the water hiding, waiting for her chance.

Just as she was about to scream again, something gripped her ankle, yanking her off balance, and Chloe ended up under water once again. That was when a pair of arms looped under hers, pulling her above water.

This time she didn't struggle for balance. She merely gasped for breath and allowed herself to be led to the creek's edge.

"Are you all right?"

Dripping with the chilled water, Chloe swiped a shivering hand across her eyes and stared with stunned disbelief into Monique's brown eyes. First Monique tried to drown her, and then she *saved* her? It made no sense.

"Wh—?" Her question was cut off by a shout from the trees.

"Chloe!" Caleb burst through the trees and scrambled down the bank to the creek. "I heard you scream. What happened? Are you hurt?"

"She fell," Monique said before Chloe could answer. "Somehow she lost her balance and the current started to sweep her away. I was able to reach her in time."

Chloe glared at Monique. The lies fell so easily from her pouty lips. "I—Monique—"

"You don't need to thank me, Chloe." Monique wiped strands of black hair out of her eyes and smiled up at Caleb. "It was no more than you'd do for me."

"I'm glad you were there for her." Caleb wrapped Monique in his arms and then, almost as an afterthought, reached for Chloe. "I don't know what I would have done if anything had happened to her."

"She's lying." Chloe pushed herself away from her brother. "She came at me with a knife. Then she tried to drown me. It was only *after* I screamed that she helped me. She knew help would be coming once I screamed, and she had to make herself look innocent."

Both Caleb and Monique stared at Chloe as if she'd suddenly gone mad.

"It's the truth." It horrified her that Caleb didn't seem to believe her. Monique had tried to kill her.

"Yes, Chloe, I did have a knife. It's right over there by our towels and soap. I dropped it when I jumped in to rescue you." Monique spoke as if dealing with an unreasonable child. "I borrowed it from Rudy so I could cut your hair."

"M-my hair?"

"Yes, your hair. You're having a devil of a time trying to keep it out of your face and I thought I'd help you. It really is easier on a trip like this if you don't have a bunch of hair to deal with."

"But what about—" Chloe's teeth chattered as she gestured toward the middle of the creek.

"What?" Monique's innocent act grated on Chloe. "You fell, and I swam out to help you. I can't believe you'd think I'd try to harm you." She glanced at the ground, but not before her eyes glazed over with hurt.

"There." Caleb turned to Chloe. "You see? Monique was trying to help you. You saw the knife and misinterpreted things. Why don't we get you back to camp so you can get into some dry clothes and warm up in front of the fire? I don't want you to catch a chill. Once you're warm, Monique can cut your hair."

"But—" Could she have been wrong and misunderstood the entire situation? It certainly appeared that way. And Caleb certainly seemed to think so. She looked at them both uncertainly and shivered. And not just from the cold.

"Come on, Chloe." The gleam in Monique's eye was victorious. "It was a misunderstanding, that's all."

"Now that I'm wet, I just want to get clean. I'll be along shortly to get warm and dry." She turned her back on them and scooped up the soap, not quite ready to believe it really was a misunderstanding. "Don't go too far away, Caleb."

She thought she heard Monique sniff in indignation but didn't care. Chloe could just imagine the hurt look in Monique's eyes and wasn't about to fall for it. If anything, Monique likely set the whole thing up so she could find favor with Caleb as the misunderstood person who was only trying to help his sister.

After her brother was out of sight, Chloe peeled off her wet clothes. Her teeth continued to chatter as she inched her way back into the freezing water. Monique soon followed, and Chloe wished she had the nerve to give the annoying woman the kind of dunking she wouldn't ever forget.

In spite of the sounds of splashing water and chattering teeth, the silence was almost overwhelming as the two women washed. Monique was out of the water and into her wet clothes before Chloe ever felt clean enough to get out. By the time she was semi-dry and back in her slimy wet clothes, the other woman had disappeared from sight, and Chloe was riddled with guilt. Maybe Monique really had been acting with good intentions. But if that were the case, why had she pulled her under the water? Or had Chloe only imagined it?

Tired of second guessing her intuition where Monique and her motives were concerned, Chloe gathered her belongings and headed back to camp. She'd only taken a few steps when something on the ground caught her eye.

Bending to retrieve it, she had to pry it up out of the dirt. Small and round, it fit in the palm of her hand. And though caked with mud, it was obviously a pocket watch. It would take some work to clean it, but she could tell it wasn't the average men's pocket watch. Even through the dirt she could see it was a brilliant blue, and it had what felt like raised jewels on one side. She'd have to get the dirt cleaned off to tell for sure.

No, this definitely wasn't a men's watch. Something about it seemed oddly familiar. She didn't own a watch, and neither did her mother. As soon as she had a chance, she'd clean it up and get a better look at it. Right now, though, she just wanted to get warm. She tucked it carefully in her towel then continued on her way.

As she drew close to camp, she sniffed her arms delicately. The scent of roses was overpowering, and her nose started to itch. She'd just have to put up with it, because she wasn't about to get back in that freezing water just to rewash with her bar of Pears lemon soap.

Cookie was stooped over a small fire when Chloe approached. But she didn't see anyone else. "Where is everyone?"

"Monique's resting, and the men are off hunting." Cookie spoke softly, keeping her face turned to the flames as she poked the fire.

"For the Sasquatch?" Despite being cold from the chilled water, Chloe's interest perked right up.

"No, not that kind of hunting. Gus thought that since we stopped early, it would be nice to have some fresh meat to add to my chili."

"Oh." Chloe couldn't help but feel disappointed. A sighting would have been the perfect way to end the day. "I guess that would be nice."

"You should probably go put on some dry clothes, honey, before you catch your death."

Though Cookie kept her attention on the flames, this was the longest conversation they'd ever had.

"While you're changing, I'll dish you up a nice bowl of chili. Unless you want to wait for whatever the men bring back?"

"Chili without their catch would be just perfect." Chloe smiled her thanks at the woman even though Cookie still refused to make eye contact. Why? Was she shy as Chloe first suspected? Or did she have something to hide? The question burned on her tongue, but she didn't want to appear rude.

"Once you've changed, you can bring your wet clothes over here and we'll dry them by the fire."

"Thank you, Cookie."

When Chloe returned to the middle of camp, not quite warm but in dry clothes, Cookie handed her a bowl of chili. "It smells delicious. Thank you."

For the first time, Cookie looked straight at her and nodded in acknowledgement. Chloe could see the kindness in her eyes. Was there a trace of a smile in there, too? As she studied Cookie's eyes, a prickle of familiarity edged her subconscious.

"Go." Cookie gestured toward the fire, and Chloe turned to see Rudy sitting there with his own bowl of chili. There was no sign of the other men. "Sit and warm your toes while you warm your belly. I'll just put your wet clothes over here to dry."

Rudy sneezed twice while Chloe seated herself on the hard ground next to him. A drift of warm air from the fire wafted over her.

"Your brother's off in the trees somewhere, with his drawing pencils." Rudy made it sound like, if given the choice between facing down a riled-up skunk and drawing a picture, he'd take his chances with the skunk.

Pressing her lips together, Chloe barely managed to suppress a laugh.

Funny, when she'd first met this man she'd been so afraid of him. Now he was rapidly turning into a friend, and because of him she was learning more about God. Not just learning. She found herself growing eager to know more.

The spicy aroma of chili teased her rumbling stomach, and she took more than a few hurried bites, knowing her mother would be horrified at her lack of manners. But she was sitting around a campfire with Rudy. There was no need to act ladylike. In fact, after she talked to Caleb, she planned to ask for a second bowl. "Did you see which way he went?"

"Over that-a way, I think." He pointed to a small patch of trees just above the creek.

"I'd love to see what he's drawing." Monique approached the fire and held her hands out to warm them. Her cooing reminded Chloe of Trina Clark. Were the two to ever meet, they would undoubtedly become fast friends.

"Monique? Do you mind if I have a few minutes alone with my brother first?"

Monique blinked and pulled her mouth into a pout. Guilt stabbed Chloe once again. She hadn't meant to hurt her. She just wanted to spend a few minutes with Caleb. She'd hardly had the opportunity to speak with him all day.

"Actually, could we talk before you go look for your brother?"

Ben had come up behind her. Chloe turned. "M-me?"

He nodded; his expression serious.

"Um, sure, but I thought you were hunting with the others."

A slow smile spread across his face. "I came back early. Skip and Gus are up to their foolishness again." He winked, and heat stole across her face, burning her cheeks. "The way those two are going, they'll be lucky if they find anything to use for bait."

Laughter bubbled up in Chloe's soul.

Uncertain what Monique would think about Chloe speaking to Ben in private, Chloe turned to gauge her reaction. But Monique was already gone—no doubt hunting for Caleb.

"Um, sure, Ben. What do you want to talk about?" She pasted a bright look on her face. It was just a conversation—nothing more. He certainly couldn't be here to see if the spark from the other night was still there, even though she foolishly yearned to explore it more herself.

"Can we take a little walk? Or are you too tired?"

Chloe shook her head. "No, I'm fine." In truth, if Ben hadn't been here she might have collapsed with exhaustion. "Let me just wash out my bowl first." She couldn't very well eat a second bowl of chili in front of Ben. Unlike with Rudy, she did care if Ben saw her sucking down her food.

"I'll take it for you, sweet pea." As Cookie held her hand out for the empty bowl, she spoke in more than her usual whisper. That sense of familiar nagged at her again, but Cookie grabbed the bowl before she could contemplate it further. "I'll take care of this. You go with Ben and when you get back, I'll fix you another bowl."

"Come on, Chloe," Ben urged.

The idea that Ben wanted to spend time with her sent the hunger pangs into hiding, and she followed him.

They hadn't gone far when he indicated a log that had long ago fallen to the ground. "This is the perfect place to talk."

He placed his hand on Chloe's back and guided her toward the log. She looked up at him, totally entranced, wanting to melt into a puddle right then and there.

"Mmm." His whisper tickled her ear, sending shivers of delight dancing over her senses. "You smell good. No more of Rudy's liniment, huh?"

Shrugging his hand off her back, Chloe didn't dare meet his eyes. One look and he'd know how much she wanted to be held by him.

What had gotten in to her? Guilt stole directly over her heart.

Worse, what had gotten into him? The man *was* Monique's fiancé, after all.

"What did you want to talk about?" Hopefully he wouldn't start in again on his insistence to send her back. Not when he was starting to accept her presence and maybe even come to like her just a bit. Besides, they'd come too far for him to send her back alone.

"Two things, actually. First, the night the men thought they found the Sasquatch. You remember?"

She remembered it well, too well; thought of it way too many times.

"I wanted to—"

"Don't!" Chloe leaped from the log as she shouted. "Don't apologize. Please."

This was so humiliating. His apology could only mean she'd been obvious in her desire for him, and he didn't want her to read too much into what had nearly happened.

"I'm the one who should apologize." She lowered her voice to a whisper. "I fear the excitement at possibly seeing the Sasquatch was too much for me. I—"

"Chloe, let me finish." Rising to face her, Ben interrupted. "I wanted to ask you not to mention that night to anyone. Especially not in an article for your father's paper."

"Oh, I see." This was just a little walk to ensure her silence. He'd felt nothing the night he almost kissed her. She'd imagined the whole thing. Perhaps he hadn't been about to kiss her after all. This was good, for Monique's sake if nothing else.

Feeling oddly deflated, she turned to walk away. "I suppose we'd better get back. You haven't eaten yet, and Cookie's chili is probably growing cold." As for herself, she was no longer hungry for that second bowl. "Besides, you have to get back to your fiancée."

Ben's hand on her elbow stopped her. His touch was light and warmth washed over her.

"Wait a minute. Fiancée? What are you talking about?" He sounded puzzled, but it could have been an act.

"I mean Monique, of course." Chloe turned and stared at him. "How many fiancées do you have?"

"Monique told you we're engaged?" His eyes widened in disbelief. "What else did she tell you?"

Chloe thought back to the mention of Ben being abandoned by his parents, and recalled the shadow of loneliness she sometimes saw in his eyes and heard in his voice when he sang; loneliness he tried so valiantly to hide. Her heart twinged at the thought. He might not appreciate knowing Monique shared such private information.

"Nothing."

"We're not engaged, Chloe. We never were."

"You're not?" A surge of relief shot through her, along with something else. Hope. Silly hope. "Does Monique know this?"

Ben laughed, though not humorously. "Of course she knows. This is just a little invention of hers. She loves to tell tales. Always has." He stopped speaking for a moment and a shadow seemed to cross his face and harden his features. It was there and gone so quickly, she might have imagined it.

"I see." Chloe fought to keep her expression impassive, though she wanted nothing more than to shout for joy.

"Maybe she should be a writer. Like you. Her propensity for storytelling is actually the other thing I wanted to talk to you about."

Chloe wasn't sure how to respond since he didn't exactly make it sound like something to be proud of.

"I knew she lied about the lynx kittens."

"You did?"

He nodded, and his lips curved up in a tender smile. "I wanted to make sure you knew I believed you. I knew you were too smart to mess with wild kittens."

"You did? Really?" Oh, glory be, he believed her!

"So you see, Chloe." Ben lowered his voice then, and it washed over her like warm honey. "If I wanted to kiss you, there is no one standing between us."

Her knees buckled. Ben's hand was at her elbow, and he guided her back to the log.

"Here." He patted the knobby, rough wood. "Sit down."

"We really do need to get back." Her voice sounded all quivery and strange to her ears.

"We aren't finished."

"We're not?" Chloe searched his eyes, so green, so mesmerizing.

Once again, he sat down on the rough wood. Unable to help herself, she followed suit.

He scooted closer. Pushed dark curls up off his forehead.

She struggled not to sigh out loud.

"You never gave me an answer."

"An answer?" She stared at him, eyes fixed on those curls as they drifted back down toward his eyebrows.

"About your article? You won't mention the bungled search, I hope."

"Oh." Disappointment snapped her back to stark reality. Of course Ben didn't want to kiss her. She was merely a reporter. Monique may not be Ben's fiancée but she *was* gorgeous. Chloe couldn't possibly compare to someone like her.

"I know you're planning to write an article, even though I'd rather you didn't. Apparently there's nothing I can do to stop you, but I do ask you to present us in a favorable light. I really can't afford an article that might portray us as a bunch of buffoons."

"I—no, of course not." She didn't know what to say.

What could she possibly say with him holding her hand and staring into her eyes like that? Chloe was quite certain that, when he gazed into her eyes, Ben could talk her into almost anything.

"Chloe, there's one more thing." His tone was husky, and his gaze never wavered as he leaned in and brushed his lips against hers. Sweetly at first, and then her thoughts burst into a kaleidoscope of joy as he pulled her close and deepened the kiss.

He let go of her hand and reached up to brush the hair away from her face. His hand was gentle as it whispered across her cheek. Then he pulled her close, his soft and mesmerizing lips never leaving hers.

Pounding in triple time, her heart soared, singing with the silly hope she'd dismissed earlier. Ben could kiss her anytime he wanted.

He wasn't engaged to Monique!

Uncharacteristically elated. That was how Chloe would describe the feeling when she wrote in her journal, though she wouldn't explain why. There was no need. Years later, when she looked back on her journal, she'd still know the reason.

After that kiss with Ben, there was nothing her father could do to force her to marry Jackson.

Journal in hand, she went in search of Caleb. Skip and Gus had not returned from hunting. Ben and Rudy sat around the fire pit singing silly songs. The longing to join them and listen to Ben sing was strong. Especially when he looked over his shoulder and gave her a warm smile. She smiled back then turned away, undeterred. She had to talk to Caleb. Rudy had said her brother headed for the trees above the creek, and she would, too. She just wanted a few minutes with him to see where his head was concerning Monique. And she really did need to warn him about the girl's knack for telling falsehoods.

She'd make it quick, though, so she could come back and listen to more of Ben's singing. It didn't matter whether he sang a ditty about Rudy's sneezing or a song about a girl who left him behind. Ben's voice mesmerized her.

While she listened, she would bask in the warmth of the fire and write down the day's events. Hardly two words had been written in the journal since the trip began. She'd been too tired. No, the tiredness had come later. At first she'd been too hurt over her father's reaction to even care about writing. Still, Chloe knew being tired wasn't a good enough excuse. She had to prove herself to her father. An accurate record of this trip must be kept so she could put everything in her article.

Well, not quite everything. She wouldn't mention Rudy shaving his head. She bit back a smile. Nor would she mention the giddy way her heart skipped out of control at the thought of Ben's lips against hers and the knowledge that no one would be hurt by their kiss.

Ben and Monique weren't engaged!

When she finally spotted her brother, Chloe ran toward him only to stop abruptly. Caleb sat under a grouping of trees, sketchpad in hand. But he wasn't alone. Chloe groaned. Of course Monique was here. She'd gone off searching for him earlier, after all.

They sat side-by-side, Caleb and Monique, gazing into the darkening sky, watching a hawk soaring overhead.

Instead of sketching the hawk, Caleb turned to give Monique a radiant smile. She stared back, gazing as if he'd instructed the bird to fly just for her.

All right, so it was an over-exaggeration. She couldn't really read Monique's expression.

Still, it was difficult to admit something ugly gnawed the pit of her stomach. Jealousy? As she slowly walked toward them, she tried to dispel the disturbing notion.

"Hi, Caleb. Monique."

"Chloe." Caleb patted the ground on his left. "Sit down. Join us. I'm trying to get inspired." He tapped at the sketchpad then locked gazes with Monique.

Monique giggled.

Clearly she was intruding. As much as she wanted to confront Monique over her lies, she didn't want to have that conversation in front of Caleb.

Chloe gave her brother a half-hearted smile. "I came to write. But I think I'll go back to camp instead. I'm not feeling well all of a sudden."

"Do you want us to walk you back?"

Though she appreciated the concern in her brother's tone, she knew the more time she spent with him in Monique's presence the more likely she was to bring up the lies. Besides, one glance at Monique's sharply pursed lips and Chloe knew it was best to distance herself from the troublesome girl.

"I'll be fine, really. You two stay and finish your bird-watching."

A thin half-smile spread up one side of Monique's face to resemble a cat that had just cornered its prey. Caleb didn't appear to notice as he nodded a good-bye to Chloe then turned back to Monique.

As they bent their heads together, a sick feeling rose in Chloe's throat. They were moving way too fast. And though she hated to admit it, she was more than a little envious. Her brother was the only one who understood her, the only one who believed in her. And if he was as serious about Monique as the look on his face indicated, she'd be left with no one to share her hopes and dreams.

Worse, and more important, was her brother headed for heartbreak? If Monique could lie so easily about Ben, what else would she lie about? And were they really lies or delusions of a person gone mad?

"Hey."

At the sound of Ben's voice, Chloe turned in surprise. "I thought you were back at camp."

"We're finished, and I thought I'd take a little walk. I needed to do some thinking."

If she was reading him right, the curve of his lips and the warmth of his gaze said he was looking for her. She smiled in return.

"It's a great place to think, Kearny." Caleb put his arm around Monique as he spoke.

Just like that, Ben's smile faded and his expression darkened. "I didn't come here *to* think." Tone harsh, he looked sharply at Monique. "I've been thinking about something Chloe told me."

Chloe sucked in a breath and sent him a pleading look. She didn't want a confrontation any more than she wanted to embarrass Monique.

Apparently Ben missed Chloe's silent begging. "I have one question for you, Monique. Why did you tell Chloe that we're engaged?"

Monique's eyes widened. Her jaw dropped along with Caleb's.

"You and Kearny are engaged?" Caleb dropped his arm from her shoulders and jumped up, heedless of the sketchpad that fell at his feet.

"We're not!" Monique stood as well, hands on hips as she defended herself to Ben. "I didn't say—"

"Chloe told me *you* told her we were getting married."

"I never said—"

"Don't bother to deny it, Monique." Ben was abrupt, angry. "I've heard enough of the tales you tell to know Chloe spoke the truth."

"No." Monique was adamant. "I didn't say that."

Didn't she? Chloe remembered quite clearly the conversation where Monique told her Ben was engaged. A horrified thought clutched at her. Had Monique actually said *she* and Ben were getting married? Or had she simply said *Ben* was getting married?

"Ben, I don't think—"

"Shut up, Chloe!" Monique planted herself in front of Chloe. "How could you lie about me like that?"

"Monique." No longer certain of the truth, Chloe searched Monique's brown eyes. The hurt she saw reflected there made her feel ashamed. Perhaps she'd jumped to conclusions, only heard what she wanted to hear. "I'm sorry, I—"

"Sorry?" Monique echoed. "I don't want your apologies." She hugged her arms to her chest, and tears spilled down her cheeks.

Heart sinking, Chloe could do nothing but listen as Monique raged on.

"I thought we could be friends. I've never had a close friend before. I liked the way you stood up to Ben. I liked the way you didn't act like you were better than me. I admired your spunk and your desire to soak in everything around you. And here all along you were plotting to lie about me!"

"Monique, I didn't mean...I thought you...." Chloe glanced up and watched helplessly, unable to come up with the right words, as Monique wiped her eyes with shaky hands.

Hot color flooded Monique's cheeks. She looked at Caleb, her pain and embarrassment obvious. Then she turned and ran into the thicket.

"Now look what you've done." Caleb practically shook with rage. "Why don't you keep your nose in your own business for once?"

The anger in her brother's voice sliced deep, and his look of scorn stabbed her heart. "Caleb, I—"

"Save your apologies for the person who deserves them. And I suggest you do it on your knees." With one last icy glare, Caleb turned and went after Monique.

After the fight with their father, this was downright unbearable. Caleb was all she had left. She had to go after him and apologize. She would grovel at Monique's feet if need be. Whatever she had to do to salvage the relationship with her brother, she would do it.

A gentle touch fell on her shoulder.

"Let him go." Ben's soft voice stopped her in her tracks.

Turning, Chloe looked up into his eyes. Regret squeezed her like a fist. What did he think of her now?

"They'll both be fine. Let them have some time."

"But Caleb—"

"He's an adult. And he's upset. I'm sure he wants to settle things with Monique."

Bending down, he picked up Caleb's sketchpad and handed it to her. "He'll be back before too long. Let's go back to camp and you can rest while you wait. Then the two of you can work things out."

Clutching the drawing tablet to her chest, Chloe nodded. With everything in her, she prayed he was right.

Ben reached out and touched her chin, then gently tilted it so she could gaze into his eyes just before he oh-so-gently brushed her lips with his own.

Chapter Eleven

The sun drew closer to the mountaintops and the brilliant blue of the sky was growing dark in color. Chloe tucked the journal into her bag and stood, her limbs stiff from sitting in one place so long. Caleb and Monique should be back by now, and she needed to talk to her brother—Monique, too, even though the thought made her stomach clench.

Rest had been impossible, and she found it difficult write. She did manage to record the memory of Monique's anguished look, followed by her brother's scorn. But that was all. Both haunted her and, though she didn't write down this part, she tried to counter each negative image with the sweet memory of Ben's kiss. Her body may have physically found a small amount of rest, but her heart certainly hadn't.

The aroma of Cookie's chili wafted across the campfire, reminding her that she'd intended to eat a second helping. As Cookie stirred the chili, Chloe remembered the vague sense of familiarity she'd had when the cook called her *sweet pea*.

Not far from Cookie, Ben and Gus paced back and forth while glaring at each other. Approaching the others, she looked around but saw no sign of Caleb or Monique.

Rudy held out a battered tin cup brimming with coffee.

"Why don't you just sit right on over here by the fire, Miss Chloe."

"Thank you, Rudy." She accepted the cup as gracefully as possible while claiming a spot near the fire. Had Ben informed them of what transpired between her and Monique?

"Did you get some rest?"

Sitting cross-legged on the hard ground, she looked up as Ben sat down next to her. Her gaze instantly focused on his soft, gently curved mouth. She blew a puff of air across the top of the steaming cup before nodding. "I think so." He didn't need to know she'd been unable to nap.

"Your brother and Monique aren't back yet." He spoke quietly, his brow furrowed in concern.

"But they've been gone for hours." Tears threatened to overtake her, and she gulped down a hefty swallow of scalding coffee. At least now she had a valid excuse for the moisture gathering in her eyes. But when Ben rubbed his hand across her shoulder, she knew she may have fooled the others but she hadn't fooled him.

"I'm sorry, Chloe. We should have gone after them when you wanted to."

Shrugging away from his touch, she jumped up and flung the bitter coffee into the fire. "We need to go find them."

"I know, but it'll be dark soon."

"That's why we need to go now." Why was he just sitting there? Didn't he care that her brother and Monique were quite possibly lost?

Gravel crunched as Gus and Skip approached them. Gus's jaw was clenched into a tight ridge, and his eyes were narrowed. He had the look of a man spoiling for a fight. Ben stood to face them, positioning himself in front of Chloe.

Skip tipped his head to peer at her around Ben's side. "Don'tcha worry none, Miss Chloe. It ain't yer fault." These may well have been the first words he'd spoken to her. Shouting at her on the trail when she lagged behind with Monique didn't count. Skip's perpetual sullen expression made his smile appear awkward and insincere.

A chill crept up the back of her neck, and she shivered. "Yes it is. I should have kept my mouth shut."

"No." Gus drew his bushy white eyebrows together. "It's the fault of that knuckle-headed brother of yours. I can't wait to get my hands on him." He had a shotgun slung over one shoulder, a hunting bag over the other, and a lantern in one hand.

"I'm going with you." Chloe stepped out from behind Ben. Gus might be angry at Caleb, but at least he was ready to go searching. And *she* was going, too.

"Gus." Ben sighed wearily. "This is no more Caleb's fault than it is Monique's. You have to admit she's partly to blame."

Gus glared at Ben. "If he so much as lays one hand on her, I'll—"

"You'll what?" Chloe marched over to Gus, glaring hard at the man she'd come to adore. Adoration or no, he wasn't going to make threats against her brother.

"Begging your pardon, Miss Chloe." Gus rubbed the back of his neck. Was it moisture, or the fire's glow that put the sudden shine in his eyes? "Your brother has sullied the reputation of my daughter, and he'll have to pay the price."

"Reputation? She's been up here for days with a bunch of men." Though she sounded like a shrew, Chloe couldn't stop herself. Not even at the thought of being stared at. Defending her brother was too important. "And to hear Monique tell it, this isn't the first time. Anyone who cares about the rules of propriety wouldn't give her a second glance."

Though Chloe didn't add this thought, she was fairly certain that, much like herself, Monique wouldn't want anything to do with a man who put propriety ahead of what was in a woman's heart and soul.

Chloe turned from Gus and stomped toward the women's side of camp, raising her voice so they could still hear her. "Right now the important thing is they've been gone entirely too long. We need to get on with the search." She rummaged through her carry-all until she found her jacket then flung it over her shoulder.

Heart pounding from the confrontation, she marched back toward Gus.

"I'm gonna search, all right." Gus kicked a hard patch on the ground, attacking a second and third time before it finally broke in to powdery dirt. "And when I find your brother, I'm gonna bust his sorry bee-hind!"

Refusing to back down, Chloe challenged Gus with a hard glare. "You'll have to bust mine, first!"

"Nobody's going to bust anything. And nobody's going anywhere right now." Ben placed a soothing hand on her shoulder. "It'll be dark soon. We won't have any luck finding them tonight. It'll be dangerous out there for us."

"What about my daughter?" Gus shouted. "She's in danger, too."

"I know, Gus." Ben sighed. His tone was one of regret and defeat. The sparks from the fire lit up his face, and Chloe could see those same emotions reflected in his eyes. He dropped his hand from Chloe's shoulder and stepped toward the older man. "Please understand. We can't risk putting everyone else in danger. Besides, Caleb *is* an experienced guide. He'll know how to keep Monique safe until morning. They'll be fine through the night, and we can search when it's light out."

A sick feeling clutched her stomach, and she hugged her jacket to her chest as if it could make things better. Ben operated on the assumption Caleb knew what he was doing. Much as she wanted to avoid it, now was the time to tell Ben the truth.

"Ben, there's something you don't understand." Inhaling hard, willing her nerves to calm, Chloe forced herself to continue. "They're in danger, too. We have to help—"

"What are you talking about, girl?" Gus stepped close as he interrupted her. Lines she'd never noticed before cut sharply into his weathered face, and he seemed far older than he had this morning. A father worried sick about his daughter.

Would her father worry about her this way? Somehow Chloe doubted it. She swallowed hard. Yes, the lie had to end. Now. Unable to bear seeing Gus's fear intensify, she forced herself to look away, at the ground.

"Uh, it's about Caleb."

"What about him? Out with it, girl."

"He's not…" She hesitated, fearful of their reaction. But the only way to convince Ben to find her brother was to just say it and accept the consequences. "He-he's not that experienced."

"What do you mean, not *that* experienced?" The hardness in Ben's tone sent a chilling creeping down her neck.

"He's—I mean, he's not really a mountain guide. Not yet, anyway. He's been hiking with some of the men in Cedar Ridge, and learning about being a guide, but technically he's a reporter like me."

There. She said it. Sucking in a deep breath, Chloe studied the coat still crumpled in her hands, waiting for an explosion that didn't come. Even Gus was silent. Willing her heartbeat to return to normal, she took another breath and looked up.

She shouldn't have.

Lips pressed together in a tight line, eyes narrowed to fierce slits that glittered from the fire's glow, Ben stared at her as if she were one of his specimens. She squirmed under his gaze. Finally, he schooled his features and spoke in a measured tone.

"And just how is it that I have two reporters along when I didn't even want *one* to begin with?"

"It's not Caleb's fault at all. It was my idea." Her words came out in a rush. "When you said I couldn't come, I hoped maybe you'd let Caleb. But you said no reporters at all, so I knew it wouldn't work. I figured you'd need a guide, so I convinced him to approach you and pretend to be more experienced than he really is."

When Ben said nothing, tears threatened. She bit her lip and willed them back.

"It was the only way I could get the story. The only way I could show my father…" She broke off and took a shaky breath. The pain of her father's rejection didn't matter now. The story didn't matter. All that mattered was Caleb and Monique's safety. "If they don't find their way back it will be my fault."

"What?" Ben's question was more of a shout. "He grew up in these mountains. Surely he'll still know how to get them through the night?"

Chloe shook her head fiercely. "We didn't grow up here. We moved here from Boston less than a year ago."

"I see." Ben turned from her, staring out at the trees.

Breathe, breathe, breathe.

Condemnation emanated from each person present, but most especially Ben. Remorse squeezed her heart.

"I'm really very sorry," she whispered.

"We're wasting precious time." Gus kicked the dirt again, this time so hard Chloe was afraid he'd go flying and land on his backside. "The devil with morning. My daughter is out there with a bumbling city slicker. I say let's find her. Now!"

"Skip," Ben said. "You go with Gus in one direction, Rudy and I will go in the other. Cookie, you and Chloe stay here in case they return. Whoever finds them, fire two shots and we'll head back here. Don't get disoriented. If you get lost, fire one shot every fifteen minutes and we'll find you. Gus, make sure you have enough oil in the lantern." While he spoke, Ben was busy attaching his reflecting lamp to his hat. When he finished, he picked up his hunting bag and shotgun and then turned to Chloe.

Breath held, she waited for angry words to rain down on her.

"Don't worry." The unusually tender tone threw her, as did his now-gentle gaze. She didn't understand. Where was his anger? He reached out to touch her cheek. "We'll bring them back safely."

"I need to go with you."

"No, Chloe. I have enough to worry about. I don't want to worry about you, too."

"Please, Ben. I *need* to go. Can't you understand? He's my brother." She locked her gaze with his while his hand lingered feather-light along her jawline. He appeared ready to relent, but before he could answer her, Skip spoke up.

"What about Cookie? She shouldn't be alone." Something about Skip's tone struck her as odd. The wiry little man was always so gruff, so abrupt. His concern felt wrong, out of place. "How's about I stay with her?"

"No." It was the loudest Cookie had ever spoken, and she side-stepped toward Gus. "I'll be just fine by myself."

"But I won't be if I'm worrying about you while I'm off looking for my daughter." They shared an indecipherable look before Gus patted her hand then turned to Chloe. "Will you please stay with Cookie?"

"My brother..." She looked at Cookie before shaking her head with reluctance. "No. I'm sorry, Cookie. I'm sorry, Gus. I *have* to go." She agreed Cookie shouldn't be alone. But she had to actively look for her brother. She *had* to.

He turned to Ben. "You're not seriously going to let her come, are you?"

"I don't know, Gus." Ben sighed and scrubbed his hand across his face.

This time Chloe didn't need to remind herself to breathe. It was her brother she was concerned about, not herself. She looked pointedly at Gus. "It doesn't matter what Ben says. I'm going to look for my brother."

"Then you'd best go pack your bag. I don't want anyone going anywhere at night without their gear. Ben, I need a word with you in private." Without waiting for a response, Gus turned and walked away from the group as if expecting Ben to follow him up the small hill near a cluster of spruce trees and overgrown weeds.

Chloe watched as Ben followed Gus up the hill. Skip, Rudy, and Cookie all stared silently at one another, the tension between them palpable.

"I-if you'll excuse me," Chloe said to no one in particular. Feeling awkward and uncomfortable, she walked the short distance to the women's side of camp and rolled up her arctic sleeping bag.

When she attempted to stuff her jacket into the carry-all, she found there wasn't enough room. She pulled things out to rearrange them, and her towel fell out. Something hard dropped to the ground.

The blue watch.

Chloe bent to pick it up and rubbed it with the corner of the towel, more positive than ever it belonged to a woman.

As the dirt began to fall away from the blue surface, she felt one small twinge of victory. But it was outweighed by something far bigger. A feeling. A sense. Hope. It had played at the back of her mind ever since she'd first picked it up.

Smaller than a man's, the face-piece was in fancy script with the word *Tiffany* engraved just above the dial. With the pad of her thumb, Chloe could make out the shape of tiny grape clusters—almost assuredly diamonds—on the back. But she didn't care about that. What made her heart leap to her throat was the certainty that the watch opened up to reveal the inner workings. And if she could trip an almost undetectable latch, she'd surely find a name engraved there.

She looked up to see Cookie approaching and that feeling tugged at her again, only this time it was stronger.

The cook stared at the ground as she walked, so Chloe couldn't see her face. It didn't matter. Chloe fingered the pocket watch and waited for Cookie's approach.

Still looking down as she stopped in front of Chloe, Cookie took her hand and squeezed tight. "I wish you wouldn't go."

A shiver skittered between her shoulder blades. "Cookie, I have to. It's my fault Monique ran off. And my brother, I-I can't bear it if something happens to him."

"Then be careful. Please?" Cookie squeezed Chloe's hand once more, seeming reluctant to let it go.

Tears burned Chloe's eyes, and she nodded. "I will."

"I'm so proud of you, Chloe. You're living your dream instead of allowing yourself to be forced into a mold."

For a moment, Chloe didn't dare breathe. Those words, spoken in that very voice, confirmed the glimmer of hope the watch had given her. A surge of excitement tripped through her and she rubbed her fingers tightly over the watch.

"I think this belongs to you." Heart pounding, she opened her palm and held it out. A painful squeeze tightened her throat.

When Cookie didn't take the watch, Chloe reached over and pushed up the brim of Cookie's hat to reveal blue eyes that were no longer hidden by shadows, and dark hair shot with strands of silver that Chloe didn't remember being there. "My father bought this for you the year Mr. Tiffany came to visit the newspaper office in Boston."

Chloe's vision blurred even more, and tears spilled unchecked down her cheeks. "Aunt Jane," she whispered as she flung herself into the other woman's arms.

"Yes, sweet pea, it's me." Aunt Jane squeezed her tight with the strength and warmth of a family hug that had never felt so good.

A dozen questions burst through Chloe's mind, and more than a few spilled from her lips. "Where have you been all this time? Why didn't you let me know you were here? Why *are* you here?"

"Shh, honey. I can only handle one question at a time." Aunt Jane stepped back and looked Chloe up and down as though seeing her for the first time, even though they'd been together the last few days. Then she brushed at the dampness on Chloe's cheeks. "I can't believe how you've grown."

"Do my parents know you're here?"

Aunt Jane nodded. "They should by now. I sent a message with the train engineer while you and Ben were arguing that first day."

Chloe felt her face flush as she remembered her behavior. "I'm sorry, Aunt Jane. I..."

The look her aunt gave her was one she'd never received from her father, one of unconditional love. "Hush. There's no need to apologize. I'm so proud of you, Chloe. You stood up for something you believe in. You're following your dreams."

"I learned it from you." Chloe couldn't keep the smile off her face. "I've missed you so much."

"And I've missed you."

"Why didn't you meet us last year like you and my father planned?"

Aunt Jane glanced over her shoulder before answering. "It's rather complicated, and we don't have much time, but the short answer is someone wants to hurt me. He also wants to hurt Gus and Ben. If he knows you and Caleb are my family, he'll try to hurt you, too."

"Who? Let's tell Ben. He'll stop them."

Jane shook her head.

"Please, Aunt Jane?"

"The less you know the better."

Chloe shivered at her aunt's ominous words.

"Stay close to Ben while you search for your brother," her aunt said. "Gus taught him everything he knows. He'll keep you safe. And as long as you continue to pretend I'm just the cook, I'll be safe, too."

"I don't understand."

"It's complicated, honey. We can talk after you get back. Just stay close to Ben. You can trust him. And perhaps when you return, your father will be here."

"But—"

"In the message I sent with the engineer, I told you father we needed his help. If the engineer delivered it as he said he would, I'm sure your father would have headed out straightaway. In fact, he shouldn't be that far behind us. A day, maybe two. Who knows, we might wake up tomorrow and see him here."

Would her father really show up? Part of her hoped he would. It could mean he cared about her after all. The other part of her was coming to like this adventurous life. Well, except for the times when she messed things up. Like tonight, with Caleb and Monique.

"You ladies okay over here?"

Aunt Jane scrambled to pull her hat down over her forehead then stepped behind Chloe as Skip approached. "Act natural," she whispered.

Skip? Could he be the one threatening her aunt? No wonder she'd reacted the way she had when he said he'd stay with her.

Chloe schooled her features, prepared to convince Skip that everything was all right even though it apparently wasn't. "We're just fine."

Skip approached Chloe, looking at the watch she still held. He let out a long whistle. "That's an expensive-looking watch you've got there. Where'd you get it?"

"It was a gift from my father." Chloe didn't like the way Skip looked at the watch. She'd give it to Aunt Jane as soon as he went away. Tucking it into the pocket of her trousers, she glanced around for Ben.

Where was he, anyway?

Almost as if she'd conjured him with her thoughts, he appeared—and looking none-too-happy. The frown line between his eyes was almost as deep as one of the mountain crevasses.

"Chloe." His voice held the same urgency she'd felt earlier. "Rudy's going to stay with Cookie. Skip will be going with Gus. We really need to go if we're going to find your brother and Monique before it gets any darker. Do you have your bag packed?"

Chloe nodded, then pulled her aunt into another hug and whispered in her ear. "I love you, Aunt Jane."

"I love you, too, sweet pea. Go find your brother. And stay safe."

After kissing Aunt Jane on the cheek, Chloe reluctantly pulled away to grab her belongings and follow Ben. She'd only gone a few feet when Aunt Jane called her back.

"Wait! You forgot something."

Her aunt bent down and picked something up off the ground. The tiny book of scriptures Rudy gave her. "Draw hope from it while you look for your brother."

"Thank you. I will."

Taking the Bible from Aunt Jane, Chloe clutched it tight, almost overwhelmed with the need to pray. But God most likely didn't want to hear from her. She was a liar. She'd manipulated her way onto this trip, and it was her fault Caleb and Monique were missing. She didn't deserve to talk to the God who'd created these mountains and all the beauty they contained.

Heavy-hearted as she followed behind Ben, she couldn't help but hope God would take the time to hear the plea her heart whispered. *Please, please, please keep them safe. Please let us find them.*

To Chloe's credit, she kept quiet as they made their way through thick brush and an area of forest so dense it seemed darker than it really was. She didn't complain about moss that brushed the top of her hat, she didn't complain about needle-encrusted branches as they slapped her in the face. For all of that, Ben was thankful.

After what Gus had just told him, he wasn't sure he could handle a conversation. Especially with Chloe. He should have sent her packing when the train had stopped in Skykomish. Now she was in danger. Real danger. Not the kind that came from conducting a search in the dark, either. It was the thing he feared the most.

It was the Rosalie situation all over again.

Ben slowed his pace almost to a complete stop.

"Ben, are you all right?"

He started to say he was but made the mistake of looking down at her. One look at the concern filling her eyes, and he was just plain lost.

He sighed heavily. "There's so much wrong, I don't even know where to start."

She nodded as if she understood and, based on what Gus had told him, perhaps she did. No matter, she deserved the truth. Especially now when she could well be in danger.

"Chloe, I need to tell you some things that are complicated and convoluted. But let me start with something good. It's about Cookie."

"I know," Chloe all but squealed. Her grin was wide, and though the light was fast growing dim, he was certain her eyes sparkled. "She's my aunt. Aunt Jane. I thought she was dead." Chloe threw her arms around Ben's waist. He didn't pull away.

"I'm so happy. But..." She reached up and scrubbed her forearm across her face.

Ben carefully extracted her other arm from his waist and turned her to face him. "But what?"

"My aunt said someone wanted to hurt her. And you, Ben, someone wants to hurt you, too."

"I know. Gus told me."

"Did he say who? Did he say why? I think it's Skip. He's the only one who makes sense. I know it's not Rudy. Rudy would never hurt anyone, despite his size. Please tell me it's not Rudy. Please—"

Ben cupped her face in his hands and tipped it to face him. She was smart, and cute, and oh so very appealing. It would be way too easy to get side-tracked.

He looked away before he said, "Gus wouldn't tell me who it was. He said it was better if I didn't know."

His gut churned at Gus's secretiveness on the subject. But Gus said he didn't want Ben taking matters into his own hands until Monique and Caleb were found.

"I think, you're right, Chloe. I think it's Skip, too."

"But Gus went with him to search for my brother. Why would he do that?"

"To find his daughter. To keep your aunt safe. I felt we should stay together; search for Monique and Caleb in one group. Cookie, too. That way no one would be alone and in danger. But Gus feels we have a better chance of finding your brother and Monique if we split up. He trusts Rudy to protect your aunt, and I..." His heart tendered as he looked at her, and he knew what he was about to say was the truth. "I'll protect you, Chloe." *Forever*, he added mentally.

Before he could do something silly like kiss her again, and before she could do something like respond, he spun her forward on the trail. "We don't have much light left. We can talk while we walk."

They walked in silence for a few minutes. He wanted to be sure they were far enough away from camp before he told Chloe about his conversation with Gus. Finally, he said, "Apparently, your aunt and Gus have been working together for quite some time. They met when she came to Florida to work on a story."

"I remember when she wrote to us about going down there. She was supposed to meet us here when she finished there. When we never heard from her, we thought the worst."

"They think they figured out who was behind the smear campaign that caused me to lose my job. Gus won't confirm that it's Skip, but he sure wouldn't leave Rudy with your aunt if he thought Rudy was the one they were after."

"Well then, we'd better get going. The faster we find them and get back here, the faster we can get this solved." She grabbed his hand, tugging it as she ran forward. "Will Gus be able to defend himself against Skip if he realizes they know who he is?"

"Trust me, I've seen Gus wrestle a gator and win. He can take care of himself." Even as he said it, Ben prayed it was true. Gus and Monique were the only family he had.

Chloe trudged along beside him in the growing darkness. She'd been quiet for at least an hour, and Ben knew she was busy blaming herself. Her silence bothered him, but each time he tried talking to her, she only gave him one-syllable monotone answers. He worried about how she'd respond if they didn't find Caleb and Monique.

When she puffed out a short, exasperated sigh, Ben was so relieved he almost rejoiced out loud.

"Tired?" He winced and turned his head when she looked at him. Somehow she'd managed to finagle her way into wearing his reflecting lamp.

"Frustrated is more like it. I don't think we're ever going to find them. They could have been eaten by bears, or fallen off a cliff, or—"

"Shh." Ben put his arm around her and pulled her close. "Stop doing that to yourself. I promise you, we'll find them." He reveled in the feel of her in his arms, the rosy scent of her skin and hair as it wafted up to tickle his nose. It was so perfect, so right. Immediately he dropped his arm.

Putting a woman in danger wasn't perfect, or right. And if he hadn't been so weak and allowed himself to be swayed by a pair of sassy blue eyes, they wouldn't be in this predicament. He'd best remember to keep his eyes, hands, and thoughts off Chloe if he knew what was good for him. The kiss they shared was dangerous, powerful, and it was just too tempting to even think about. Then when she threw herself into his arms after he agreed she could come on the search, well, it was nearly his undoing. The woman was causing him to lose his mind.

A quick blast of gunfire burst through the night and echoed in the air. Beside him, Chloe froze. He could feel the hope permeating from her as she sucked in a sharp breath, waiting for the sound of another shot. The second shot filled the air, and beside him Chloe shouted for joy.

"Thank the Lord, he's safe!"

"Amen." Ben uttered the agreement before he even realized it. Perhaps Rudy's prayers were influencing him more than he thought. As he unleashed a laugh, Chloe looked up at him, temporarily blinding him once more. But it didn't matter. Feeling every bit as joyous and relieved as Chloe, Ben threw his arm around her. Her hat, with his reflecting lamp, thumped against his chest.

"Sorry." She turned in his arms to gaze up at him. When he winced again she pulled off the hat. Warm light surrounded them, but this time it didn't blind him. Her hair spilled down around her shoulders, glowing a warm shade of golden brown. The smile she gave him was absolutely radiant. "I guess I got a bit too excited."

Tightening his arms around her, Ben rested his cheek atop her head. His pulse quickened, and his heart thumped as he fought the urge to kiss her.

He pulled away from her. "Shall we go back? I know you're anxious to see your brother."

When she looked up at him Ben swore he could see perplexity on her face. She felt something, too. The very thought made him want to turn and run like a scared jackrabbit. That door needed to shut, and quick. There could be absolutely nothing between him and Chloe. She was not the kind of woman to have a casual dalliance. And for him, a man with no home, to ask anything more of a woman was a silly notion.

Somewhere along the way, the path they followed had blended into trees and bushes so thick Chloe feared they'd never find their way out.

"Ben?" Carefully, she extracted her hand from his. He'd been holding it while they wandered the trail back to camp. But as right as her hand felt in his, she knew they were lost, and she wanted to hear it straight from his mouth with no distractions. "Do you honestly think we're headed in the right direction?"

"I...uh...we just need to follow the creek downhill." He didn't sound very sure of himself.

"*If* we can even find it. We've been looking for it so long I think my legs are going to collapse."

Ben was instantly the gentleman. "Do you need to stop and sit down for a while?"

"No. I don't need to rest. I need for you to admit we're lost and shoot that gun so the others will come looking for us." Thus far Ben had adamantly insisted they weren't lost. This was the first time he'd shown the least bit of hesitation. She didn't know why he was so stubborn. Must be that capable field biologist image he had to be certain to portray. Maybe this time though, he'd finally admit they needed help.

"I suppose you're right." He huffed loud enough to be heard, and Chloe knew he was disgusted with himself. Reaching into his jacket, he pulled out his revolver. Then he handed her his pocket watch. "Here. You be the timekeeper. Every fifteen minutes I need to fire off a shot. You can sit right there on the grass."

Chloe smiled up at Ben as she sat, then she opened the timepiece and ran her thumb across its face. Twelve-forty. It was after midnight. It had been a couple of hours since they heard the shots indicating Caleb had been found. Surely Aunt Jane revealed herself to him after he returned to camp. A pang of regret struck her heart. She would have given anything to be there for the reunion.

When Ben shot the gun, she winced and covered her ears. "Ouch!"

"Sorry. I'll walk away from you before I shoot the next one."

The fifteen minutes slowly crawled by, during which time Chloe continuously rubbed the face of Ben's pocket watch and thought about Aunt Jane's. It was still in her pocket.

Chilled air breezed across her arms just then, and she shivered. It seemed she'd been sitting in the damp grass for hours.

"Cold?"

She nodded. "As long as we were moving, I was fine. But now, well, it's not exactly hot up here even in the daylight. I do have a jacket in my carry-all, though."

"Ladies', or hunting?"

"Hunting, of course. Waterproof and down-filled. It's fairly heavy, so I'll wait a while before I put it on."

Ben's nod of approval filled her with a sense of satisfaction. She'd actually done something right.

"I think we should go ahead and build a fire," Ben said. "Let's walk down here a ways and see if we can find a good spot. You keep watching the time though, and let me know when I need to fire another shot."

Half an hour and three shots later, there had been no return shots or sound of voices calling them. But they had found a spot with enough of a clearing to build a fire.

Chloe searched for stones to ring the fire pit while Ben gathered wood. There weren't many stones around, and she found herself having to go deeper into the brush each time.

"Five feet. Don't go any further than that." Ben dropped some branches into a pile.

"Not a chance." Lost in the woods with Ben wasn't so bad, but alone at night—she didn't relish the thought at all. Especially if that weasel, Skip, was lurking somewhere nearby. She tapped her hat, thankful for Ben's reflecting lamp. "And if I did happen go too far, I've got this trusty thing so I won't get lost. All you'll have to do is follow the light."

"Just be careful, Chloe."

Chloe's heart warmed at the protectiveness in his tone. "I will, Ben."

"Don't go any further than the sound of my voice, and if you even think someone is nearby, scream as loud as you can."

"I will, I promise."

A crack of a twig sounded to the right of her, and she whirled around. Thankfully Ben was close enough to be seen. The hair stood up on the back of her neck. "Ben, I don't think we're—"

Strong hands shoved at the center of her back, and Chloe's feet slipped out from under her.

"Ben!" Chloe screamed and grabbed for a branch. She missed, grabbing nothing but air. The world tilted and whirled uncontrollably. When she finally hit something hard and sharp, her breath was torn from her. A bright light exploded at the back of her eyes, followed by a quickly growing dimness and sensation that awareness was fading away.

"Chloe!" Frantic, Ben shouted until his throat was raw. He'd heard her scream, heard her voice fade away to nothingness. He'd dropped the wood and jumped up immediately, quickly scanning the area. All he saw was darkness. No sign of light. She couldn't have gotten so far away there'd be no light. Why had the light on her reflecting lamp gone out?

Sick with worry, desperate for a beam of light, a noise, some indication of where she might be, he ignored the stinging nettles and sticker bushes as he tromped through the brush.

His toe caught on one of the massive tree roots, which poked up from the ground, and he stumbled. He caught himself and watched his step a little more closely. As soon as he stepped over the last bit of root-gnarled ground, Ben stopped short. He'd arrived at the edge of a cliff.

Did Chloe come this way? Dear God, he prayed not. Heart slamming against his ribs, Ben sucked in a sharp breath and carefully kneeled at the edge. His fingers dislodged small rocks and dirt, and they spilled downward. When he didn't hear the debris hit bottom, Ben's blood roared in his ears. Had it landed on something else? Chloe, perhaps?

Cautiously, lest the earth give way beneath him, he lay flat on the ground and scooted forward an inch at a time until he was close enough to peer safely over the edge.

With nothing but the moon to light the area, Ben had to strain to see. But there, on a thin precipice, halfway down the sheer drop, he could just make out the figure of someone lying in a heap. His stomach plummeted, and the air *wooshed* from his lungs. No one could survive a fall like that.

"Chloe!" His throat tightened painfully. "Chloe, answer me. Can you hear me?" No answer. She didn't even stir. And the moonlight was not bright enough to illuminate her face.

It was just like Rosalie all over again. Only this time, the blame rested solely on him. A sickening lump formed in the pit of his stomach. He should never have let her come along. He had to get to her, make sure she was alive. He had to keep her safe.

Even without daylight to show him, Ben knew years of hard weather left the bluff in a state of decay. There wasn't much to assure a sturdy foot or hand hold. Still, there was no question in his mind. He had to get to Chloe.

This couldn't happen again!

A wave of unresolved emotions slammed into him, leaving him dizzy. Guilt, helplessness, anger, and the painful, ragged cut of a breaking heart.

The long-ignored feelings nearly paralyzed him. But he steeled himself, forced the feelings back to the dark place they belonged, and whispered a fervent prayer. He could not give in to pain. If he did, his resolve would dissipate. Chloe was the important one. She was all he could think of.

Slowly, Ben lowered himself over the side. For one sickening moment his legs dangled there. His arms dug into the ground in order to keep from slipping over the side. A slow, cold trickle of sweat trailed down his back. He scrambled his feet against the wall of dirt in a mad search for his sense of balance. Finally, he lowered one foot and one hand at a time, making sure with each movement that he was secure before continuing.

When Ben finally dared look down, he'd only gone halfway. His arms were like lead, a streak of numbness ran down his left leg. All he could smell was the strong scent of earth—and fear. Chloe had neither moved nor uttered a sound since he'd begun his descent.

The grim reality of the situation settled with a lurch in the pit of his stomach, and Ben once again steadily, though too slowly, continued toward the ledge to Chloe.

Finally, his foot touched bottom. Limp with relief, Ben collapsed at Chloe's side.

Thank goodness she hadn't stopped to take her carry-all and sleeping bag off her back when they'd found the clearing. She'd gone hunting for rocks with the burden on her back, and it looked to be what broke her fall. She lay on her side, curled up like a sleeping child.

Only he didn't know whether she was unconscious or...dead.

Ben reached out a shaky hand to brush aside the hair that spilled across Chloe's face. Her hat and his reflecting lamp were nowhere in sight. Wherever they'd landed, thankfully the flame hadn't started a fire. Gently, he stroked her cheek. Her stark paleness seemed to glow harshly in the moonlight.

Placing a hand to her breastbone, Ben held his breath. He couldn't feel her heart beating; he could only hear his, thrumming in his ears. She must not be dead. This could not happen again. His heart couldn't bear it.

"Come on, sweetheart," he whispered. "Be alive, please be all right."

He moved his hand to her neck, just below her jaw, and waited—perfectly still. It was faint, but the pulse was there.

Overwhelmed with relief, Ben leaned back and looked to the sky. "Thank you." Staring at the night sky filled with only a scant few stars, he whispered his thanks several times over. "Thank you."

Scanning the dark, shadowy shape of the mountainside above him, Ben knew there was no way he'd be able to get her back up. Not at all. He'd drop her for sure. He looked down. The bottom didn't seem to be that far away. The rocks jutted out like steps. They'd have to go down. But the darkness could be masking the true depth, and he didn't want to chance even carrying her down until it grew light. And even then he'd have to wait until she regained consciousness.

Keep her warm. He had to keep her warm. Ben loosed the straps that kept her sleeping bag over her shoulders then gently eased her up enough to pull it and her carry-all out from under her. He unrolled the sleeping bag and, as he did, something slipped out and hit the ground with a soft thump. Ignoring it for now, he pulled out her pillow and placed it beneath her head.

Next, he undid each and every tie that kept the bag closed then unfolded it and spread it over Chloe. Before he climbed under it himself, he carefully removed her boots and set them aside. After taking off his own boots, he scooted down as close to her as possible without moving her and gently wrapped her in his arms.

Ben's nose twitched when the faint scent of roses tickled it. He burrowed closer to Chloe, intent on keeping her warm. A tender wave of admiration and protectiveness began a slow curl around his heart.

Thank the good Lord for her sleeping bag. Ben remembered laughing at her that first night, teasing her that she was too good for a simple bedroll. A bedroll might not have been padded enough to save her life. He shook his head, feeling like a silly fool. All the times he'd teased her, or made snide little comments, he'd only been doing it to protect himself. He never wanted to let himself like her. But heaven help him, he did.

More than he even wanted to admit to himself.

He brushed his lips across the top of her head and then squeezed his eyes tight against the hot moisture threatening to spill. She'd be warm now.

As he moved to get comfortable, Ben's hand struck the object that had fallen from Chloe's arctic bag. Picking it up, he realized it was a book. Her journal? He ran a hand over the cover. The feel was soft, not quite smooth. Leather? He opened it and thumbed through the pages. There were too many to be a simple journal, and the pages were much too thin and delicate to allow someone to write in the book without the fine pages tearing. Could it be a Bible?

Though it was a journal he'd always seen her with and never a Bible, that didn't mean anything. He reached for Chloe's bag, intending to stuff it inside, but something stopped him. It wasn't as if the Bible had healing properties, but just holding it gave Ben a small measure of comfort, as if merely due to its presence everything would be all right.

Shaking his head, he tried to talk himself out of the silly thought. But he'd

heard Rudy preaching one too many times in an attempt to convert Ben and Gus while on the trip out from Florida.

"Lay your burdens at the cross."

"Jesus died so you may live."

"Forgive, just as your heavenly Father has forgiven you."

"You have a Father who loves you. Seek His will above all else."

Admittedly he didn't understand all of what Rudy spoke of, but some of it was familiar. Some of the words were reminiscent of his childhood—words his father taught him in those happy and adventure-filled days before his parents left him.

He'd dismissed Rudy time and again, especially where it came to that God-as-a-father business. But where he'd scoffed at him a week ago, this time Ben had to wonder. What if Rudy were right? Even if praying to God had never worked when he'd prayed for his parents to come back for him, it would be senseless to ignore the fact that praying might help Chloe.

Wouldn't it?

Please God, please. God had spared Chloe's life with that heavy arctic bag, and now Ben needed to beg Him to let her live through the night.

He gripped the Bible in his hand and prepared himself for a vigil.

Chapter Twelve

He murmured the prayer over and over. And as daylight began to edge the black sky like a burning match to the corner of a page, Ben could see that it really was a Bible he held. He wanted to kiss the soft leather binding, thankful Chloe breathed through the night and thankful for something else—something he wasn't sure he was worthy of. Rudy's God was real.

Rudy's God was his God now. He didn't feel good enough. He didn't feel worthy to call on God's name, or to call himself a Christian. But he had heard Rudy talk about that plenty. If one subscribed to Rudy's way of thinking, sinners—the unworthy—were the very reason Jesus walked the earth and died.

Taking a deep breath of fresh morning air, he had to hope Rudy was right, because this newfound warmth pulsing through him was something he wanted to hold on to forever.

Perhaps he could find answers in the Bible. There was enough light now that the dawn was breaking—Ben released his grip on it and opened the leather cover.

To Rudy Thatcher,
"He came to save the lost."
Always, your loving wife, Adele

Rudy was married? True, Ben didn't know him well—he was someone Gus had come across. They'd worked with Rudy on that fateful South American expedition, but Ben had never met him before that, nor seen him since. Not until Gus suggested he join them for the Sasquatch hunt. But it was odd that Rudy never once spoke of his wife on the long train trip from Florida while he was forever talking to Ben and Gus about his faith in God.

Perhaps she died, and Rudy didn't want to talk about her? He gently thumbed through the delicate pages until he came to the page that listed family births and losses. Sure enough the name Adele was inscribed under the heading entitled *Deaths*, the ink on the second 'e' smeared slightly as if by a tear.

Chloe stirred slightly, and Ben set the Bible aside.

"Chloe?" he whispered, stroking her soft cheek.

Her eyelids fluttered, but her eyes remained closed.

"Chloe, wake up, sweetheart." He continued stroking her cheek, praying all the while that she'd open her eyes soon.

Sometime during the long night, their souls bonded. Not that Ben planned to share the notion with anyone else. His buddies would scoff and call it sissy stuff, malarkey. But he knew it with every breath he took. He could no longer deny the truth, finally had to admit what he'd been fighting for days.

Attraction, or mere *like*, didn't describe this hungry yet tender feeling that stirred his blood with each thought of her. Thoughts he simply could not get out of his head. And it had nothing to do with holding her all through the long night, murmuring softly in her ear, tightening his arms around her each time she moaned or stirred. These thoughts had been plaguing him, slowly but surely, since the first day he saw her. He was only just now beginning to realize their depth. He'd spent the night reflecting on these things, as well as praying. That was another thing his buddies would scoff at. But now, as her eyelids fluttered once again, Ben realized the fact that she'd survived the night was a gift from God Himself.

Coming to that realization was a surprise in itself—but he couldn't ignore all the times he'd felt an internal push to pray for Chloe throughout the night. It could have only come from one source. Given the way his parents abandoned him to Gus's care when he was a young boy, he wasn't naturally inclined to pray.

His parents had been missionaries. But they'd cared more about their mission work than they did their own son. He'd been six or seven when they'd gone off to Africa to teach the natives about God. They left him with Gus so they'd have more time to concentrate on their mission. Ben would have only been in the way, they said. And apparently he would have been in the way the rest of his childhood, because they never returned and their letters eventually faded to a trickle. The letter with the article about Jacko was one of the last ones he ever received. Because of that, he hadn't really had much use for God. Until last night.

"Caleb?" During the night, Chloe had shifted, and her head now rested on his chest, his arms pulling her tight. Now he tilted his head, trying to see her. As she stirred and attempted to sit up, the chilly morning air brushed Ben's chest where she'd lain. He shivered.

"Caleb is that you?"

"It's me. Ben." He sat up rather awkwardly, helping Chloe to sit as well, careful not to jar her. She was sure to be in pain. His own joints were stiff and sore from huddling immobile for so many hours. He brushed his fingers along her cheek. "How are you feeling?"

"Ben?" She looked into his face and blinked, as if trying to clear her focus. "What happened? Why are you here? Where are we?"

"You fell. Last night. Are you hurt?"

"Hurt? I-I'm not sure." She shook her head as if shaking off his touch. Then she laughed—a faint tinkling sound that lifted the edges of his heart. "Everything hurts. I feel like I was thrown from a moving train."

"You might as well have been. Don't you remember falling?"

Still looking dazed, Chloe turned her head and stared up the steep incline. Her eyes widened, and once again the fear that had gripped him when he'd first

glanced over the side to see her laying in a crumpled heap gripped him again. He pulled her close.

"I remember gathering rocks for the fire pit."

"That's right. The drop-off was well disguised with bushes and trees."

"I'm glad you found me," she said softly. "Otherwise, I might have died."

Ben's heart stuttered as she echoed the thoughts he'd had all night. "We were lucky. God was watching over us." He smiled down at her, and the edges of her mouth slowly turned upward. "I hope He has some more of that in store for us now, because that's as far as our luck goes. Thus far no one has found us. I haven't even heard them out looking for us."

"They never heard the gunshots?"

"No."

"Oh." Her face seemed to crumple, and she sounded so dejected, so perplexed, he had to tell her.

"I didn't fire any more shots last night."

Her eyes widened and she drew back in surprise. "Why not?"

"I left the shotgun and my hunting bag near the fire pit. Then, when I heard you scream, I didn't bother to go back for it. If it was protection you needed, I had enough right here." He patted the revolver he wore under his vest. "Still, it wasn't the smartest thing I've ever done."

"I don't understand. Why didn't you shoot off the revolver then?"

"I don't have much ammunition left. I figure it's better saved for emergency purposes."

Shrugging out of his arms, Chloe looked around her in disbelief. "This doesn't constitute an emergency?"

"Not when you consider we could be days out here without food and need the ammo to hunt. Or..." He eyed her steadily. "...to keep us safe."

"I see." She spoke in a tone that belied her words and stared everywhere but at him.

"Chloe, look at me." She shook her head in refusal.

Stubborn woman.

"Fine then. Don't. But know this; we're going to be fine. I promise. I've survived much worse situations than this. And remember, they found Caleb and Monique last night. He's not going to stop until he finds you. And then there's Rudy and his prayers. I'm certain those prayers, and ours, are going to sustain us."

Instead of answering, Chloe giggled.

Ben lifted a brow, puzzled. A head injury? Was she hysterical?

"Chloe?" Still sitting beside her on the ground, he put a questioning hand on her elbow. She stopped giggling and turned to him.

"I guess I was lucky you didn't throw me off the train that first day. I really thought you would. I was glad you didn't. This was really important to me. Only now, now I'm not so sure it was worth it." Tears pooled in her eyes, and she dashed at them with the backs of her hands. "You know this is my fault All of it. If I hadn't been so bull-headed, none of this would have happened. I deserve to be down here. But you..." She broke off as she looked up into his eyes. "You, Ben, you don't deserve this."

There was such sorrow etched on her face, Ben could hardly bear to see it. He pulled her tight against his chest and murmured in her ear, "Don't blame yourself. It's no one's fault."

After a moment of resting her head against him, not speaking, Chloe pushed out of his arms. He wanted to pull her back, tighten his arms around her, but he didn't.

"What do we do now?"

"I don't know, sweetheart. I just don't know." The endearment slipped out before he realized it. Ben wished he could call it back, wished Chloe hadn't noticed. But she had. Her eyes widened ever so slightly. He swallowed, hard.

Chloe's stomach chose that moment to grumble, and she laughed nervously. Even though a touch of scarlet blossomed on her cheeks, Ben couldn't help but laugh too. Not to embarrass or tease her, instead it was a release of all the pent-up emotions he'd dealt with through the night.

"Ben?" Her voice was questioning, hushed.

Did that mean she felt it too? This feeling that had started with a spark of interest when he'd first laid eyes on her?

He was going to kiss her. There wasn't a doubt in his mind as he leaned closer to her. He was going to kiss Chloe, and there was no stopping it.

Until he noticed the look of pure astonishment on her face and realized she wasn't even looking at him.

"Look." Her whisper was hushed wonderment. She pointed at something behind him that he couldn't see, something down the hillside.

Ben found it difficult to tear his gaze from Chloe's face, but he did angle to his left and followed the direction of her finger.

Too far away to be seen distinctly, a large dark figure stood in the shadow of the Douglas firs. Ben's first guess would be a grizzly. He squinted to try and get a better look. It certainly wasn't a man. It was much too tall. But whoever or whatever it was, the color was all wrong for a grizzly. Instead of a rusty, golden brown, this creature was dark, almost black. *Jacko? Could it really be?*

"Is it...?" Chloe was breathless.

"I don't know yet." Ben jumped to his feet, trying to still the hammering in his chest. Man, grizzly, creature, he didn't know. Nor would he get his hopes up. He knew better than to second-guess nature and her creatures. But that didn't still his growing excitement.

Never taking his eyes off it, Ben rummaged through several of his vest pockets before finally finding his field glasses. He put them to his eyes, but they were out of focus. A glint of morning sunlight caught the lenses as he tried to bring them into focus.

It must have alerted the being to their presence, because without a moment's hesitation, the creature, if it really was a creature, ducked into the woods.

Chloe let out a painful sounding breath, as if she'd been holding it the entire time.

"Could you see it?"

"Not clearly enough. He—it—left before I could get the lenses into focus."

"Well then, we'll just have to sit here and watch until he—or it—reappears."

Sit and watch? Chloe sounded optimistic the creature would return. Not Ben.

His first instinct was to scramble down the cliff-side and run pell-mell into the woods right behind it. Of course that was neither logical nor feasible. He had Chloe and her injuries to consider.

The funny little quirk of her mouth reminded him of his earlier desire to kiss her. The desire was still there, heightened by what he hoped they'd just seen. Never taking his eyes off her, Ben sat back down.

Suddenly he was optimistic too, filled with enthusiasm for more than just chasing after a supposed Sasquatch. He looked at Chloe and leaned back against the cold, hard granite mountainside. He'd sit up here with her for a while and listen for sounds of Gus and the others searching for them. They could pray, eat whatever they could find in her carry-all, and just see what would happen next.

Kisses?

Jacko's cousins?

A newfound faith in God?

Life was full of surprises, and Ben intended to savor each one.

Chloe couldn't recall a time in her life where she'd ever been so sore. It was like—well, like she fell off a mountain. Every bone and muscle ached. Even her eyelashes hurt. Of course, there wasn't a chance in blazes that she'd say anything about it to Ben. Not one chance. If it was stupid, stubborn pride, so be it. Ben wouldn't know a thing about her pain. It would only feed that crazy notion of his that women belonged at home. Besides, she'd seen genuine concern in his eyes earlier. She didn't want to worry him.

After taking a short amount of time to eat some dried jerky and a tin of the plum pudding from Chloe's pack, they called for Caleb and the others for what seemed like hours. In reality, though, it had probably been less than one. Time crawled along, most certainly due to the painful twinge in her bladder. There wasn't a tree or bush in sight, at least not one that didn't involve climbing the cliff. Up or down, neither was an option she wanted to consider right now. Her stomach churned at the very thought, and she quickly decided to do her best to concentrate on other matters—like getting someone to answer their calls.

"Caleb!" She screamed so loud it caused her throat to burn. "I wish we could just use the gun to fire off a shot."

"I have a feeling that if they were anywhere nearby, we would have heard *them* calling for *us*. I'm sure they want to find us just as much as we want to be found."

"You're right." Chloe's throat was so raw she sounded like a bullfrog. "They've probably gone off in another direction."

Ben nodded. "If they had found the shotgun and my supplies, they'd have surely headed this direction by now. You sound pretty bad. Why don't you rest your throat and have a drink?"

He fumbled in her pack for the canteen, watching her all the while. He looked almost tender, and yet, there was something else. It was almost as if he wanted to devour her. Her pulse quickened. She wished he'd quit looking at her like that.

"Here you go." He uncapped the canteen and tenderly placed it in her hands. "Drink."

This was the Ben she'd imagined that first night she'd listened to him sing, the Ben she'd caught only occasional glimpses of since then. He tried so very hard to hide it, but he was such a gentleman, and so protective. If she didn't watch out, her heart could—

No, don't think like that. She let the cool water wash down her parched throat, as if washing away thoughts of something that could never be. She couldn't take her eyes off the goal. Not for one minute, not even for someone like Ben.

The article on the Sasquatch, and the path it would pave for her, dangled before her. She stood on the threshold of a promising future, no matter what her father thought.

And Ben...well, he had his life and she had hers. The two didn't mesh. They never would, and she'd best be forgetting his gorgeous eyes and heart-stopping voice. When they were back in Cedar Ridge, Ben would go off on his search for the snow gorilla, and she'd write her Sasquatch article. And even if things changed in her journalism career, if she managed to attain the same status as Nellie Bly, everything else in her humdrum life would be the same.

Everything except her heart. Her heart would be changed forever, and she had the awful feeling it wouldn't be for the better.

No, a hollow empty heart was something she could do without.

Chloe handed the canteen to Ben. He tilted his head back to drink, and she watched as a drop of water trickled off his chin and down his throat. She closed her eyes for a brief moment, fighting her attraction to him. When she opened them again, he was wiping his chin with the back of his hand.

"Here you go." He handed her the canteen again.

"But you only took one drink."

"Put it back in your bag. We don't want to deplete the supply since we don't really know how long it'll be before we can replenish it."

He stared at the trees below, perhaps searching for a creek. Chloe wasn't sure. But finally she could stand the silence no longer.

"We have to go down, don't we?"

Ben nodded. "If you're feeling up to it, we have to do something. They haven't heard us yet. Chances are they won't. I don't know how much longer we can stay here. And I don't think you want to try and climb back up."

Chloe turned and looked again at the steep, sheer wall of rock that towered behind her. That Ben had been able to reach her was nothing short of a miracle. The thought of trying to climb it made her almost physically sick. But then, so did the thought of going down from here. To go back up, though, would be nearly impossible. However, from what she could tell, there appeared to be enough jutting earth on the way down to get a good hand and foothold.

It truly was a miracle she'd survived the fall. "Thank you, God."

"Amen."

Chloe looked at Ben in surprise then realized she'd spoken her thanks aloud. Her lips twitched before breaking into a smile. "Rudy," she said simply.

Ben nodded and pointed at the Bible still sitting next to their belongings. "He's been quite the influence on me as well."

In spite of their precarious situation, Chloe couldn't help but smile. The sight of Rudy's Bible filled her with hope. God was with them. He protected her during the fall. They would be all right.

"Once we're down, I don't how long it'll take us to get back to the camp. Assuming they stay where we left them. There's so much terrain and so many different trails, it could take a couple of days to find the right one. We have to find food, water, and maybe even shelter if we can't reach them by evening."

"You really don't think they'll find us here?"

Ben pressed his lips together. "They haven't so far." He pointed toward the sky. "It was a long drop. And either they didn't come this far to look for us, or they can't hear us." He shrugged. "I don't know."

Chloe hadn't realized they were so bad off. Spending another night out here, separated from the others? Being alone with Ben wasn't a distasteful prospect, not in the least. But what if they never found their way back?

As if he read her mind, Ben reached out to touch her cheek in a gentle gesture. She closed her eyes and leaned her face against his hand.

"Chloe, sweetheart." His whispered words brushed softly against her ear. "Try not to worry so much. We'll be fine. And they've found Caleb and Monique. It won't be long before you see him again. Maybe even today. No. You know what? It *will* be today."

He called her sweetheart again. Did he mean it, or was it an endearment he used loosely? It didn't matter, because however she fought it, her bones turned to mush.

"I'll let you decide when you're feeling up to it."

Chloe nodded.

"So..." She peered over the edge, fighting a wave of dizziness.

They had to do something, and they had to do it soon. The pain in her bladder was growing too sharp to ignore.

"Well then." Her voice rang oddly in her ears, high, unnatural. "Now is as good a time as any. I guess we'd better get started."

Ben nodded and took her hand. He squeezed it, as if to confirm she'd made a wise choice, and gazed into her eyes. Chloe searched his face and found what she sought—strength, warmth, and the assurance that they would be fine. There was something more too, a spark flickering deep in his eyes, and her heart longed to explore it.

Chloe tore her hand from Ben's and turned away, angry with herself. She had to get a firmer hold on her feelings. She dug her hand in the pocket of her trousers and gripped Aunt Jane's watch. Pulling it out, she was relieved to see it survived the fall intact.

"Chloe?" Soft, deep, Ben's voice washed over her, heightening her sense. He gently took her by the shoulders and turned her to face him. With a soft touch, he tilted her chin so she would look at him.

"I'll be fine." Though she said it, did she really believe it? Not really. But one thing she did believe. In that moment, as Ben stood there cupping her chin in the palm of his hand, stroking stray hairs out of her eyes, everything between them changed. It was much too late for her heart to forget she'd ever known Benjamin Christopher Kearny.

Swallowing hard, she looked him in the eye and then at their destination below.

"Whenever you're ready." Her words came out in a croak. An air pocket clogged her throat, making breathing painful. "But you go first."

Ben took one step toward the first jutting rock then stopped. He turned to Chloe.

"Here. Give me your things."

After rubbing her fingers over the watch once more, she held it up. "First I want to tuck this safely in my bag." After carefully wrapping it within the layers of her clothing, she held her bag out to Ben. "You take the pack, and I'll sling the sleeping bag over my shoulder. That way neither one of us will be loaded down."

"Fair enough." His smile was soothing, gentle. "Do you still want me to go first?"

"Yes." She nodded emphatically. Still looking at her, Ben took his first cautious step.

"Oh, wait." He scrambled up to stand beside her again. "Give me a piece of paper out of your journal. We should write a note to the others in case they come this way."

"Oh. Good idea." Chloe dug into her bag once more, and tore a sheet of paper from the pages of her journal. It took her another second to find the pencil, and she handed both to Ben. She watched while he quickly scribbled the note then asked, "What are we going to do with it? They won't know to look down here."

"I'm going to put it in this." He reached down and stuck the note into the empty pudding tin, leaving enough of the paper to be noticed if someone saw it on the ground. "Now stand back." Ben wound his arm in a circle just like Kid Nichols of the Boston Beaneaters and hurled the tin up the side of the cliff. It only went three-fourths of the way before it bounced back down.

"Quick, catch it." The can rolled toward the ledge. They both made a quick scramble, and Ben rescued it before it went over the side. He threw it again. This time the tin disappeared from sight.

"Great throw. And great idea." Chloe heard it hit against something. "When the others come along, they'll be sure to recognize the can and know to wait for us to double back."

"Right. Now let me get a ways ahead of you before you come down. Aside from the rocks that might come tumbling down, I wouldn't want you stepping on my head or anything."

Chloe smiled. Funny that he could keep a sense of humor at a time like this. It helped. Yes, something had definitely changed between them. Something she liked way too much for her own good.

The wary, edgy, and apprehensive feelings that had been replaced with her excitement over the note quickly returned to churn in her stomach. Her nervousness over scaling the cliff-side only increased the urgency in her bladder. She had to get down the mountainside fast, yet she had to go slowly enough that she didn't fall and kill herself. She might not be so lucky a second time.

Ben inched down the mountain face excruciatingly slow. He had to go slow for Chloe's sake. Though she wouldn't admit to very much, he knew she had plenty of aches and pains from her fall. Her fall was his fault. If he'd only thrown her off the train when he'd had the chance, she wouldn't be in this predicament. He thought again of Rosalie.

Women shouldn't be exposed to such dangers. They belonged at home, where it was warm and safe, doing women's stuff like cooking and knitting. Not falling off cliffs, risking life and limb for the sake of a newspaper article.

He looked up at Chloe, amazed that she was doing as well as she was. She never complained. Funny, when he first met her, he figured her for the whining and complaining type like Monique. "How are you doing up there?"

"I'm doing fine as long as I don't look down."

He smiled at that. No matter her circumstances, he knew Chloe would always search deep within herself until she found something good to hang on to. No matter what happened, she'd be fine.

The first thing he did when he made it to the bottom was to watch until Chloe was within arm's length. Then he put his hands around her tiny waist and lifted her down.

She turned in his arms and rested her head against his chest, breathing heavily. The frantic beat of her heart vibrated through his senses.

"We're down." She leaned against him while she caught her breath, and he buried his face in his hair. "Thank goodness."

"You smell like a flower garden," he commented. "Or a girl from gay Paree."

"Monique's soap. Roses." She muttered something else, but not loud enough to be heard. He thought all women liked roses. Of course Chloe wasn't like all women—a thought he had way too often lately.

"I always thought Monique smelled a little too prissy to go out in the wilderness. Now she's got you smelling the same way."

With an indignant *hmph*, Chloe pulled out of his arms.

"I'm not complaining." Ben drew her close again. "Just teasing. If I didn't think you smelled good, I wouldn't have held you all night, remember?"

Chloe shrugged out of his arms. "I've got my breath back now." She disappeared like a lightning bolt behind the nearest clump of bushes.

Ben took the opportunity to study his surroundings, heavily wooded Douglas firs, cedars, larch trees, and the mountain they'd just descended. He turned and studied the line of the mountain, and a sinking feeling overtook him. There was no way back up as far as he could see. No path, no trail up the mountain. It was sheer rock in either direction.

"Oh, no." Chloe gasped when she returned and saw him staring at the wall that seemed to go on forever. "What are we going to do?"

"I don't know." It was a definite predicament. Ben had a sinking feeling, because he knew that what he wanted to do and what was best for Chloe were in total opposition. He *wanted* to head through the trees in search of whomever, or *whatever*, they'd seen while they were still up on the ridge.

"The terrain on the mountain is bound to change sooner or later. Our best bet is to follow it around until it does." As he spoke, he saw Jacko's cousins and his dream of discovery slip away.

Chloe nodded, but she didn't look too sure. "What about the others? How will they find us?"

"Don't worry." He tried to assure her as well as himself as he pulled his compass from his pocket. After finding true north, he determined the direction they would head. North-by-northwest. "Once we find a path back up the mountain, we'll head southeast and it'll bring us back to this very spot." He tilted his head toward the rocks above. "Only up there."

"I'm so glad you thought to leave that note."

"With any luck, they'll be sitting there waiting for us when we return."

"I hope you're right."

So do I. Ben took a deep breath and prepared to lead her in the opposite direction from his dream. His first responsibility was to get Chloe up the mountain then see her safely home with her brother.

Then he'd come back.

Alone.

And with any luck at all, the Sasquatch would still be here when he returned.

"What is wrong with you?" They'd walked a couple of miles through a dense thicket of fir and cedar, and Ben's tone was grouchy.

"Wrong? What makes you think something is wrong?" Was she walking too slowly? She'd been concentrating on trying to ignore the itchiness that had been driving her crazy almost since she woke up after her fall. Because of all the commotion after she'd bathed with Monique's soap last night, she never had time to dwell on it or go back and wash off. Now, it seemed the more time passed, the more irritated she grew. She'd been doing her level best to keep him from knowing. And truth be told, the itching was worse than her sore muscles.

"You're scratching like a dog with one too many fleas."

So he'd noticed. And he mentioned it so gentlemanly. "One flea is one too many."

"Well?" He glanced over at her, and her heart did a flip-flop. "Do you have fleas or don't you?"

"No." She laughed. "I don't have fleas. It's the soap. Ever since I washed with it, I've fantasized about water. You would probably say it's necessary to hydrate our bodies."

"Your assessment of me is correct. That's exactly what we need the water for. However, I wouldn't mind exploring this little fantasy of yours." He raised one eyebrow and grinned.

Chloe ignored her racing pulse, as well as his comment. "I need it to get this soap off of me. It's plain making me crazy. I think I'd rather choke to death from lack of water, than scratch my skin raw."

Truth to tell, her physical discomfort—pain included—had almost veered her thoughts away from her guilt. True, Ben had said the incident wasn't her fault, but she knew that if she'd only listened harder and not been so quick to jump to conclusions, none of this would have happened. A good reporter never jumped to conclusions. They searched out all of the facts, no matter their personal feelings.

The facts.

Each and every time.

More than anything she wished to be back up mountain, tolerating Monique's questions about Caleb. A friend, she'd said with those hurt eyes. All Monique had wanted was for Chloe to be her friend. Ironic, really, when one considered that all Chloe had wanted for as long as she could remember was a friend.

Forgive me, Lord. And please give me the chance to make it right.

Her cheeks burned with shame. She'd given no thought to matters of safety when they'd embarked on this journey. The only thing that mattered was the story. Never mind family relationships, safety matters, hurting other people's feelings. The story was the most important thing, and this was going to be a good one.

Not anymore. Chloe no longer believed it. If only she hadn't been so short sighted, so focused on her goals to the point of ignoring all else. Chloe sighed in self-disgust.

"There's something else wrong, isn't there? Something besides your itchy skin?"

A few steps ahead of her, Ben stopped and turned to stare at her.

"No. Why would you think that?"

His tender smile caused her stomach to flutter. "Aside from the fact that you're trudging along at a slug's pace, your heavy-hearted sigh might be a good indication. Your pain must be worse than you've let on. Maybe we should stop and rest."

"No." She was quick to assure him. "I'm not in much pain. You're right about there being something else, but I really don't want to talk about it."

"All right." He shrugged and looked at his compass. The compass that he'd use to lead them back to the others. And Caleb. She closed her eyes. *Dear God, please let Caleb forgive me.*

No matter her personal feelings of disgrace, she couldn't show weakness to Ben. She'd done enough damage already. She opened her eyes to find him staring at her. He quirked one brow, and the corners of his lips twitched.

"You'd rather brood?" There was no mistaking the amusement in his tone.

"Yeah." She nodded then looked at the ground, waiting for Ben to start walking again.

He didn't.

After an uncomfortable pause, Chloe looked up to find Ben still staring.

"What?" She was unable to keep a slight giggle out of her voice.

"Brooding isn't good for you. It eats you up inside and blinds you to your surroundings. As I recall, you recently went over a cliff. Maybe if you talked about it, we can prevent that from happening again."

Ben looked as though he was trying very hard to be serious. Chloe lips tugged upward. It was nice they were talking. They'd developed a comfortable rapport after she'd awakened on the ledge, and Chloe found it easier to talk with Ben than with anyone else—with the exception of Caleb.

A fresh wave of pain rippled through her, and she knew she was dangerously close to tears.

No. Chloe shook her head trying to shake off her fear and sadness.

Ben took a step closer, and before she was even aware of his intent, he gathered her in his arms.

"I know you're worried about whether we'll get back." Ben tightened one arm around her waist and the other across her shoulders. Her face pressed against the warmth of his chest, and she inhaled the piney, outdoorsy scent clinging to him. She could get entirely too comfortable in his arms.

Instinctively, she attempted to pull away. But Ben held her tight and rested his face against the top of her head.

"It'll be all right." Ben murmured in soothing tones. "I promise."

"I know." Chloe's throat was painfully tight. "It's not just that. It's Caleb. He was so angry at me. First my father, and now him. I'm alone. More alone than I've ever been."

As soon as she mentioned her father, Chloe knew she'd made a mistake. Ben's body went rigid, and she knew he would ask her about it even though it was a subject she'd rather not discuss.

"Caleb will get over it." He smoothed his cheek against the top of her head.

Surprised when he didn't mention her father, Chloe tilted her head and searched Ben's face. His smile was gentle and his eyes sincere.

"I don't think so." The thought of her brother never forgiving her was way too painful to consider.

"Caleb's thinking with his, uh... affections. As soon as reality takes hold, he'll realize you care about him."

"His *affections*, huh?" She tried to smile, knowing exactly what Ben was talking about, and hoped he was right that Caleb would come to his senses.

"Now, what's this about your father? What happened with him?"

Ben's eyes searched hers, and she looked away, content to rest her head against his chest once more. He was so strong, yet so gentle. She fit against him as if it were meant to be, and though it was a betrayal to her earlier self-lecture, Chloe knew she would gladly stay this way forever.

"It's a long story. I'm not sure where to start."

"With the beginning."

With shaky emotions, she drew a deep breath and pulled away from him. She could only pray, as she prepared to tell him about her father, that he didn't share his views.

Chapter Thirteen

Trying to tell Ben about the confrontation with her father was nearly as difficult as when she'd finally faced her father with the truth. Her stomach knotted up, and she couldn't quite get the first words out. Of course Ben staring at her with that unwavering green gaze, like he'd just discovered some woodland creature previously unknown to science, didn't help matters any.

"Stop," she said finally.

"Stop what?" Ben sounded puzzled, though he shouldn't be. Chloe was certain he knew exactly what he was doing to her.

"You know what." She rubbed her upper arms and turned away from him. "Staring. Quit looking at me. I can't talk to you about this if you keep staring at me like that."

She bit her lip, waiting for his response. It wasn't verbal. His touch was light on her shoulder, and Chloe caught her breath.

Still grasping her upper arms, she whirled around. "What!" As soon as she shouted, she was sorry. But stubborn pride wouldn't let her call the words back.

"If you've got your back to me, how can you know if I'm staring?"

Because I can feel your eyes burning into me.

"I just know." She was much too testy. She needed to get herself under control. "Look over at the hillside and I'll tell you."

"Only if you sit back-to-back with me." The teasing grin on Ben's face was impish and caught at her heart in such a way she was helpless to do anything but agree.

What a mistake. As Ben rubbed his back up against hers, his body heat wound through her and wreaked havoc with her concentration. This was no good. She scooted away.

"Hey." Ben's protest only disconcerted her further. "You're breaking your promise."

"We're still back-to-back. We don't have to be touching."

"My, my, my. If I didn't know better, I'd think you were a little disturbed. Maybe, uh, thinking with your *affections* like Caleb's been doing?"

"Fine," she snapped, then slapped her knees. "I won't tell you a thing."

"All right, I'll behave." Ben's tone was contrite now, and Chloe could just imagine the teasing gleam in his eyes turning tender. He was so gentle, so caring at times, it almost made her heart hurt.

"See?" he said, "I'm staring out at a gorgeous green hillside. My back is to you so I can't see your face, and I'm not touching you in any way, shape, or form. You remain undisturbed. Now tell me what happened with your father. Why do you hurt so badly when you mention him?"

The gentleness in his voice tore at her heart. She'd been doing fine in Ben's presence, feeling completely at ease. Too much so, really. If she let herself get too comfortable, it would be way too difficult to say good-bye when the time came. And it would come. No man like Ben would settle down in a dink-town like Cedar Ridge.

Now where had that thought come from? Ben settling in Cedar Ridge? Never. She'd best get thoughts like that out of her head right now.

"My father got angry at Caleb and me because we lied to him." The words weren't as hard to say as she thought, though they sliced through her with a cold hurt. "Remember that first day of the trip? The day Caleb was to meet you at the train?"

"How could I forget? In my point of view, you tricked me then proceeded to ruin my trip."

His simple words, though spoken without malice, filled her with guilt. Once again she was faced with the realization that it was her fault they were down here, lost from the others. She deserved every bump and bruise she'd suffered.

"We were late because we told our father the truth that day."

"I remember thinking you must have been crying. Your face was blotchy and your eyes were red."

Just the way she wanted Ben to think of her. Blotchy skin and red eyes.

"Yes." She closed her eyes with a sigh, unhappy to admit it. "I had been. Crying, I mean. I hate to cry, but it was so terrible. Suddenly we were homeless. Then you didn't want us either. It was an awful feeling. I think I fought with you so much about going because I was just as afraid of having nowhere to go as I was afraid of not getting the story."

The rumble of laughter that rose in Ben's chest brought fresh heat to Chloe's face.

"That's my Chloe. The story is always right up there with life's major events."

My Chloe? He'd said it, but did he mean it? Her stomach fluttered.

"I used to think it was something to be proud of, but not anymore."

"Don't be too hard on yourself, Chloe. As I read somewhere recently, He came to seek the lost. And once we're found, there's always room for grace and forgiveness." Rudy had said something similar when he handed her his Bible, and the thought curled around her heart.

As Chloe continued to tell him about the fight with her father, she found herself leaning against Ben's back the same way he'd tried leaning against hers. His strength and warmth surrounded her, and she found it easier to tell him about the argument with her father.

When she finally concluded her tale, she blinked back tears, determined not to show any further sign of weakness.

Though he still kept his back to her, Ben reached back for her hand. It was warm, comforting, and decidedly sensual.

"Chloe." His voice was a gentle rumble, and she closed her eyes, loving the sound, loving the way his words made her feel. "Like your brother, your father will come to his senses. He's just hurt because you lied to him, though I really don't see how you could have done things any other way."

"You don't?"

"True honesty is the best way to go, I'll never believe otherwise. I know for a fact what it's like to be lied to by someone you love. But in this case, I understand completely. You have a dream, and your father refused to let you fulfill it, no matter how good you are."

Stunned at what he said, Chloe leaned forward. As soon as she did, cool air rushed across her back, leaving her feeling empty. She scooted around to face Ben, and he did likewise, though she stared at the ground instead of his face. Feeling the way she did, she feared she might fall right into his arms.

"Once he thinks about things and realizes how valuable you are to him, he'll apologize."

"Do you really think so?" Though her heart leaped unexpectedly, she refused to hope.

"Yes." Ben nodded. "I'll bet by the time we get back to Cedar Ridge, he'll be waiting for you and Caleb with open arms."

"I hope you're right."

"I am." Ben spoke with certainty. "Your father won't be able to turn his back on you."

When Ben stopped speaking, Chloe looked up to see him staring into the treetops. A faraway expression touched his face, and she knew he was thinking about his own parents and how they'd abandoned him to Gus's care. She was about to say something when he shook his head slightly and glanced back to her.

"There's no way a father can just shut the door on his daughter. A son maybe." Chloe wondered at the bitterness in his tone. "But not a daughter. Especially not one who is so valuable an asset to his business."

"Valuable?" She hesitated. What did he mean by valuable?

"No doubt once he thinks about it, your father will realize how important you are to him. Not only as a daughter, but as a reporter."

"Oh, no." Chloe's laugh was harsh even to her own ears. "My father will never see me as a reporter. He's like you. He doesn't think women are good for anything but wiping dishes and scrubbing floors."

The edges of Ben's mouth twitched ever so slightly. "Did I say that? When did you ever hear me say anything like that?"

He sounded so incredulous, Chloe could only stare. He *had* said that, hadn't he? Now, looking at his unwavering stare, Chloe began second guessing her earlier impressions of Ben.

"What exactly did I say, Chloe?"

It was a challenge. She could hear it in his voice. A direct, unmistakable challenge.

"I—well—you said, um..." She flustered a moment before declaring, "You didn't want me along!"

He fixed her with an unwavering stare. "You're right. I didn't."

"Well!" She straightened her spine in indignation.

"Now wait a minute." Ben was quick to protest. "You've got it all wrong."

"Did you or did you not want me along?"

To Chloe, the expression flickering across his face made him seem almost regretful. "Well, no, I didn't, but—"

"Ah, ha!" Chloe leaped to her feet, remembering too late how badly her body hurt. "How can you sit there and tell me you don't think like my father when you've just admitted it?"

"I only said I didn't want a reporter on this trip. I didn't say women couldn't be good reporters. Look at Nellie Bly."

That he mentioned her hero, that he even knew who she was, gave Chloe hope. "If that's truly how you feel, why wouldn't you let me interview you before you left town?"

"Trouble." A spark lit Ben's green eyes, and his face hardened. "One interview with you, and reporters would be crawling all over this mountain. The entire project could have been in jeopardy."

"I don't understand."

"Of course you don't. You're one of them." Sarcasm laced the edges of his words. "Reporters only think of one thing. The story." The tone in his voice left her feeling ashamed.

Chloe wanted to deny it, but she couldn't. The story *was* the most important thing. She opened her mouth to say just that, but the look in Ben's eyes stopped her cold. The spark was gone, replaced by a deep wave of pain.

"Consequences are just as important as the story." His whisper was thick, pain-filled. "Reporters never stop to think about that."

Avery. This was about Avery and the headhunters. Prickles skittered across the back of Chloe's neck as she remembered the story Monique told her. Maybe if he talked about it, got his feelings out in the open, that lonely haunted look she caught glimpses of now and again would leave his beautiful eyes.

She reached out and touched his hand, and he swallowed hard.

"Why don't you tell me about it, Ben? It had to have been a horrible experience."

He jerked his hand from hers and stared, wide-eyed. "You know?"

Chloe nodded. "Monique told me."

"She did?" Ben appeared surprised. "I didn't think she'd ever admit to it. Maybe there's some hope for her after all."

Chloe was puzzled, but she didn't let on. Ben was beginning to open up, and that's what mattered.

"Since all I have is Monique's version, why don't you tell me from your perspective?"

"It was nothing. I don't want to discuss it."

"Nothing?" Chloe was incredulous. How could he say it was nothing when he so clearly carried it with him night and day?

Ben shook his head, his lips pressed together firmly. He was shutting down before her eyes. Chloe had a sudden desperate need to reach him and a sudden desperate fear that if she didn't, he'd be lost to her forever.

154

She reached for his hand again, this time lacing her fingers with his, hoping he wouldn't pull away. He didn't. The light pressure of his fingertips dancing on her knuckles sent waves of awareness skipping through her. He was warm and firm, strong, yet in need of comfort.

And she wanted to offer it to him.

She leaned closer to him, her eyes never leaving his.

"Why don't you talk about it, Ben? Admit how you feel?"

He glanced downward, his smoky lashes brushing the upper curves of his bronzed cheekbones. He tried to pull his hand from hers, but she held fast.

"Why are you so stubborn? If you would just talk about it, maybe that sad haunted look would leave your eyes once and for all."

When Ben looked up his expression was unreadable. But his pupils were wide, and Chloe's breath hitched.

Without warning, Ben grabbed her other hand and yanked her toward him. Caught off-guard, she lost her balance and fell into his lap, which knocked him off balance.

They landed in the most indelicate position, and it threatened to send Chloe's senses reeling out of control. She stared down at Ben, not sure whether to be shocked at her feelings or indulge them.

Reaching up, Ben cupped her face with strong, gentle hands and traced her cheekbones with his thumbs. Then he trailed one thumb down the side of her face until it found the corner of her mouth. He raised his head just enough to reach her lips with his.

It was a light kiss, feathery, quick. But it turned Chloe's insides to liquid and, instead of pushing away from Ben and sitting up as she should by all manner of propriety, her body acted of its own accord and melted against him.

The pounding of Ben's heart seemed to flow through her veins. She could feel it thumping against her ribs, vibrating its way to her own heart. The warm liquid feeling grew in intensity, and she caught her breath when Ben laced his fingers through her hair.

He meant to kiss her again.

The second kiss was neither light, nor feathery. It was demanding, hungry, deep, and soul shaking, and ended much too quickly for Chloe's liking.

Ben gently rolled Chloe to the ground at his side, his arms cradling her as he looked up at the sky. On her side, in his arms, she stared at him, barely able to breathe. His face was flushed, his eyes glimmered. He breathed as raggedly as she did. Chloe wondered if he, too, felt like he'd been transformed into a heart-pounding puddle.

"You want me to admit something?"

His words were as husky as Chloe was breathless, and she nodded. Had she been standing, Chloe most likely would have swooned.

"How about if I admit I've spent most of my time up here preoccupied? Dangerously so. And not with finding the Sasquatch. All I seem to be able to think about is how I want to spend my time kissing you senseless."

Certainly her cheeks must be glowing like a beacon. They burned hot enough. That Ben even thought about kissing her senseless left her knees feeling like jelly.

"You play with my senses. You distract me. And look where it got us."

"This is hardly your fault, Ben Kearny."

"It would never have happened if I'd have been paying better attention to the project instead of thinking about you."

Chloe's pulse did a crazy kind of dance, all the way to her heart. She had to clear her head. This kind of talk could very easily lead them to dangerous territory, a place she wasn't ready to go. Not now, not even with Ben. Especially now that she knew God as more than just an unseen entity. This was definitely not behavior God would approve of. She had to think of something else, had to change the subject and refocus her thoughts.

"Reporters, I understand. Me, I understand. But what about Monique? Why did you want her to leave?" The soft tenderness vanished from Ben's eyes, and Chloe wished she could call back the words.

"She hasn't been in the field for three years. She's out of shape and has always been lacking in her field skills. Gus sprang her on me at the last minute. He threatened not to come if I didn't give in. Rudy went along with his demand and said he wouldn't come either. I had no choice."

"So you didn't have time to find another team?"

"Right. Plus, Monique is getting over a broken heart. Not the best emotional condition to be in when your safety and the safety of those around you rely on good judgment."

Curiosity got the better of her and she had to ask. "Who broke her heart?"

"A fellow by the name of Avery." Ben's scowl was as ferocious as his tone of voice.

"Avery? But I thought he was dead."

"Dead?" Ben seemed surprised. "You know of him?"

"Only what Monique told me. He was killed by headhunters."

"Headhunters?" Ben laughed as if she'd told a joke.

"He wasn't?"

"No. I can't believe Monique..." He broke off and shook his head. "Yes, I can. She is so full of—"

"She told me you didn't want reporters along because of what happened with Avery."

"Avery has absolutely nothing to do with it, and neither do headhunters. He's alive and well, but he won't be when Gus catches up with him. He left Monique at the altar. He's nothing but a black-hearted scoundrel." Ben took her hand and stared into her eyes. "I really don't want to discuss it anymore."

Chloe swallowed hard and stared back, her gaze never wavering from his face.

"I didn't trust myself to keep you safe, and obviously I was right."

"No, Ben. No. This is my fault. I should have—"

"Shh." Ben brought the back of her hand to his lips and gently kissed it. Chloe gasped softly. She could have sworn the green in his eyes darkened with passion, the same passion that flamed to life within her.

"Never doubt your self-worth." He gazed at her with his deep green eyes, still holding her hand. "I feared I'd come to care for you. Which is exactly what's happened, and I'm glad." He gave her hand a squeeze, and she bit her lip, aching for him to kiss her again. She wanted his kiss so bad, she almost missed his words.

"Y-you are?"

His smile and nod of affirmation made her want to jump up and spin in a circle, but she forced herself to remain calm.

"So you really don't care that I'm a reporter?" She asked the question hesitantly.

"Care?" He took her hand and winked—a heart-flipping, mind-soaring wink. "I think it's wonderful that you're doing what your heart tells you."

Right then, Chloe's heart was telling her to let Ben in. She leaned close, and this time he did kiss her again.

Chloe allowed her heart to soar just a bit before common sense took over. She pushed Ben away. "Ben, we can't do this."

He looked dazed. "Why? What's wrong?"

"No respectable young woman goes around kissing men she barely knows. Especially not in the woods."

"I won't tell if you won't." His mouth formed an impish pout.

Much as she was tempted to trace it with her lips, Chloe shook her head. "That's not it, and you know it."

Ben pulled his arms from around her and pushed up on his elbows. He turned to her, his expression serious. "This certainly changes things then."

"What do you mean?"

"I mean..." The impish look was back. "I'll have to spend the rest of this trip making sure you know as much as you need to about me. By the time we get back to Cedar Ridge, you'll know everything there is to know about Benjamin Christopher Kearny—so you'll feel quite comfortable kissing him. In the woods, out of the woods, in the mountains, and out. Anytime, anywhere your heart desires."

When Ben stood up, Chloe noticed he looked right pleased with himself.

"We'll just see about that." Though she teased, her heart skittered with anticipation.

"This looks like a good place to stop and rest a while."

Ben halted and turned in time to see Chloe lean against a monstrous fir tree. Her face was pale, and a purple smudge stood out on the tender skin under her eyes. Ashamed, Ben realized they should have stopped to rest long ago. A glance at the sun told him they should have stopped to eat a couple of hours ago.

"I'm sorry, Chloe. I should have asked you sooner if you wanted to stop."

"Don't be sorry. I could have spoken up sooner if I wanted. I just need to rest a bit."

She dug through her bag and pulled out the canteen and Bible. She opened the canteen and held it out to him. "Drink?"

Ben took it from her and swallowed gratefully, forcing himself to stop lest he deplete what was left of their water supply. He handed it back to her. "Try to save some for later just in case we don't come across a creek or river for a while."

He watched as she took a drink before opening the Bible. "What are you reading?"

"I wanted to read back over the creation story. I've heard it before of course, but I never really considered the reality of it before. And after being up here, I don't know how anyone could look at these mountains and everything we've seen and not believe God created it. Not only that, but to me it speaks of His incredible love. I want to know Him more."

After what he'd experienced during the night while he prayed for Chloe, Ben wanted to know Him more as well. He sat across from Chloe and listened while she read aloud.

"And the Lord God made all kinds of trees grow out of the ground—trees that were pleasing to the eye and good for food."

Ben leaned against the tree, the warmth of Chloe's voice wrapping around him, and his eyes grew heavy. He could listen to her forever....

"Who is Jacko?"

The question startled him, and his eyes flew open. Where had she heard the name? Had he mentioned him at some point? Caught off-guard, Ben sat straighter and asked, "Where did you hear about Jacko?"

"Earlier, when we saw the creature from up on the ridge. You whispered his name."

"Jacko is a—was a baby Sasquatch. He was heralded across British Columbia by rail. Poked at, mocked." He told Chloe about the newspaper clipping his father sent and how it had fueled both his imagination and his lifelong desire to find the Sasquatch.

"I'm so sorry," she said when he'd finished. The compassion shining in her eyes seemed to come from deep within her soul. Ben reached over and squeezed her hand as she continued. "I didn't mean to hurt you by bringing up your father. Monique told me about your parents leaving you. I should have been more sensitive."

He should have figured. Monique never kept anything to herself. What else had she told Chloe?

Ben stood and reached out his hand to help her up. "If you're ready, we'd better get on our way."

If he spoke a little harsh, he was sorry. But he didn't say that to Chloe. He didn't want to open himself up to any further conversation about his parents.

Some wounds cut too deep.

Sometime late that afternoon, the sky darkened and rain began to fall. This time Chloe led the way, and at first Ben found himself entranced with the small drips of rain that formed speckles on her trousers. But that didn't last very long at all. Without the warmth of the sun, and with the wind blowing against his back, it wasn't long before Ben felt the chill right to his bones.

"I think we should find shelter and sit this one out."

Chloe stopped and turned to him. "Don't tell me you're afraid of a little rain?" Her smile was wide and bright, and it sparked the still warm memory of her lips against his.

"I was, um, thinking about you. I don't want you to get too uncomfortable." *And I want the chance to keep you warm.* As soon as he thought it, shame washed through him. His mind went back to the Bible and the scriptures Chloe read to him earlier. He knew God wanted him to be honorable in his thoughts and deeds. Right now he wasn't sure he could be that way where Chloe was concerned.

"I won't melt." She gave him a saucy tilt of her head. "Ben, I may not have lived in this part of the country long. But it's been plenty long enough to know that the weather will change in five minutes. Rest assured it won't be long before the sun will be out again."

With that, Chloe turned her back on him and began trekking onward up the path. Remembering his desire to be pleasing to God, Ben forced himself to keep stride with her so he wouldn't be tempted to go back to counting the rain-splattered speckles on her backside.

Surprisingly, she was right, and the sun did come out before long. That the weather changed frequently was a fact he should have known before embarking on this journey. He usually took such care to obtain details on the area he was planning to visit. This time, though, it was different. Since this wasn't a normal scientific venture, he'd been more caught up in the money aspect of finding the Sasquatch. What the money would mean to him for future projects, how the find would endear him to the trustees at the university, and the excitement of actually heading the project.

That the air in the Cascades was so damp was an unwelcome reality for Ben. He had been in plenty of mountains, plenty of jungles. He was used to flash rainfalls, wind, and foggy mist. But none of it had ever seeped into his bones the way it did up here. He wasn't sure whether to curse the mountains or love them. For now, with Chloe next to him on the trail, knowing her newfound enthusiasm for God's creation, he'd choose to love them.

Thinking about her impromptu teasing, his heart warmed. Every time she teased him, he saw the unmistakable proof that she was comfortable in his presence. The spirit and zeal for life that he'd noticed from the beginning were still there, but there was more. Her words flowed from her in that sassy manner that had him wanting to crush her against him.

With each step he took, Ben cursed himself a fool. Why had he gone and kissed her? Why had he given in to the temptation? Now he had to figure out how to keep his hands off her the rest of the way, as well as figure out how to tell her there was no way he was seeking a relationship. He knew better, he just didn't know what had gotten in to him.

His behavior only complicated matters, and he could actually see the wisdom in Rudy's teachings. Ben should have taken more care with his manner. Now Chloe would think he was interested in her. Truthfully, he was—hopelessly. But there was no chance it could be anything more than a flirtation. Three years ago he'd had what he thought would amount to a permanent relationship with Rosalie. It had ended in tragedy. He wasn't about to go down that road again. His battered heart couldn't bear any more bruises.

Though her rain-soaked clothing was an added irritant to her already itchy skin, the clammy feeling could not dampen Chloe's sprits. Nothing could. The injuries from her fall no longer seemed as painful. The intimacy with Ben, something she'd treasure forever, renewed her spirit. It gave her a joyful, zesty feeling, and she couldn't help but continue forward with a jaunty step.

Everything seemed right, and she knew that when they found their way back to the others, Caleb would be safe and he would forgive her. While she was thinking with the optimism Ben's very presence instilled in her, she also told herself her father would forgive her and maybe even give her her own column at the paper. *Please, God, let it be true.* Not the column part, but the forgiveness part. More than her own column in the paper, she wanted her father's forgiveness.

Ben's attitude when it had started raining brought a smile to her face. It appeared in this one thing at least, she had the upper hand. She'd finally shown him, by not giving in to his suggestion that they stop, that she was quite capable of being on this journey. Of course, it didn't mean she liked the rain and clammy clothes. It just meant she was determined to keep pressing on so Ben wouldn't think she was some silly goose looking for a lark. She was most relieved when the sun finally peeked back through the clouds, and hoped it wouldn't be much longer before her clothing dried out.

As the trail veered sharply to the left, and into the trees, she looked back, alarmed. "Ben, this is taking us the wrong direction. Away from the mountain."

"Don't worry. These mountains are full of switchbacks. I'm sure it'll swing back around eventually."

She nodded, reluctantly agreeing that he knew better than she. He had, after all, studied the map with Caleb. The sudden smile that lit his face had her curious though. What could he possibly be thinking about?

Men. It took so little to make them happy. Nothing like being lost in the woods to make them feel important.

Shrugging, Chloe went back to searching for signs of a river or creek so she could wash the traces of Monique's soap off her skin. Ben had assured her the amount of snow that accumulated in these mountains every year had to run off somewhere.

Besides, he'd said with a wink that had her wanting to smack him, he was beginning to take a cotton to roses.

Then it started. A slow resonating sound that touched every fiber of her being. A low pulsing sound that radiated her senses. Ben was humming. His sound washed over her, making her weak. She wanted to cover her ears, to block out the sound that stirred her so much, but she couldn't. Helpless to do anything but listen, Chloe let Ben's tune wash over her.

Like his voice, the sound of his hum was mesmerizing. Haunting. It was the same tune he sang that night at Trina's birthday party. His *lonely* song. At least that's what she dubbed it. It may have had a totally different meaning for him, but to Chloe it was a haunted lonely tune and it drew her heart toward his.

Perhaps because she was a full-grown woman who, until a few days ago, was still living with her parents? That wasn't the total reason. Truthfully, old maid or no, she was just as lonely as Ben looked and sounded whenever he sang or hummed that song or any other.

She turned back, wondering if his eyes would reveal his true feelings. He smiled and held his hand out to her. She took it gladly and studied his eyes. She may have detected a hint of loneliness there, but she wasn't entirely sure. No matter. She'd happily fill the void for him.

As they walked and Ben hummed, she was struck once again with the disturbing realization that when they found the Sasquatch it would all come to an end. He would go on his way, and she would go back to Cedar Ridge with her big story. She tried to force the unpleasant thought out of her mind so she could enjoy trudging along next to this man, listening to the low, melodious rumble as he hummed his tune.

Because, for perhaps the first time in her life, the thought of getting *the* story didn't excite her as it usually did.

"Listen." Ben stopped in his tracks. After slogging up the path for half the afternoon, searching for a sign that it would swing back toward the mountain, Chloe was glad for the respite, however short it might be.

She held her breath, listening, concentrating, though it was extremely hard to do given that all she wanted to think about was Ben. Ever since he'd come to her rescue, he'd gone out of his way to comfort and assure her that things would be fine. Both his tone and general attitude toward her had softened, and it was obvious he was attracted to her. And the feeling was mutual. She really had to be careful not to allow temptation to get the better of her. Here, away from other people, it would be way too easy to compromise herself. Her reputation, such as it was, most likely was ruined, but acting on her feelings still wouldn't be right in the eyes of God. And something about her talks with Rudy, and then reading from the Bible he'd given her, made her want to be pleasing to God.

"Are you listening?"

"Listening?" She really needed to stop thinking about him. "Oh, yes. What am I listening for?"

"What are you thinking so hard about that you've forgotten to listen to your surroundings?"

"Nothing important." Embarrassed, she didn't allow herself to meet Ben's eye. Her dastardly conscious called her a liar.

Then she heard it. The unmistakable rush. Water.

She clapped her hands together and ran toward the sound. Finally, she could get some relief for her itchy skin.

"This way." Certain he was behind her, she kept running.

When she saw it, she stopped and stared, only vaguely aware that Ben had caught up to her and now stood at her side. An entire creek thundered toward her in a downward race to the bottom of the mountain. Fresh water.

"Oh glorious day." She stared at the beautiful sight. Then, without giving it another thought, Chloe plopped herself down on the bank and pulled off her boots.

"What are you doing?"

"I'm going to take a bath, silly. What do you think?" She dug around in her carry-all for her lemon-scented bar of soap. "I'm itching to death, not to mention the fact that you've been riling me about smelling like a silly flower. Don't you think it's time I did something about it?" She finally grasped the soap and pulled it out of the pack. "There. I think you'd better just disappear now. Go on. Turn around. Go look for some more tracks or something."

"Chloe, the sun's going down. It's not very warm. I really don't think—"

"Never mind what you think. I'm getting in that creek even if it decides to snow. Now go away!"

"Confounded bossy woman." He muttered so low, he most likely hadn't intended for Chloe to hear.

But she had.

Feeling triumphant, she pulled a towel from her bag and removed her socks. "Why don't you go set up camp? If you're worried about me getting cold, you can go start a fire. I'll be along in a bit."

She saw the corners of his mouth twitch, and she wanted to reach up and pop him in the jaw.

"Chloe, the creek is cold. Extremely. It's snow runoff from the mountains."

"I know that." She hated that she snapped at him. But honestly, didn't he think she knew anything? "I'm not going to luxuriate, just soothe my skin and wash with something that won't make me itch." She turned her back to him and reached up to unbutton her shirt.

Turning to look over her shoulder, she watched until he walked away. Then she stuck one toe in the water and bit back a scream.

Steeling her nerves, she took a deep breath.

She wasn't about to give Ben the satisfaction of knowing he was right.

Chapter Fourteen

The air was cold as Chloe pulled off her shirt. Goose flesh gathered on her arms and the back of her neck, sending shivers all through her. She wasn't surprised to find her arms and chest covered in a red rash, which only made her more determined to rid her skin of the itchy rose-scented residue. With her mind made up, and despite the cold, she aimed her feet toward the creek.

When her toes came in contact with the icy water, she shrieked and jumped backward, wondering if clean was worth it. She thought of Ben's piercing green eyes, of his haunting voice, of the kisses they'd shared.

How could he possibly be attracted to a woman who continually scratched at her arms and itched her nose? Is that how she wanted him to remember her when this was all over?

Over. A sharp pang sliced through her at the raw truth. It would be over eventually, and she would have to hold her chin up and accept it. Determined to leave Ben with a good impression of her, Chloe took a deep breath and plunged herself into the icy water.

In a matter of seconds she was chilled to the bone and had a difficult time hanging on to the soap. The water was too cold to waste time, so it was a quick scrub at best. Chloe dressed as fast as her numb fingers would allow, satisfied that she no longer smelled of roses and praying the itchiness would soon depart. She wrapped the soap in her towel and stumbled back to camp, relieved that Ben had indeed built a fire. Good. That meant she could tumble right into her sleeping bag and get warm. Her feet were numb as well as her hands, and she tripped over a rock. She would have lost her balance if Ben hadn't reached out and caught her.

"I've got you, Chloe." His voice flowed over her, with a warm smoothness she ached to reach out and touch. "My goodness, you're colder than I feared." He held her close with one arm while using his other to bundled her in her down-filled hunting jacket.

Chloe leaned against him as she stumbled toward her sleeping bag. She stared at it and shivered, not quite ready for a night on the cold, hard ground.

"Here, drink this." Ben crouched before her after she sat down and pressed a cup of hot liquid in her hands once she was settled. "I made some nettle tea while you were gone. I figured you'd be cold, but not this bad. I'm glad I made it."

"Me, too." She hated the way her teeth chattered. Ben helped guide the cup to her lips, and Chloe took a grateful sip.

"Thank you." She resisted the urge to make a face. Nettle tea would most definitely never become her favorite.

"Um, Chloe..." He sounded nervous and when he cleared his throat, she looked up.

Chloe shrieked and leaned back when she realized he was reaching toward her shirt buttons. "What are you doing?"

Ben jumped with a guilty start and dropped his hands to his lap. "Sorry." He sounded embarrassed.

"Sorry?" He tried to unbutton her shirt and now he was sorry? "What kind of man are you? What were you thinking?" Her voice rose to a shout. "Were you trying to take advantage of me while I'm freezing?"

"No, Chloe, that was never my intent."

"What then?"

Though he cleared his throat again, his whisper was still husky. "Your hands must have been so cold when you were dressing. You, um...."

The last thing Chloe ever expected from Ben was for him to flush and look away. Then his words struck her with startling clarity. *Hands, cold, dressing.*

"Oh my goodness." Looking down at her front, she gasped, and her face burned. Her shirt gaped open, exposing her chemise and the bare skin above. She dropped the cup of tea and quickly did up the buttons.

"Why didn't you tell me, Ben?"

He looked up, his cheeks still red. "I didn't want to embarrass you."

"Well, what do you think you just did? Aside from scaring me, that is?"

"I'm sorry. I just wanted to help." He seemed so earnest and an unexplained—though not unpleasant—sensation tugged at her heart.

"I know. I'm sorry, too. I overreacted and shouldn't have."

Instead of meeting her eye, he reached for the cup of spilled tea. "Can I get you some more?"

"No," she said quickly. Perhaps too quickly. She didn't want to hurt his feelings, didn't want him to know she couldn't stand the dirty, earthy taste of nettle tea. "I'm feeling much better now."

"You are?"

"Yes." Her teeth chattered at the same moment she spoke. "Oops. I guess maybe I'm still a little cold, but not much."

"Let me see if I can help warm you up." Ben's voice was lower than usual, and it didn't take Chloe but a second to guess his intent.

The kiss was so light, so quick, if it hadn't warmed her right to the toes Chloe would have wondered if it really happened. She gazed up at him, aching to be kissed again, even though her better judgment warned her against it.

Ben must have read something in her face because he sat beside her on the sleeping bag and drew her into his arms just before his lips claimed hers.

"Now that you're finally warm," Ben murmured against Chloe's mouth, "I'll set about making supper." He released her and pulled away, though he continued to stare with contentment shining in his green eyes.

Chloe flushed under his gaze. "I'm not hungry." But she was definitely warm.

"You're sure?"

"Yes. I just want to go to sleep. I'm too tired to wait for supper."

Not that I'd be able to eat a bite anyway. She was too worried about her feelings toward Ben. They'd been sparking from the moment she laid eyes on him. Sparking, and now igniting. What worried her was the possibility that they might burst into flame, and she definitely wasn't ready for that to happen.

Part of her longed to explore her feelings, but there was no logic in it. As long as she planned a career in the newspaper business, there could be no man in her life, so she might as well not even dwell on any possible feelings she may have for Ben. Even though he claimed the opposite, she knew men wanted to banish their women to everyday drudgery. *Don't think, don't talk, just cook, clean, and make babies.* A pain, swift and sharp, cut through her at the thought of babies. The feeling surprised her, caught her off-guard. She always told herself she wasn't about to be subjected to that, but for perhaps the first time in her life she realized how wonderful it would be to hold a baby. To guide and nurture another human being, to love unconditionally and receive that same love back.

Tears burned beneath her eyelids and tickled at her nose. *Oh, dear Lord, why does it have to be this way? Isn't there a way to fulfill my dream and still be a wife and mother?*

Eyeing Ben as he prepared his own supper, she wondered if he was really as antiquated as her father. Had he been telling the truth? He'd said he hadn't wanted her here because she'd be a distraction to his concentration. But there, too, was an example of women being good only for serving a man's needs. She hardly thought his underlying motive for being attracted to her was due to her sterling conversation. Nor was it for her brains. He really was like her father. Just the thought had her disloyal heart skipping a beat.

Then another thought struck her. Ben had said Monique hadn't been on a hunt in a few of years, which meant she'd been before. Could that mean there might be hope that Ben would accept Chloe's presence on another trip?

"...so I guess I'll just lean against this tree trunk."

"Huh?" Chloe looked up to find Ben waiting for a response. And she hadn't heard a word he'd said. "Sorry. I guess I wasn't paying attention."

"I said since I don't have bedding of any sort, I'll just lean against this tree trunk and hope to get a good night's sleep."

Oh, that's right. Chloe had completely forgotten Ben left most of his belongings back at the fire pit when he went looking for her. This would never do. He would freeze if he was left to sleep without covers. It might be warm enough in the daytime, but as soon as the sun went down in the mountains, it was downright cold.

"I'll stay pretty warm here, I think." He wrapped his arms around himself as he said it.

Chloe thought she detected a bit of self-pity in his tone, and she bit back a smile.

"Somehow I doubt it. But don't think you're going to climb in with me. You can use this." She indicated the sheepskin liner that she had yet to fasten back into her sleeping bag.

"Thank you." Ben's hand brushed hers when he took the liner. When he flashed her one of his devastating smiles, something she'd thought about earlier that day flashed into her mind. A dread feeling built up within her, along with the knowledge that she'd be spending the night alone with Ben.

True, she'd spent last night alone with him. But that was different. She was injured and totally unaware of his presence. Tonight she was much more than aware, and it had nothing to do with propriety. Who cared about that at this point? It wouldn't do any good because any reputation she might have had was certainly ruined by now.

After climbing into her sleeping bag, she took her time fastening each tie—all the while trying to focus on her task rather than Ben's smile, his voice, his touch, their shared kisses, and the passion that had flared within her.

Turning to get comfortable, Chloe sighed. How, oh how would she ever get to sleep?

"Something wrong?" Ben's voice was husky, an instant reminder of the way he'd kissed her.

"I'm fine." A small spark of guilt pricked at her over the untruthful answer.

An owl hooted just then, and she shivered. Some unidentifiable animal far up in the mountains bellowed to his mate. The wind, though not blowing overly hard, still sounded ominous as it whistled through the trees. She turned to stare at the fire's glow, only to notice the bats flying overhead.

"This is ridiculous." She scooted farther into the sleeping bag. If only she could work up the courage to scoot closer to Ben.

"Are you sure there's nothing wrong?"

This time, Chloe thought she detected a hint of amusement in his tone. She tightened her jaw. "Everything is just perfect."

She burrowed further under her covers, leaving just a tiny opening to breathe through. The bats wouldn't be able to get to her if she was totally covered, would they?

Someone had pushed her!

Chloe sat up with a gasp and stared into the darkness. Though she could barely make out his shape in the shadowy night, she could see that Ben was sleeping nearby. Should she wake him up? No. She could tell him tomorrow. He needed his rest. Besides, it was just a dream. That was all, just a silly dream.

She was safe.

Wasn't she?

Ben awoke to the fragrance of tangy evergreens and crisp mountain air, but something was added to it. A sweet scent, yet tart and delicious. It drifted past his nose and wrapped around his senses.

Chloe.

He rose up on his elbows and looked across the springy grass to where she lay only a few feet away, her face bathed in the soft morning light. She faced him, sleeping peacefully, a gentle smile curving her lips.

It came from her. The lemon-scented soap she'd bathed with clung to her, mingling with her body's natural sweetness to send him reeling.

This was no good. Getting involved with her would mean breaking her heart at the end of this hunt, because as soon as they found the Sasquatch, he intended to journey off to Africa in search of the snow gorilla.

Chloe sighed in her sleep and her lips parted, all soft and beguiling.

She was restless, tossing, turning, and stirring the air around her. The bewitching lemon scent was heightened. He turned his back to her and punched the air with his fist. Why him?

There was no room for another person in his life, especially not a warm, good-smelling woman, especially not after what happened before—with Rosalie.

A chill settled around Ben's heart just then. He wrestled with his thoughts.

Chloe, warm and tantalizing. The type of woman who would insist on going to Africa with him.

Rosalie, stone cold dead because of him.

Chloe.

Rosalie.

Chloe...

Finally, with considerable force on his part, the window to Ben's soul slammed shut.

Exhausted before the day had barely begun, he climbed out of the itchy wool bedding and scooped up the soap and towel Chloe had laid out for him before they'd gone to sleep last night.

The dratted lemon soap. Like an idiot, he brought it to his nose and sniffed.

Chloe, sweet-smelling Chloe.

Ben swore under his breath. If he'd had the foresight to grab his hunting bag before he'd taken off looking for her, he'd be able to bathe with his own soap and smell like a man should. He didn't want to smell sweet. And he certainly didn't want to be reminded of how he'd been wide awake most of the night thinking about how good Chloe felt in his arms, how good she tasted when he kissed her. How she moaned ever so softly...

"Forgive me, Lord." In spite of the cool morning air, Ben didn't waste any time jumping into the creek. It was the only way he knew to send any thoughts of Chloe by the wayside.

"I had a nightmare during the night." Chloe was just tying the last strap of the bedroll as he returned from the creek.

He noticed a slight tremble to her hands as she drew closer. Obviously the dream upset her.

"I think it might have been my subconscious trying to get me to remember. I did some research for an article once, about the subconscious—"

"Chloe, the nightmare?" Alarm prickled at the back of his neck, and he didn't have the patience to listen to her talk about an article she wrote for her father's paper.

"I think someone pushed me off the ridge. As I was trying to catch my balance, I think I felt someone's hands on my back. I must have forgotten because of the fall. I read an article once—"

"Are you sure?"

She nodded. "Pretty sure. I can't believe I forgot about it."

"You were hurt, as you said. And when you woke up in the morning, we had a lot of things distracting us. Like how to get back to camp."

"And Monique's itchy soap."

Ben laughed, glad she could break up the tension without getting hysterical. But his thoughts churned, trying to come up with a reason why someone would want to push her. It had to have been Skip. There was no other explanation. Was there? He clenched his hands into fists.

"Don't worry, Chloe. We'll find out who it was."

"I think we both know who it was." She pressed her lips together and tipped her head to the side.

His next words were spoken to assure himself as much as Chloe. "I'll keep you safe."

But could he really? He had no idea what sort of danger they would face before they finally caught up with the others.

And then there was Skip. What kind of danger would he present?

Ben couldn't take his eyes off Chloe as he climbed the hill, drawing ever closer to where she sat on a grassy knoll with her feet tucked under her. They'd stopped for lunch, and she'd gone off to look at the view while he broke camp. He knew there was a breathtaking view of a nearby lake in front of her, but she wasn't looking down at the lake. She stared off into nothingness. Her hair wafted around her face, which was lifted toward the sun. The closer Ben drew, the more certain he became that she was singing.

His heartbeat quickened and he picked up his pace. He hadn't realized Chloe liked to sing. He loved music as much as he loved the wild, untamed forests and jungles, as much as he loved studying animals. Music kept him sane.

Chloe's speaking voice had such a lilting, sweet essence to it. Ben was quite certain that when lifted in song, it would have the quality of a nightingale.

Anticipation filled him as he headed toward her. He quickened his pace, eager for this treat to his ears. He caught the familiar strains of one of his very own songs as he neared, but it had no impact on him. He was momentarily stunned. Chloe was no nightingale. She was more like a mockingbird with a throat infection.

Ben shook his head in disbelief. Chloe's speaking voice played over and over in his mind. It had captivated him, and yet she couldn't sing a note! Flat, toneless, he wished he could drown out the sound. He swallowed back his laughter and gazed into her face, praying she wouldn't be able to read his expression.

Staring directly into her clear blue eyes was a mistake, for the emotion hidden there captured him. The same emotion flooded his chest and his throat tightened painfully.

She was lovely. The soul-deep longing on her face tore at him, stealing his breath. His heart lifted past the edges of disappointment, and he heard the ache in her voice as she sang his song, the song he'd written as he'd lain awake one night yearning for, and certain he'd never find, someone to fill the void in his heart.

"...empty..."

If she was aware of him, she gave no indication, so caught up was she in the words she sang.

"I need someone..."

There was such heartache, such feeling and emotion in her voice, Ben was certain the depths of the words touched her just as they did him, and the certainty overcame her off-key tone.

The familiar tune pierced his heart, and before he even realized it, he was repeating the words with her, his gaze never leaving hers.

"Lonely..."

Ben lowered himself to his knees, his rich voice rising to blend with Chloe's awkward one.

"I need someone..."

The corners of her mouth lifted somewhat, the only indication he had that she was pleased to see him, but it wasn't enough to take away from the seriousness of the words she sang.

"Lonely." His song. She sang it like she'd written it. She sang it like she'd lived it. Like she felt it.

The thought stopped him short. Had she? Was that the secret hidden in the depths of her blue eyes?

Without thinking, he reached out and took her hand. Small, delicate and warm, it fit perfectly in his.

He reached out his other hand, and brushed his fingertips across her cheek. Her voice quavered, but only slightly.

There were no musical instruments, but suddenly Ben could hear them. He could see the pulse thrumming at Chloe's throat, and his own heart picked up a beat. His eyes fell lower then quickly rose back to her face.

Her eyes were bright. Did she feel something too? The same thing he did?

How had things changed so quickly? He didn't know. He just knew that by the time the song was over, Chloe was as breathless as he was.

The last bars of Ben's song hung in the air, filling the silence. Chloe's surroundings had faded so completely, the waterfall ceased rushing, the tree branches weren't rustling, and the creek stopped thundering. Her only awareness was of Ben, kneeling in front of her.

His face was so near hers, Chloe searched every inch of it. From the fine lines that accented his eyes, to the sensuous curve of his lips. Her heartbeat quickened.

Ben reached out and buried both hands in her hair before pulling her to him. His lips were warm as they claimed hers, seeking, needing, giving.

All of her senses were off-kilter, floating, spinning, drifting, until breathless, they both hesitatingly broke free.

While she caught her breath, Chloe studied the pale yellow flecks sprinkled through the green of his eyes. She longed to slip past those flecks, through his eyes, straight to his soul. She could see that he wanted to love her with more than just kisses. As much as she wanted the same thing, she knew it couldn't happen. When she gave herself, it would be forever. And she knew as soon as they got back to Cedar Ridge, he'd be gone from her life.

Slowly, the chirping of birds pricked the edges of awareness, and bit by bit the sounds and smells of the forest crept in. She had wanted to languish in it forever, but Chloe knew the magic was past. Frightened by the intensity in Ben's eyes, and confused by her own feelings, she looked away.

When Chloe tore her gaze from his, Ben felt like he'd lost something important. Something wonderful. Something he couldn't yet name. He hadn't wanted to stop at mere kisses, and the intense passion shook him to the core.

He could tell by the way she stared at the ground and plucked the grass with her small delicate hands that she was nervous. This was no good, these feelings that kept pulling them toward each other. Not for either of them.

They couldn't be distracted by feelings that could go nowhere. They had to stay alert to their surroundings and the dangers of the mountains. Especially him. He had to be aware of every detail and pay special attention to getting Chloe home safe and unharmed. He'd never be able to live with himself if something happened to her. As it was, her ruined reputation already weighed heavy on his heart. He couldn't bear the thought that people would be gossiping about her and making assumptions based on their time alone.

A lengthy and uncomfortable silence passed while Ben tried to figure out what to say, how to gently put a stop to this craziness.

"Ben, it's time to talk."

He almost sighed with relief when Chloe spoke. It meant he wouldn't have to. She'd set it right, say they shouldn't be doing this, quote one of Rudy's Bible scriptures. He'd nod mutely in agreement and they could get back to their business of finding the right trail.

He swallowed hard and nodded. He'd go along with whatever she said.

"Who is she?" Chloe's voice was shaky and faint, like a whisper on the wind.

He blinked, surprised by the question. "Who?"

"The woman who broke your heart." She ducked her head, as if embarrassed to even bring up the subject.

"I don't...understand." A slow dread settled in his stomach.

"We've already established it wasn't Monique. You said you were never engaged to her. So if Monique wasn't the one who broke your heart, it had to be someone else."

Rosalie. Just thinking her name speared his heart. He swallowed past the sudden tightness in his throat. Guilt assaulted him. "I really don't want to talk about it." His voice came out harsher than he'd intended.

"Ben, maybe if you talk about it, it'll help."

He stiffened. He thought he'd kept his feelings fairly well hidden. He clenched his jaw, saying nothing.

"And that haunted look in your eyes and voice whenever you sing; talking would be good for you."

"I don't..." He stopped himself. *Did* he have a haunted look? He was haunted, that was for sure. Haunted by things he should have done, things he didn't do. "I should have...I mean..." He broke off, not sure what to say.

"I'm sorry I brought it up." Chloe reached out and took his hand, and her gentle touch threatened to overwhelm him. Then she lifted her head, and he saw something flicker in her eyes. Pity. He didn't like it. Especially not coming from her.

"Don't be." He pulled his hand from hers. "I just don't want to talk about it."

"All right." She spoke softly, gently. "But when you're ready, I'll be here."

Her willingness to help touched him deep in the heart. He was a cad to ignore the offer. But he needed time to think. He stood, never taking his eyes off her. "I think it's time to pack things up so we can move on."

"I'll be along in a minute." Chloe didn't move. "I just want to enjoy this scenery for a minute longer. I know I said it before, but how can anyone look at this and not see the loving Father who created it?"

He nodded, though he couldn't see God's glory at the moment, and turned toward camp. Emptiness overtook him as he placed one foot in front of the other. He didn't like walking away from her after she'd so generously offered to give him solace from memories that ate at his insides. It was like he'd slapped her in the face.

But he just wasn't ready to open up. Heaven knew a part of him wanted to though. Maybe Chloe was right, and it would ease the torment deep inside him. But at the same time he didn't want to burden her, and he couldn't bear to see any condemnation in her eyes.

No. He shook his head. If he could just keep himself from thinking on it too much, it would go away. It had to, because he wasn't about to let it get the best of him. Just like this attraction to Chloe. He couldn't give his heart to anyone. He'd already learned the hard way. Don't trust people, don't love, don't...anything. It only brought hurt, hurt his bruised heart could no longer bear.

A shrill scream snapped Ben out of his reverie.

Chloe.

Even before he leaped to his feet and began running, Ben's heart was slamming against his chest.

Chapter Fifteen

She was going to die. Chloe knew it as certain as she knew her own name. She should have been more careful.

The snake had come from nowhere. He must have been sunning himself on the other side of the rock she rested on. Recalling the way it stared at her, slithering, stretching up before striking, Chloe shuddered. Revulsion shook her. She tried to keep the panic at bay but it wasn't enough to stem her tears. There was nothing she could really do except sit still and try to stay calm.

She'd known before taking off on this journey the chances were high that she'd come across a snake somewhere along the way. She'd been so caught up in her thoughts of Ben, she'd forgotten to check the area before she sat down on the rock.

Would she go to heaven? The thought that she wouldn't terrified her. Though she'd attended church her entire life, she knew now that she hadn't really been there spiritually. She hadn't known the meaning of true worship. But did she now? Thanks to Rudy and their morning prayers, she thought she did. But her faith, her *real* faith, was so new, she didn't know if it was good enough to wipe away her multitude of sins.

"Please, Lord, forgive me for lying to my father. And Lord, thank you for sending Rudy into my life so I could come to know you, no matter how short the time was. Please, Lord, let Rudy comfort Caleb and lead him to you so that he won't be lost like me. Please, Lord, help me." If Ben found her in time, he could get the poison out. Perhaps he had a snakebite kit hiding in one of his vest pockets.

She fought the urge to run to him. Having learned from an article she wrote for her brother, she knew staying still was best. That way the venom wouldn't race as quickly to her heart. Still, that hadn't stopped her from running from the rock and to the shelter of the nearest trees when the snake first struck. Instinct alone had prompted her to get as far from the forked-tongued creature as possible.

As she rested against the scratchy bark of a towering tree, its cones scattered all around her, she knew she was going to die up here, in the mountains, all alone. And Ben would be the one to find her. An image danced in her head, a picture of green eyes and a not-truly-happy smile.

"Please be with him, Lord. Please don't let him blame himself." The fault had been hers alone, and yet she knew Ben would blame himself.

"Chloe."

She looked up at the sound of Ben's voice. He rushed over, his face and voice full of concern. "What's wrong? What happened?"

She started to speak, but was so relieved to see him, she started to shake. "S-s-snake." She pointed at her foot.

"It bit you?"

"Y-y-yes."

He was on his knees instantly, his eyes filled with concern. Gently, he removed her boot and her stocking. His hands were warm and gentle. Comforting. It was nice to know his was the last face she'd see before she died. His was a nice face.

"How come you lied to me, Ben?"

Lied? Ben couldn't take the time to answer. Her voice was high, shrill, and her question made no sense. The poison must be rushing through her bloodstream, making her delirious. He had to find the wound, get as much poison out as he could so he could save her.

Hurriedly, he searched her slim, delicate ankle for any signs of redness. There were none. He pushed the hem of her pants up over her calf. When it didn't appear it would go any farther, he tugged at the fabric above her knee and pulled the hem upward.

With as much tenderness as he could, Ben ran frantic fingers over Chloe's satiny smooth skin, searching for bite marks.

"Are you sure it was this leg?"

Chloe opened her mouth to speak but only nodded.

Ben worried that in her fear she'd become confused. They were wasting precious moments while poisonous venom raced through her veins. He shuddered at the thought of the venom piercing its way to her heart.

It must be the other leg. His fingers were like oversized thumbs as they fumbled with the laces of her other boot. He dug in his pocket for his knife to cut the knot. The same knife he would use to cut her tender flesh and suck the poison. His stomach clenched.

"Ben?"

At the light touch on his shoulder, he looked up into her frightened blue eyes.

"You don't need to cut my boot. It wasn't that leg."

Her bottom lip quivered, and Ben knew she was scared.

"You're sure?"

Chloe bit her bottom lip and nodded.

"You'll have to take your pants off then. I can't get the cuff over your knee."

"It was below my knee. I can still feel where it struck."

Ben shook his head. How could she be certain? She'd been so frightened.

There wasn't even a red mark on her exposed skin.

She shuddered.

"He was so ugly, Ben. Just staring at me, those beady eyes never moving. It's nothing I'll forget anytime soon."

Ben's hands never stopped running over her skin, searching for something he might have missed.

"Everything was quiet. It was like I was in a dream. A nightmare, really. I had been running, and stopped to rest on a huge rock. The only thing I could hear was the pounding of my heart."

Ben's hands stopped. "What?"

"It was like a dream."

"Wait, wait. Not that. You said you couldn't hear anything?"

"N-no. Just my thudding heart. And I guess my panting breath."

"No rattle?"

"No." She sounded puzzled. "I told you—"

"Chloe, you never heard a rattling sound? Not once?"

"I don't think so." She looked uncertain.

"Believe me, you'd know if you had. It's not a sound you'd ever forget. Kind of like those beady eyes. It sends chills right up your spine."

"You sound like you know."

Ben's hands were stroking her bare leg again, and his lips formed a slight smile. Chloe looked at him with a questioning gaze.

"I do know, and I should have known."

"Huh?"

"I was so worried about you when you said you were bitten I never stopped to give it any thought. There're no rattlers on this side of the mountains. Don't you remember me telling you that when we first started on the trail?"

"Well yes, but when I saw the snake I just figured you didn't know what you were talking about."

Ben pressed his lips together. Bad enough that she would doubt his credibility. Worse was that in his worry over her, he forgot it was too cold for rattlers here. He should have remembered immediately. What was it about her that caused him to forget such simple things?

"The snake wasn't poisonous. And as far as I can tell, it didn't bite you either."

Tears sprang to Chloe's eyes, and Ben resisted the urge to brush them away.

"I feel so silly." Her voice was a shaky whisper. "You're absolutely sure?"

"Yes." Ben grinned at her and slowly pulled her stocking back over her leg.

"But—"

"There are no marks on you anywhere. The snake might have struck, but he didn't bite through your trousers. And it wasn't a rattler. I'm telling you, it's too cold for them to survive here. We have a lot of ground to cover before we would make it into their territory."

"You mean I'm not going to die?"

He smiled at her. "No."

"Oh!" Chloe threw her arms around Ben's neck and buried her face in his shoulder.

It was too much for him suddenly. The fear and relief they'd just shared, their previous kisses, days of walking together. He ran his hand from her ankle to her thigh, before returning her embrace. He fell back onto the grass, taking her with him.

Chloe didn't realize she'd shut her eyes until all movement stopped. She lay perfectly still, knowing Ben was underneath her, trying not to feel anything. Finally, she dared peek her eyes open and sucked in a sharp breath.

She stared into Ben's eyes, transfixed by the pleasure dancing through their green depths. When he blinked, thick lashes fanned his cheeks. Impulsively she brushed her lips across that same spot.

This time it was Ben who sucked in a sharp breath.

His hands, which had been at her waist, moved down her hips.

In spite of the heavy fabric of her pants, she could feel the searing heat of his hands struggling to pull her closer, heat which intensified a thousand times as her lips sought his.

The kiss was hurried, demanding, eager with need, and more intense than anything Chloe had ever imagined. A bevy of feelings swirled in her, threatening to overtake her. She knew she could fall in love with this man. Then tomorrow would come, and he'd go back to his swamp in Florida, or his jungle in Africa, and she'd be left with a broken heart.

It was Ben who finally broke the kiss. He pulled away from her but held her face in his hands. He stared into her eyes.

"Oh, my." Chloe could scarcely breathe.

Ben smiled and her heart skittered. "Yes. Oh, my. Is that all you have to say?"

"I'm not sure what to say. I've never felt like this when I've been kissed before."

"Have you been kissed by a lot of other men?"

"A few."

Ben set his jaw in a grim line, and she decided not to tell him about Jackson. He searched her eyes, and Chloe opened her mouth to speak but found herself with nothing to say.

"Chloe." Ben spoke with a ragged whispered. "You're so good for me. If only…" His voice trailed off, and Chloe's hope died.

If only? If only what?

She opened her mouth to ask him, but the look on Ben's face as he caught her hands in his indicated there would be no more to say on the subject.

Chloe held tight to Ben's hand as they walked up the trail. They'd quietly gathered their belongings and were once again on their way, Ben seemingly as lost in thought as she was. Were his thoughts on her the way hers were on him?

Ben surprised her by breaking the silence first. "Let's talk a little, shall we?" He brought Chloe's hand to his lips and brushed a feathery kiss on the palm. Shivers of pleasure danced up her spine.

Chloe couldn't help but smile. He finally wanted to talk. "Of course, Ben. Talking will do us both good."

"I don't want to talk about my troubles."

Chloe sighed and pried her hand from his. He would never get rid of that haunted look if he didn't talk about it. But she had to be careful not to push. She didn't want him to retreat into himself. "What do you want to talk about then? The Sasquatch?"

"No." There was a trace of a smile on Ben's face as he recaptured her hand. He lowered his voice. "I want to talk about kissing you some more."

A sudden warmth, the same passion she'd felt earlier, flowed through her veins.

"Ben, we can't."

"Why not?" He looked disappointed but determined to persist until she gave in.

But she wouldn't give in. "Because." *I'm afraid.*

"Are you afraid of me?"

Had he read her thoughts?

"Are you?" Still holding lightly to her hand, he turned it palm up and slowly brushed it with his lips.

"No." *Liar.*

"Tell me the truth, Chloe."

"I'm afraid of you."

"Don't be," he said gently. "I won't hurt you. Ever." And for the second time that day, she was carried away by the sensation of his hands around her waist, lifting her so her mouth could meet his. The only thing she felt, the only thing she heard before she melted against him was the thundering of her heart.

After that, Chloe's perspective was all out of whack. Part of her longed for more kisses, longed to be carried away on the clouds. She wanted to swoon and coo like Trina and her silly friends, wanted to look deep into Ben's eyes and get lost in their depths, sing with him again, share her deepest emotions with him, her dreams...

But it couldn't happen again. Next time, they might not stop with kisses. And that would be more than her heart could bear. She couldn't endure giving her love to Ben without giving herself in marriage. In the short space of a few days, she'd given her heart to the Lord, and for the first time in her life she wanted to seek Him and His will before her own desires. She wasn't sure she'd succeed, but she wanted to try.

And marriage...it wasn't anything she ever really thought she wanted before. Until now.

Until Ben.

She loved him.

Well, maybe it was too soon to know for sure, but given that she was totally and irrevocably in love with his voice, and just being near him caused her heart to do flip-flops, it was the closest she'd ever come to love in her life. And since he didn't feel the same way about her, kissing him again would be a mistake.

And as for her dreams...she would pursue God's will and pray she didn't have to give up on them. It would hurt too much if being a journalist wasn't in God's plan for her life. She'd told Ben about being a reporter, but she hadn't told him the rest of her dream. Nor could she.

True, he'd said he believed a woman capable of being a reporter. But she didn't believe he meant it. He still went out of his way to protect her. If he thought she was tired, they stopped for a rest. If he thought the ground was too uncomfortable, he offered her the wool liner to fasten back into her sleeping bag. Of course she refused.

His protectiveness, while it touched her, showed her he still didn't think she was capable of more than dabbing perfume behind her ears. If she told him the rest of her dreams, he would laugh at her the way Jackson had. He would laugh like her father.

No. She couldn't tell Ben her dreams and risk his scorn. Her soul wouldn't be able to withstand it.

So now, torn between so many conflicting emotions, she could barely look Ben in the eye. To do more would only open her heart to the rawest hurt possible.

But oh how she longed for more of his kisses.

Early the next morning, as they headed up the trail, Chloe thought some of the twisting curves looked familiar. Or was it wishful thinking? Hopefully they were heading in the right direction. There were so many trees, so many trails, they all looked alike. They could wander around here for years and never cross the same path.

Most of the time Ben studied the ground, though occasionally he glanced up into the treetops and at the mountain peaks towering all around.

"I don't think you'll find any tracks up there." Chloe wondered what he was looking for.

"Just admiring the scenery." He flashed his heart-melting smile. "It's so beautiful up in these parts, I swear a man could get sunburned tonsils from looking up all the time and trying to take it all in."

"Is that why we're walking so slow?" If Ben expected her to laugh, he'd have to be disappointed. She was tired and thought she'd probably feel better if they kept up a quicker, more normal pace.

Of course if they walked too fast, Ben wouldn't be able to take such care with nature. She admired him more and more with each step they took. He examined every set of prints, explaining them to her, and she wrote them down in her notebook, sketching pictures here and there. It would all fit together into an interesting story or article. In spite of her weariness, Chloe was fascinated by her surroundings. And by Ben.

"I'm just trying to open my eyes to some of the scriptures we read and what you've said about the glory of God's creation. How only He could have created something so beautiful. And only He could have created all of Earth's creatures. How does that reconcile with my life as a scientist?"

"Can't you be both? A scientist *and* a man of God?"

He shook his head, brow drawn. "I don't know. My parents believed in God, but I don't think they lived up to their beliefs by dumping me on Gus. And Gus doesn't believe in God. He believes in science. My parents knew that. Gus told me once that they tried repeatedly to 'save' him, but that he just didn't buy into it. If they really believed, if their mission was to bring lost souls to Christ, how could they leave their child with someone who didn't believe? If they didn't intend to come back, there was nothing there to assure them I'd be raised in faith."

The sadness in his eyes tore at Chloe's heart. "Do you know for a fact that they didn't intend to come back?"

Lips pressed together, Ben shook his head. "I always thought they meant to, but then the letters grew further apart until they stopped coming all together. I figured their mission was more important than their son."

"Ben, did you ever try to find them? Did Gus?"

His steps slowed, and Chloe slowed her own to match his pace until they came to a complete stop.

"No, we didn't. Gus just figured the same thing I did." As he studied her face, Chloe saw his eyes brighten, saw the hope settle in them, and knew he'd come to the same conclusion she had. "You think something happened to them, don't you?"

"I think it's possible. If they loved you as much as you say they did, if they were as committed to God as you thought they were—then no, I don't think they deliberately abandoned you."

He reached for her hand, clasped it in his and gazed into her eyes. "Then we have two mysteries to solve."

"Two?"

"Who pushed you off the ridge, and what happened to my parents? As soon as we get back to camp, we'll work on both."

As they walked, they discussed possibilities of who could have pushed her.

Both of them agreed it couldn't be anyone but Skip. There wasn't a sign of anyone out in this wilderness, and really, Skip was the only one of the group that could have possibly wanted to hurt Gus and Ben. Rudy and Monique were both part of the fateful trip, and Caleb and Aunt Jane certainly weren't suspect. That left only Skip.

But why? Or was there a darker menace in the woods—a stranger no one knew?

"There's something else we need to talk about, Chloe." The seriousness in Ben's tone stopped Chloe in her tracks.

"What is it? What's wrong?"

"Nothing is wrong. Don't look so alarmed." Before she realized his intentions, he dropped a kiss on her forehead. She closed her eyes, reveling in the feeling, then opened them abruptly and chided herself for her foolishness.

"What do you want to talk about?" She hoped Ben wouldn't jump to the silly conclusion that she might be swooning over him.

"I just think we need to make some plans."

"What kind of plans? What for?" Chloe shook her head, confused.

"Our food, *your* food, will only last so long."

"You're thinking we'll be here longer than you originally thought?" A sinking feeling filled the pit of her stomach.

"Yes." Ben nodded and drew his brows together. "The trail seems to be taking us farther from the other mountain. I thought it would eventually lead us down and around to a trail on the wooded side of the peak we were on. However, the trail just keeps leading us higher and farther east. It could be quite a while before there is a fork in the trail that will take us where we want to go."

"Oh, I see." Further from the peak, further from Caleb, further from home. They really were lost.

"We could just head off in the direction we want, but it's not the safest thing to do. We should stay on the path and plan to take a little longer. But we need to be prepared for our food to run out. I'm going to show you some things to keep an eye out for—different plants and wildflowers that we can eat for survival."

After looking all around her, Chloe had to laugh. "I don't see anything around here I'd even attempt to eat. What will we do? Peel bark off the trees?"

"Actually, if you we get desperate enough for food, I'm sure we will."

"All right then. There." She pointed at a pinecone on the ground. "There's some food for you. Why don't you just pick up that pinecone and stick it in the pack?"

She watched in amazement when Ben did as she asked.

"You're not serious?"

"The nuts. A little dry, not too tasty, but if you need nourishment—"

"Ben! I'm not eating pinecones!"

The smirk on his face was so recalcitrant, she wanted to smack him.

Then he laughed.

"What are you laughing at?"

"These aren't pinecones. Look around you. Do you see any pine trees?"

"Yes." Puzzled, she stared at the trees that surrounded them. "Everywhere."

"No you don't. You see different varieties of fir trees, some cedar trees, and lots of Douglas firs. I won't say you'll never see a pine tree on this side of the mountains, but they're few and far between. On the east side, pine trees are everywhere—along with the rattlesnakes." He looked pointedly at the cones on the ground. "Those are fir cones."

"Smarty. Pinecones, fir cones. It really doesn't matter. A cone is a cone and a tree is a tree."

"Don't be too sure of that. Some trees are conifers, some are deciduous, and some can make you very sick."

"All right, O Great and Mighty Mountain Expert," Chloe declared with a half-bow. "Lead me to yon edible trees."

While Ben was able to point out several different edible plants, and Chloe thought she'd recognize them again if need be, they were disappointed not to see any sign of tracks—Sasquatch or otherwise.

It was pleasant though, walking beside him, listening and learning from him. He showed her how fern could be used as an antiseptic, and that wherever stinging nettles were found, fern grew nearby. He explained how to make a shelter out of large, fallen trees and tree branches. He even pointed out different plants she could eat if no other food could be found. And for protein, he pointed out the black slimy disgusting slugs that could be found in the darker parts of the woods.

By the time he was ready to stop for lunch, Chloe was grateful for the chance to rest. She removed the burdensome pack from her shoulders and dropped it to the ground. "It's beautiful here." She rubbed at the twinge between her shoulder blades. By the time this trip was over she'd be a permanent hunchback.

"We can sit here." She spread out her bedroll and then realized how he might possibly interpret her actions. She'd intended the blankets as a comfortable resting spot, but would Ben think it just a ploy to get him near her?

"Don't sit there." Ben's tone was quick, snappy.

She knew it. He did think she was just trying to get close to him. "Sorry," she mumbled.

"It's just that you spread the blankets over some foliage, and had you sat there, you would have crushed it."

"Oh." Foliage. That was all.

"Here, let me move it for you." Her heart jumped as Ben stepped closer to her. Cursing her reaction, Chloe watched him gently tug the blankets to a clearer spot then walk over to examine the wildflowers as if measuring any damage that had been done.

He muttered something about pixie-cup lichen and haircap moss, and though she wanted to ask about it, she remained quiet. Other thoughts were taking precedence in her mind.

Nature, Ben's gentle way with it. The way he cared. Oh, she'd known it before. Nature, after all, was his life's work. But in that instant, Chloe saw that nature was much more than Ben's work. It was his love, his life, it meant everything to him.

And she was envious.

Chloe made herself comfortable on top of the sleeping bag and pulled out the last tin of plum pudding.

"Thank goodness."

"What?"

"It's the last of the pudding." She looked up at Ben and forced a smile. Then she handed him the pudding and the opener. "I'm so sick of it I'll likely never eat it or another plum as long as I live."

"You may live to regret those words when all we find to nourish our starving bodies are..." Ben tossed the pudding up in the air, caught it, opened then presented it to Chloe with a gallant smile and a half-bow. "...plum trees!"

"You're the expert." She smiled sweetly. "Surely you can find something for us to live on besides plums."

"You mean you want something else to eat? A gourmet meal, perhaps?"

"Gourmet would be good, yes. Anything would be better than this." A movement caught Chloe's eye. "Look Ben. Over there."

Holding her breath, she watched as a porcupine lumbered out of the brush to slowly make his way up the hill from the creek. His quills resembled long pine needles, and she was surprised by their color. This was the first real live porcupine she'd ever seen, and somehow she thought they'd be smaller and darker. With the sun shining on his quills, he was almost yellow in color. Not wanting to spook him, she remained perfectly still. Regretfully, she couldn't risk digging in her bag for her pad and pencil so she could do a quick sketch. Not that she had the same skills as her brother, of course.

Try as she might, Chloe couldn't figure out what the animal was doing out of his habitat. To the best of her knowledge, porcupines were nocturnal. Maybe he was on his way home from a night out.

"Shh. Stay still." Ben's voice in her ear startled her, and she turned to look at him. "That's my cue." He rose slowly, reaching inside his vest and pulling out his revolver.

Chloe stared after him, horrified. Surely he wasn't... "No!" She jumped up. "What are you doing?"

"You said you wanted something besides pudding. You said you might be interested in something a little different." He looked over his shoulder, and his next words were ominous to Chloe's ears. "This is different."

"I didn't mean I wanted to eat a porcupine." She felt ill.

Ben didn't look at her. He just kept aiming at the porcupine, which had stopped to listen to the sounds around him.

"I don't know about you, but porcupine meat doesn't exactly sound appetizing. Look at him." She was appalled that Ben would even consider killing the little critter. "You're telling me you could actually eat him?"

"Yup."

"I don't believe you." She reached out and shoved his shoulder. "Go catch a fish."

"No, sorry. The porc is mine."

"I won't allow it. It's murder, pure and simple." She shoved him again.

"Murder? What about the poor fish you just instructed me to catch? That's not murder?"

"It's a little different. God put the fish here for us to eat."

"And what is the porcupine for?"

"I—well, I don't know. But it's not for food."

"God told you that Himself, did He?"

Chloe reached out to shove him again, but Ben grasped her hand in his. "Do it again," he warned in a low voice, "and you can be sure I'll exact suitable payment from you."

He stared directly at her lips, conveying his meaning with his eyes and causing shivers of anticipation to thread through her heart and down to her stomach. Chloe did the only thing she could. She jerked her hand from his and turned back to the porcupine.

"Shoo!" She stomped her foot loud enough to startle the lumbersome animal, but he didn't run. She stepped a little closer to him and stomped her foot again, clapping her hands together to make more noise. "Scram, scat!"

"I'd be careful about getting so close, if I were you." Ben sounded amused.

"And I'd be careful about pointing that gun at him." Chloe stomped her feet at the little creature again. The porcupine wasn't frightened enough to run, though he did lift his tail and pull it back as though getting ready to swing it at her. She squealed and jumped out of the way.

"Are you sure you don't want me to shoot it?"

"Of course not." She picked up a large branch and shook it at the porcupine, prodding him gently until he finally lowered his tail and trudged out of sight. He was a stubborn little creature, not the least bit scared of her or Ben. Satisfied that the porcupine was safe, she turned to Ben. He was staring at her as if she'd grown another head.

Sitting down, scanning his face and looking into his green eyes, her heart skipped a beat. What was it about the depths of those eyes? She couldn't even glance at them without feeling as though she'd hopped on a runaway train headed down the mountain.

Chapter Sixteen

Bang, bang, you're dead. Bang, bang, you're dead. The childish phrase played through Chloe's mind, accented by each step she took.

It was Ben's gun. All right, so she'd known about it all along and had even been grateful for it when they were looking for her brother and Monique. And she knew that its presence meant not only protection, but food when their current supply ran out.

That wasn't the problem. The problem was, once Ben pulled the gun out to try and shoot the poor porcupine, she recalled Monique's taunting about preservation. How could she have forgotten? Because with the memory came the horrifying realization that Ben intended to kill the Sasquatch. *What did you think he would do, you measle-brained dingbat? Take it by the hand and lead it all the way down to Cedar Ridge?*

Fine, so the thought had never occurred to her. It really should have, especially after Monique made that comment about Ben preserving it. Somehow she'd conveniently put that thought out of her mind. But now that awareness had crept back in, she needed to figure out how to stop him. Under no circumstances would she let him kill the Sasquatch.

She forgot that vow when she glanced to the side of the trail scant moments later.

"Ben, look!" She grabbed his arm, stopping him abruptly.

Both the excitement in Chloe's voice and the searing sensation of her hand on his arm startled Ben. Had he missed something?

The expression on her face was barely confinable glee. Her eyes sparkled. Her lips curved ever upward. She gestured wildly at something on the ground off to her right. Something very interesting. He sucked in a breath.

A print.

A very large print.

"Is that what I think it is?" Chloe's voice was breathy, and Ben's own excitement grew. She grabbed his arm once again.

"Could be." Ben nodded, only halfway acknowledging what she said, unable to take his eyes off the print.

"Oh, Ben! This is so exciting."

Ben was almost knocked off balance when Chloe threw herself into his arms. He regained his balance then managed to push her aside, still staring at the print, only vaguely aware of a huffing sound.

This was no ordinary print. It wasn't one he recognized as belonging to any animal indigenous to these parts. Though it was almost the same shape as a human footprint, the impression was deep—too deep to have been made by man, or any animal on this continent.

The foot was flat with five toes, no discernible arch, and most importantly— no claws. The print, almost twice the size of his own footprint, appeared to be a left foot, though he couldn't be positive. It took two of his own strides before he found the second footprint.

"What does it mean?"

Ben glanced at Chloe. Her blue eyes were so wide he could get lost in them. Curiosity certainly had the best of her.

"I'm not sure what it means, but I'd like to find out."

"Could it be from a bear?" Chloe shivered, her eyes round with concern.

"No, definitely not. Even the largest of bears has a fourteen-inch print at the most. Around here, most bear prints are going to be about the size of yours. And there would be claw marks. This print is much the same as a human's. Rather strange, wouldn't you say? Unless there's a giant running around these woods, I'd say we've found our first Sasquatch tracks."

Chloe's smile was wide, and Ben could almost feel an arrow pierce his heart. What would it be like to have that smile be meant for him, not the prospect of a story?

"Shall we follow them?"

Ben nodded, and if possible, Chloe's smile grew larger.

"What will we do if we find the creature?"

Ben patted the revolver at his side and his blood raced. Chloe's enthusiasm was contagious. If he brought back a Sasquatch, the pieces of his life might fall back into place. His name would be on the tongues of every scientist in the country. Country? Forget that! *The world!* He started into the brush, following the tracks, reveling in this newfound excitement. Until he felt the hand on his shoulder. Until he saw the look on Chloe's face.

"No!"

Ben knew what she was talking about, but he couldn't let it go by without a comment of some sort. "No?" He raised one eyebrow and fixed her with a challenging stare.

"No." Her voice was controlled, almost dangerous. "You're not going to shoot it. I won't let you."

"And just how do you propose to stop me, Chloe? Are you going to scare it off with a branch?" He knew he must sound childish, but this was his *dream,* confound it all. She wasn't going to spoil it for him.

"If need be, yes, I will." She was so matter of fact, and her bottom lip stuck out just enough to tease his senses. He wanted to do his own teasing. He wanted to press his own lips to hers, draw her sassy bottom lip into his mouth, and see if it tasted as delicious as it looked.

Instead he said, "I can guarantee you this. One look from that Sasquatch, and it'll be you who runs away. He won't run from you."

"How can you be so sure? Some of the reports I've heard—and most of them come from an old Salish man—say the creature is shy. Not frightened of us at all. He just doesn't want to show himself. So, no, I won't be running away from the Sasquatch. I'll do everything I can to scare him off."

There was nothing he could say to that. As was happening quite often with her, Chloe had the last word.

Not sure whether to kiss her senseless or just ignore her words, Ben turned to follow the prints. He'd deal with Chloe and her threats another time.

Not that he took her seriously. Scare the Sasquatch indeed.

Ben couldn't help but laugh out loud. He'd be willing to stake his reputation on a bet that Chloe would take one look at ol' Sassy and run screaming in the opposite direction. He laughed again then glanced over his shoulder at Chloe.

"Is something funny?" She stood a few feet away, staring at him. Her lips curved sensuously upward, enticing him as they always did.

"No." Ben stepped toward her, wishing he didn't sound like he was choking. "Nothing's wrong at all. Let's see where these lead us. Shall we?" He stepped past her, not looking back, not wanting to admit just how close he'd come to kissing her again.

Six, twelve, eighteen, twenty-four, thirty. Ben silently counted off six feet for each stride the creature had made. He stopped, dismayed, after seventy-eight feet. Thirteen strides and the tracks stopped. If he'd have been the superstitious sort, he might have said it was an omen. He brushed at the imaginary prickles on the back of his neck.

The Sasquatch had apparently disappeared into thin air. How or where, Ben was at a loss to say. The tracks simply ended.

Stumped, he looked all around. There was no cliff, no drop off. The ground was soft, and had the Sasquatch continued on there would, theoretically, be an indentation of sorts. He glanced into the trees overhead. Certainly the creature couldn't climb a tree. The thought was ridiculous.

"What are we going to do now?"

Pulled from his thoughts, Ben stared at Chloe. She stood beside him, apparently as puzzled as he was, with one hand on her hip. Her face was scrunched in concentration, and soft curls tickled her cheeks. She was quite a fetching picture, and it didn't take much to imagine her in something a little more revealing and decidedly feminine.

No. Ben shook his head. He had to stop thinking this way.

"Ben? I asked a question." She sounded annoyed that he hadn't answered her right away. "What are we going to do now?"

"We're spending the night here." He didn't even have to think about it, the answer was so clear in his mind.

"Do you think it'll come back?" There was no mistaking the spark of hope in Chloe's blue eyes.

"No." Ben pulled his gaze to the ground, to the prints. "I want to cast these prints, and I don't have my plaster. It's in my pouch, which was left behind when I went looking for you."

It wasn't until Chloe flushed and looked at the ground that Ben realized he spoke more harshly than he ever intended. When he realized it, he wanted to kick himself. He knew she felt guilty over the entire situation.

"I'm sorry. I didn't mean it like that. What I need to do is mix up some mud and make a casting with it. We're waiting for it to dry completely before we move on. That's why we're spending the night here. This is too good to ignore."

"Can I do anything to help you?"

"Yes, you can pull out your canteen to help make the mud." He thought for a moment. "Actually, I think we'll fill up two prints in case one doesn't turn out."

He glanced at Chloe to find her staring intently at the bush next to him. "What do you see there?"

She scrunched up her face and stepped closer to the bush. "I'm not sure what it's from, but it looks like an animal of some kind snagged their fur on the branches here."

It took Ben half a second to push Chloe aside so he could take a look. He reached down and extracted the clump of coarse brown hair. "This is no ordinary animal fur. I think this might just be from the Sasquatch." He whirled around and pulled Chloe into his arms.

"You're my lucky charm," he murmured softly, sincerely. "First you find the tracks, then you find this. I can't believe I wasn't observant enough to notice it."

"Reporters have to be observant of everything."

"Yes, but I think there's something special about your brand of reporting." As he said it, Ben realized the truth of his statement. Maybe it wasn't so bad having a reporter along after all.

She shrugged and looked away from him, but not before Ben saw a look of pure pleasure sparkle in her eyes. He had the feeling she wasn't used to receiving compliments. He'd have to remember to do it more often. But in the meantime he had the perfect way of thanking her for her discovery.

"Look at me." When she didn't respond, he released her from his arms to cup her face in his hands and tilt it toward his own. "Thank you for being here with me, Chloe. Thank you for your find. You'll never know how important this is to me, or how much I appreciate it."

"My pleasure." There was a trace of huskiness in her soft tone, one that Ben echoed in his response.

"No, Chloe, this pleasure is all mine." He lowered his face to hers and claimed her lips with his own.

Would it really be so bad if his heart got just a little bit involved?

Chloe was nearly asleep when it started. A low moan followed by a cough. Was Ben sick? Or was he having a nightmare?

The sleeping bag twisted around her feet as she turned to face him. He slept on his side, facing her. They were much too close for Chloe's comfort, but Ben insisted she stay near enough that if something happened he'd be right there. Protective, ever protective. While part of her wanted to buck that and argue with him, the other part was deeply touched.

The cough came again, followed by another moan. The hair on the back of Chloe's neck prickled with alarm.

Ben hadn't stirred. The sounds weren't coming from him.

Could it be the person who pushed her?

Beyond his feet, the campfire had died down to glowing embers. Carefully Chloe inched out of her covers and crawled to the fire pit. She looked at the rocks surrounding the fire and reached for one.

"Ouch!" She dropped it, blew on her fingers then picked it up again. Her hand clasped around the hot rock, and she pulled it toward her. Would it be enough protection?

"Ben?" She whispered as loud as she dared.

He didn't move.

The congested sounds grew louder, the moans lengthier and more pain-filled.

Torn between the urge to jump up and scream or pitch the heavy rock toward the bush where the sound was coming from, Chloe chose to do nothing.

She was afraid any sudden move on her part would startle whoever it was into some sort of action. Shoulders tense, fists clenched, she scarcely dared to breathe. When the next bout of coughing started, she jumped. Thankfully, so did Ben.

Startled, he sat up. Chloe met and held his gaze, too frightened to say anything. A finger to her lips indicated he should keep silent. Lifting the rock with her other hand, she raised her eyebrow at the same time and hoped Ben would understand that he too should pick up a rock.

They had to be ready to act when the intruder made his move.

Ben listened for a moment, crawled out of his covers just as she had, then reached over and pried a stone from the fire pit.

He held it, staring at Chloe as intently as she stared at him. Was he frightened too? She couldn't be certain.

Then the corners of his mouth twitched the slightest bit, and he tossed the rock back at the fire. Unexpectedly, Ben burst into laughter.

Chloe clutched the rock tightly to her chest and debated throwing it at Ben. Had he lost his mind? She held her breath, waiting for the moaning intruder to jump out at them.

In one fluid movement, Ben caught her hand with his and gently pried her fingers from the rock. He was warm and strong, and his presence overwhelmed her. She looked up at him, unable to move.

"There's someone in that bush." Her whisper came out as a croak. "Can't you hear the coughing?"

"It's okay." Ben appeared to be amused. "Remember that porcupine you so valiantly did battle over?"

Chloe nodded. Why was he babbling about the porcupine?

"It's probably not him, but I'll bet it's his brother or cousin or some other long lost relation."

The porcupine? Chloe straightened her shoulders. "Are you serious?"

Ben nodded.

No one was skulking around waiting to do them in. "The porcupine." Relief flooded her, and she laughed, though she wasn't amused.

"They often cough and moan at night. Don't feel bad, they've scared many a miner and trapper."

"I'm not scared." Chloe's voice seemed a bit high, and she wondered if Ben noticed. He must have, because suddenly she was in his arms. She should have pulled back, retreated, but instead closed her eyes and leaned into him. Resting her cheek against his hard chest, she reveled in his nearness and the safety that enveloped her.

She remembered how he'd warmed her after her dip in the creek, how he ever so gently kissed her. And again, when they found the prints and the tuft of hair. She wondered if he'd kiss her now. Would it be joyful and gentle, or urgent and fevered? She pressed tighter against him, aching with a need she didn't understand.

Ben cleared his throat and moved away, taking the warmth with him. "We'd better get some sleep. Tomorrow is another long day."

Chloe watched him poke the coals with a stick before he went over and climbed under his covers. Unable to take her eyes off him, she felt cheated. She thought he winked at her, though she wasn't sure.

Embarrassed at the blatant way she'd stared, Chloe ducked her head under the covers.

Nearby, the porcupine continued with his noises. Chloe tried to block out the sounds by thinking of other things. She thought of her family and attempted to draw a picture of them in her head.

All she could think about was Ben and the unbidden feelings he stirred in her.

Early the next morning, Ben sat in front of the fire. It crackled and spit, and smoke wafted toward his face. Heavy-hearted, he sighed.

The mud casting hadn't turned out as well as he'd hoped. Probably because he hadn't used the proper material. The dampness in the air didn't help, and he shouldn't have messed with it before it was completely dry. He knew better. But he'd been looking for something, anything to make himself feel hopeful. Maybe it would look better when it dried more completely. And while it was disappointing, he had to keep telling himself it was better than nothing. But he wasn't sure how he could begin to convince the colonel, and the science world, that this was the footprint of a Sasquatch. He traced his fingers over each toe print and each crease in the foot hoping the act itself would muster some of his enthusiasm. It didn't work.

And if that weren't bad enough, he'd been feeling melancholy ever since

Chloe had mentioned his parents. Though he was certain it hadn't been her intent, she'd reopened a wound. Thinking about his parents made him think of Gus and Monique, and thinking about Monique made him think about the last expedition he'd been on. The past was something he thought he'd put behind him, but almost from the beginning of the trip, it had been haunting him again. And then there was Chloe.

Her safety was the only thing that mattered right now. He wouldn't be satisfied until he delivered her back to her brother, and then to her parents. That would mean telling her good-bye. And there was a part of him that wasn't ready to do that. He tossed the casting aside.

"Hey, be careful. You went to a lot of trouble to get that. You don't want to break it."

"I guess."

"What's this all about?" Chloe's voice was filled with concern, and she came to sit beside him. "Didn't it turn out?"

"Not really."

"Let me see." She bent down and picked it up. After she scrutinized it front and back, she fixed her gaze on his. "I think it will pass, but if you're not happy with it, why don't you make another one?"

"Chloe, we'll be here for days waiting for it to dry properly. I don't know what I was thinking when I cast it in the first place."

"Ben, it sounds to me like you've stopped believing in yourself." She reached over and touched his shoulder, giving him a shy smile. "You're good at what you do. You've proven that to me over and over. You've shown me how to survive up here. What to eat, what not to eat. What to stay away from, how to take the sting out of stinging nettles."

That elicited a half-hearted laugh from him.

"You also saved my life. If the Sasquatch exists, you'll find it. I know you will."

"If?" Was she having doubts?

"That was just a figure of speech. It exists, I know it does. Just as Jacko was on that train in Canada, I know *you'll* be the one to find it." The smile she flashed him was sincere, and so painfully alluring, it quickly brought to mind the way she'd felt last night as he held her in his arms.

The blush that stole over her face let Ben know she was thinking the same thing. Suddenly hungry for her touch, he reached for her, but she shook her head and folded her arms across her chest.

"I want to talk."

Ben sighed, resignedly. He knew what she was referring to, and he still wasn't ready. But perhaps she was right, and it was time.

"Did you love her?"

"Who?" To ask was dumb. He knew who. *Rosalie.* She wanted him to talk about Rosalie, about the past.

"I don't know *whom.* Whomever you dream about, whomever you sing to. The woman who put that haunted look in your eyes..." Her voice trailed off as if even she didn't want to talk about the subject.

Panic seized him, and he sat there, silent, staring into the fire as the tortured memories engulfed him.

What would Chloe think of him when he told her? Would she despise him, be repulsed by the very sight of him, or would she perhaps...understand?

"Come on, Ben." Her touch was gentle on his arm, and his heart thundered. "You picked the perfect place to stop last night. It's beautiful here. I want to show you something I found. When we get there, we can talk. I promise it will be all right."

Ben studied Chloe for a moment, her sparkling blue eyes, her fresh face—the mountain air had given her a healthy, attractive glow—framed by her soft tawny hair, curling in gentle wisps. His glance kept going back to her eyes. Gentle eyes, sincere eyes. He'd find no other listener more caring and understanding than Chloe.

He swallowed hard and turned away from her, not quite ready to reveal his inner turmoil.

Standing, he took a breath to compose himself. He scooped sand over the fire. Once it was reduced to a smolder, he nodded and turned back toward her. "Okay. Let's walk."

As they walked through the trees, bright rays of sunshine sliced through to bathe their path in warmth. Dirt, gravel, and broken twigs crunched beneath their feet.

"It's over there." Chloe pointed to a group of downed trees. They crisscrossed each other like a pile of branches in the middle of a giant fire pit. "There must have been a huge windstorm up here."

Without her even saying a word, he knew her intent as she headed toward the deadfall. "Be careful. They might not be as sturdy as you think."

"Don't worry, Ben. You just follow me. I'll be careful."

Before long, they were seated facing each other on the trunk of a fallen cedar. They were positioned so they could see mountains in every direction. Snow-capped peaks toward the west, and dusty brown ridges far off in the east. The tree's diameter was large enough for them to sit cross-legged, comfortably facing each other. They'd used other deadfall as stepping stones and were a good six feet off the ground. It was...nice.

But nice wasn't what Ben needed right now. He needed to bare his soul. He needed redemption. And even in a God-touched place like this with a woman who held his very soul in her hands, Ben wasn't sure he'd find it.

"Rosalie." His throat was tight with emotion. "Her name was Rosalie Faulkner. She was a student at my university, along with Monique and Avery."

He hesitated and pulled at a broken piece of bark.

"Go on. It will help you put the past to rest." The soft urging, the gentle concern in Chloe's eyes, gave Ben the assurance he could tell her anything and it would be all right.

"Gus, Avery, and I worked as a team. We needed money to fund the South Pacific project. Unless a scientist is independently wealthy, there's always a need for funds. Rosalie's father, Professor Faulkner, happened to chair the funding committee. He didn't really care for me. Didn't like my background or the way I was raised. Called me an upstart all the time and said I was a wiseacre because I was always one step ahead of him and the rest of the class."

"He just didn't like that you were smarter than him." Chloe spoke in a playful manner, but there was more truth in her words than she knew.

"He also happened to be on the scholarship review committee and had my scholarship revoked after..." *After Rosalie.* "After my last semester. That's why I didn't graduate, and why I don't have my doctorate."

The lost degree was one more reason Ben wanted to succeed on this trip. No matter how much he tried to convince himself otherwise, he had something to prove.

"Does Monique have her doctorate?"

"No. She never was a scientist. She was always along as an assistant. It was the only way Gus could justify having his daughter along. Anyway, Rosalie was a journalism major."

"Journalism?" Chloe eyes rounded in surprise. "She was studying to be a reporter?"

Ben nodded. "She and Monique were friends. Monique figured if she introduced us, she could talk me into taking Rosalie on the South Pacific assignment. She thought Rosalie could write such an impressive paper, the professor would fall at our feet with funds. I didn't think it would work, nor did I think Professor Faulkner would approve of his daughter going along with me. So I took it one step further."

"You asked Rosalie to marry you."

He nodded slowly, shame-filled. His selfishness had cost an innocent life.

"I courted her first, so it wouldn't seem so obvious."

"But if Professor Faulkner disliked you as much as you say, what made you think he'd let you take his daughter into the jungle? Much less marry her?"

"That's where Monique came in. She's such a charmer she could talk a man into doing anything. She already had the professor in the palm of her hand. I figured it wouldn't be hard for her to convince him to let Rosalie go with us. I mean, my name was kept out of everything. I figured by the time we got back, Rosalie and I would be married and there wouldn't be anything he could do."

"Then the money would start flowing in."

"Yeah. Only...only..."

Chloe finished the hateful sentence for him. "Rosalie never came back."

Ben groaned and buried his face in his hands.

"Ben?" Chloe's hand brushed his cheek, her touch tender. "You don't have to tell me the rest if you don't want to."

"I have to." He raised his head, aching to reach out and take her hand. "Now that I've started, I have to finish. Everything was fine for a while, but then Monique decided to be jealous of Rosalie."

"She wanted you for herself?"

"I don't really think so. She brought Avery along, and had him twisted right around her finger." He sighed. This was really wearing on his emotions. He felt drained. "I think she couldn't stand the fact that there was another woman along. Monique likes to be the center of attention."

Chloe nodded as if she knew exactly what he meant. "What did she do?"

"At first she tried hanging all over me, trying to divert my attention from Rosalie."

"Were you tempted?" Something flickered in Chloe's eyes, and Ben tensed, searching for the right answer.

"Monique's a very beautiful woman. And underneath that catlike exterior is a sensitive and vulnerable person. So yes, there were times I was tempted. I mean, we grew up together. Ninety percent of our lives have been spent together, and there usually weren't any other females around. How could I not be tempted? But no, I was long past the temptation by the time Rosalie came along. Besides, I wouldn't have been able to do that to Avery."

He searched Chloe's face, hoping she understood. She reached over and squeezed his hand.

"Monique did anything and everything she could to undermine Rosalie and make her feel incompetent, out of place. And I was too caught up in my studies to realize what was going on. But the worst thing was when she started making up stories to scare her. Poor Rosalie."

"Ben." Chloe feathered kisses on the back of his hand, and his heart did a loop-de-loop. "It wasn't your fault."

"Yes it was." She winced at the angry blast of his tone, and Ben pulled his hand away, ignoring her hurt look. "Don't you see? I used her. Tricked her. Not a very forgivable act, was it? Especially when I tell you Monique scared her so bad with one of her stories, Rosalie ended up running off a cliff. *And I wasn't paying any attention!* She died because of me, because of *my* negligence. Because I deceived her and took advantage of her good nature."

Chloe gasped and looked downright horrified.

He wouldn't blame her if she never spoke to him again. And somehow, he felt a hollow emptiness at the thought. If only things were different. If the thing with Rosalie had never happened then maybe...no. Even if it had never happened and he wasn't so guilt ridden, Chloe still couldn't be part of his life. She wasn't someone he could say good-bye to every couple of months after having only spent a few days together between assignments.

He stood and balanced himself on rough bark, then carefully picked his way back down to the grassy floor of the forest. When he reached the bottom, he turned to watch Chloe step from one fallen tree trunk to another, and he held out his hand to help her down when she reached the last one.

"Thank you." Chloe gave him a gentle smile and squeezed his hand. "You have to stop blaming yourself for something you weren't responsible for."

"But I was," he said. "I was responsible. I failed to protect her. I didn't keep her safe."

"How could you?" Chloe's firm demand took him by surprise. "You couldn't be there every minute. You're human, remember?"

She wrapped her arms around him and rested her head against his, their cheeks just brushing each other. "You're human." This time she said it gently.

Relief raced through him. Chloe hadn't turned away in the wake of his confession. She seemed to understand and care.

A warm peace seeped into his heart.

The Lord our God is merciful and forgiving....

The scripture from Daniel... Is this what forgiveness felt like?

Chloe turned and kissed his cheek, then whispered in his ear. "Don't worry. What happened with Rosalie won't happen with us."

Us. She thought there was an *us.*

"No." He shook his head. "There *is* no us. There can never be an us. My life is exploring new places, studying wildlife. I couldn't ask you to come along with me."

"But I would go with you anywhere. Just think of the stories I could—"

He put his hands to her lips to silence her, and she gently kissed his palms as if acting instinctively.

"No," he whispered.

The tears in her eyes tore at his heart.

"I've already put your life in danger once. I can't do it again. I could never bear losing you like Rosalie."

"I'm not her. Nothing will happen to me."

There was some logic in what she said. Chloe wasn't Rosalie, and just because Rosalie died on an exploration didn't mean Chloe would. However, she couldn't promise that. Rosalie certainly wasn't the first person to ever get killed on an expedition, nor would she be the last. And he couldn't risk Chloe being added to the list. Even if it meant losing her forever, so be it. At least he'd know she was safe in Cedar Ridge, even if she wasn't his. He closed his eyes to the fresh surge of pain.

"I'm sorry, Chloe. I can't change who I am and what my life stands for. And I can never, *ever* put your life at risk."

"It would be a risk of my own choosing." Quiet determination overtook the gentleness in her tone, and he saw fear in her eyes. The same fear he felt. The fear of losing each other. Still, he couldn't give in.

He shook his head and let out a pent-up breath of sadness.

"Don't you understand?" Her voice rose in anger. "I want to be with you! These last several days have been the most special of my life."

"Chloe, I don't know what to say. I—"

"Don't," she said harshly. "Don't say another word. You really are just like my father. And just like Jackson, too." Chloe clenched her jaw and pressed her lips together. She shook her head with fury. "You think women are only put on this earth to serve you. You can deny it if you want, but your actions prove otherwise."

Whoever this Jackson was, he seemed to incite pure venom in her. She turned from him and stepped toward the sun-dappled woods. "I'll meet you back at camp. But don't worry," she yelled over her shoulder. "I'll be extra careful not to walk off a cliff."

Her words, hurt-filled and angry, cut him to the core. He swallowed hard and blinked to clear his vision. But his vision only blurred again as she quickly walked away. He swore he could hear a whispered *"I love you"* trailing on the breeze she left in her wake.

A painful lump filled his throat, threatening to choke him as he whispered words he didn't think he dared say out loud. "Heaven help me, I love you too."

Chapter Seventeen

Bright and blue, the sunny sky was in total contrast to Chloe's mood. Rain and thunder would have suited her just fine. At least then, she wouldn't have to smile and be cheerful. But it was hard to mask her feelings as she marched along the dry and rocky trail that edged a treacherous and steep precipice.

They'd packed up their things and headed the direction Ben thought was the right one. But even his comment that they should be getting close to the camp where she hoped Caleb and Aunt Jane still waited didn't shake her out of this melancholy.

"Chloe, talk to me." Ben's plea tugged her heart, but she didn't answer. "Please?"

"I don't feel like talking." Chloe hated to snap at Ben. It wasn't his fault.

The truth was she still burned with guilt over her nasty comment about not falling off a cliff. It was a vile, hateful thing to say. Especially after Ben had bared his soul to her about Rosalie. She knew it hadn't been easy for him to do. She was sorry. Deeply sorry. But she couldn't bring herself to say so.

Because not only did she feel horrible about her comment, she hurt over the realization that no matter what fire sparked between them when they touched, Ben had no intentions of making room for her in his life when this trek was over.

It was probably just as well, since he'd undoubtedly try and turn her into a drudge who dutifully waited at home for her husband to return from his adventures.

As close as she held her dreams, she'd meant what she'd said about giving them up for him. This feeling she felt for him, the ache deep inside, the longing for his touch, was so strong she'd happily wait for him. No. She shook her head adamantly. It would never happen. Ben was too entranced with the outdoors. He'd never be willing to make room in his heart for a wife.

Where was all this silly nonsense coming from anyway? Chloe clenched her fists at her sides and charged ahead of Ben, up the trail.

"Chloe?"

While Ben called her name, she ignored him. She had nothing to say to him at the moment. Not until she could snap out of this grumpy mood. Anything she might say would be out of her control.

"Chloe, hold up. Why are you walking so fast? What is wrong with you?"

Ben sounded irritated. As well he should. She ought to be able to put her silly dreams aside and face the day with a smile. For Ben's sake, she really should try. Determined, she stopped and waited for him to catch up. It was obvious he wasn't going to give up until she told him something, and since she couldn't tell him what she was truly thinking, she brought up the other thing that weighed heavily on her mind.

"Please tell me you weren't serious yesterday when you said you'd kill the Sasquatch? Monique mentioned your plans to preserve it, but I thought she was making it up." The downward curve of his mouth made her stomach drop. "Please tell me that isn't your intent. Please?"

"Chloe." Ben sighed and stepped close. "I'm a scientist. Specifically, an ethologist. Remember? Surely you knew we preserved specimens when you came on this trip?"

As a journalist, and as an educated woman, she really should have known it. But she hadn't. Chloe looked up into his eyes, her own eyes pleading with him. "This is different, Ben. It's like killing a man."

"No." Ben's lips tightened. He shook his head. "This is what we do. It's how we study creatures. It's how we learn about animals." His voice was firm, steady, unswerving.

"I can't be part of it, Ben." She looked into his eyes, looked for some sort of understanding. "I'll have to find my own way back if that's what you intend to do." She turned and walked away.

Behind her, Ben puffed out a breath. "It's my profession, Chloe. My career is at stake. I can't just ignore that because of your sensibilities."

Chloe clamped her lips together and kept walking. Behind her, she heard Ben's boots crunching the ground as he matched her footstep for footstep. Why did she have to go and bring up killing the Sasquatch? That was hardly the way to make peace.

"I swear to you, Ben Kearny, if you so much as point your gun, I'll—" She broke off and came to a halt as the trail ended, leaving her to face a slow-moving creek.

Rocks of all sizes jutted forth, and some of them seemed to form a slippery walkway.

"It appears there's nowhere else to go." Ben studied the water, and Chloe watched in dismay as he stepped past her.

"Where are you going?"

Ben stopped and looked at her over his shoulder, his lips pressed together in a flat line. It was the same look her father wore when he thought she was either stupid or just plain bothersome. She couldn't stand the thought of being either one.

"Across the creek, of course." His tone was as short as her mood, which made Chloe feel all the worse. It was bad enough for her to be sour without drawing Ben into it too.

"Ben, I'm—"

"I don't want to discuss it with you any further, Chloe. I make all the decisions regarding the Sasquatch, and that's that. Now, are you coming?" He prepared to step across the rocks.

"Fine," Chloe snapped. "You make all the decisions regarding the Sasquatch."

But you don't make all the decisions about me! She'd only wanted to apologize. Chloe shouldered her way past Ben and stepped out onto the first stone. She reached the second and third stone without problem, and didn't turn to Ben until she was halfway across the stream. He was two stones behind her.

"You just remember as you're staring into Sassy's soft, gentle brown eyes before you pull the trigger, he's just another *decision* to you. Just another project, just another way to make money and build your name."

The dark glitter in Ben's eyes and the square set of his jaw told her his mood had finally matched hers. Good. It served him right to have his fine mood ruined. He had no right to take the life of the Sasquatch. None at all. Chloe took another step and her right foot slipped, throwing her off balance.

With both arms outstretched, she did a funny sort of wave and eventually regained her balance. She turned to see if Ben had even attempted to come to her rescue.

If he had intended any such thing, the smirk on his face indicated otherwise.

"Were you waiting for me to fall in?" She spoke sweetly and resisted the urge to flutter her lashes.

"I thought it might cool you off a bit, yes." His sugary tone almost rivaled hers.

"Just be careful when you get to this spot. That over-inflated ego of yours will be too much for you to balance. You'll be lucky if you don't end up drenched." With that, Chloe made the final hop to the other side of the bank. She turned to Ben, to watch him scale the remaining rocks.

Before he did he asked, "Just what makes you think his eyes are soft and gentle?"

"A conversation I had with the Salish man I told you about. He told me the Sasquatch is a curious creature and nothing to be feared. In spite of the dangerous tales surrounding him, he only wants to be loved and understood. It's we humans who make him out to be scary because we don't understand him."

"Hogwash." Ben moved two stones closer to the bank.

"Ben, I don't want to fight with you about this. I just wish you'd reconsider—"

"No! And I don't want to discuss it anymore." He stepped toward the final rock; the very one Chloe had slipped on. "If you say any more, I swear I'll leave you up here to your own devi—" Ben's eyes widened with alarm and he did that same kind of funny wind dance Chloe had done, to try and regain his balance.

Unfortunately, he slipped right into the shallow, rocky stream.

It would have been funny had he not hit his head on the very rock he'd been standing on.

Horrified, Chloe dropped her sleeping bag and sloshed into the water.

"Ben?" Chilled water filled her boots as she rushed to his side, but she tried to ignore it. Her boots would dry, her feet would warm up. It didn't matter. All that mattered was Ben, and right now his eyes were closed and his neck tilted at a funny angle.

She reached down to pull his head up out of the water, but stopped.

Would she hurt him worse if she moved him? She thought she read once that in one of Aunt Jane's articles. She didn't want to hurt him. But neither could she let him lie in the icy water.

First she had to wake him up. She placed her hands on either side of his face. One hand dipped into the water, since his right ear and that side of his face skimmed the creek.

"Ben, wake up." She stroked his cheeks gently, careful not to splash water up his nose. "Ben?"

There was no response.

"It's okay Ben, it'll be okay." Frantic desperation rose in her heart. At the same moment, the sun slipped behind a cloud, and a shiver ran down her spine.

For one desperate eternity, Chloe wasn't sure what to do. She looked at Ben then up at the bleak clouds darkening the skies, and knew she had to get him out of the water despite the possibility of injuring him further.

No. She couldn't think that way. There would be no further injuries. She would get Ben out of the water, and he'd be fine.

"Fine." Chloe spoke with desperate determination. "You're going to be just fine."

The sloshing water was the only sound she heard as she moved around to loop her arms under his armpits. Somehow, she had to drag him out of the water and up the short bank.

A sharp tug, followed by a burning sensation in her low back was her only answer when Chloe attempted to pull Ben to shore. His head lolled to the left, and a soft moan escaped his lips.

"That's right, Ben. Wake up. Help me. I need your help." Chloe shook his shoulders, dismayed when there was no response.

Please Lord, please. Let him be all right. Help me help him.

Water seeped up her pant legs, as she knelt in the stream. It was the only way. Put the strength in her legs and pull on his shoulders as she stood up. The water thoroughly soaked her pants and threatened to weigh her down, but she still gained enough momentum as she stood to pull Ben backward to the stream's edge.

It didn't matter that, as she fell onto the grass, Ben's weight knocked the air from her lungs. He was out of the water, Chloe thought as she struggled painfully to regain her breath. That was all that mattered. At least now she had a chance to get him warm and dry.

After a few moments, her breathing returned to semi-normal and she set about in an attempt to roll him onto the ground without hurting him. She pushed him a little and scooted the opposite direction, repeating this several times until she was finally able to ease out from under him.

Scrambling to her knees, Chloe knelt over Ben. He looked so still, so peaceful, one might think he was merely sleeping. She ran her fingers across his face, hoping her touch might finally wake him up. When it didn't, she gave a small cry and slipped her hands beneath his head, searching for the spot where he hit it on the rocks.

"Please, God. Please!" She hoped to find a goose egg, but instead felt a damp stickiness.

Horrified, Chloe stared at her bloodied fingers before reaching into her shirt pocket to search out a hankie. The action was merely reflexive since she never carried a hankie. Not in her shirt pocket anyway. *The carry-all!* Rather than waste precious moments dwelling on her foolishness, she jumped to her feet and raced back to the stream.

The carry-all dangled half in and half out of the water. One strap was caught on the rock Ben had slipped on. His revolver was at the bottom of the stream. It must have fallen in during her struggle to drag him out of the water.

At least now she wouldn't have to fight with him about killing the Sasquatch. The stray, unwelcome thought found its way to Chloe's mind before she could do anything to stifle it. She grabbed for the gun and pulled it, dripping wet, from the water. Was it ruined? She felt like she should know the answer, but didn't. If it was, that would mean there'd be no fresh meat other than fish. It would also mean no protection should they come across a bear.

An ominous feeling settled in the pit of her stomach as she tried to shake the water from the gun. She'd made such a stupid fuss about it before, never taking the time to consider that its purpose was for more than just killing an innocent creature. What if they needed it now? It was all her fault. Everything. If she hadn't needled Ben so much about killing the Sasquatch, if she hadn't plotted to be included on this trip in the first place...

No!

Chloe shook her head angrily, refusing to send her thoughts down that self-destructive path. She was not a weakling, despite what the men in her family thought. Ben had spent hours as they walked, tutoring her in the ways of nature and the means available to her for survival. She'd treat his wound with the best of her ability, get him warm and dry, and set about doing whatever it would take for them to survive.

Determined now, Chloe rushed back to Ben's side and fumbled through the bag searching for the pile of handkerchiefs she'd purchased that day at the general store. When looking at Ben's pale face, that day seemed so long ago.

An ugly bruise was beginning to form on his right cheekbone, and a cut marred his upper lip. Chloe dabbed at his lip with the hankie, but it was a small cut and by now the blood had already dried. The cut on the back of his head was the one she must worry about. She ran back to the creek and doused the cloth in the cold water then dashed back to Ben and pressed the cloth to the wound. All the while, she prayed the blow to his head wasn't life-threatening and that the cut wouldn't become infected.

Glancing around at her surroundings as she held the cloth to Ben's head, Chloe felt an immutable sense of hopelessness. Still her gaze roved her surroundings and her thoughts whirled furiously. What did she expect to find? Fern. Fern! What was it Ben had said? The fern acted like an antiseptic.

She laid Ben's head gently back on the ground and rose to conduct a thorough search of the area. When her eyes landed on some stinging nettles, hope surged within her. The ferns had to be nearby. Hadn't Ben said God planned it perfectly when He put the two so close?

Sure enough, the delicate feathery plants were nestled nearby. Careful not to step in the nettles, Chloe tenderly broke off several small fronds. Small was better, she remembered Ben saying. Tender, young, more potent.

She hurried over to Ben and gently swiped at the wound with a few leaves.

Next, she crushed a frond in her palm the way she'd seen Ben do, and she rubbed the crumpled leaves with her fingers, rolling them over and over in her palm until they made a coarse paste.

Leaning over Ben, she smeared the green mush on the cut over his eye and again on the wound at the back of his head. Then she scrubbed her hands over her pant legs. She'd think about washing them later. Finally, she let out the breath she hadn't realized she was holding until that moment.

One task out of the way. The bleeding was stanched and an antiseptic was protecting the wound. Now she had to figure out where they'd spend the night. Later she'd worry about why he wasn't opening his eyes. Right now she had to get him someplace warm and comfortable.

Think. Think. *Think!* She scanned her surroundings again while trying to quell her desperation. She shook her head and bit her lip to keep the tears at bay. There weren't any caves or crevices anywhere, no cubbyholes. The only thing she saw was a fallen tree. A fallen tree. Hadn't Ben told her...?

Rushing over, she wrenched her ankle with a sharp twist as it caught on a rock. Walking all around the tree, she studied it carefully. Old and large, it was weighted down by last fall's leaves and pine needles and heaven knew what else. Probably bugs, but hopefully no animal droppings.

She shuddered, determined to dispel unpleasant thoughts. A raindrop hit her nose. It was starting. She had to hurry, or Ben would catch his death of cold.

Was it better to leave Ben in the rain while she made the shelter? Or drag him to the tree and then build it? If she hesitated, the shelter floor would be soaked.

The arctic sleeping bag! It would keep him warm while she went to work on the shelter. She raced down to the creek to retrieve it from the bank, only to find it gone. It must have rolled into the creek and washed away.

Racing back to where Ben lay, Chloe dug her ladies' hunting jacket from her pack. Gently, she placed it over him. She'd have to wander down the creek later to see if the sleeping bag turned up. Right now, it was more important to build a shelter.

First things first. Tree branches. *"With enough of these,"* Ben had said, *"you can sit out a rainstorm and never get wet."* She hoped he'd been right.

Dead tired, Chloe set straight to work gathering fir and cedar boughs and hauling them to the deadfall. The wind and rain stormed around her, but she didn't let it stop her.

The boughs had to be placed wrong-side up and just so against the trunk of the fallen tree. This would keep out the rain. Layering them shingle-style would protect them from the wind. It was tough work, but she stuck to it, determined to make a warm dry place for Ben to recover.

By the time she was finished, she was covered with mud. It was raining so hard, she considered lifting her face heavenward and standing still long enough for the rain to wash her off. She couldn't. She had to think of Ben.

Rushing back over to his side, Chloe studied him with dismay. He was still unconscious.

"Come on, Ben. Wake up. Please. We have to get you warm. I've built the shelter. Come on. I need your help. I've never done this before." He stirred slightly, and so did the hope she forgot she had.

His eyelids fluttered. He opened his mouth and moaned.

"That's right, Ben." Chloe shook him. "Come on. Open your eyes. I need to get you to the shelter."

Ben's eyelids fluttered, and his lips parted. He groaned again.

Chloe held her breath, anticipating the next step where Ben would open his eyes.

It didn't happen.

Very slowly, she exhaled. Somehow she would have to get Ben to the shelter on her own.

She crouched at his head and once again looped her arms under his armpits.

"Come on," she muttered. "If you can hear me, help me out."

No response. She dug in her heels and tugged. The only one who moved was Chloe. She stumbled backward and struggled to catch her balance.

Again. Hands looped under his arms. "Come on, Ben." Deep breath. Tug. Nothing. But this time she didn't lose her balance.

Again. Hands looped, mutter, tug. And...he budged. Chloe whooped for joy and it gave her the gumption to try it again.

It would work. If she had to do it an inch at a time, if it took her all night long, she would get Ben into that shelter.

Thankfully, it didn't take all night. It took less than an hour to get Ben to the shelter. But even so, it was dark and she was exhausted. Chloe looked at the woven branches that formed a lean-to roof, amazed she'd actually built it herself. Ben had been right when he'd explained it all to her. She pulled a few branches off to make an opening. No rain leaked through.

But of course *she* was wet. Shivering, she tugged Ben inside. She didn't wait to get him situated. The rain was coming down harder, and she didn't want the ground where they would lay to get wet.

Quickly, with cold, numb fingers, she re-covered the shelter with the branches. Satisfied they wouldn't get any wetter than they were, she ducked down and crawled in, carefully replacing the last branch.

There was nowhere for her to lie except halfway on top of Ben. In order to do its job and keep them warm, there couldn't be much room in the shelter. She'd made it small like Ben had said. She had to get him warm.

With his back flush against the shelter's only wall—the underside of the fallen tree—Chloe knew she had to get as close to him as possible to generate heat. She pressed against him, cold herself.

Two bodies, a small close space.

Under any other circumstances, it would be improper to crawl into such a small place with a man. But worry for Ben's condition overrode her discomfort.

Why hadn't he stirred enough to do more than groan?

Chloe's head rested on his chest. At least he was breathing evenly. She lay there, listening to the steady breaths and thrumming of his heart, and wondered how long the rain would last.

What would she do if Ben never woke up?

Chapter Eighteen

Late the next afternoon, Chloe stood at the creek watching the water thunder and churn. The chilled mist that rose off it to brush her skin was the perfect match for her mood. Never had she felt more alone. Not when her father threw her out, and not when Caleb disappeared. Nothing compared to this emptiness, this dread that Ben might not survive. He'd been right all along. She didn't belong here, had no business here. If she hadn't argued with him about the Sasquatch, if she'd not distracted him from his footing...

The canteen she'd brought to the creek dropped from her hand and landed with a *thunk* on some rocks near the edge. She stooped to retrieve it, but just as her fingers brushed it, the water swept it away. "No!" She bit back a sob, determined not to cry. It wouldn't do any good. A chill wound its way down her neck and seeped into her limbs. She shivered and rubbed her arms to generate warmth. Her comfort was inconsequential at the moment. All that mattered right now was Ben and the predicament she'd gotten him into.

She was thankful the wind no longer raged. She'd waited all morning for it to die down so she could go in search of food for Ben. It worried her that he had yet to regain consciousness, but she felt compelled to have nourishment at the ready when he did.

Space in the shelter was cramped just as he'd taught her, and Chloe had spent the long stormy hours sandwiched next to him while the wind howled outside. From time to time he would moan in pain, and she'd whisper to him in soothing tones. She'd taken his cries as a good sign. Hopefully that meant he'd awaken soon.

Now though, she began to have her doubts. He'd been asleep too long. She prayed with all her might his body was merely mending itself and that his hours of unconsciousness meant nothing ominous.

No, she couldn't think that way. Ben would be fine. And when he awoke, he'd hate her for getting him into this situation.

Feeling dejected, Chloe decided she'd best be off in search of food. She might even try her hand at catching a fish. She had Ben's fishing line and hook, having rifled through the pockets of his hunting vest in search of anything that might prove useful.

Most of what was in his pockets, she'd seen before. What had surprised her though was a metal telescoping cup. She'd never seen him bring it out and use it. Perhaps it wasn't really water-worthy. His compass was useless, having been broken in the fall. Its paper dial was torn, the brass needle bent, the glass shattered.

In hopes of filling her canvas bag with berries and such, she had emptied it of all its contents save Aunt Jane's pocket watch and Ben's field glasses. They were the last thing she'd grabbed before leaving the tiny shelter. There was a little water under the lenses, but hopefully they would dry out soon.

As she walked, scouting out a variety of plants in the area, Chloe also kept her eyes open for the sleeping bag. She still held out hope that it might have washed up the bank somewhere.

Several times, she had the eerie sensation that someone was nearby. But each time, she glanced around and was unable to spot movement of any kind. Even the breeze was unusually still. A shiver of uncertainty crept up her spine, and she remembered the feel of hands on her back just before she fell off the bluff.

Indecisive when she reached a fork in the trail, Chloe looked behind her. She needed to be cautious, to remain oriented as to in which direction the shelter lay. Finally, she chose the path to the left. It appeared to be a good choice because the first thing she spotted as she rounded the bend was a raspberry patch. Eagerly plucking the berries from the vine, she filled her bag and enjoyed a few mouthfuls along the way. Their tart sweetness slid down her throat as she savored the taste. At least if she couldn't find anything else, these would sustain Ben for a while. She contemplated the fact she might have to leave him and go for help. Would the shelter keep him safe?

Once again, she thought about how alone she was. It seemed years had passed since she and Ben had been separated from the others, and even longer since the terrible fight with her father.

Enough time to fall in love.

Enough time to know that once Ben got better, if he did, and they made it back to civilization, he'd be on his way.

Without her.

But Ben wouldn't be able to go on his way if something happened to him because of her idle daydreaming.

Sighing and overcome with dismay, she went back to the work of gathering nettles for tea, ferns to take away the burns she received from the nettles, and a variety of edible wildflowers. At least she thought they were edible. She was careful to gather only the ones she was sure Ben had pointed out to her as safe for human consumption.

Eventually, growing more exhausted, Chloe seated herself on the grass under a tree to rest a bit and eat some berries before heading back to the shelter.

It was beautiful here, a paradise, but she couldn't sit for very long. She had to get back to Ben. She stood and lifted his field glasses to her eyes, frustrated to discover she'd managed to get berry juice on the lenses. Once she wiped them clean, she had a perfect view of the woods that scaled the mountainside. The trees seemed to go forever heavenward. Even with the glasses she couldn't see the top of the mountain. It probably went on for miles. An eagle flew overhead, circling something on the ground that Chloe surmised to be his evening meal. She spotted a waterfall and, peeping out from a grove of trees, an elk. The sound of birds chirping filled the air.

"Perfect," she murmured. Even more perfect when shared with someone you loved. Her fanciful thoughts turned to Ben, and all she'd learned about him in the past several days; his gentleness with nature, his love for the outdoors, his protectiveness. Then, there was the way his voice made her knees buckle when he sang. How had her life ever seemed full without him? The urge to please her father was still there, but wasn't nearly as strong since Ben assured her that she was every bit as capable of writing for a newspaper as the next person. She loved him...and her life would seem so very empty without him.

She needed to remember every detail of the scenery here, as well as all the newfound feelings she'd discovered about Ben, so she could record them in her journal after she returned to the shelter. After she knew Ben would be all right.

She put the field glasses back in the bag, gently so as not to smash the berries. As she did, her hand brushed Aunt Jane's watch. She pulled it out of the bag and ran her fingers over the shiny diamonds that lined the bright cobalt blue coloring. Her nail caught on a tiny bit of metal. Rubbing it again, she was surprised when the face snapped open. Just as she knew it would be, Jane's name was engraved inside with a fancy script. The inner workings were fascinating in meticulous detail, but not nearly as fascinating as the small piece of paper she found sticking out from behind the flat metal piece opposite the clockworks.

Flipping at it until it opened, Chloe pulled out the paper.

Rosalie's brother. Those words never would have made sense before, but now that Ben had told her about Rosalie, they made perfect sense. Her aunt had figured out that not only was Skip the one behind the sabotage on Ben's career, he was doing it because Rosalie was his sister.

She couldn't wait to tell Ben. The thought brought her up short. For the briefest second, she had managed to forget his condition.

What if he never woke up?

Brushing a pinecone, or rather a *fir* cone, out of her way, she recalled Ben teasing her about possibly having to eat one. Perhaps she should gather some into the bag. Just in case.

"Oh, Ben." She wanted nothing more than to tease him back. "Please God, let him wake up soon."

Cold. It was the first awareness Ben had as he started to wake. *Cold and alone.*

What about Chloe? He shivered and rubbed his arms. If only he could get warm.

"Chloe?" Ben knew there'd be no answer. Wherever he was, there was a sense of emptiness. He could feel by the discomfort that he was in a small, tight space. It seemed whichever way he moved he was penned in on all sides. Bit by bit, he gathered the strength to open his eyes. At first he saw only darkness, but when his eyes adjusted he realized he was in a hole somewhere. A shelter of some sort.

His last awareness had been of skipping across the creek on the rocks, arguing with Chloe about whether or not he should kill the Sasquatch. Then he'd fallen into the water. Had she pulled him out? How had she managed? And had she built the shelter where he now lay? If so, where was she now?

"Where are you? And where am I?"

There was a crick in his back and no matter how he turned, he couldn't get comfortable or warm.

Where was Chloe, and why did he feel so empty when he thought of her?

She'd left him. Chloe had left him just like his mother had left him, and like his father, like Rosalie.

Everyone always left him.

A thick layer of fog swept toward her, and a chill pricked at Chloe's skin. Why hadn't she noticed it sooner? With a sense of alarm, she realized it was much thicker than any she'd ever seen. They had a lot of fog in the lower mountains near Cedar Ridge, but it didn't compare to this. She hurried back toward the shelter, nervous that she couldn't see more than a few feet in front of her.

It's all right. It's not as bad as it seems. But the sky was growing dark faster than usual.

It was okay, she knew how to get back. She'd been very careful in noting the direction. But as she walked, the fog grew thicker, and before long she couldn't see her hand in front of her face, let alone which direction to head. Panic set in.

Ben. She had to get back to him. But which way should she go? Goose flesh rose on her arms. The fog was damp, misting around her, and before long she was soaked to the skin.

Her leg hit something sharp. She reached out and touched the outline of a giant boulder. She didn't remember seeing it before. Was she lost? Who would take care of Ben?

"Ben?" As soon as she called out his name, she realized the ridiculousness of it. He was still unconscious, and even if he did happen to wake up, he'd be too weak to answer.

Chloe refused to give up. She stumbled around, determined to find Ben, unwilling for him to be alone. Her fingers and toes grew numb with cold, and her clothes were damp and chilled. Her nose was starting to run.

Finally when she could barely put one foot in front of the other, she knew she had to stop and rest. Maybe, just maybe if she rested a few minutes, she'd restore her strength and regain her sense of direction. Or maybe, if she was lucky, the fog would lift and she'd be able to find Ben.

Chloe fought to keep her eyes from closing. She couldn't fall asleep, could merely take a brief rest. Ben was more important that her own comfort.

She was so cold.

Her eyelids were so heavy.

Was Ben safe?

Chloe's eyes drifted shut. She fought to open them, but they were like lead. She was so cold.

She dreamed. In her dream, she was vaguely aware of someone tucking a blanket around her. She tried to peep her eyes open but couldn't bring her vision into focus. It was a large person, with hairy hands. No one she recognized, but she wasn't frightened. The person was gentle, so gentle, while tucking the cover under her chin.

"Thank you." She managed to whisper the words just as the warmth seeped around her.

Startled to feel the sunlight on her face, Chloe's eyes flew open.

Ben! She'd been away from him all night. She prayed he was all right. How could she have fallen asleep without getting back to him? She pulled aside her covers and jumped up.

Covers? Frozen in place, she stared in disbelief at the sheepskin lining she recognized as part of her sleeping bag. Where was the rest of it?

More importantly, *where had it come from?*

Chloe leaned against the tree and shut her eyes for an instant, thinking back. She remembered sitting down to rest, closing her eyes for just a moment then trying to open them again. But they'd been so heavy. Then she remembered a sense of awareness that someone was nearby. She remembered struggling to open her eyes to see a large figure bending over her, tucking the blanket around her. Who was it? Whoever it was, they were wrapped in what appeared to be a bearskin coat.

She remembered thinking, right before she'd drifted off, how hairy the person was.

Her eyes flew open and she jumped up. Could it be? No. *Ridiculous!*

There was absolutely, positively no way a Sasquatch had come and covered her up while she'd been sleeping. It was a dream. That's all. Just a dream.

She must have forgotten something. She must have stumbled across the sleeping bag, or at least the liner, before she sat down to rest. The odd thing was, she'd forgotten all about it.

Suddenly stricken with fear, Chloe glanced around. There didn't appear to be anybody nearby. It didn't matter. She had to hurry back to Ben.

She walked up the hill a short way and stood looking in all directions, trying to get her bearings.

Which way was the shelter?

Off in the distance she saw what might be the shelter. She reached into the bag and pulled out Ben's field glasses. Lifting them to her eyes, she squinted to get a better look. Chloe whispered a prayer of thanks as she recognized the area near the creek where Ben had fallen. And just beyond it, the shelter. Thankful, she hurried toward it as fast as possible.

"Chloe?"

At the sound of Ben's weakened voice, she turned. He sat at the edge of the creek, his face and hands wet.

"Ben?" He was awake. He was all right. "Ben. Oh, Ben." She hurried to him and threw her arms around him. "I was so worried. I thought you were going to die. Then I went out to find some food, and the fog came in and I got lost and... oh, never mind." She rained kisses first on his head then his face, his beautiful battered face. "You're awake. You're alive. Thank you, God. Thank you."

"You went to find food?"

She nodded, still unable to keep from touching him. "I just can't believe you're awake."

"When I woke up, I found your canteen filled with water."

Chloe pulled back and stared into his eyes. "What did you say?"

"The canteen. I—"

"By the shelter?"

"No, in it. Right next to me. Filled with water."

"But I lost it in the creek. How...?" She shook her head. "It can't be. I had the strangest experience. I'll tell you about it later, when you're stronger."

"I'm strong enough now." Ben made as if to stand, and Chloe helped steady him until he stood on shaky legs. Though his face blanched from either pain or weakness, he still gave her a determined look. "Now what were you saying?"

"I got lost in the fog."

"After that fight we had, I was certain you'd left me."

Chloe shook her head in horror. "No, Ben. I could never leave you."

There was a touch of sadness in his eyes as he smiled down at her, and he looked as if he weren't quite convinced. He started to say something then shook his head as if it didn't matter. But it did. Chloe wanted to hear it.

"Ben, is there something you want to talk about?"

"You said you had a strange experience. What happened? Tell me about it."

"You won't believe me." They walked toward the shelter as she spoke. "While I was lost in the fog, I grew so weary I had to sit down and take a small rest. I fell asleep and had the strangest dream, like someone was there. When I woke up, I was covered with the lining of the sleeping bag."

"So that's where the rest of it was. You took it with you. That was smart, Chloe. Especially since you ended up getting lost."

"What?" Chloe shook her head. Ben must be slightly disoriented and not know what he was saying. "Ben, the sleeping bag was lost in the creek. This is the first I've seen it since you fell."

"Then how...?"

"That's what I'm trying to tell you. Someone brought it to me. They covered me with it. I couldn't see whoever it was, but they were big and had hairy hands. *Very* hairy, as in..." She felt so stupid saying it out loud. "...Sasquatch hairy."

A funny thing happened. Ben didn't laugh at her. He looked incredulous. Not like he didn't believe her. It was something else, and she just didn't want to grasp it. However, when Ben pulled the branches from the shelter to reveal what was inside, a chill went through her, and she stood there with her mouth gaping open.

In the opening of the shelter lay the outer cover to the sleeping bag. She snatched it from the ground.

"How? Where did you get this?"

Ben grinned, looking quite pleased with himself. "Until this very moment, I thought you covered me with it."

"Are you sure you feel up to leaving right now? Don't you think we should wait until you're a little stronger?" Chloe had been hen-pecking him since he'd announced they'd better be on their way. Ben appreciated her concern, but she was beginning to aggravate him.

"Will you quit prattling on about it? How many times do I have to say yes?"

"Prattling on? Is that what I'm doing?" Though her face remained passive, her voice was chilling, and the spark disappeared from her eyes.

Humbled and contrite, he reached out to touch her cheek. She jerked her head back, her eyes as hard and cold as glacier ice. "I'm sorry, Chloe. I know you're only asking because you care. But please, I'm fine. Really, I am. Will you forgive me?"

One short, curt nod was his only answer before Chloe stood up. Ben also stood, sensing all was not really forgiven. Was what he said really *that* bad, that unforgivable?

"Which way do you want to go?" Chloe looped the sleeping bag over her shoulders and handed him her pack. There was a definite chill in her voice.

"Why don't we head up that trail over there?"

"That's where I got lost in the fog. Why do you want to go that way?" The chill in her tone gave way to suspicion, and he knew exactly what she was thinking.

Certain he was grinning like an idiot, he reached for her hand. She slapped it away. Still, her mood couldn't quench his excitement. They were about to find Jacko's relatives.

"Chloe. The entire purpose for this fiasco was to find the Sasquatch. Humor me, and let's just head that way. Okay?"

Instead of answering, Chloe turned on her heel and headed for the trail.

What had he done?

Was there a man on earth who would ever understand women?

Chloe walked so quickly and furiously, she thought her legs would fall off. Her face ached with tension.

Prattling on, prattling on.

Over and over the words rang in her ears, until she no longer heard Ben's voice, but her father's.

Shut up, Chloe. Just shut up. Why do you have to prattle on all the time? Why can't you just be a good girl and shut up?

Prattling on, prattling on.

Finally, unable to bear it any longer, Chloe covered her ears, stepped off the trail, and leaned against a tree.

"Enough!" The word tore from her throat, startling her.

She sensed Ben's presence beside her but didn't look up at him. She knew there were tears in her eyes, and she didn't want him to see them. She knew he hadn't meant the words the way her father always meant them. She knew Ben was merely reacting to being asked the same question over and over again. Still, his reaction brought back all the feelings of her failure with her father. Of how she could never make him proud, no matter how hard she tried. How she wanted nothing more than to write, the simple pleasure it brought her, and how it would only serve to help her father in his business. And mostly, she thought about the rift between them now and how she couldn't go back home even if she wanted to.

When Ben touched her shoulders, she shook her head and looked at the ground. Then he gently drew her into his arms, as if instinctively knowing he shouldn't force her to look at him, as if instinctively knowing she didn't want him to see the tears. He held her close, sprinkled kisses on the top of her head, and murmured something she couldn't hear. It wasn't until he whispered her name that she finally looked up.

"Chloe," he said again, then reached out and gently wiped the tears from her cheeks. "I'm so sorry I hurt you. I really didn't mean too."

"I-I know you didn't, Ben. I'm sorry if I made you believe it was you I was upset with."

"It's not me?"

"No, what you said, I knew you didn't mean. But it reminded me of my father, of something he used to say to me all the time, of our fight, of not having any place to go when I get back ho—" She broke off as a fresh wave of pain tightened her throat.

"You have someplace, Chloe. With me." He tightened his arms around her. "Stay with me. I'll take care of you."

"I don't want to be taken care of Ben. I just want to belong, to fit in."

"You belong with me. You fit in with me."

"No, I don't." She struggled against him, but he held her fast. She wanted to be enveloped in his warmth. She wanted to lose herself. But she couldn't. She had to make him see things for what they were.

"You were quite clear before. You want me, but on your terms. You want me to be waiting for you when you get back from your adventures. It won't work that way for me, Ben. I want all or nothing."

"Chloe, I'm sorry. I just can't take you with me. You see what's happened here. Everything is my fault. I've put you in jeopardy just by letting you be here. If something happened to you, I'd never forgive myself. The way it is, your reputation is ruined. But don't worry. I'll—"

"Stop!" She knew what he was about to say, and she couldn't bear to hear him say he'd marry her just to salvage her reputation. Instead she tried to divert him back to the blame he'd placed upon himself. "You spend too much time worrying. When I fell, it was because I was pushed. And we both know it was Skip who pushed me. Skip, who is Rosalie's brother, by the way. But I survived. And you've proven that even experienced people can have accidents."

"Skip is Rosalie's brother?"

Chloe ignored the question. There'd be time to answer that after she made him understand. "Look, Ben. Didn't I pull you out of the water? Didn't I build the shelter and make a safe haven for you? Find you food? Didn't that prove anything to you? Anything at all?" She tore from his grasp, terribly afraid she'd burst into tears once again.

He stood rigid, his expression unreadable. Why couldn't she make him understand?

Almost as if he discerned her thoughts, Ben pulled her toward him with a gentle hand. He tilted her face, cradling it gently in his hands.

"Did you know that when I woke up in the shelter, alone, I thought you'd left me? Abandoned me like everyone else." He leaned forward and brushed his lips gently against hers. "All I could think was how empty my life would be without you."

Tears blurred Chloe's vision, and hope took flight in her heart.

"Don't ever leave me, Chloe. Please? We'll find a way to work things out. I love you."

This was more than she ever dared to hope. Unable to speak, for fear the moment would disappear forever, she smiled up at him. They stood that way, satisfied to simply gaze at each other, until Ben reached down and slipped his finger through the black scrap of Chantilly lace that Chloe used as a belt.

He tugged until it came untied.

She swallowed hard, watching every move his hands made. Her lace belt whispered along her waistline as Ben pulled it free. Her heart pulsed, and she swore she could feel it deep in her belly.

After Ben looped the lace around her neck like a scarf, he gave a quick tug on the ends, and she fell against him.

There was a question in Ben's eyes, and an answer in Chloe's. He reached out and touched her hair, and she knew they were about to kiss, knew she wanted more than just a kiss, knew that this time their kisses would be more than she could ever imagine.

When his lips finally met hers, Chloe sighed. This was the answer to all her dreams.

"Chloe?"

"Yes," she whispered. "Yes."

He purifies us... The words came unbidden to her heart, reminding her of who she wanted to be and why.

Slowly, regretfully, she pulled away.

"No. I'm sorry, Ben. I can't do this. I-I want to, but it's not right. Everything I've learned about God lately tells me it's not right without marriage."

Tears pricked her eyes as Ben sighed and dropped a kiss on her forehead.

She closed her eyes, willing her heart to hold on to this moment forever, praying he wouldn't take it as a rejection of him.

"What in blue blazes is going on here?"

Chapter Nineteen

The booming voice, surprisingly close to Ben's ear, seemed to come from nowhere. Chloe pushed away from him in a heartbeat.

"Father!" Chloe's startled shriek pierced his ears as well as his nerves. "What are you—? How did you—?" She shrieked again, and before Ben could recover, she was heading toward the creek.

"Answer me, son. And while you're at it, you'd best tell me your intentions toward my daughter."

Ben stared into a pair of eyes as blue as Chloe's, but colder than the glacier water flowing from the mountain. The balding man with the mustache of a walrus was doing his best to look fierce, but even though Ben knew Chloe's father was about to slug him, he wasn't afraid. Given her disheveled state as she scrambled away, it was no less than he deserved. A tender wave of warmth flooded the center of his chest as he recalled her flushed cheeks and mussed hair.

Before he could finish that thought, Ben saw stars.

He fought through the wave of dizziness and rubbed his jaw, blinking to try and clear his vision. He wouldn't have thought the smaller man could hit quite so hard.

"Mr. Williston, I—"

"Think carefully before you speak, son." Williston's warning was rife with danger.

"I don't have—" Ben stepped back. "I mean I didn't have—it was innocent in the beginning, but now my feelings have changed. I'm not sure what my intentions are. I know what I'd like them to be, but I'm not sure what they can be."

A soft gasp drew his attention, and Ben turned to his right in time to see Chloe disappear over the slope that led to the creek. He started to run to her, only to find his way blocked by a younger, beefier version of Chloe's father. And there was no mistaking the fire in his eyes. Ben braced himself as another Williston prepared to unleash fury on his face.

"What are your intentions toward my sister? And I'd be careful how you answer that."

Before he could even answer, Ben saw stars again. This time, though, he had to pick himself up off the ground. When he finally stood and stared into the eyes of the man who could only be Chloe's older brother, Charles Jr., he didn't hesitate in his answer.

"I love her." He worked his sore jaw and mumbled the words. "I just have to figure out a way to work things out so I can give her what she deserves."

"I'm not sure what my intentions are."

Ben's words, his uncertainty, placed Chloe's heart in turmoil. She sat at the edge of the creek and dashed cold water on her cheeks. Her hair and clothing were put back together. If only she could say the same for her emotions.

But he'd said he loved her. He'd said his life would be empty without her. How could he have changed his mind so quickly? *Why* had he changed his mind so quickly?

Or had he been lying all along?

Ben didn't know his intentions, and yet she'd given him her heart.

She was a fool.

Thank the Lord her good senses had taken over before she gave him more than her heart. She brushed her hands together and stood. There would be no making that mistake again.

Perhaps her father had been right to punch him.

In spite of herself, Chloe's heart lifted at the thought of her father. She knew Aunt Jane sent a message to him through the engineer. But she never really thought he'd come. Or maybe she never really allowed herself to hope he'd come. Did his presence mean he'd forgiven her and wanted her to come back home?

Not that it mattered any longer. Just by being alone with Ben overnight, even though it was the result of an accident, she disgraced her family. There was no going back now.

Forgiveness and strength—she needed both. "Please, Lord, please." She closed her eyes as a soft breeze carried her whispered prayer down the creek.

An intimate relationship meant committing her heart. Chloe might have committed her heart to Ben, but obviously he hadn't committed his heart to her. She'd wanted to give her whole self to Ben, body, heart and soul. He'd acted as though he wanted the same.

And yet he didn't know how he felt.

She, on the other hand, knew exactly how she felt.

Like a fool.

The chill in Chloe's heart seeped to her fingers and toes. Shivering, she knew she couldn't sit by the creek forever. She had to muster enough dignity and courage to head back to Ben and her father, where she knew heartbreak and disgrace awaited her.

Dread built in her chest with each footstep, and as she drew closer it nearly overwhelmed her. Ben stood face-to-face with Charles Jr. What on earth was *he* doing here? That he would actually leave his bottle of whiskey and come all this way for her was nothing short of astonishing. She drew in a deep breath and slowly approached. As she did, Ben and her older brother turned to face her.

Ben's face was scraped up and battered, just like her heart. Chloe ran toward him, aching to kiss his hurt away. He may not know how he felt about her, but she loved him so much. She would never love anyone else. Dashing her fists against her eyes, she drew up short and struggled to hold the tears at bay.

"If you put those tears in her eyes, so help me..." Charles Jr. clamped his hand down on Ben's shoulder, but Chloe's heart lifted with pride as Ben shrugged it off and stepped toward her.

"Are you all right?" His voice was but a whisper as he approached, and Chloe could see the concern in his eyes. After what her family put him through, he was still concerned for her. If possible, her heart soared even higher.

"I think so." She cast a wary glance toward her father and braced for a slew of angry words. When they didn't come, she turned back to Ben. "What about you? Your face...." She reached up and touched his battered jaw. It looked worse up close.

Ben gazed down at her, his eyes warm in spite of the way her family just treated him. He reached up and covered her hand with his own.

"Chloe, about what I said." He drew in a deep breath. "I'm so sorry. When your dad startled us, I—"

A noise sounded behind her, and Ben looked up. Likely her father or brother, and a new anger filled her at what they'd done to Ben.

She whirled around, incensed. But the shout on her lips, the anger in her heart faded at the sight of the woman standing just beyond her father.

"Mama?" Hot tears blurred her vision before she could fully soak in the sight of her mother. Chloe swiped at her eyes with the back of her hands, aching to run to her. Torn, she looked up at Ben, reluctant to leave his side until he finished what he wanted to say.

"Go ahead, Chloe." His voice was low and intense. "Go see your mother. I'll still be here." He reached for her hand and gave it a squeeze. "I promise."

She hesitated before turning toward her mother. Then she broke in to a run, stumbling across half-buried tree roots. "I've missed you so much!" Chloe flung herself into her mother's arms, hugging her tight while she tried to control these all-consuming inexplicable emotions.

"Chloe." Her name was a caress on her mother's lips. "It's all right, sweetheart. Hush." Her mother stroked her hair and spoke in soothing tones.

Chloe imagined herself as a young child again, where her mother truly had the power to make everything all right. She sighed. If only...

After a moment, Chloe pulled away and studied her mother's face. Concern pinched her lips and furrowed deep lines in her brow. Concern caused by Chloe's reckless behavior. Guilt pricked Chloe's heart, even as she tried to tell herself that had none of it happened, she wouldn't have gone on this amazing adventure and fallen in love with Ben.

To assure herself he was still there, Chloe glanced at Ben and was rewarded with a smile. Maybe things weren't as bad as they seemed after all. She smiled as well, then turned back to her mother.

"Mama, I'm so sorry I caused you pain."

"It wasn't your fault, dear. The important thing is we're here, now. And we're together."

"I know Aunt Jane sent a message to Father, but I didn't expect for you to be here." The thought of her mother trekking through the wooded mountains amazed her. Wearing boots, trousers, and carrying a backpack, no less. Even more amazing was the fact that her father let her do it.

Behind her, someone cleared his throat.

"Chloe?" Her father. "Come on, honey. Walk with me. Let's talk a bit."

Talk? Her father wanted to talk to her. He didn't even sound angry. Why? Apprehension gripped her, almost crippling in its power, and she hesitated.

"Go on, sweetheart," her mother urged. "He needs to do this."

Reluctant, but struggling not to show it, Chloe allowed herself to be led away by her father. As they walked past Ben, his smile was one of encouragement. Why, when he didn't know how he felt about her?

When they finally came to a stop, they were far enough from the others for privacy, but close enough to see the hopeful looks on their faces.

"I'm so proud of you, Chloe."

Rooted to the spot, she stared at her father. Gaped was probably a more apt verb.

I'm so proud of you. Words she'd longed to hear her entire life. Had he really said them? Or had she imagined it? She cast him a hopeful look and, when he nodded, bit her lip to ward off the tears.

Her daddy loved her.

A sudden ache to feel his arms around her propelled Chloe forward. She was rewarded with a bear hug the likes of which she hadn't felt since she was a small child. When she stepped out of it, he pressed a kiss on top of her head.

"Chloe, my sweet daughter. I hope you can forgive me for ever doubting you. If you hadn't pushed me to the edge, I never would have realized it. The minute you walked out the door—no, the minute I told you not to come back—my heart broke. I wanted to go after you, but my stupid pride wouldn't let me. If anything had happened to you…" His voice shattered into a muffled sob, followed by a broken whisper. "I'm so thankful you're safe. Can you forgive an old man for his foolishness?"

Hot tears flooded Chloe's eyes as she thanked God for giving her father back.

"I want you to take over the paper."

That was the last thing she expected to ever hear. She could do nothing but stare at him. Her mouth went dry, and she swallowed hard, attempting to moisten it. Was this really happening? More tears threatened to fall as she struggled for words. "You…want…me?"

"That's right, honey. I'm ready to retire. It's only natural to want to leave the paper in the hands of someone I trust and respect."

"You…respect…me?" This couldn't be real.

Her father nodded and smiled. "While you were down at the creek, Ben told me how you saved his life."

"Did he tell you about Caleb? How we got separated from the group?"

"He did, sweetheart."

"They're in danger, Father. There's a man who wants to hurt Ben and Gus and anyone connected with them. Aunt Jane said he's dangerous. We have to get back to them."

"We will. Don't you worry. And Charles Jr. is here to help." He squeezed her hand. "I'm so proud of you, honey. You've battled your shyness and replaced it with a newfound courage. You went after your dream even after I tried to squelch it. Not only that—" He broke off suddenly and practically beamed. "You're a top-notch writer, too. Nellie Bly had better watch out."

"But what about Caleb?"

Her father cleared his throat. "Caleb isn't happy in the newspaper business, and since I want my children to be happy, I decided not to push him."

He paused and glanced tenderly at Chloe. "Ben told me Caleb plans to travel around the country, drawing whatever he sees, with plans to someday compile his pictures into a book. Maybe, by then, you'll be so successful, you can publish it for him."

Chloe was stunned. The dream she'd had for years was coming true. But her heart failed to lift and soar the way she always imagined it would if this day ever came. It was difficult to imagine her heart ever soaring now. Not when the man she'd given her heart to had inexplicably changed his mind.

In that moment, she saw life for what it really was.

Unpredictable.

Crazy.

Changing, ever changing.

Things didn't always turn out the way you dreamed, and you had to be ready to accept and change with it. If you couldn't, you would hurt forever.

Chloe suspected she would hurt forever.

"Well? What do you think?"

Her father's approval meant so much to her, and she didn't want to hurt him with her answer. The joy of finally winning his acceptance was bittersweet, but she would push past the pain and give him the answer he sought.

"Oh, Father, of course I will." No longer able to hide her tears, she threw herself back into his arms. But she immediately lifted her head up off his shoulder and stared up at the mountains.

She finally did it. She finally won her father's approval.

But without Ben, it meant nothing.

Chapter Twenty

Sandwiched between her parents, Chloe's heart was conflicted. Her joy at being with them, having reconciled with her father, was dampened by the ache in her heart every time she looked up and saw Ben.

After a meal of bread, dried meat, and apples from her parents' packs, they had finally started off on their search to find the others. It seemed they'd walked for hours, and now the sun was just beginning to slip from view. It would soon be time to set up camp, and another night would pass without knowing if Caleb was safe.

Charles Jr. walked in front of her, keeping a constant, wary eye on Ben, who walked beside him. It was better to keep her eyes on the ground, because it seemed like every time she looked up, Ben turned to glance at her over his shoulder. Uncertainty filled her. Could it be he figured out where she fit in his life after all?

At the next turn in the path, Chloe realized this stretch of the river looked familiar. "Ben!" Certain they were only about half a day from the camp where they'd left Aunt Jane, she stopped.

Ben turned and flashed a grin. He recognized it, too.

"Mother, Father, this is where we were before we were separated from Caleb." She should feel excited, but apprehension crawled up the back of her neck. She rolled her shoulders, trying to regain focus. "Our last camp was right up this bank."

"Then this is probably the best place to stop for the night."

Chloe wanted to argue with Ben, but she knew he was right. They couldn't search in the dark. It would be better to build their camp now and get a good night's sleep.

Before settling in for the night, Chloe longed to talk to Ben. She didn't want to go to sleep without knowing where she stood with him. But that would be impossible under her father's careful scrutiny. There was one thing she could say in front of the others, though.

"Father, remember the watch you gave Aunt Jane? The one you got from Mr. Tiffany?" Before he could answer, she turned to Ben.

"Ben, I never did get to tell you how I figured out Skip was Rosalie's brother." Chloe explained about the scrap of paper she'd found in the workings of Jane's watch, and how it led her to believe Skip was Rosalie's brother.

"I think you're right, Chloe. It makes perfect sense, and it gives him a motive to go after Gus and me." Ben gazed at her with a look that warmed her all the way down to her toes, and for the briefest of moments, she wished her parents weren't here.

Ben must have had the same feeling, because he turned to her father. "Mr. Williston, may I have your permission to talk with Chloe in private before we all turn in for the night?"

"No, sir, you may not." Her father's voice was stern, but Chloe could tell he was only trying to appear that way.

Still, Ben didn't press the matter. Instead, his eyes were full of promise as he simply smiled at her and said good night. And for the first time since her parents had found them, Chloe felt a bit of unease finally lift from her shoulders.

Awash with warm feelings of reassurance, Chloe stretched and climbed out of her arctic sleeping bag. She cast a quick glance around the camp, her heart singing with the reminder that her father cared enough to come looking for her. And her mother had left the comfort of her home to hike these trails with him. Love bathed her heart, but uncertainty still hovered.

Caleb. Aunt Jane.

Were they safe? Warm? Or was Skip causing them to suffer?

Today, please Lord, please let us find them today.

They had to. They would. A strong sense of hope battled with the uncertainty.

Chloe wandered down the short trail to the river to freshen up. When she returned, perhaps the others would be awake so they could hurry and be on their way.

Less than ten minutes later she turned to step back on the path, only to see a dark shadow where the sun had just been. Unease grabbed her stomach, but before she could react, something cold and hard bit against her throat and sharp fingers dug into her arm.

"Make a sound and you're dead." Skip. She didn't have to turn to know it was him. He gripped her arm harder, and she bit her tongue to keep from crying out. "Do you understand?"

"Yes. Please, just don't hurt my family."

"Just get walkin'." He eased the gun off her neck then ground it into her back without the least bit of gentleness. "And be quiet about it." He pointed her away from the path and down the river, shoving her so hard she almost tripped.

Fear for her family kept Chloe quiet as she trudged along, a gun occasionally jamming the center of her back when she didn't walk fast enough. After they walked for about ten minutes, the trail grew dense, and it wasn't long before they left the river behind and angled into the woods.

When the gun poked her in the back again, Chloe picked up the pace only to be jerked by the arm with sharp fingers and shoved face first against a wide fir tree. Her face scraped against the bark, and she bit back a cry. She was determined not to let Skip know she was afraid.

"Take off your belt."

The demand took her by surprise, and her belly clenched. "Why?"

"Just do it!" The gun slid up her back toward her temple.

Fingers trembling, Chloe untied the piece of black lace and tugged it free.

"Give it to me." Skip snarled the words and Chloe shook harder, but she managed to hold out the lace.

"Now put your hands behind your back, wrists together."

Chloe almost sagged in relief. He wasn't going to do the unthinkable. He was merely going to bind her hands.

Once Skip finished tying her hands, he prodded her in the back, and they were on their way. Not long after that, Chloe caught sight of her brother and Monique seated on the ground at the base of a massive Douglas fir. Her heart lifted, but just as quickly fell as she realized they weren't free to run toward her any more than she was to run toward them. Skip had them bound to the trunk of the tree, with her aunt, Gus, and Rudy tied to the tree opposite them.

It sickened her to realize they hadn't been that far from finding them. If she'd only wakened Ben and her parents before heading down to the river, they could be capturing Skip at this very moment. Skip shoved her toward the tree where Caleb was tied, and she stumbled. Tears blurred her vision, but not from pain.

"Caleb," she whispered.

"No talking!" Skip's command was harsh, but no harsher than the shove he gave her. She couldn't quite catch her balance and fell shoulder first into the tree. "Sit!"

She sat, not daring to turn her head to the side to see if she could see Caleb. She concentrated instead on her aunt, who was within her line of vision. While Skip busied himself lashing her to the tree, Chloe gave her aunt a tender gaze and let her eyes drift closed for a second before opening them again. Hopefully Aunt Jane understood the unspoken message that Chloe loved her.

Once Skip was finished testing the rope that he'd looped between Chloe's bound hands and had tied her securely to the tree, he took off the way they'd just come.

To try and catch her parents and Ben unaware? A sick feeling stole over her, and she fought the tears threatening to spill over. "Father in heaven, please be with them." Chloe fidgeted, trying to twist her wrists apart, determined to free herself and the others before Skip could return.

"Caleb. Oh, Caleb, Monique, I'm so sorry for everything."

"It's not all your fault," Caleb whispered. "I'm sorry, too."

A lump welled in Chloe's throat, and instead of answering, she tried rubbing her wrists against the rough bark behind her.

"Me, too." Monique's apology was quiet, but sincere.

"I know," Chloe answered.

Across the way, from next to her aunt, Gus cleared his throat. "I wish we could all hug it out, but we really need to concentrate on getting free."

"I know, Gus. I'm so sorry, you're all in this mess because of me." A lump tightened Chloe's throat, and she couldn't say anything more. Everything was her fault. If Skip hurt anyone, she would never forgive herself. When Skip returned, she'd make whatever bargain she had to in order to keep everyone else safe.

Please, Lord, either help us to get free, or give me the right words to convince Skip not to hurt anyone. But whatever happens, please don't let anyone get hurt because of me.

Guilt and sorrow mixed in Chloe's heart, and she struggled against its weight. She needed to stay strong, needed to continue trying to free her hands. Sharp splinters of tree bark bit into her skin, but it didn't hurt as bad as the thought of losing someone she loved. She couldn't let it stop her.

A moment later she was rewarded when she felt lace give way. Once her wrists were apart, it was easy to pull her arms free of the rope Skip looped between her wrists instead of across her chest. He must not have thought she was strong enough to tear through the lace.

He was wrong.

Chloe stood, then hurried over to Caleb. She thought she heard a chuckle from either Gus or Rudy. But she ignored it for the time being. After kneeling next to her brother, she pressed a kiss to Caleb's cheek and busied herself with the knotted rope that held him and Monique against the tree.

"Mother and Father are here."

"What? Where?"

"They're about three miles from here, I think."

"I knew they'd come," Aunt Jane said.

"They caught up with us yesterday. Charles Jr. is with them."

"Unbelievable." From beside her, Caleb laughed. "How did he sober up long enough to make the trip?"

Struggling to loosen the knot, Chloe didn't answer right away. "We don't have much time. I need to get these ropes free before Skip returns. Then we can catch him by surprise."

"Miss Chloe?" Rudy's voice was like the light of Ben's reflecting lamp, illuminating the obvious.

"Where is it, Rudy?"

"Over by the campfire, next to Cookie's, er, Jane's cooking gear. Skip snatched it from me while I was sleeping last night."

Relieved that they hadn't been tied up and suffering for days, Chloe busied herself searching through the pots and food staples for Rudy's machete.

When she came across it, she grabbed it and quickly set about severing the ropes that bound the others. "We weren't far from here when Skip grabbed me. So we have to hurry. We need to be ready when he comes back."

Once everyone was free and they'd all taken their turns hugging Chloe, they arranged themselves around the trees again so they could try and catch Skip off-guard when he returned.

Ben wasn't awake long when he realized Chloe was missing.

At first he figured she'd gone down to the river to wash up, but too much time had passed. A quick trip down the path produced a towel and a bar of lemon-scented soap that Chloe had undoubtedly intended to wash with. But something, or someone, had kept her from it. They had to find her. He turned and ran back to the camp.

"Mr. Williston, Mrs. Williston, Chloe's missing." Ben didn't waste time with niceties or a gentle voice. He shook both of Chloe's parents awake then apprised them of his suspicions. "We need to hurry up and find her."

Charles Jr. grabbed the front of Ben's shirt, pulling him close. "If anything happens to my sister because of you—"

Cecily shrieked, and it was only out of respect for her that he didn't flatten Chloe's brother.

"Now isn't the time, Williston. Your sister has a way of wandering into trouble, and we need to find her before something happens." Even as he said it, Ben couldn't shake the unsettling feeling that this time was different. He glanced down at the towel and soap he still held in his hand.

Chloe hadn't wandered into trouble. This time, trouble had found her.

But they'd barely taken three steps outside of camp when Ben became aware that trouble had found them, too.

Chapter Twenty-One

It seemed to Chloe that she'd just settled back against the tree when the top of a head bobbed in to view. But it wasn't Skip's. It was Ben's!

A cry of joy tore from her, and she scrambled from her spot against the tree to race toward him.

Caleb's cry of warning came too late, and a chill rushed through her as she realized both of Ben's hands were behind his back. As were her father and brother's.

Skip was right behind them, a gun in one hand. He grasped her mother by the arm, and her terrified expression filled Chloe with rage.

"Get back," Skip yelled. "If you come any closer, I'll kill her."

Chloe stopped in her tracks.

"All of you get over there." Skip pointed at the tree where Gus and Aunt Jane pretended to still be tied.

Ben gave Chloe a look of regret as he obeyed Skip and sat on the ground next to Gus and Jane. She understood. He didn't want to get her mother killed. No one did.

Her father and Charles Jr. sat down as well.

"Please don't hurt her, Skip. She hasn't done anything to you."

Skip turned the gun toward Chloe and waved it toward Caleb and Monique. "Sit."

"Please, Skip. Let her go."

"I said, sit."

While Skip's attention was on her, Chloe realized she provided enough distraction that Rudy was able to inch away from the others. If she could keep Skip distracted just a little bit longer, Rudy might be able to jump Skip from behind.

"Take me instead. Please?"

"No, Chloe," her mother begged. "Do as he says."

"It'll be okay, Mother, I promise."

"Shut up, both of you."

Chloe stepped closer to Skip, hoping Rudy would be able to do the same. He was out of her line of vision now, so she couldn't be certain how close he was to Skip. And when Skip motioned Chloe closer, she obeyed. When she was within arm's reach, he shoved her mother away, and reached out and grabbed Chloe.

His fingers dug into her arm, but she didn't care as long as her mother was safe.

"Don't any of you move a muscle, or she's dead." His menacing tone buzzed across her ear. Then he whirled to one side. "You neither, Rudy. Get on back over there by the others. And drop the knife, too."

Chloe's heart sank as the knife clattered to the ground, and she winced as Skip pulled her away from the others. She prayed for a way to grab it before he could.

Just a few feet from where the knife lay, the exposed root system of a massive Douglas fir stretched onto the path. If she could cause him to stumble, perhaps she could get free.

Praying Skip wouldn't notice the obstacle, Chloe sucked in a steadying breath and pretended to trip. When Skip didn't release his grip, she forced herself to sway forward. Then she planted her feet and ignored the pain in her arm as he tried to hold on to her.

Skip lost his balance and hit the ground. The gun was knocked from his other hand. He scrambled toward it, but Chloe was faster, and as she held it tight she breathed her thanks to the Lord.

Skip inched his hand toward the knife and Chloe leveled the gun at him. "Don't you dare move, or you'll regret it." But Skip didn't reveal a hint of fear as he grabbed the knife and jumped to his feet.

"I mean it." Chloe pointed the gun toward the bushes next to Skip and fired. The sound blasted her ear and her hands stung, but she tried not to show it. She swung the gun back toward Skip's face, and he dropped the knife.

"Great work, Chloe. I'll take it from here. You go check on your mother." Relieved to hear Ben's voice from behind, Chloe resisted looking away from Skip until the gun was firmly in Ben's hand.

"Ben, did he hurt you?"

"Nothing a little loving wouldn't cure."

Her heart skittered, but the sound of her father clearing his throat caught her attention.

"Do we need to have another talk, son?"

"No, sir. But Chloe and I do, just as soon as we get Skip taken care of."

Before she could think about what Ben might mean, Caleb barreled toward her. Her mother was right on his heels, with her father close behind, and Chloe was caught up in a family embrace the likes of which she'd never experienced.

Things were finally as they should be for her family. She prayed she could say the same thing for Ben and herself.

There was too much excitement around the campfire that night, too much celebration. And to Ben's dismay, Chloe was at its center.

It wasn't that he didn't want her to have her moment, but he'd waited patiently for a different moment, one when they could be alone. But since it didn't appear it would happen anytime soon, he contented himself by sitting as close to her as he dared under the scrutinizing glare of her father.

"I have an announcement," she said. As she spoke, Ben couldn't help but notice the way the firelight reflected like diamonds in her eyes, and he had to force himself to focus on what she was saying.

"My first order of business as editor will be to report on the courageous undercover reporting of Jane Williston." She turned to her aunt and beamed as she pressed the Tiffany pocket watch into her hand. "I think this belongs to you." Jane clutched the watch to her heart and gave her niece a smile.

"Thank you," Jane murmured.

"Now, Aunt Jane," Chloe said, "please tell everyone how you stumbled upon the story."

It didn't escape Ben's notice that Jane reached over and took Gus's hand. Nor did he overlook the encouraging smile Gus bestowed on her. "If you remember, Charles, Cecily, before I could meet you out here I had to go to Florida to do some research. That's when I met Gus." An intense look passed between the two before Jane continued.

"As most of you know, Ben was the subject of a scathing series of articles that he claimed were false. My publisher wanted me to try and set the record straight."

Rosalie. A lump formed in Ben's throat, and he stared into the fire. Would he ever get over this guilt? *Please, Lord,* he begged silently, *please help me forgive myself.*

Chloe nestled her hand in his, and he soaked in the comfort of her touch. If only they could leave the campfire so he could talk to her. Instead, he had to pull his attention back to what Jane was saying.

"Not long after that, someone tried to kill me."

Chloe gasped and squeezed Ben's hand.

"No, don't get alarmed," Jane said softly. "Everything is fine. Thanks to Gus. After the second attack, he convinced me that it would be safer if I left Florida. Joining the expedition seemed perfect, until we were on the train, and I recognized Skip."

Jane's voice hardened. "He was a pesky little reporter I once worked with at the *New York World.* Something told me he might be the one behind the attacks, but at that time I wasn't sure why. All I knew was I couldn't let him recognize me, so I tried to hide my identity. I remembered he had a sister who'd been killed on a science expedition, and it wasn't that much of a leap to realize it was the same girl who was killed on Gus's expedition."

Chloe's father cleared his throat then speared Jane with a narrowed glare. "Why didn't you go to the sheriff when you arrived in Cedar Ridge?"

"And tell them what? That Skip wrote an expose on Ben? Charles, you know full well that isn't something the sheriff would involve himself in."

"But he tried to kill you."

"I didn't have any proof it was him."

"Then why didn't you just come to me?" Mr. Williston's voice grew louder. "You were in Cedar Ridge for a few days before you headed up the mountain."

"Charles," Jane sighed. "I should have. I know that now. And I'm sorry. But I wanted to do it on my own. I wanted to find the proof somehow. And I didn't want to do anything to reveal my identity to Skip. But when Chloe showed up at the train, I knew I had to get word to you."

Mr. Williston nodded, seeming satisfied.

Jane turned to Chloe. "I'm sorry I put you in danger, sweet pea."

"You have nothing to be sorry for, Aunt Jane." Chloe leaned over and hugged her aunt. "I think everyone will agree that things worked out well." She practically beamed as she turned to Ben. "Now if we can just get the University to restore your career."

"It's a nice thought, but I'm not sure I want that career back."

Chloe's eyes widened, but he simply smiled at her. It was one of the things he wanted to talk to her about, when they were finally able to be alone.

"There's one more thing." Her voice was strong and confident, and Ben marveled at how much she'd changed since the day he first met her in Cedar Ridge. He thought she was beautiful then. But she was more so now.

Chloe stood and walked over to Rudy who was near the tree, guarding Skip. She handed him the small Bible he'd lent her. "Rudy, I don't have the words to thank you. This Bible, your friendship, the scriptures you taught me. All of those things helped my faith grow. They helped me stay strong when I was afraid. They helped me survive everything that happened after I was pushed off the cliff."

She was so graceful and poised with her newfound self-assurance, and the center of Ben's chest warmed with his ever-growing love for her. He couldn't wait to tell her everything in his heart. But first, he had to offer his thanks to Rudy as well.

He cleared his throat. "Rudy, everything Chloe said goes for me, too."

"Well, um..." Rudy gave a curt nod and looked at the ground. A blush swept up his neck and washed over his face. He waited a beat before glancing back up. "Ben, Miss Chloe, I'm glad I could be of help. But I think the good Lord did most of the work." Rudy reached out and took the Bible from Chloe. Then he planted a kiss on the top of her head.

Ben swore he saw the man swipe at a tear. He blinked rather rapidly himself then stepped toward Chloe so he could steal her away. To his disappointment, she was already being drawn into a conversation with the other women. Shortly thereafter, it was Ben's turn to guard Skip. By the time he'd exchanged duties with Caleb, Chloe was fast asleep.

Would he ever get a chance to talk with her?

Biting back his frustration, Ben looked up at the stars and pled his case to the Lord.

The next morning, Ben stood just off the path that led to the river, waiting for Chloe to finish washing up. He intended to tell her what was in his heart. And if possible, he'd be able to make up for not spelling it out when initially confronted by her father.

No one would notice him wandering off with Chloe, because everyone else was preoccupied.

Caleb and Monique were holding hands and gazing into each other's eyes.

Charles Jr. sprinkled dirt over the remaining embers of last night's fire.

Jane and Chloe's mother packed up the last of "Cookie's" pots and dishware.

Gus and her father stood apart from the others, talking animatedly. They appeared to get along well, which was good, as they'd soon be fathers-in-law to their respective children's spouses.

Ben was still disappointed in Gus for not telling him all the details about Skip from the beginning, but he knew Gus thought he was doing the right thing. It would be hard to stay angry at the man who'd been like a father to him.

Not far from where Ben stood, Skip tried to loosen his bonds, but they held fast.

Rudy, as usual, sneezed and blew his nose, while he occasionally pointed the gun at Skip.

Finally, after minutes that seemed to stretch on forever, Chloe appeared on the path.

Ben's heart quickened, and he grinned so hard his face hurt. He knew she was happy for the turn her life had taken with regard to her father, but he also saw uncertainty in her eyes. He worried it was because of him and prayed he'd be able to erase it.

"Chloe, will you walk with me so we can talk in private?"

Her smile faded, and when she shook her head, Ben's heart began to break.

Chapter Twenty-Two

"Chloe?" Ben's voice was soft and gentle to her ears, but uncertainty infused her, almost paralyzing her, bringing her to a halt.

"Please, will you walk with me?"

She knew he wanted to finish the talk that they'd started after he told her father he didn't know what his intentions were.

They were leaving to head back to Cedar Ridge in a few minutes and he wanted to tell her how he felt. She wasn't sure she could have this talk with him before they arrived home. Better to be there and be heartbroken, than to try and hide her pain from everyone the entire step of the way.

She'd tossed and turned on the hard ground all night long, thinking about him and about her father's proposal. Making her father proud, taking over the paper, was her dream come true. But no dream would be complete without Ben.

When he placed his hands on her shoulders, she ached to lean into him. Instead she closed her eyes and steeled herself from the fresh wave of pain.

"I can't do this now, Ben. Can it wait until we get back to Cedar Ridge? Please?"

"I don't think so, Chloe." He sounded so disappointed, her heart twisted. "We'll have to do this a different way."

As soon as his hands left her shoulders a chill took their place. As he walked away, she longed to look up and see where he went. But stubborn pride wouldn't allow it.

So she stood stock-still and waited until she was certain he was gone so she could quit standing here like a statue, feeling totally conspicuous.

"Are you saying you want to marry my daughter?" Startled by her father's booming voice, she jerked her head up.

Ben? Marry her? Chloe straightened, ignoring the hopeful feeling leaping in her chest. But yesterday he said he didn't know how he felt. Hardly daring to breathe, she strained to hear Ben's reply.

"Well, sir..."

So he didn't mean it after all. Otherwise he would have said, "yes, sir" right away instead of stammering like a lame schoolboy.

"You'd better be saying that." Her father's voice was almost a growl. "After spending all this time alone with her up in this wilderness, that's exactly what you'd best be saying."

One thing was for certain. Much as Chloe loved Ben, she wasn't about to let him be forced into a marriage because of her father's tender sensibilities where she was concerned. Especially not to protect a reputation she couldn't care less about.

Chloe swiped at her face to make sure it was free of stray tears, then ran toward her father.

"No, Father! I won't let you force Ben into marrying me."

"Are you saying you don't want to marry him?"

"Chloe, didn't you hear a word I said to your father?"

Her father spoke at the same time Ben did, but it was Ben's words she chose to focus on.

"No." Though her voice sounded shaky to her ears, she looked at him with unwavering eyes. "I didn't hear a word you said. But yesterday, I *did* hear you say you didn't know what your intentions were toward me. And that was after you told me you loved me. Did you say it just to—just to—?"

She couldn't say it. Not here, not in front of everyone. But she may as well have, because they all stood watching. Gus and Rudy stood just beyond her father. Her mother and Charles Jr. stood next to Ben. Her mother's eyes were unusually bright, her cheeks flushed pink. Monique stood right behind her mother, brown eyes fixed on Chloe but her hand holding tight to Caleb's.

Her humiliation was complete.

Ben sighed and looked uncomfortable. "No, Chloe. I didn't say it for any reason other than the truth. And yesterday, when your father confronted me, I don't know why I didn't tell him I loved you the instant he asked. I'm sorry. I did tell him later, though."

The truth? "What?" Chloe's heart began to thrum. Was he saying he loved her? She wanted to be clear this time.

"I love you." Ben's mouth began to curve upward. "And if you're doing this just to make me suffer humiliation in front of everyone, I'm going to…"

Had he really just said he loved her? In front of her family? "What will you do?"

In two swift strides, he stood before her. "This," was all he said before he pulled her to him and kissed her senseless.

Finally, breathless and senses reeling, she pulled away. "What did you say to my father?"

"I asked him…" Ben paused and took her hand. "I asked if he knew of anyone who would be willing to run the paper in your absence."

"My absence?" She closed her eyes, not allowing herself to hope. When she opened them a second later, he still stared at her, eyes wide. She swore she saw a twinkle in those forest green eyes.

"Yes, your absence. I believe we have a snow gorilla project to tend to in Africa. And then perhaps a trip to the South Seas. You're going to be one successful journalist with all the adventures you'll be writing about."

"Africa," she said uncertainly. "The South Seas. I thought…"

Did he mean it? Had he changed his mind about her going on another field expedition?

The twinkle sparkled brighter.

He meant it! Oh, glory be, he meant it!

Delirious with joy, she flung herself into his arms, her head resting against his chest. After a brief moment he pulled away and kneeled at her feet.

"Chloe, I can't live my life without you. Life is full of risks, I know that now. Anything can happen, even in your quiet little town."

"What else do you know?"

"That you're quite adept at survival skills. So I'll do my best not to hover over you, worrying about your safety all the time. And..."

"And?"

"I'd rather give up a life of adventure and stay in Cedar Ridge running the paper with you, than wander through mountains and jungles alone."

"You wouldn't be alone, Ben. You have Gus and Rudy."

"Look. My knees are starting to lock up. Will you hush and let me propose so I can kiss you properly?"

Chloe's heart skipped a beat then more than made up for it in the next few moments as it pounded erratically while she stared open-mouthed.

"Good," Ben said. "You've finally stopped talking." He paused to lift her hand to his lips. He feathered kisses on the back of her hand then gently brushed his lips over each finger.

She caught her breath, her heart thundering out of control.

"Chloe." His voice was husky, a low rumble that sent wisps of awareness skittering across the hand he still held. "Stay with me forever. Go with me to Africa, Australia, and anywhere else we can think of."

Forever.

With Ben.

Chloe sighed.

"Chloe, will you be my wife?" His green eyes were full of tenderness, and she realized there was something different reflected there. Something she'd not noticed before.

"Wife?"

"Yes," he breathed. "Wife."

"And you'll take me everywhere you go?"

"Everywhere. I'm even hoping one of those trips will be to find out what happened to my parents."

"I'd be happy to help you find your parents, Ben. And I'm praying we'll find them safe and sound."

"Me, too, Chloe. Me, too. And I'll expect you to report on it."

"You will?" she asked cautiously. "Does this mean you no longer care if you have a reporter along with you?"

He couldn't keep the grin off his face. "Only one reporter. You."

She finally dared to believe everything would be all right. "What if I wanted to take a vacation from work and come up here to look for the Sasquatch again?"

Ben rubbed his chin and looked up at her mischievously. "As long as you don't let us starve to death and you promise to keep me warm at night, I guess that would be all right." He bit his bottom lip and raised one eyebrow before kissing her hand.

She dropped to her knees before him and brushed her lips against his. "Do you promise not to shoot any innocent porcupines?"

"Promise." Ben's eyes never left hers.

"Even if he swats you with his tail, leaving your leg full of quills?"

"Even if." His tone was so serious, she knew he meant it.

"What about the Sasquatch?"

"Chloe, I swear to you, if the Sasquatch shows himself to me, the only thing I'll shoot him with is a camera."

"What?" She tilted her head to the side. Had she heard him correctly? "Your camera?"

"I've been thinking about getting myself one of Mr. Eastman's newest Kodak cameras. It seems like he comes up with a new idea every year to improve on the one before."

"But what about the funding you're sure to get if you bring the Sasquatch back? I'm sure they'll want more than a photograph."

Ben reached out and captured her hands in his and her heart skipped a beat. "You're all I need."

"You would give all that up for me?" She was still having a difficult time believing it.

Ben nodded, stood, and pulled her to her feet. Then he kissed her again, so soundly she melted against him. "We'll be happy, Ben, I promise."

"Chloe, I love you so much. I plan to spend every day of the rest of our lives showing you how much."

He loved her. Really truly loved her. "I'm so sorry you didn't get to see the Sasquatch."

"I'd much rather look at you than any hairy old Sasquatch," he said with a grin. "Besides, I have that tuft of hair and the mud casting of his footprint. I still can't believe they survived with the pack getting soaked."

As Chloe gazed at him through her tears of joy, she realized that for the first time since she'd known him, Ben had a smile captured in the depths of his eyes.

"Well then," her father shouted. "Let's get on with it so we can be on our way. Are you going to marry him or not?"

She tore her gaze from Ben's and looked over at her father. "Yes."

Ben squeezed her hand, and she looked back at him, love overflowing her heart. "Yes," she murmured again a fleeting second before his mouth claimed hers and her heart was swept away in a flurry of feelings. Her mother's sighs and her father's *harrumph* floated through the air and added another layer to the cocoon of love surrounding her.

Overcome with the dizzying sensation, Chloe rested her head on Ben's shoulder and looked heavenward, giving thanks to God for this precious gift. She also thanked Him for Rudy's friendship and gentle ministering at the river that led to her renewed faith.

She couldn't wait to get home to begin her new life as the editor of the *Cedar Ridge Reporter* and, more importantly, as Mrs. Benjamin Kearny.

A movement caught the corner of her eye, and she turned her head to get a better glimpse. When she did, she gasped.

Was it? Could it be?

"Ben. Ben, look."

He turned and as he did, he straightened. "Don't move. We don't want to scare it away."

As he spoke, a dull ache settled in Chloe's heart.

If he squinted just right, Ben could almost make out the shape of the figure standing behind the fat trunk of a Douglas fir. Whoever it was, *whatever* it was, it was far larger in girth than the ancient tree. The figure was dark, but too far away to tell if it wore dark clothes or was covered in fur. His heart leaned toward fur. He *wanted* it to be fur, wanted it to be the Sasquatch so he could be vindicated in the eyes of the University and his former peers.

Taking one careful step forward, Ben silently willed the figure to stay in place. Surprisingly he, or it, did, but Ben still couldn't be certain if it was the Sasquatch. If it was, the creature was far too trusting, because Ben knew at this distance he could pull out his gun and finally be vindicated.

"Caleb. Over here. Hurry."

Beside him, he heard Chloe suck in a breath. He turned to give her a reassuring smile and dropped a kiss on her forehead. "Don't worry, Chloe. Everything will work out."

And Ben knew he spoke the truth. He was a changed man.

"I need you to sketch the figure at the edge of that tree," he said to Caleb. "I think it's the Sasquatch, and it will put your sister's newspaper into direct competition with the *New York World*."

Chloe leaned into him, a radiant smile on her face. An overwhelming sense of peace settled over him then, and Ben wasn't even tempted to step closer to what could possibly be the Sasquatch. The dream he'd been chasing all this time was right here in his arms, and he never intended to let her go.

Epilogue

"Good morning, Mrs. Kearny." Ben slapped the early morning copy of the *Seattle Post Intelligencer* down on the bed. His grin was larger now than it was yesterday afternoon when he'd kidnapped her from their wedding reception and whisked her off to Seattle.

"Look at this headline!" He picked up the paper and waved it in her face. "What do you say we skip the snow gorilla project for the time being and go in search of the story of the century? Gold!"

Chloe grabbed him around the neck and pulled her toward him. She lifted the covers and patted the spot next to her.

"What do you say you climb back in here and forget about everything else for the time being?"

Not quite certain he believed her, Ben wriggled from her grasp. "You don't want to chase the story?"

"I want to chase you!" She reached for him again, but he backed even further away.

"What would your aunt Jane say?"

"I believe she'd say my man with the green eyes is a great deal more important than any old story."

"Even if it means scooping Nellie Bly?" Ben stepped close again, and this time when she reached for him he let her pull him forward.

"Even if! Besides, after meeting her, I know she'd understand."

Later, as the sun rose on Seattle and the rest of Washington, a new song played through Ben's head. Gone were the strains of the lonely song he used to sing, replaced by pure and utter joy, and his heart sang with new knowledge.

He would never be lonely again.

Acknowledgments

I am blessed to have so many wonderful people who encourage and support me on a daily basis.

I owe a great big bouquet of thanks to some very special ladies. Each one of you helped this book along the way, some in its rawest form and some in its later form, but you each helped mold it into an adventure that I hope others will enjoy: Marti Bodley, Vera Belaoussoff, Gabrielle Luthy, Kassandra Stirling, Narelle Atkins, Susanne Dietze, Debra E. Marvin, Stacy Monson, and Niki Turner.

Barbara Smith, Pamela Mynatt, and Tiffany Van Ingen—mother, sister, and niece—your love and support means everything to me.

Kyle Mynatt and Rich Mynatt: two special guys. Kyle, you are about to go on a big adventure of your own. Always remember you are loved. Rich, I've never seen you without a smile, and I'm thankful to God for the ever-present joy you bring to our family.

Sharon Gillenwater and Diane Langley: two dear friends who encourage me whenever I feel like giving up. Thank you for all of the years of laughter and friendship.

The ladies of Inkwell Inspirations: you inspire me daily as I strive to become a better person.

Dina Sleiman and Roseanna White, you are both amazing at what you do. I am humbled by your belief me, and in this book.

Love, blessings, and many thanks to each one of you for the way you've touched my life.

Soul Painter
by Cara Luecht

Miriam Paints the future...but can she change it?

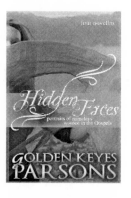

Hidden Faces:
Portraits of Nameless Women in the Gospels
by Golden Keyes Parsons

A compilation of four biblical novellas.
Trapped: The Woman Caught in Adultry
Alone: The Woman at the Well
Broken: The Woman who Anointed Jesus's Feet
Hopeless: The Woman with the Issue of Blood

CPSIA information can be obtained at www.ICGtesting.com
Printed in the USA
LVOW09s1449051114

412174LV00008B/1125/P